I Am A Survivor

Sex, Lies, and Abuse

By. MsNikk

Tell Her She's Beautiful LLC.

Columbus, Ohio

Copyright © 2025

Tell Her She's Beautiful LLC.

All rights reserved.

Cover Illustrations by. Wanikki "MsNikk" Cabell

Published in the United States by

Tell Her She's Beautiful LLC.

Columbus, Ohio

ISBN: 978-1-7365739-9-0

Library of Congress Control Number: 2024927580

Printed in the United States of America

Dedication:

Though this may not be a true story it is a familiar story and if you or anyone you know have been through this understand you're not alone. You can and will get through it. You are a survivor. You're valued, loved, and most importantly you're beautiful.

I Am A Survivor: Sex, Lies, and Abuse

"You have no idea what I've been through."

"For the record my name is Detective James Moon; Deja do you know why you are here today?" he asked, as he opened up a folder to show me the pictures.

Here I was in the interrogation room at the Columbus Police Department. I have had enough and Detective Moon was not going to be ready for what I had to say.

"Well, Deja Thomas, are you going to answer me?" he asked, irritated.
"My name is Deja Anderson," I said, with an attitude. "And yes, I know why I'm here. I can see the pictures you just laid out."
"Anderson? So, you're divorced already?"
"No, not by law, but when I left him, I went back to using my maiden name."
"Okay, so, tell me what happened? Did you have something to do with this?"
"It doesn't matter what I say. I am a suspect and you are going to find a way to take my words and use them against me, because that's what police do to get what they want even if it isn't the truth. I know how you do things," I said angry.

I was more than angry. This man ruined my whole life and now I am still being blamed and tortured. I had enough.

"Alright, I get it, we are the bad guys. But that's not true. All I want is the truth, Deja. I know from past reports you have been the victim of Xavier Thomas's abuse. And even though he was an evil man we still have to find out what happened to Mr. Thomas and yes, the first person we normally like to talk to is the spouse," Detective Moon said in a calmer voice.

I sat in silence for a minute with my head down. I could tell Detective Moon was getting annoyed, but he tried to stay calm and patient as he waited for me to say something.

"I didn't have anything to do with it," I said as tears rolled down my face.
"So, what do you know? When was the last time you saw Mr. Thomas."
"I don't know nothing. And I have not seen X since yesterday when I called the police, because he found out where I was and you guys took forever to get there. By the time the police showed up he was long gone and I didn't see him again. But he made sure to leave a lasting impression on my damn face," I said angrily, talking about the bruises X put on me when he beat the shit out of me.
Detective Moon paused for a minute. "So, you may have been the last one to see him."
"I couldn't have been the last one to see him, because I had nothing to do with this," I said, pissed off now, because Detective Moon was trying to be slick.

"Deja, let me be real with you. You called the police yesterday at 9:20pm saying Mr. Thomas found your location and he was trying to bust in your house. You disconnected from the dispatcher at 9:30pm. At this point we can assume Mr.

I Am A Survivor: Sex, Lies, and Abuse

Thomas busted in, because the dispatcher heard a loud noise before the phone disconnected. And from your bruises I can see Mr. Thomas was very violent with you. Our officers were on the scene by 9:45pm and Mr. Thomas was already gone. When the police talked with you, you mentioned Mr. Thomas had only left about 2 minutes ago on foot. My officers report that when they showed up, they had another patrol unit circling the block and did not see anyone in a 10-mile radius. Now how is that possible if Mr. Thomas was on foot? So, tell me Deja what am I missing?"

"WHAT DO YOU WANT FROM ME? Huh, Huh?? You have no idea what I've been through."

I Am A Survivor: Sex, Lies, and Abuse

Chapter One: Trap
"He's playing on my innocence."

"Girl, are you ready for this trip? I am so excited to be leaving boring old Columbus, Ohio for 2 weeks. I swear I'm going to move away from here one day and never look back. This vacation is well needed," Liz said as she laid foolishly on my bed.
"Just because we are roommates and friends does not mean you can be all up in my room and on my bed," I said being funny.

Liz was my best friend and I just loved her. We met in college and after graduation we decided to be roommates. Liz's real name is Elizabeth Sawyer, we have been friends for like 5 years now. She works in IT and I work in accounting. We were lucky when looking for employment after college, because we both snagged a position at a law firm downtown. We were excited to be working at the same place just in different departments. Even though we were both living in Columbus, Ohio, Liz was from New Rochelle, New York not too far from Manhattan. I was born and raised in Columbus. She hated Columbus, but I think she was sticking around until she could talk me into moving. I wasn't sure I wanted to move though; I liked boring Columbus.

Liz was excited for our vacation. It had been a while since either one of us had been on a vacation. I can't lie, I was excited too. The plan is to go to New York for the first week. Liz's friend Tamara or Tammy, was letting us stay with her for the first week while Liz caught up with her family since she had not seen them in a long time. And though, I knew some of Liz's family through video calls this would be my first time meeting them in person. The second week me, Liz, and Tammy would be flying to Paris, France. This was going to be a much needed, full of excitement vacation. I didn't know Tammy well, but I saw her in a few video calls with Liz. Liz always talked about how cool she was, but she didn't talk to her much, because Liz said she was wrapped up in her boyfriend more than anything. Liz was actually shocked that Tammy said she would go on the trip. Liz said Tammy couldn't come to Columbus, because her boyfriend would always agree then change her plans by surprising her with a vacation somewhere else. Liz was afraid that it would happen this time, but so far Tammy is still going. Liz and I would be on our way to New York tomorrow.

"Deja, so I was thinking instead of staying with Tammy the whole week we can stay with my mom the first two nights. Tammy's boyfriend lives with her and he is supposed to be there this weekend. He will be out of town the rest of the week. So, we can just let them have those two nights and stay with my mom. Then we will be with Tammy, who also wants us to tour Manhattan, because she knows you have never been to New York. She loves showing people the city," Liz said excitedly.

I Am A Survivor: Sex, Lies, and Abuse

"Okay Liz, you know I'm down with whatever. I can't wait to see mama Ruth. I just love her and I finally get to see her in person."
"So, are you packed? You have clothes all over the place in here," Liz said, judging my messy room.
"Shut up and get out," I said, pushing her off my bed.

Liz laughed, got up off my bed, and left my room. She definitely knew me. We took Friday off to have a day to clean the house. I needed today to also get packed, because Liz knew I was not packed. "Ughhhhhhh," I stretched as I stood up from my bed. I looked at the time it was 9:15am. I knew we would be leaving super early tomorrow, since we were driving to New York. I had to get on the ball with packing, cleaning, and running some errands before we left tomorrow. I looked in the mirror just to check my hair and my eyebrows. I was able to get my hair done yesterday after work. I went with box braids so it would be easy to manage. And yeah, that hair was tight, but it still looked fresh even though my bonnet came off last night. My eyebrows were freshly done too. One of my errands today is to get a Mani and Pedi. I had an appointment set for 1pm. So, I figured I had some time to get this room put together and get my packing done.

I didn't waste any time either. I may be a procrastinator and do things at the last minute, but I do get things done. I straightened my room, vacuumed, packed my suitcase, and even cleaned my bathroom before 11:30am. I still had to clean the kitchen. It was my assigned area for the week, me and Liz would switch common areas each week to clean. But since it was close to 12pm at this point I knew I would just jump in the shower and head to my nail appointment.

I checked the clock when I got out of the shower it was 12:15pm. I was doing good, and on time since my nail salon is only 15 minutes away. I threw on some jogging pants and a T-shirt, put my hair in a ponytail, did a once over in the mirror. I was still gorgeous. For me to be 26 years old I still looked like I was 21. I was 5'2 and 130lbs. I was slim in the waist and heavy in all the right places. My breast size was 36C and my booty had some curve to it. Liz always said I was in some kind of committee just not the big booty committee. She always told me she admired my skin tone. She would say my dark brown skin was flawless and looked silky. She was so silly. Liz was light skin yellow bone Hispanic ethnicity. She was gorgeous too. She had that "Puerto Rican" hair. I would always tease her about that. Her hair was thick and beautiful. She was taller than me. She stood about 5'9 and she was a "Slim Thick Mami" which is what her boyfriend nicknamed her. Her boyfriend Eddie wasn't happy about us being gone for two weeks either, but he let us know we deserved to have our girl time. At least that's what he said.

I was ready to walk out the door. I let Liz know I was headed to the nail salon and would tackle the kitchen when I got back. She was in the shower so she just yelled okay.

I Am A Survivor: Sex, Lies, and Abuse

I made it to the salon on time. I sat in the massage chair as the nail tech started with my pedicure. I laid back and enjoyed the massage as she worked on my feet. I started thinking about how much fun we were about to have. I was thinking about meeting Liz's family. Recently, I've been talking to her brother Randy. Liz introduced the idea of me dating someone out of the state, when we were joking about how my man is probably not in Columbus. I think she only said that as a reason to get me to move with her. Randy is older than me and Liz by 2 years. So, Liz called him and brought up the idea to her brother and we've been talking ever since. I haven't really had a relationship since high school. I mean I dated people in college but they never lasted. I know mostly due to me being a virgin, and a lot of times the guys I dated weren't up for waiting. The longest I dated someone was like 3 months. After that they would find a reason to be done, because I would explain that I was not in a rush to give it up. I come from a Christian home and I'm a daddy's girl. And my dad always said if it doesn't feel right don't do it. Liz always said, "Deja, that's your dad, he wants you to be a virgin forever." And she is probably right, but hey I listen to my daddy. I believe when it's right I will know. Liz always says I just need to do it to get that first experience over with and then I would know why sex is what keeps the relationship going. I told her I still plan to wait until I find the one who makes me feel comfortable about it and not rush me.

Even though I'm talking to Randy, and I get to meet him soon. I also told him I will not rush into anything. Besides, we've only been talking for two weeks and we are just friends. He seems cool though, and he said when I see him, we will get away to have some alone time. He promised to take me out for dinner.

I began to doze off during the massage, when my phone rang.

"Hello,"
"Deja,"
"Hi, daddy," I said.
"So, your mom said you are leaving tomorrow."
"Yes sir. I am packed, I just have to finish some cleaning and I will be ready."
"I know you weren't going to leave without seeing us, right?"
"Of course not. I figured I would see you and mom this evening. Mom said you had to work until 5pm today."
"Yes, that was the plan, but I actually finished early today. I just had to finish sending off some new contracts and getting the team prepared for next week. We have a few new clients. We will be starting work on their houses next week."

My dad owns his own contracting company remodeling houses and rental properties.

"Oh, that's cool. I'm getting my nails done now, but I will swing by when I'm done so I can see you and mom. Is she home too?"

I Am A Survivor: Sex, Lies, and Abuse

"Yea, she is in the kitchen cooking us some lunch. I will tell her you will be over soon."
"Okay, see you in a little bit daddy."
"Okay, I love you."
"I love you too," I said, hanging up the phone.

My dad is big on making sure I see him especially since I will be gone for two weeks. I normally see my parents every Sunday for dinner. It's like our ritual. If I miss, I have to make sure I see them on Saturday or Monday after work. So, with me being gone for two weeks it's probably going to drive them crazy. I'm sure they will be fine, but we are so close that they always check on me. Another reason why I don't want to leave Columbus, because then I would always have to plan trips to come back just to see my parents. I guess if I do decide to move it better be somewhere close enough to visit often. I am an only child so they keep me close, and I love the bond we have.

I finished up at the nail salon, and headed to my parents' house. It was 2pm, I texted Liz to let her know I would be stopping by my parents before coming home and to check to see what she had on her agenda. She texted me back and said she was going to Eddie's house for a little bit so she would see me later.

I made it to my parents' house and ate lunch with them. We talked and watched movies until about 6pm. I figured I would hang with them for most of the day so they would feel good not seeing me for a while. I know being a daddy's girl he couldn't wait to give me the lecture on being safe and not going places alone especially when I got to Paris. I tried to reassure my mom and dad that I would be safe and Liz was not going to have me go anywhere alone. I didn't even think to mention that I was talking to Liz's brother. I knew my dad would get worried and start talking about how he needed to meet him first and then we would have to have the sex talk. I knew I wasn't going to rush into anything with Randy so I would save myself from having to have that talk with my dad. I know he was just being my dad but if I even mentioned I was talking to someone and going to meet him for the first time in New York my dad would be worried. I wanted to enjoy my trip. So, I didn't bring it up, but if things continue to go well with Randy, then I will let my parents know. I just don't want them freaking out while I'm away. Even though I'm 26 years old, I know in their eyes I'm still their baby girl.

I gave my parents a hug and they wished me safe travels. We don't normally say "goodbye". It's normally "see you later". My dad always told me don't say goodbye that means forever. I left and headed home.

I made it home at about 6:45pm. Liz was not home yet. I went ahead and cleaned up the kitchen. I checked and made sure I packed everything and had my clothes picked out for the morning. I sat down to watch some TV, when I heard Liz coming through the door.

I Am A Survivor: Sex, Lies, and Abuse

"Hey girl," Liz said.
"Hey,"
"So, I was thinking, do you want to leave tonight?"
"What, why?"
"Well, I was talking to my mom and she said if we wanted, we could leave tonight and she will keep her phone near her, so she can let us in when we get there. The drive is only 8 hours. We will get there around 4am if we leave around 8pm."
"What time is it now?" I said, turning around to look at the clock.
"It's 7:30pm," Liz said.
"Why in a rush though?"
"Well, I'm excited for the trip and to see my family. We got everything already done here. I mean we probably would have been leaving around 4am tomorrow anyway to get on the road. My mom is having the whole family over to welcome us. So, this way if we leave now and get there around 4am or 5am we can sleep and be ready to see my family by the afternoon. You know how us Puerto Ricans party," she said laughing.
"Well, that's fine. Let me get my stuff. I guess it's okay to leave now," I said, going to my room to grab my things.

I did a once over to make sure I had everything. Liz was already at the door with her stuff waiting on me. We locked up the house and headed to the car. Liz ordered a rental so we had a black Honda Pilot. Liz said she would drive first since she was wide awake. She would let me rest and we would switch off if she got tired. We headed out and I closed my eyes to get some rest.

I woke up to Liz cursing at someone on the phone. She was trying to keep her voice down, but I could hear she was upset.

"What the fuck man? I did everything you asked and you are still coming at me like this. I thought we were better than this. You know you are a piece of shit."

I lifted up and looked at the car clock. It was 3am. We had to be close to New York and Liz drove straight through. Liz hung up the phone once she realized I was up.

"Is everything okay?" I said with concern.
"Yea, we are almost there. Do you need me to stop or anything?"
"Are you tired? I can drive if you want me to."
"No, I'm not tired. Do you need to go to the restroom?"
"No, I'm good right now but I will probably have to go soon."
"Okay, I will stop at the next exit if they have gas stations close."
"Okay, so are you okay though? I kind of caught the end of your conversation."
"Yea, I'm fine. It's just Eddie being an ass."
"Is that why you wanted to leave so early?"
"Yea, and no, I mean I really am excited to see my family. It's been forever. But Eddie got me all fired up, because he is so jealous. I was at his house, we were

I Am A Survivor: Sex, Lies, and Abuse

chilling, I fucked the shit out of him, hoping that would satisfy him while I'm gone. Right before I was about to leave my phone rang. It was my brother's friend calling to ask me when we were leaving. And without a doubt Eddie starts going off talking about are you fucking him is that why you going to New York. And it just irritated me so much I just left. I figured if we would have stayed until morning his ass would have shown up trying to argue. So, of course he has been calling since we left, because why, he came to our house looking for me. I was ignoring his calls, but I figured I would answer the last call only for him to still be pissed off. When I saw I woke you up, I just hung up the phone, since he was still going off. Like, he can't understand that me and my brother's friends are close too, they treat me like their little sister. Ugh, he just gets mad if any dude calls me. He is so annoying. Like, I spend all my time that I can with him and do everything for him and with him. He's just annoying," Liz said, upset.

"Yea, I noticed Eddie definitely likes to be with you as much as he can. And he gets mad easily if you can't spend time with him."
"Yea I know. And it's probably my fault, because I thought that shit was cute at the beginning, but now it's just annoying. Like dude I'm not cheating I don't spend that much time away, for me to be cheating. When I'm not with Eddie, I'm with you and he knows I'm with you, because he will video call me when I'm not with him. Or I'm at work and he knows that too, because his ass video calls me at work too. He knows I'm going to video call him on this trip too. Ugh."
"True, but don't stress it. Maybe he will calm down and this time away will help him see things clearer. Maybe," I said, laughing.
"Whatever you get on my nerves too," Liz said, smiling.

We stopped at the next exit to get gas and use the restroom. Liz didn't want to switch off on driving, because she said she was still wired from being angry and driving helps. So, I let her continue with driving and I went back to sleep for the remainder of the ride.

I woke up to Liz nudging me. "Get up girl, we here."

I looked at the clock again. It was 4:45am. I did a long stretch and got out of the car. Liz's mom came outside. Liz screamed and ran to her mom and hugged her. I started to get our bags out of the car when I saw more people come out of the house. The whole family must have been here waiting for Liz. It was a beautiful sight, her dad, her little sister, and her brother all embraced her with love. The family welcomed me as well with hugs. Her dad and her brother helped with our luggage. Her brother smiled, gave me a hug, and whispered in my ear I looked even better in person.

Liz said we would sleep once we got to her mom's house, but we did not. We were talking and laughing all morning. I was well rested from the car ride of course but Liz was going on no sleep at this point. Liz looked so happy to be around her family. Her brother Randy sat by me and we talked. Her mom was in

I Am A Survivor: Sex, Lies, and Abuse

the kitchen making a feast. She was so happy her daughter was home. I was enjoying the beautiful aroma of Mrs. Ruth's cooking and the happiness of the family. After we ate what seemed like a 4-course meal, Liz showed me where I would be rooming, for the next couple of days. Randy helped me bring my luggage to the room. Liz's room was right across the hall from me. I was in awe of the house. It was pretty big. It was a ranch but huge, it had two living room areas, a big kitchen, dining room, and a basement. They had 5-bedrooms in this house and 3 bathrooms. Randy showed me around while Liz said she was finally going to lay down. It was probably around 7am.

I wasn't tired as I slept in the car. So, I stayed in the living room with Randy just talking and watching TV while everyone started to settle back down. Mrs. Ruth and Liz's sister Emily cleaned up the kitchen and went back to their rooms once they were done to get some rest. Liz's father Mr. Peter talked with me and Randy for a bit until he got tired and went to the room to get some rest as well. Mr. Peter stated for us not to stay up too long or we would be tired by the time family arrived. Mr. Peter mentioned Liz's aunts, uncles, and cousins would be coming around 1pm.

Randy and I probably stayed up talking another two hours. We were talking about life, goals, and getting to know each other more. I felt comfortable around him and he was definitely fine. He stood about 5'9" same as Liz. He was a little darker than Liz, and he also had the beautiful dark thick hair. His hair was probably a little past his shoulders and he wore it in a ponytail. He was beautiful. He was tall, thick built, and stalky. My conversation with him seemed to flow and he seemed very interested too. I was feeling like this could really turn into something. We figured we should hit the bed since we knew more family would be here soon. He walked me to my room and kissed me on my cheek like a gentleman and said he would see me later. I was definitely blushing.

I went into the room and laid down. I was hoping to fall asleep, but I couldn't. I texted my parents to let them know we left early and I was already in New York at Liz's family's house. My dad texted me back saying okay, but asked why we left earlier than expected. I explained to him how Liz couldn't wait to see her family. My dad said okay, he loved me, and told us to be safe. I laid there for a while playing on my phone until I finally dozed off.

I woke up to voices in the hallway.

"Yea, she is sweet, the innocent type. I'm not sure she's ready for what's next."
"Who are you talking to?" I heard Liz voice say.
"I'm on the phone."
"Well, go somewhere else with that. You are probably waking Deja up, she sleeps light."
"Nah, I'm not backing out, it's still a go." I heard the voice say as it became distant.

I Am A Survivor: Sex, Lies, and Abuse

It sounded like Randy talking, but I couldn't tell since my door was shut. It got quiet in the hallway and I got up out of the bed. I heard a low knock on my door.

"Deja," Liz said, opening the door slowly. "Oh, you're awake."
"Yea, I'm up. What time is it?"
"It's almost 12:30pm. My mom is already in the kitchen cooking and my family is in the living room. I think some of my aunts and uncles are already here. I'm about to jump in the shower and get dressed. You can use the bathroom right next to your room when you're ready."
"Okay," I said wanting to ask who was in the hallway earlier, but I figured I wouldn't.

I got up and picked out some clothes and went to the bathroom to take a shower. I could smell the sweet scent of Mrs. Ruth's cooking. I was thinking if I stay here too long, I'm going to gain a lot of weight. I got dressed and came out to the living room. Liz was entertaining her family. Liz saw me and started introducing me to everybody. They were lively, having a good time, and playing music. It was a party.

We ate, they shared with me some of the family stories, we played games, and danced. I didn't see Randy, so maybe he wasn't the one on the phone. It was probably close to 3pm when I saw Randy come into the house. He came up to me and kissed me on my forehead.

"Hey beautiful," he said sitting next to me.
"Hey, where have you been hiding?" I said making conversation.
"I couldn't sleep after talking with you this morning, so I stepped out for a bit. I was wondering if we can sneak away for a while?"
"Where are we going to go?"
"We can go to my place if you're okay with that?"
"Oh, you don't live here?"
"Nah, I just stayed last night since I knew Liz and you were coming to town."
"Oh, okay."
"So, you cool with stepping away. My family will be here all night so you won't miss much," Randy said smiling.
"That's fine, just let me tell Liz."
"Okay, cool. I'll meet you outside."

I let Liz know I was leaving with Randy. She gave me that "go girl" look. I just laughed and told her I will be back. I went outside and Randy was waiting out front. He drove me to his house and we talked the whole way. I really felt comfortable with him so I wasn't too worried about leaving with him. I was just hoping he wasn't thinking this was that moment, because I was going to have to let him know I was not feeling it.

I Am A Survivor: Sex, Lies, and Abuse

But nonetheless we made it to his house. He had a ranch as well, much smaller though. He had a 2 bedroom, 2 bath with a basement. It was spacious and cute. We sat in the living room watching movies and talking. He stated he just wanted to get me by myself so he could get to know me better. We talked for hours. He told me about his job. He had already told me he worked for a construction company. He talked about how he was working on starting his own construction company and he really liked what he did. I told him about my job and how I wanted to branch off and do accounting on my own as well. He joked and said I could be his accountant once he got his company established. I started to think that would be cute. I would be following in my mom's footsteps as she is my dad's accountant for his company. But I was just thinking that, not trying to get ahead of myself I didn't know Randy that well to see where this would lead.

He kissed me on my lips and we cuddled with each other. I laid on top of him while we got comfortable and snuggled under the blanket. I was feeling him. He started rubbing on my stomach while we were watching the movie and his hand went up to my breast. He started massaging my breast. He turned my cheek to face him and he kissed me. I felt my body getting tense and covered in chills. I started to think to myself, is this about to happen? Was I ready? The feeling was amazing and I could feel my body yearning for more. I was beginning to feel my heart beating faster and I was getting wet down there. I could also feel his penis rising as I was laying on him. My body was telling me this was happening and I was ready. His hand started working its way to my pussy. I felt him unbuckle my pants and his fingers went in to massage my clitoris. My mind thought wow this is happening. I moaned with every massage and I could feel my body getting hotter. "I wanted this, I wanted this" I chanted to myself as I could feel the intensity of every movement. I was about to cum. He whispered in my ear "tell me when you are cumming." I felt a sensation hit like never before, I moaned "I'm cumming" and I felt my body explode in ecstasy. He removed his hand and licked it. He whispered, "You taste good". I smiled.

He began to lift up and so, I moved for him. He reached in his pocket and pulled out his phone. He answered it.

"Hello," he said. "Yea, alright. I'm good. Everything is good. What do you mean?"

He sounded irritated. I couldn't hear who was on the other end of the call, but he got up and walked out of the living room. So, I couldn't hear his conversation anymore. He came back about 15 minutes later and said he had to take me back to his family's house. He had to go handle something. He never said what it was, but he took me back to his family's house. He gave me a kiss and stated he would be back to finish what he started. I smiled and he left out.

I collected myself outside trying not to think about what just happened. I just knew this was going to be it. But nope not right now. I figured it must not be the right moment or maybe he will come back and finish what he started like he said.

I Am A Survivor: Sex, Lies, and Abuse

After a few minutes outside, I went into the house and the family was still having a good time. It was around 8:30pm when I checked my phone. Liz was not lying, her family parties all night and starts early. I think everybody finally started to leave around 10pm. Me and Liz helped her mom clean up and then we all headed to our rooms. Randy never did come back, but when I checked my phone, I had a text from him saying he would see me in a little while. I texted back okay. I took a shower before laying down just in case Randy came through. I was feeling him even more now and I wanted him to finish. Oh, lord what was I saying my thoughts were all over the place. I was rushing this myself. I mean, it was so weird that I felt so comfortable to let him go that far. I never did foreplay with anyone. Well, I masturbated before but no foreplay with someone. Maybe I was ready or Liz was just in the back of my head pushing me. I put my nightgown on and made myself go to sleep.

I was startled awake about 2:30am as I checked my phone because it was vibrating. I answered the phone.

"Hello," I said, clearing my throat.
"Come outside beautiful," I heard Randy say. "Don't put nothing on, just grab some shoes."
"Okay," I said as I hung up and thought to myself, he wants me to come outside in my nightgown. I did.

He was sitting in his car parked in the driveway. He rolled down his window and told me to get in the backseat. I stared at him with confusion but I got in the backseat. He climbed over the driver seat to sit in the back with me. He didn't say anything, he just pulled my nightgown up and pulled my panties off. My pussy was already secreting in wetness when he placed his fingers down there to massage my clitoris. What was he doing? My body was going crazy with every touch. If this is what I was missing wow, why did I wait? And we didn't even have sex yet this was just foreplay. He kept his eyes on me watching me as I moaned with every touch. My body was covered with sensations flowing like crazy. He whispered cum and like clockwork my body exploded. He was doing something to me and I was all in. He pulled his pants down and I thought okay this is happening now. I was preparing for this moment, I think.

"Come here I want you to rub on my dick."

I got closer to him. I had no idea what I was doing. I mean I saw movies and stuff but it was different actually being present in it. But I think he caught on. He took my hand and made me lick it. He guided my hand to his penis and started moving my hand up and down on him. He began kissing me and he slid his hand down my back to massage my pussy again. He then whispered "suck on this dick." I moaned as the words did something to me. I was in the moment and I went in on his penis. He whispered things he wanted me to do and he took control teaching me how to suck on his penis. I was all in. I started cumming and he whispered for me to moan on his penis. As I was cumming, he came with me.

"Damn, baby that was good," he said. "Now lay on your back and open them legs."

I laid on my back and before I could even get my legs open, he was already pulling them apart. He placed his mouth on my clitoris and I moaned so loud from the feeling I knew I was experiencing something amazing. He went in and I was losing it. I was hoping I wasn't too loud, but I couldn't stop moaning. It felt so good. My body was shaking and his tongue was sending chills through my whole body. His hands came up to squeeze my breast and I felt myself cumming over and over. I couldn't control it. Damn, I was ready. He stopped after I came one more time.

"How are you feeling?" he asked.
"I don't even know what to say. I feel amazing."
He smiled. "Good, because I'm going to take my time with you."

I didn't know what that meant, but it gave me chills. I could tell he knew what he was doing, because he just kept watching me. Like, he knew his words were doing something to me.

"Well, you better go back inside. I think you had enough for tonight," he said, giving me a kiss on my forehead.

Was he serious? What the hell is happening? I didn't even know what to say. I leaned in to kiss him. He grabbed my ass and kissed me hard. I felt chills again. This dude was doing something to me and I was feeling it for sure. I went back inside and he pulled off. It didn't take me long to doze off and I slept well too.

"Yo, I think she's ready now, it's just fucked up I can't be the one to do it."

I jumped up thinking someone was in my room. Was that part of my dream? What was going on? I got out of bed and opened the door to see if I saw anyone. There was no one there. And it didn't sound like anyone was up yet. Maybe I dreamed it.

I looked at the clock next to my bed. It was 10am. Man, I slept late and well. I looked out the window and saw Randy's car was outside. He must have come back. I saw he was standing by the house on the phone. He looked my way and waved. Then he hung up the phone and headed in the house.

"Well, you slept in. Did you have a good night?" Randy said, smiling as he came into my room.
 I smiled back. "I did have a good night, did you?"

I Am A Survivor: Sex, Lies, and Abuse

"It was amazing," he said with a smirk. "What's on the agenda for today?"
"I don't know Liz didn't say what we were doing today."
"Oh, Liz is already gone. She went with some of her friends to breakfast. She said she tried to wake you, but you were out. So, she called me to come over to keep you company for a while. She didn't know when you were going to get up and she mentioned you normally sleep light so she figured you must have been worn out from the party," Randy said laughing.
"Oh wow, I didn't hear anything. That party sure wore me out," I said jokingly.
"Oh yea, it did huh," he said, being flirty.

Randy bent down and kissed me on my forehead.

"Well get dressed. I'm going to take you to breakfast and maybe tour you around the city and make a day of it. Liz went with her old high school buddies. She will probably be out for a while anyway."
"Okay that's cool with me," I said, getting out of the bed. "I'll be ready in a little bit."
"Okay, I'll be waiting in the living room," Randy said, smacking my ass on the way out of my room.

I picked out my clothes and jumped in the shower. I started thinking about what happened yesterday and early this morning. I just can't believe I am so comfortable with Randy. I just can't explain it. Like, am I going to lose my virginity on this vacation. I'm just so lost on how open I am being with him. And he is making me want him. I have never been like this with anyone or even felt like this. I keep telling myself this is okay, as I can hear Liz in my thoughts "just get it over with," but then I keep saying to myself maybe I'm moving too fast. I don't know anymore.

I got dressed and met Randy in the living room.

"Where's your family? Is anyone here?" I said observing the house being so quiet.
"Nah, they went to church this morning and probably out to breakfast now," Randy said getting up. "You ready?"
"Yea, I'm ready," I said thinking to myself "in so many ways, I am ready".

We drove to Manhattan to have breakfast. Randy showed me around. I told him not to tell Liz as I know Tammy wanted to be the one to show me around. We went to Central Park, Time Square and Chinatown. We spent all day viewing the city. We ate, saw some more main attractions, talked and enjoyed each other's company.

We started heading back around 6pm. I checked my phone and Liz texted me asking where I was. I responded with "we are on our way back to the house". I told her Randy took me to Manhattan; she didn't seem too upset about it. She

I Am A Survivor: Sex, Lies, and Abuse

responded 'okay I'll see you when you get here.' We arrived at the house and Randy didn't come in. He gave me a kiss and said he had to go meet up with his friends. He mentioned one of his friends was a rapper and he was performing tonight in a downtown Manhattan club. He said he was going to link up with his friends and then go home to get ready for the show.

Randy left and I went inside the house. Mrs. Ruth already had the house smelling good as she was cooking dinner. Liz's sister Emily and her dad Mr. Peter were in the living room watching TV. I said hello to everyone and went to find Liz.

"Hey girl, you made it back. Did you have fun?" Liz said, picking out some clothes from her suitcase.
"Yes, I did. Manhattan is huge and a busy city. What did you do today?"
"Oh, nothing much. I went out with my old high school friends and Tammy. We went to breakfast and the mall. We are actually going to go to Andre's show tonight, one of Randy's friends."
"Oh okay, Randy was just telling me about that. He said he's going to go meet up with his friends now."
"So, you really like my brother huh? Are you still a virgin? I see you had some alone time with him and all."
"What? I don't know what you are talking about," I said, joking with her.
"Deja??"
"Yes, okay I'm still a virgin. But I like your brother and I feel comfortable with him. I mean we did some things, but we didn't have sex," I said hesitantly.
"Deja, okay I don't want details, because that's my brother, but I WANT DETAILS," Liz said, pulling me to the bed to sit down and talk.
"Okay," I said with excitement. "We did foreplay and lots of it. Omg Liz, your brother is amazing. I don't know what to say, because I don't want to give you too many details."
"OMG, Deja he is reeling you in. You are about to be going crazy for my brother."
"Uh, I think I already am. I like him a lot, Liz," I said covering my face and falling back on the bed.
"OKAY! My brother is putting it down. Not that I want to imagine that but he got you wrapped around his finger," she said laughing.
"I know and he is so gentle. I mean he made me feel so good. I thought I was ready to let go and then he said I'm going to take my time with you. Like what is that? Am I tripping? I just knew it was about to happen."
"Ooh Deja, he got you all the way in. Honey, your virginity is about to be LOST!"
"Shut up."
"I'm serious, I didn't know my brother be doing that. Not that I wanted to know, but in terms of what he is doing you are going to be whipped my friend."
"Damn," I said, putting my hands over my face again.
"I mean don't feel like that. My brother is a good dude or I wouldn't have introduced him to you, but you're going to want to move to New York," Liz said laughing again.
"Whatever, Liz."

"Anyway, go get you something cute to wear tonight so my brother can drool over you like you're drooling over him. Oh, and get your stuff together too. We are going to Tammy's first, since we will be out late, and we will stay with her tonight."

"Wait, I thought we weren't staying at Tammy's until tomorrow. Isn't her boyfriend still here?"

"Well, she said he is leaving tonight instead, that's why she is going with us to the show. She said X's plans changed so he will be gone tonight."

"X, that's his name?"

"Well, Xavier but everyone calls him X," Liz said. "We will eat dinner with my family, head over to Tammy's once we are ready, drop all our stuff over there, then ride with her to the show."

"Sounds like a plan," I said heading to my room to pick out an outfit and get my things packed up.

I ate dinner with Liz and her family. We talked and laughed. Around 9pm we started getting dressed. I jumped in the shower and put on this slim fitting black dress with the back out. I thought to myself if tonight is the night maybe I shouldn't wear panties. I did a once over in the mirror to check me out. I was rocking the dress and I was feeling good. Then the thought came in my head in my dad's voice "this could be a trap". No, Deja Randy seems like he is level headed and Liz said he is cool. What am I thinking? Okay maybe I'm overthinking this. I slipped on my black open toe sandals and thought to myself again. He's playing on my innocence.

Chapter Two: Confused
"What the fuck is happening?"

After getting dressed and grabbing our suitcases, Liz and I headed to Tammy's house. We got there around 10:30pm. Tammy lived in an apartment complex on the 3rd floor so we had to take the elevator up. Liz knocked on the door once we made it to the apartment.

"Bitch, I was wondering when the hell you were going to show up. I've been drinking and I am ready to party," Tammy said as she let us in.
"Tammy, this is my college friend, roomie, and bestie Deja."
"Hello Tammy, nice to meet you and thank you for letting us crash here."
"Oh, aren't you a cutie. Well, welcome Deja. We about to turn up in this bitch. I am so glad to finally meet you. We are going to enjoy this well needed vacation," Tammy said with a bottle of Hennessy in her hand.
"Let me get some of that," Liz said, grabbing a cup off the counter.
"Yes, ma'am," Tammy said while pouring Liz a drink. "So, yawl can put your stuff in the two rooms on the right in the back. I don't care who gets what room. There are twin beds in both rooms. So just pick a room. And I'll get you a drink started too Deja."

Me and Liz walked to the back to find our rooms. Tammy's apartment was cute. From the front door you walked into the living room with the kitchen off to the right. The kitchen had a bar style island that separated the living room from the kitchen. Tammy had a leather sectional in the living room that took up most of the space, but she had her dining room table behind the sectional right by the patio back doors. Since she was on the 3rd floor she had a balcony. When we walked past the kitchen there was the hallway to the rooms, on the right. The bathroom was first, on the left, Tammy's room was right next to the bathroom at the end of the hall. There was a bedroom next to Tammy's room on the right and then the third bedroom was in the corner to the right of the second bedroom. Me and Liz picked a room and put our stuff in there.

We came back up front to Tammy playing music and dancing in the middle of the living room. I took a sip of my drink, because we could see that Tammy was ahead of us on being buzzed. As she glided across the floor, I could see she was tall, maybe 5'7", and she was slim and curvy. She was very beautiful. Light skin with curly hair. She seemed pretty outgoing and cool to hang with.

We sat in the living room talking for a little bit while me and Liz played catch up on being lit like Tammy. Tammy got up around 11:30pm and said we should

I Am A Survivor: Sex, Lies, and Abuse

head out. At this point me and Liz both agreed we were feeling good. Tammy drove.

We arrived at the club called Essence in downtown Manhattan around 12:15am. We walked in and the place was packed. It was live and the DJ was jamming. Tammy waved at someone at the bar. Me and Liz followed Tammy. Tammy talked to someone at the bar and next thing I know we had a waiter showing us upstairs to the VIP section with two bottles of Hennessy and glasses.

"X is very well known here. So, I can have whatever I want when I come here." Tammy shared with us.

The waiter showed us to a table with a good view of the stage, we could see everything. We danced, drank, and were having a good time. The DJ spoke around 12:45am and announced that the show would be starting soon. I saw Liz get up and wave at someone. I couldn't see who she was waving at so I just kept talking to Tammy and sipping on my drink. I was feeling good like I didn't have a care in the world. I didn't even notice we were already on the 2nd bottle of Henny until I saw Randy and he whispered in my ear; "I didn't know you drank". I guess that's who Liz was waving at.

Randy and a few of his friends came up to our VIP section. Randy sat by me. And I don't know if I was still jonesing or if I was drunk, but him sitting next to me was making me hot. I kept trying to think differently, but my body was saying find a low-key spot and just do it. Deja no you are drunk. Snap back. Randy stood up once the DJ came back on and announced Andre to the stage. He grabbed my hand and had me stand in front of him as we watched Andre perform from the balcony. I was trying to listen to the music but Randy standing behind me and holding my waist was my focus.

Randy whispered in my ear, "You having a good time baby," as his hand moved to my ass to squeeze it.
I turned and said "yes baby."
"You ain't wearing panties, are you?"
I just smiled at him and started moving to the music.
"Damn, you sexy as hell," he whispered in my ear.

I just smiled to myself as we danced and watched his friend perform. He just kept kissing my neck and rubbing on me. I was feeling it and he was making me feel even better. I just knew tonight with the liquor, with him rubbing all over me, and him telling me I was sexy, it was going to happen. And I was ready for it to happen.

I Am A Survivor: Sex, Lies, and Abuse

We watched Randy's friend Andre perform until he finished. Around 2am we were getting ready to go. We went outside and Randy walked with us to Tammy's car. In my head this was not going how I wanted it to go. But since I had a little liquor courage, I thought I would change the scenario.

"Hey baby, I want to go with you tonight," I said hoping to get him to let me go back to his place. He looked at me with his sexy smile and leaned down and kissed my lips.

"I told you I'm going to take my time with you, baby," he kissed my forehead and opened the car door for me. I felt my insides crumble but I held myself up and got in the car. He was reeling me in for sure.

I don't know if Tammy was speeding or not, I was so drunk and lost in my thoughts, but we made it back to her place pretty quick. It was around 2:30am when we got in the house. I was so done with myself and drunk. I went to the room, threw on my nightgown and passed out.

I woke up at 3:30am and had to go to the bathroom. When I stood up, I knew I had too much to drink as my head was spinning. I opened the room door to head to the bathroom. It was quiet so everybody must have come in and called it a night too. I opened the bathroom door holding on to the knob as I felt I was going to fall.

"Oh my God, I'm so sorry," I said in shock, quickly covering my eyes, when I realized there was a naked man in the bathroom.

I couldn't help but to notice his penis; that is where my eyes went after looking him in the eyes. I don't know if I covered my eyes fast enough. I slowly walked out of the bathroom backwards still covering my eyes and only looking down to the floor to guide myself out of the bathroom. He never said anything. I turned around and headed back to my room and closed the door. I stood against the door thinking to myself "what the hell". I thought Tammy's boyfriend was out of town. My mind began to think about what I saw and how big he was. His penis was thick, long, and halfway down his thigh. The man stood tall, maybe 6'0", dark skin, handsome, and his body was muscle built. Damn, Tammy had good taste in men for sure.

No, what am I doing? I have to go to the bathroom. I slowly opened my room door after collecting my thoughts. I saw the bathroom door was open and he was no longer in there. I hurried into the bathroom and locked the door. I used the bathroom and realized I needed to clean myself up. I was super wet down there.

I Am A Survivor: Sex, Lies, and Abuse

I couldn't believe it. I cleaned myself and slowly opened the bathroom door hoping I didn't see him again.

I went back to my room and opened the door. I saw him sitting on my bed. I stood in the doorway for a minute not sure what to do. He was not naked completely; he did have on boxers. He didn't say anything, he was just staring at me. I could feel my body being covered in chills and my breathing was increasing. I didn't know what I should do or say or if I should go somewhere else. He got up off my bed and walked towards me. I was getting nervous. He grabbed my wrist and I felt tingling in my pussy. What was happening? He pulled me into the room and closed the door. He pushed my back against the door and grabbed my neck. Without a thought his tongue was almost down my throat before I could even catch my breath. The feeling was mind blowing. No words, just feelings, blood pumping, and chills all over me. This was crazy, but it felt so good. He took my nightgown off and I had nothing underneath. He took his boxers off and I looked down to see his penis. I looked back at him amazed and he smiled. He kissed my neck working his way down to my breast. He sucked on my nipple while I felt his hands touch my pussy. I let out a quiet moan not trying to be too loud. This was wrong but it felt so good. He kissed my belly button on his way down. He lifted my leg to put on his shoulder and he squeezed my thigh and then his mouth went to work. I couldn't stop the overflow of chills, and I could no longer keep quiet. My body felt like it was exploding. I was shaking with every touch his tongue made as he massaged my clitoris. And once again I felt like my body was exploding. What was he doing, and why? I never thought this would be my first time. I was hoping this was not Tammy's man. What am I doing? Oh no my body was exploding again and my moans were uncontrollable.

He stopped and came back up. He looked me in the face and smiled at me. I was just in shock. He grabbed my wrist again and I could feel the chills coming through. He slowly turned me around and pushed my stomach to the door. He kissed me on my cheek and then I felt his hands between my legs. He lifted my ass and I felt him enter my pussy, quickly and hard. I screeched as it did not feel so good at first. But he kept pounding harder and harder. And before I knew it, I could feel my body exploding again, the chills were intense, and I couldn't be quiet. It felt so good. My body began to shake again and he continued to keep pounding. I could feel all of him inside me. He leaned in to kiss my cheek again.

He whispered in my ear. "It feels good doesn't it."
I moaned the words "Yes."
"I didn't know you were a virgin," he whispered, still pounding and not skipping a beat.

I Am A Survivor: Sex, Lies, and Abuse

I couldn't believe this was happening. He was fucking me for what seemed like forever. My body was just exploding like every 5 minutes and the feeling was out of this world. I didn't know if I wanted it to stop. My pussy was soaking wet and getting wetter. He pounded harder, went deeper, and I heard him moan as he released. He finally pulled out and I felt my legs go weak. He grabbed me by the waist to stop me from falling. He grabbed my wrist again, and walked me to the bed. He had me lay on my back. He spread my legs while still standing and began to massage my clitoris. He was staring me in my eyes while he continued to massage my clitoris. I was shaking and my eyes started to roll up as I could feel that explosion coming again. What was this man doing to me? I couldn't get enough and the feeling was amazing. I didn't even know until he leaned down to kiss my face, I had tears rolling down my cheek. What was happening to me? I exploded and as I was trying to moan, he leaned down again and put his tongue in mouth. The feeling of him kissing me sent even more intense feelings to my pussy while I was exploding.

After my last explosion he grabbed his boxers and put them on. I laid on the bed not sure what I should even do now. He opened my room door and went into the bathroom. He came back to the room with a wet rag. I had my legs bent and closed. He came over to me and spread my legs and looked me in my eyes as he wiped my pussy clean. I felt the chills again. He cleaned me up and then handed me my nightgown. I got up to put my nightgown back on. I tried to stand but my legs were a little wobbly. I had to regain my balance. I was hoping he didn't pay me any attention, but he was watching me. When I looked up at him, he just smiled. Once I was dressed, he grabbed my waist, pulled me towards him, and started kissing me again.

He kissed my neck and then whispered in my ear. "You're mine now."

I didn't even know what to say to that. He walked out the room and closed my door. What the hell just happened? Oh, my lord, what about Randy? Why didn't I stop him? Tammy is going to kill me if she finds out. Randy is going to kill me if he finds out. What the hell am I going to do? I began to panic not knowing what just happened. I tried to lay down but I couldn't go to sleep. I started counting to calm my breathing and then I started crying. I cried myself to sleep.

"THIS SOME MOTHER FUCKING BULLSHIT. WHAT THE FUCK YOU JUST GOING TO COME IN MY HOUSE AND DISRESPECT ME LIKE THAT. LIKE YOU LET THIS BITCH COME IN HERE AND DISRESPECT ME. I'M ABOUT TO BEAT SOME ASS STRAIGHT UP."

I jumped up when I heard the yelling. Shit Tammy knows. Fuck what do I do. I jumped out of the bed to grab some clothes. My phone was on the floor. I picked it up. I thought I put this on the charger. I checked the time it was close to 12pm. Then I heard banging on my door. Fuck!

"Deja it's Liz, open up," Liz said. I opened the door not remembering if I locked the door last night, maybe he did. "What the Fuck is going on?"
"Liz, I don't know. I went to the bathroom last night. And this man was in there and I walked out and I, I," I said as I started to panic trying to explain to Liz what happened. "I didn't mean to do it, I was drunk, he was in my room, oh God what did I do?" I started to cry.
"Well, at this point whatever the fuck happened you need to get your shit, because we got to go now," Liz said irritated.

She left out of my room. I continued to get dressed. I could still hear Tammy going off. I could hear a man's voice too so obviously she was yelling at him. I was freaking out. I grabbed all my stuff and opened the door. Liz was waiting on me. Liz walked in the living room and I could see that X was holding Tammy.

"Don't say nothing just get the fuck out of here," X said, looking at me.
"YOU BITCH. JUST WAIT I'M GOING TO BEAT YOUR MOTHER FUCKING ASS BITCH." Tammy continued to yell trying to get out of X's hold.

As we went out the door, I guess I was whispering to myself, but the words "I'm sorry" came out. I felt so ashamed. Liz didn't say nothing to me in the elevator or in the hallway. I kept my head down until we got to the door outside. I saw Randy and my heart dropped.

"Liz, you called Randy? Did you tell him?" I whispered.
 Liz didn't even look at me, she just said, "he already knows Tammy did that."
"Fuck," I said to myself.

Randy didn't even look at me. He helped Liz put her stuff in the rental and closed the trunk. I thought to myself oh shit what do I do now. It doesn't even look like I'm going with Liz. I can't go with Randy, he's going to kill me. I didn't know if I should even do or say anything, but I definitely didn't want to be stranded outside of Tammy's apartment.

"Liz," I yelled her name before she closed the car door. She didn't even look at me, she just pulled off. "Randy, I'm so sorry. I didn't even know what was happening until it was too late."
"Deja, save it. Get in the car," he said as a black sedan pulled up and he opened the door.

I Am A Survivor: Sex, Lies, and Abuse

I stood there for a minute too scared to get in, not sure what was happening. I pulled out my phone thinking this would be a good time to call my parents and maybe get me to the airport. But when I looked at my phone, I saw I had a text from an unknown number. I opened it.

Get in the car. You will go to the Haven Hotel, let them know your name at the desk and they will get you a room key. I'll be there shortly.

X

What in the world? How did X have my phone number? What the hell is going on? I hesitated for a minute. Thinking I could still call my parents. But Randy had already put my bags in the trunk of the car and he was now at this point pulling me to the car. Okay just go, I told myself. Once you get to the hotel you can call your parents and leave. I got in the car and Randy closed the door. I saw him walking in the apartment complex before the car pulled off. I felt so horrible. My first-time having sex and it was a whole nightmare. I lost my friend, Randy, and now here I was in New York and no way home. I was so lost and confused. I was hurting, because I messed up. I liked Randy. Why would I do that to him? Why would I do this to Liz and her friend? I am a horrible person. I couldn't shake the feeling. I began to cry again. What the fuck is happening?

Chapter Three: Frustrated
"What do I do now?"

The driver stopped at the front entrance of the Haven Hotel. I hesitated on getting out of the car.

"Excuse me sir. I think I changed my mind. Can you take me to the airport instead," I said. I was a little nervous now, and too afraid to go inside the hotel. I didn't know what was going to happen next.
"Sorry, ma'am I was given strict orders to bring you here nowhere else."

I was devastated. I got out of the car and thought I could just order a rideshare. Yes, once he leaves, I will order a rideshare. He got my bags out of the trunk and then he left. I waited for him to leave and I pulled out my phone. I was thinking if I just go to the airport I can stay there until I can get a flight back home. What did I get myself into? I ordered the rideshare and waited for it. It will be arriving in 5 minutes, the app read. Wait, what? The rideshare was cancelled. How? Why? Order it again Deja. Okay one is coming in 2 minutes. Nooo! The rideshare was cancelled again. Why? What the fuck??

"Deja, I told you to go inside and get the room key," I heard a familiar voice say.
"Shit," I whispered to myself. It was X he was already here.
"Here, I'll take your suitcase," he said as he grabbed my suitcase and my wrist to pull me inside.
"You know that was some real foul shit you did. I really don't think I should be here with you. Did you know I was talking to Randy? I mean I don't even really know anything about you for me to be here," I said while he was still pulling me.
"Oh, really that's why you were trying to catch a rideshare to the airport."
"What," I paused. What in the world is going on? I thought to myself as we reached the hotel front desk. This man is crazy.
"Hi yes, I have a reservation under Deja Anderson," X said, still holding on to me.

What the hell. How does he know my full name? Did I lose my ID or something? I checked my purse and wallet. I still had my ID, money, and cards.

"How do you know my name?" I said, still shocked.
"Don't worry about that right now, let me get us checked in first," he whispered.
"Sir, will you be using the card on file for the charges," the hotel clerk said.
"Yes, that's fine," X said.
"Okay Mr. Thomas you will be in suite 1000," the hotel clerk said smiling and handing X the room keys.
"Thank you," X said.

I Am A Survivor: Sex, Lies, and Abuse

He was still holding my wrist. At this point I was thinking I must be about to die or something, because I can't seem to understand what is happening right now. Maybe this is just a bad prank or a joke on me. Not funny okay snap back to reality now. X pulled me on the elevator. I couldn't even think of what to say as we stood quietly waiting for the elevator to reach the 10th floor. I quietly whispered "so this is how I die." Not realizing the words came out.

"You're not going to die Deja," X said. The doors to the elevator opened and he pulled me into the room. Which happened to be the whole floor as we walked right into the suite from the elevator.

I'm not sure I could say it enough. But now I was really confused about what was happening. The suite was beautiful. Not sure why I was admiring the rooms but I didn't know what else to really even think about. It had a whole window view of the city outside. The suite had a full kitchen, dining area, living room area, and 2 bedrooms and bathrooms. The owner suite was huge and you could access the ensuite bath from the bedroom. Very pretty. I was trying to keep my mind focused but I was scared and had so many questions.

"You like it?" X said standing in the living room. I didn't speak. I just looked at him.
"Say what's on your mind Deja," X said, taking a seat on the couch.
"What you did hurt a lot of people. My friend, your girlfriend, and the guy I was dating," I said, irritated.
"You mean what we did, because I don't recall you stopping me."
"Okay smart ass. What we did."
"We are grown, and shit happens. I saw a fine ass, no sexy ass woman standing in front of me. Well, hell you already saw me naked. I figured what was left for us to do but explore the vibe I know you were feeling too," X said, standing up and walking towards me. "Hell, and if I was Randy, I would have never let you stay anywhere but with me."

X walked up on me towering over me and looking me dead in my eyes. I backed up until I hit the wall and he moved closer. He pinned me to the wall. I could feel my heart beating faster. I was scared but my body was sending mixed signals. I felt the chills and the sensation running through me. He just stood staring at me. I could feel my body touching his and I could feel his penis rising. I still had so many questions, but I already knew where this was about to lead. I broke the staring contest trying to refocus my mind back on the problem. He lifted my face up back towards him and started kissing me. Damn, I was not good at this.

I finally found some strength and pushed him. "No, I'm saying no this time."

I Am A Survivor: Sex, Lies, and Abuse

He backed up. And I walked away from the wall so he wouldn't corner me again.

"I should have said no the first time, but you caught me in a vulnerable moment. I was drunk and it was late. My mind wasn't thinking right," I said finally getting some words out. "I like Randy and you just came out of nowhere. You were supposed to be out of town. And Tammy is your girlfriend."
"You don't even know Randy all like that."
"I DON'T KNOW YOU," I yelled, irritated.

He grabbed my wrist again. I pulled away.

"No, we're not doing this again. I shouldn't have done anything with you in the first place."
"Tell me right now that you didn't feel good fucking me. And for your first time. Tell me it wasn't good and you can leave right now. I ain't holding you here."

I walked to the elevator and pushed the button.

"So, you just ain't going to say anything. That's not fair."
"It wasn't good. I mean it was, but it was only good because I was vulnerable and the way you came at me. Oh man, what am I saying. I have to go." I said pushing the button to the elevator hoping it would come quicker.
"You have to use the key to call the elevator," he said, holding the key in his hand.

I smirked at him then I walked towards him to grab the key. He grabbed my wrist again.

He whispered in my ear "Well, let's try again. If you don't like it, I will let you leave."

Before I could say anything, he turned my back towards him and started taking my pants off. Fuck this was going to happen and I just couldn't stop it. He leaned me over the dining room table. He wasted no time. He pulled his pants down and he was fucking me hard within minutes. I was already so wet my pussy was cumming before I could do anything. The chills and the sensation were hell of crazy. I couldn't stop moaning. I was cumming again every 5 minutes as he just went deeper and deeper. He kissed my neck and whispered "tell me you like it." Fuck, I came so hard the words just came out my mouth. "I love it, fuck me harder." What the hell was I doing? How was he doing this? My pussy was throbbing in ecstasy and I didn't want him to stop. He fucked me for what felt like two hours and I just kept cumming. My shit was dripping wet. My legs began to shake and he went in deep as hell and I started cumming as did he.

I Am A Survivor: Sex, Lies, and Abuse

"Shit, that pussy is something else."
"Fuck you," I said pulling my pants up. I was so irritated with him.
"We already did that baby," X said, fixing his attire.

I just looked at him with anger. I sat down to catch my breath and recollect myself.

"So, how did you know my full name downstairs? How did you know I was trying to get a rideshare to the airport? Did you tap my phone? What is really going on?" I said ready to talk.

"Oh, now you feel like talking?" he said sitting down in front of me. "I knew your name because Tammy told me. I guess she asked Liz what your last name was and it came up in conversation when she said you would be coming over with Liz. And yes, I downloaded an app to your phone, to track your whereabouts and to see what you are doing on your phone. To answer your question what's going on, I told you the first time we fucked you were mine now," X said that with so much confidence he almost sounded arrogant.

"Are you serious? How and when did you have my phone?"
"I took it when I left your room this morning. I put it back before you woke up. That's what started the whole mess with Tammy, because she caught me coming out of your room this morning. And since you were still asleep, I locked the door before I shut it so Tammy wouldn't try to come in."
"Why would you even do that in the first place?"
"I like to know where my girl is at all times and what you are doing on your phone. Like ordering rideshares to the airport when I told you where to be."
"You can't control my every move and I'm not your girl."
"Why can't I and I already told you, you're mine now."
"I didn't agree to that."
"You did when you fucked me."
"So, me fucking you just makes it official? Where they do that at?" I said angry.
"Hmmm, you know you lucky I like you. I normally don't let any girl get fly at the mouth with me," he said standing up. "Look I'm about to go take a shower so we can go get something to eat. You coming?"
"I'll take my shower when you're done."
"I already saw you naked, what you worried about?"
"I don't want to take a shower with you. I don't even know why I'm still here."
"Oh, I get it, now you want to take things slow. Okay well there are 2 bathrooms you can use the other one."
"I'll do that."

What the fuck am I doing? I thought to myself as I walked to the 2nd room taking my suitcase with me. I just want to take a shower. Once we leave this hotel and get something to eat, I will try to get away from him. I went through my suitcase to find something to throw on after my shower. I found some jogging pants and a t-shirt. I figured I will try to look undesirable at all costs and comfortable enough to run if I need to. I jumped in the shower and came back to the room to get dressed. X was already sitting on the bed half dressed. He had on some dress pants and a button-down shirt but it wasn't buttoned up yet. He was holding a red satin dress slim fitting in his hand with some red bottom black sandals.

"What's this?" I said holding my towel tight around me hoping he wasn't trying to fuck again.
"This is what you are going to wear."
"Where you get that from?"
"I had the ladies downstairs pick something nice out for you."
"When did you book this hotel?"
"This morning, why? Did you think I had this plan for months?"
"I was just asking. Where are we going for dinner?"
"Somewhere nice, where jogging pants and a t-shirt is not allowed."
"Hmmm," I said, grabbing the dress and shoes.
"What?"
"Nothing. Thank you for the outfit."
"Oh, she can be nice," X said as he stood up and kissed me on the cheek. "Get dressed, I'm hungry."

X left the room and I closed the door. I put on the damn dress and shoes. It's like he was doing the most, for what. I needed to get away from him. I needed to call Liz and make this right. I tried calling her number but the phone was going straight to voicemail. She must have blocked me. I came out of the room and X was standing by the kitchen counter next to a bouquet of red roses and he was holding one in his hand. How romantic I thought. He was really doing the most.

"Cute," I smirked.
"You don't like roses."
"I said they're cute."
"You said cute and smirked about it."
"You would notice everything."
"Well, you look beautiful," he said, handing me the single rose he was holding.
"Thank you." I said as we walked onto the elevator.

I didn't say much as we walked through the hotel lobby and to a car that was waiting for us. I guess he already had this planned too. He opened the door and I got in the car. I just stared out the window at the fancy city lights. I didn't look his

I Am A Survivor: Sex, Lies, and Abuse

way once. I guess I was just trying to figure this all out in my head. I didn't even know what the hell I was still doing with him. I really needed to go find Liz and Randy and talk this out with them. I started to feel so horrible. I could feel the tears rolling down my face. I tried to wipe them without X noticing, but he was already handing me a tissue.

"Thank you," I said, grabbing the tissue.
"You know if you're worried about your friend, we can go see her tomorrow. I'm pretty sure she just needs some time to cool down."
"Yea, right. You didn't see her face. She looked like she was through with me."
"She's not."
"How do you know?"
"Well, if she is your best friend. She's not done with you, she just needs some time to clear it out of her head and really think about it. You didn't sleep with her man," X said laughing.
"You got jokes. I hurt her brother though."
"I bet that doesn't even matter either. And besides he's a man he will move on too. And you weren't even talking to him that long. Hell, he didn't even fuck you."
"You know you're real horrible on the sympathy part."
"I wasn't trying to sympathize with you. I was just stating facts."
"Whatever."

It went back to silence. We pulled up to some fancy spot called Devinos Steak House. X got out of the car and came to my side to open my door. We walked into the restaurant and the host greeted us.

"Hello Mr. Thomas, welcome back. I have this section reserved for you," the host said as he walked us to a section with no one in it.
"You reserved this whole area?" I said, shocked.
"I did, is that okay with you?"
"I guess, how much did that cost?"
"Don't worry about it I know the owner."
"Is it okay if I ask what you do for a living?"
"I think you just asked me," X said smiling.
"You know what I meant."
"Don't be afraid to ask me anything. I don't bite. Well at least not in public," X said laughing.
"Ha, ha not funny. So, what do you do?"
"I do a lot of things. I run a successful marketing firm out of Brooklyn. I also have a few small businesses around the city that I partner with like some local grocery stores, local cleaners, a coffee shop, and a corner store. And I'm working on expanding my partnership with a few other places in Jersey. Where I was supposed to be, but I had one of my partners go."

"Oh,"
"What?"
"Nothing, you just seem like you have a lot on your plate."
"It keeps me level headed and busy. I like that."
"How old are you?"
"I'm 36."
"You look younger than that."
"So, what do you do?"
"I'm an accountant at a law firm back home in Ohio. But for some reason I think you already knew that." I said, confused as to why he asked.
"I didn't know it was at a law firm."
"Right,"
"Are you ready to order Mr. Thomas?" the waiter said.
"Oh, I didn't even look at the menu yet," I said, picking up the menu.
"Would you like me to give you a minute?" the waiter said.
"Ye-," I started to say until X interrupted me.
"No, I will order for us. I will have the steak medium, with asparagus, and she will have the shrimp and steak medium with a baked potato. And please send out a bottle of your best red wine," X said, giving the waiter our menus.
"Sure thing Mr. Thomas it is always my pleasure to serve you," the waiter said before walking away.
"Do you always order for people? How did you even know I would like that?"
"I always order for my woman, and if you don't like what I ordered I can inform the waiter."
"I'm not your woman. And I will eat what you ordered," I said thinking why am I still sitting here.

Why didn't I just get up and leave what was holding me back? He planned all of this didn't he?

"You seem like you want to say something but you are not saying it. What's on your mind?"
"I guess I am just trying to figure this all out still. I mean I'm confused about what we are doing? I should be checking on Liz," I said, worried about my friend.
"Liz is going to be okay, like I said earlier she just needs a minute. And what we are doing is getting to know each other better. Whether you agree or not, you're mine and you will agree soon."

The waiter came back with the wine, filled our glasses, and left the bottle.

"And what's that mean?"
"Deja, you will see."
"And what if I can't see us being together. Then what?"

I Am A Survivor: Sex, Lies, and Abuse

"Then I guess I have to move on, but I doubt it."
"What about Tammy?"
"What about Tammy? I'm done with her and you saw she was done with me."
"Didn't you love her?"
"I have love for her for sure. But Tammy and I were on the verge of breaking up. I didn't mean for it to happen like that, but you just happened to catch me at a vulnerable moment too."
"I don't like this."
"You don't like what? The wine," X said tasting the wine.
"No, I don't like that-," I paused.
"Just say it, Deja."

The waiter came out with our food. I waited for him to leave before I started to speak again.

"I don't like that I feel like I can't walk away when I should really walk away. It's like I feel connected to you and I want to know so much more about you, but I keep thinking that this could be all wrong and I should run at the same time," I said, sounding stupid. "Does that make sense?"

X started to laugh and I started to feel stupid for saying it. I knew I should have just kept that to myself. I frowned at him as he continued to laugh.

"No, don't take it like that. I was laughing because you really are sweet and innocent," X said, trying to lighten the mood. "It's because you lost your virginity to me."
"What?" I paused. I thought about it and I remembered my parents trying to talk to me about this when they called themselves having "the sex talk". "Never mind."
"What? Why you say never mind?" X said interested in knowing.
"I get it now. It's the transfer of energy when you lose your virginity or have that intimacy with someone. And it's heightened when it's your first time."
"Smart girl," X said, taking a bite of his food.

We ate and continued talking. I still wasn't sure about all of this, because of how we met. But I was really intrigued by X. He was definitely keeping my attention and it wasn't all bad. I just needed to figure out some things or clear my mind from all the madness that happened. I just kept going back and forth in my head about "what am I doing?" "Why was I entertaining him like this?" I just kept thinking I really need to go see Liz and get away from him so I can think better.

We finished eating and headed back to the hotel. I kept thinking I have to find a way to leave. I mean he seems cool, maybe I should just tell him I really need to go. I can go get my things and leave right? We made it back to the room. I saw him put the key on the kitchen counter. I figured this is my time to go. I can grab the key and this time when he says I can leave I just leave.

"X, this was fun and all but I really should get back to check on Liz."
"And what happens when she doesn't let you in the house or better yet maybe she is at Tammy's house trying to comfort her. Give it a day, we can go see her tomorrow."
"I don't want to stay here with you. I know things are going well, and I do like you, but I really just want to clear my head. I mean maybe I should just go home right now."
"You go home right now and then what? Or better yet don't you live with Liz. How is that going to work out? Are you going to move in with your parents until you can figure it out?"
"Why does that matter to you? I have no clue what I am going to do."

"So, just hear me out. If you stay tonight. I will go with you and sort things out with Liz. And I know you were supposed to go to Paris next week. Well, you probably don't want to go with Tammy anymore. I will get us tickets in the morning and we can catch a flight out on Wednesday. That way you can still say you enjoyed your vacation. Then when we get back, I will help you break your lease with Liz if things don't work out. I will get you a place here in New York."

"So, you are buying me out of my problems to move here with you to New York. I don't think so," I said walking to the 2nd bedroom to get my suitcase.
"Deja, if you want to leave the key is on the kitchen counter. I'm not forcing you to stay. I was just wanting you to still have a good vacation."

I grabbed the key off the counter and walked to the elevator. This time I swiped the key before I pushed the button. Hurry up the elevator. Why was I thinking about his option? I mean besides the moving to New York part it sounded doable. Right? I need this elevator to move faster.

"Deja, it's late. You're not going to catch a flight to Columbus tonight," X said. I could feel him standing right behind me.
"Why are you trying to force me to stay with you?"
"I'm not forcing you to stay. I'm just letting you know what you may be leaving behind if you walk out those doors."
"If I choose to stay tonight. I can't move to New York. And this does not mean you are buying me, you can't control me, and you really need to take the app off my phone too," I said. I handed him my phone.

He paused for a minute.

I Am A Survivor: Sex, Lies, and Abuse

"Okay," X said, taking the phone from me.

I watched as he showed me the app and removed the spyware app.

"Thank you," I said, getting my phone from him.

I put my suitcase back in the 2nd bedroom. I explained to him I would be sleeping in there tonight alone just so I could clear my head of everything that happened today. He agreed with no hesitation. I closed the door and put my pajamas on. It was close to midnight and I wanted to lay down from all of the stress today. I was so frustrated. I didn't even know what to say anymore. All I was thinking is, what do I do now?

Chapter Four: Damaged
"Everything is going to be okay."

I woke up in a panic. I screamed. "Shitt!" I looked around. Oh, good it was a damn nightmare. But my chest was hurting horribly. I grabbed my chest. It was tight and it hurt so bad. I heard X open the door.

"Deja, are you okay?" he said sitting on the bed next to me.
"I don't know. I had a horrible dream. I woke up panicking and my chest is hurting."
"Here let me see. Lay down on your back. I'm going to push on your shoulders to stretch you out. Let me know if the pain gets worse or better."

I laid down and he pushed on both of my shoulders and within seconds I felt something move and the pain stopped.

"Wow, it feels better."
"Good."
"Thank you, X."
"You're welcome," he said as he got up to leave. He turned back. "Come lay with me. I'll keep you safe."

I hesitated, but that nightmare was so bad I didn't want to say no. I got up and followed him to the owner's suite. We laid down and he wrapped his arms around me. I was asleep in no time.

I woke up to X talking on the phone. I couldn't hear what was being said because he was in the bathroom with the shower running. But I could hear him talking. I looked at the clock and it was 10am. I grabbed my phone and tried to call Liz again. The phone was going straight to voicemail. I was about to text when I saw my dad calling.

"Hi daddy."
"Hey, baby girl. Are you having fun?"
"Yes, daddy Manhattan is amazing."
"That's good. Liz must have really been missing her family. You guys left earlier than planned."
"Yea, Liz was so excited to see her family. And they were happy to see her too."
"So, what's on the agenda today?"
"Probably some shopping, not for sure."
"What's wrong baby girl? You know daddy can hear it in your voice. Are you having men troubles?"

I Am A Survivor: Sex, Lies, and Abuse

"No, dad you know I'm single," I said, trying to convince myself. My dad was good at reading me even on the phone.
"Baby girl,"
"Daddy, I'm fine. I just woke up, that's all."
"Alright now, well you girls have fun and make sure you text us when you get to Paris, and remember, be safe."
"Yes, sir always. I love you daddy."
"I love you too baby girl. Talk to you later," My dad said before hanging up.
"So, you're single now?" X said standing at the bathroom door in a towel.

I didn't even pay attention to the shower cutting off.

"Why are you listening to my phone call?"
"You didn't answer my question."
"Good morning, X, don't start today."
"Good morning, Deja, I just asked a simple question."
"Ugh, yes X I'm single."
"Okay, was that hard to answer? You said it, pretty easy on the phone with your dad."

I threw the covers over my head to hide my reaction. It was too early and I didn't know how to answer that question, because I still didn't know what the hell I was doing.

"Deja," X said as he pulled the covers down and was now on top of me.
"X," I said, staring him in the face.
"How old are you?"
"26," I said, irritated.
"Then act like it," he said, kissing my lips before standing up. "Go get dressed. We are going to meet up with Liz for lunch."
"You talked to her," I said as I jumped up in excitement.
"Yeah, she agreed to meet us for lunch."
"What," I jumped on X's back and hugged him. "THANK YOU, THANK YOU!"
"Get your ass in the shower, and you're welcome."

I ran to jump in the shower. I was so excited. How did he get through to her? I am so happy right now. I was dancing and singing while I was taking my shower. I knew I had to calm down, because I didn't know what mood she would be in or what he said to get her to meet me. I now knew I must be blocked if he was able to call her. I took a deep breath after I got out of the shower. I realized I was going to have to walk to the other bedroom. I forgot my suitcase was in that room. I wrapped my towel around me. I came out into the owner's suite and to my surprise X had some clothes laid out for me. They had tags on them. It was a white button-down shirt with a white tank top to go underneath with some ripped jeans. He even bought me a new bra and underwear. And some white sneakers and socks.

"X, what is this?"
"I bought you some clothes to wear."
"You know I have clothes. You don't have to keep buying me clothes."
"You know just a simple thank you would be nice."
"X,"
"What?"
"Thank you," I said, grabbing the clothes.
"You're welcome."

X left the room. I got dressed and we headed out to meet with Liz. I was so nervous. I didn't know what I was going to say. I kept moving my hands while we were riding in the car. I couldn't sit still.

"Deja, relax."
"I can't. You know me and Liz never fight. I mean I can't even remember a time where she got mad at me or I got mad at her, even in college. Like we always see eye to eye."
"It's going to be fine."
"But what if she hates me now. That's my best friend. I don't want to lose her."
"And you won't."

We pulled up to Jazzy's, a brunch restaurant. We walked inside and Liz was already seated at the table. She didn't look too happy. I was preparing myself for this. It will be okay.

"Well, I see you both made it okay," Liz said, pretending to look at the menu.
"Hi, Liz," I said as I sat down. X sat next to me.
"Hello," Liz said.
"Should we order first?" X interrupted.
"Sure, why not," Liz said with an attitude.

Liz gave her order to the waiter and X ordered for me and him again.

"Oh wow, it must be serious. He knows what you like already."
I looked at X. "Liz, it's not like that. I mean. I don't know. I just want to say I'm sorry. I didn't mean to do anything to hurt you, your friend, or your brother. I love you Liz, you are my best friend."
"Do you know how embarrassing that was, bringing you into my friend's house and you fucking her man. And then you're still with him in my face."

I Am A Survivor: Sex, Lies, and Abuse

"I tried calling you myself. You have me blocked. I didn't know he was going to call you and set this up."
"Why are you still with him?"
I paused and looked at X. "I don't know Liz. I'm still trying to figure this out myself. I mean I talked with X and we just have this really good connection. And I mean you pretty much left me to figure it out myself when he was there to help."
"I left your ass, because you embarrassed the shit out of me. And then you bring me here to show off your new dude the one you fucked in my friend's house," Liz began to yell.
"Okay, hold on now Liz, you need to calm down and hear Deja out."
"Oh, now he's fighting your battles too. You know what I don't know what I was thinking. I'm out of here," Liz said as she got up to walk away.

This did not go well. X got up and followed behind Liz. I just sat there and put my hands in my face. I knew this was not going to go over well. Why am I still with this man? I look so stupid thinking I can be with him. A few minutes went by. I turned around to see Liz and X talking. She looked frustrated but she was shaking her head yes to him. I wasn't close enough to hear what they were saying. I saw X pull out something and started to write something down. He handed it to Liz. Liz looked shocked and began to smile. She hugged X. What just happened? Liz and X came back to the table.

"I'm sorry Deja. X just told me everything and you're right I should have listened to you." Liz said, sitting back down.
"I'm confused. What just happened?" I said, lost.
"Like I said, X told me everything and I get it you were drunk and my brother just shot you down you were vulnerable and X went for you."
"What made you change your mind? I'm so lost. What did you write on that piece of paper X?" I said getting upset.

The waiter brought the food out.

"Let's eat. I'm starving and this food looks good." Liz said, ignoring my frustrations.
"What is going on right now?" I said angry.
"Look, Deja, I told her the truth. It wasn't your fault it was mine. I took advantage of you. I knew Randy pretty much shut you down before you came back to the house. Tammy said something about how she saw him shut you down when you asked to go back home with him. I didn't tell you I knew that and when I saw you standing there, I couldn't believe that he would turn your sexy ass down. I wanted you the instant I saw you," X said.

I Am A Survivor: Sex, Lies, and Abuse

At this point I was annoyed. He was lying and Liz all of sudden was cool, because X told her the truth. I couldn't help but to think there was something more going on. I just ate my food and played along, because obviously they thought I was dumb enough to fall for the bullshit. I just didn't understand how Liz would just lie so easily and act like she was good all of a sudden. I was ready to go home for sure now. I didn't care what I had to explain to my parents. I wanted to get to the airport. This was some true fake ass shit I was dealing with. She started talking about how she unblocked my number. We can still go to Paris together, because Tammy's not going. I was annoyed.

After lunch we rode back to the hotel in silence. I was just so upset with Liz and how she switched to fake so quickly, that I didn't even care about making her my friend again. We made it to the hotel and as soon as we made it to the room, I couldn't hold it anymore.

"You paid her, didn't you? So, now you're buying my friendships?" I said picking up the couch pillow to throw at him.
"Deja,"
"No, be honest X," I said, trying to hit him, but he was holding my hands.

I just wanted to punch him. He wouldn't let me go. He turned me around and started holding me so I couldn't move. I started screaming and trying to break away. I was so angry. Like what the hell was he doing this for?

"Deja, calm down," X said.

I started to cry and he let me go.

"Yes, I offered her some money not just to lighten the mood or buy your happiness, but I know Tammy mentioned Liz being upset when she first got here. And I just thought some of the frustration Liz may have been mad about was her family troubles and not really about you. Liz didn't know until she was on her way here Friday night that her father made some bad deals recently gambling and it's going to cost them her family's house. Tammy mentioned that to me before you and Liz arrived in New York. I figured her being mad at you just put the icing on the cake. So, I figured if I could ease some of her worries then maybe she would see things a little better. I'm sorry."

"You can't buy happiness X. She was so fake with it you could see it clearly." I said, still angry.
"You're right, it was a stupid idea. I will have my bank rescind the money in the morning."

I Am A Survivor: Sex, Lies, and Abuse

"No, give her whatever the hell you promised her. It doesn't fucking matter now. I'm over this shit." I said going into the 2nd bedroom and shutting the door.

"Deja,"

I sat on the bed looking at flights to Columbus on my phone. I didn't see any leaving today, but I saw they had one leaving in the morning. I called the airlines to book it. I figured I still had my Paris ticket. Maybe they could exchange it for a ticket home, or I would just pay extra if I needed to. The representative on the phone was super sweet. She cancelled my flight to Paris and emailed me my confirmation that I would be leaving to go to Columbus at 9am tomorrow. I didn't care anymore. I was going home. I laid down so frustrated with everything, I cried myself to sleep.

I woke up around 7pm to my phone ringing.

"Hello," I said, clearing my throat.
"Deja, are you alone?"
"Randy?"

I sat up and realized X was sleeping right next to me. He must have come into my room after I went to sleep. I got up quietly and walked into the living room, shutting the door to the bedroom.

"Yes, I'm alone now. Randy, I don't even know what to say. How are you?"
"Don't worry about all that. I need you to meet me tonight. You need to get away from X, Deja. Come by yourself."

I looked on the kitchen counter and dining room table to see if X left the key out. He did, it was on the kitchen counter. I grabbed the key.

"Okay, where do you want me to meet you?" I whispered as I looked around the room hoping X didn't wake up.
"Meet me at 26th and 3rd. I will pick you up from there. Just make sure X doesn't follow you. He's dangerous Deja."
"Okay, I'm grabbing my shoes and leaving now." I whispered, putting my shoes on, grabbing my purse, and heading to the elevator.

I kept looking behind me hoping the elevator would open before X woke up and caught me. The doors opened and I hurried in the elevator. I made it to the lobby and ran out the doors. I waited until I was across the street at another hotel lobby before ordering the rideshare. The rideshare came within 2 minutes and I got in the car. I kept checking my phone and looking behind me to make sure no one was following me or trying to reach me. I know X showed me he took the spyware off but I kept checking my phone to make sure I didn't see it back on there, since he showed me what it looked like.

I started thinking to myself I knew something wasn't right about X. Randy said he is dangerous. I'm pretty sure this is why I have been feeling so lost, confused, and not sure what to do. I was getting worried about all of this and thinking it's a good thing I left out tonight. I will just have Randy take me to the airport in the morning and forget about my suitcase. Or maybe I should go to the airport now. I can call Randy when I get there and let him know I'm safe. As I was thinking that the rideshare pulled up to the corner of 26th and 3rd. Shit, I was here now. I got out of the car and looked around to make sure I didn't see any suspicious cars. I wasn't followed. The rideshare left and just as I was about to go into the coffee shop, I heard Randy calling my name. I turned around and saw his truck.

"Get in the car," Randy said.

I got in the car and he pulled off.

"Where are we going?"
"Just to a little spot up the street. I just want to make sure no one is following us."
"Okay," I said, looking around to make sure I didn't see anything either.

We pulled into what looked like an abandoned garage. It may have been an old car shop. Randy turned the car off and we sat in the car for a minute in silence. I kept watching him. He looked upset and frustrated. He finally got out of the car and I followed suit.

"Are you going to tell me what's going on?" I said, a little nervous.
"You know I really can't even believe I'm trying to help you, after the shit you did?" Randy said with anger in his voice.
"Randy, I'm sorry," I said, scared of what he might do.

He walked towards me and I backed up, nervous that he might hit me. He turned around and then turned back around towards me again.

"You know this was fucked up," he said getting in my face.
"Randy, I didn't mean to hurt you," I said, trying to back up again.
"The fucked-up part about all of this shit is I really started to like you," Randy paused. "And then you go and fuck X. Like I didn't even mean shit to you."
"It wasn't like that, Randy. I was drunk and he caught me off guard. And I know that doesn't make it right, but I didn't know what was happening until it happened. Oh, God I'm so sorry," I said, trying not to cry.

I Am A Survivor: Sex, Lies, and Abuse

"Hell, I should have known. X's sorry ass probably had this planned from jump. And to think I thought that dude was my friend."
"What? You were friends?" I questioned.
"Not anymore," Randy said, walking back towards his car.

I was missing something here. I didn't know if this was the time to try and figure it out, because I was getting scared of what Randy really was trying to do to me. He opened his car door and I started looking to see if there was another way out of this building, because I was afraid this was going to be where I died. He closed the car door and came back towards me. Shit, what do I do now?

"Randy," I said, trying to sound calm.

I was watching his hands to make sure he didn't get a weapon out of the car, but I didn't see anything in his hands. But he reached in his back pocket. I flinched. He pulled out his phone. Thank God.

"X, was at the club Sunday night. My boy sent me the pictures. He was scoping you out from the get go. And your dumb ass fell right in his trap," he showed me the pictures on his phone and the video.
"This doesn't prove anything he was probably checking on Tammy. She was right next to me," I said, trying to convince myself.
"Watch the full video, Deja."

I took his phone. From the video you could see a man I couldn't really tell if it was X, but he was the same height and built from the back. His boy videoed X with his phone out, zooming in on a close up of me dancing beside Tammy. He zooms in close enough to where Tammy is no longer in the view and it's just me. He watched me for a few minutes on the video and then he left. I handed Randy the phone back.

"And that's not all. Word on the street is X is planning to move you to New York. Liz told me today he gave her enough money to pay off my father's debt, the family house, and for her to pay off the apartment lease so she can move back home too. And he's planning to have you move here with him. But you already knew that didn't you?" Randy paused. "You're planning on moving here with him, aren't you?"
"No, I never agreed to that."
"You still fucking him?"
"Randy, that's not why I am here. You said he was dangerous, what do you know?"
"You still fucking him. I can't believe this shit. You bitch. You just fell right into his trap and said fuck me huh?" Randy said, getting angry again.

"Randy, you are scaring me. Please just tell me what you know."
"Fuck you," Randy said as he grabbed me by neck.
"RANDY," I screamed trying to break free from his grip.
"You gave him my pussy and now I'm going to take it," Randy said, pinning me against the wall and trying to take my pants off.

I screamed. I tried to break free from his grip, but he was starting to choke me. I pushed him but he wouldn't let go. I kneed him in his balls and he let me go. I started to run but he grabbed me from behind and threw me on the ground. He started kicking me in the stomach. I covered my stomach and then he bent down and punched me in the face. I screamed in pain. This was it, I was going to die. He started tugging at my pants again.

"Bitch, I'm going to take this pussy," he said as he punched me in the side, because I was trying to stop him.
"STOP, RANDY," I screamed out trying to keep him from pulling my pants down.
"SHUT UP, BITCH," he yelled, hitting me over and over again.

I was tiring but I wasn't going to give up on stopping him; as he almost had my pants down. He just kept hitting me in my stomach, my arm, and my face trying to get me to stop fighting him.

"YOU LET X TAKE IT WITH NO FIGHT, BUT YOU TRYING ME," he yelled, still punching me every chance he could.

I was giving up. I couldn't hold off anymore. I was in so much pain. I knew this was it. I saw car lights and heard a loud screech noise. It was a car pulling into the garage. I tried to scream but nothing came out. Randy noticed the car too and finally lifted off of me. I looked up to see X running towards me and Randy. X punched the shit out Randy and they went at it. I tried to move to get up, but my stomach was on fire. My arm was throbbing in pain. I could hear them tussling, but I was trying to get up so I could leave. I could hear what sounded like another car pulling up and a couple of people running towards us. At this point I knew I couldn't move so I just curled myself up in a ball hoping that no one tried to hit me again. I could hear X yelling.

"Get this lame ass dude the fuck out of here. I got her. Take his car too. Clear this area," X said.
"You got it boss," I heard someone say in all the commotion going on around me.

I felt someone grab me and I screamed.

"Deja, it's me X. I'm going to pick you up and put you in the car," he said.

I Am A Survivor: Sex, Lies, and Abuse

I looked up to make sure it was X. It was. I put my arms around his neck even though I was in pain. I let him pick me up. I screamed, but I held as strong as I could.

"It's okay baby, I got you," I heard X say.

He drove us back to the hotel. When we got there, I saw a few guys waiting on X. He got out of the car and started talking to them.

"I need you to tell the hotel clerk that we need to go in from the back. I don't want to carry Deja in looking like this so everyone can see her. And get a blanket or something so I can cover her," I heard X tell one of the guys.

X got back in the car and two of the guys got in the back seat. X drove to the back of the hotel. When we got back there, I saw one of the hotel staff holding a blanket and the door open. The other guy X was talking to earlier came to the car. X got out of the car and he took the keys from X. X grabbed the blanket from the hotel staff and came and opened my door. He wrapped the blanket around me and picked me up. One of the guys in the back seat got out and got in the passenger seat. I saw them pull off as X carried me through the back door of the hotel. The staff guided us to the staff elevators and up to our suite.

X laid me on the couch and wrapped the blanket tight around me. I wanted to cry, but I knew any movement would hurt. X went into the bathroom and came back out with some wet rags and alcohol. He sat next to me and poured the alcohol on one of the dry rags. He put it to my lip. I screamed.

"Deja, I'm sorry I'm just trying to clean up the cut. You're probably going to be swollen tomorrow."

I tried to say something but I just started crying. And then I started screaming, because it hurt to cry. My stomach was on fire. X ran to the kitchen to grab ice and he put it in a bag. He placed it on my stomach. And then he walked away. He looked pissed.

"FUCK." He yelled.

I jumped.

"I CAN'T BELIEVE HE DID THIS SHIT," he yelled pacing back and forth.

He paced for a while talking to himself. Then he looked at me. He didn't say anything. He walked towards me and picked me up. I screamed in pain. He carried me to the owner's suite and sat me on the bed. He unwrapped the blanket from around me slowly, since he knew I was in pain. He took off my button-down shirt and left the tank top on me, but he slowly took off my bra. I screamed again. He took my shoes and socks off and my pants. He lifted my legs up after he took off my pants and covered me up with the blanket on the bed. He picked up my clothes and the blanket that was wrapped around me and cut the light off and left the room. He never said anything else. I laid there with tears in my eyes. I couldn't believe what just happened. I didn't know what to think. I closed my eyes and fell asleep.

I woke up the next morning. It was now Wednesday and the clock read 9:10am. I had missed my flight. Not that I would have been able to move to get anywhere. I realized X was not in the room with me. The place seemed quiet, so I don't know where X was. I knew I had to get up though, because I had to pee. I slowly tried to lift up, but started panic breathing as the pain was hitting harder than yesterday. I felt like a train hit me. I finally made it to my feet. I leaned on the nightstand to make sure I could move my legs okay. I made it to the bathroom, it hurt to sit on the toilet. It hurt to stand back up as well. After I washed my hands, I walked over to the mirror and lifted my tank top up. I could already see the bruises on my face and arm, but my stomach looked like he used me as a punching bag. I tried to touch my stomach and instantly felt sharp pain. I began to feel queasy and I made my way back to the toilet to throw up. I was crouched down by the toilet when I saw X out of the corner of my eye standing in the doorway watching me.

"Damn, Deja."

I forgot to pull my tank back down so I'm pretty sure he was noticing the bruises. He crouched down beside me and pulled my braids back as I continued to throw up. He started rubbing my back as I leaned over the toilet. After I finished, I leaned back on the floor and rested my back on his chest. He pushed his head into the back of my braids and I felt him kiss my head. He reached around to touch my stomach.

"Please, don't," I said as I jerked, scared, he was going to touch me. "It hurts."
"Let me get you back to bed."
"No, I don't want to move right now everything hurts."

We sat on the bathroom floor for about 20 minutes. He was rubbing my legs to make me feel better, because he couldn't touch my stomach. Finally, I let him carry me back to the bed. He put the covers back over me and he left the room. I closed my eyes again and dozed off.

I Am A Survivor: Sex, Lies, and Abuse

I was awakened by voices in the room. I opened my eyes to see X and some strange man standing by the bedroom door. I grabbed the blanket to cover myself since I only had on my tank and panties.

"It's okay, Deja, this is a good friend of mine. He is a doctor," X said once he noticed I was awake.
"Hi, Deja, my name is Dr. Aaron Saunders. I was told about your bruises and I just want to check you out. Is that okay with you?"

I shook my head yes, because I didn't want to talk. He pulled the covers back and looked at the bruises on my arm and face. He asked X if he could lift my shirt. I looked at X.

"It's okay, Deja, he just needs to see the damage," X said.

That word stuck in my head… I was damaged. I couldn't even think straight anymore. I just wanted this to be over with. How can I stop this pain? I was mentally, emotionally, and now physically damaged. I began to cry as I felt the doctor gently pressing on my stomach.

"I think she needs to go to the hospital." Dr. Saunders said. "I will call the ambulance."

The doctor walked out of the room to call 911.

I found the courage to screech out some words. "X's what's happening?"
"Deja, you have to go to the hospital," X said, sitting next to me holding my hand.

I began to freak out.

"Don't worry I will be with you the whole time and Dr. Saunders will meet us there to take care of you," X said, trying to calm me. "Everything is going to be okay."

Chapter Five: Furious
"This shit just keeps getting better and better."

All I saw was bright lights and people towering over me. They were pushing me in a bed and X was right there with them telling me I was going to be okay. They were rushing me somewhere and I didn't know what was happening. I could hear a lot of talking, but I couldn't make out anything they were saying. I was going in and out of consciousness. And then everything went black.

I woke up to machines beeping. I was in a hospital room and I could see they had a saline bag attached to me. I saw Dr. Saunders and X standing at the foot of my bed.

"I don't think we should worry her with everything right now. I don't want her to panic," I heard X say.
"What are you not trying to tell me?" I said clearing my throat so X can hear me.
"Deja," X said, coming to my side.
"What's going on doc," I addressed the doctor, because I knew X wasn't trying to tell me something.
X looked at me. "Go ahead, tell her doc," X said.
"Deja, how are you feeling?" Dr. Saunders said.

I actually didn't feel any pain at this point. I figured they must have given me some pain meds. I just felt heavy and my eyes felt heavy too.

"I'm feeling fine. What happened?"
"Well, the bruises in your stomach were concerning. I wanted to bring you in to do some tests and get some blood work to make sure you didn't have any internal bleeding. It's not too alarming but you did have some minor blood vessels burst in your stomach. It only caused bleeding into the skin, no real major damage. But I want you to get plenty of rest and take things easy for a few days," Dr. Saunders said looking at X.

He wasn't telling me everything. I could tell.

"X, don't keep things from me what's going on," I asked, getting upset.
"Deja, listen to the doc. I think right now the best thing to do is just get some rest and I'll take care of you," X said, rubbing my hand.

I pulled away from X. I began to breathe hard. What the fuck was happening? I began to panic. Why are they keeping secrets? Am I dying? X grabbed my hand again, and Dr. Saunders checked me out. I calmed my breathing trying not to freak out. I was losing it though. I didn't know what to feel right now.

I Am A Survivor: Sex, Lies, and Abuse

"Am I dying, what's wrong with me?" I said angry at this point.
"No, nothing that serious about your health. I just know you really should stay off your feet for a while and get rest. You have to let everything heal," Dr. Saunders reassured me before stepping out of my room.

What the fuck is happening? What was X hiding?

"X, please tell me. I won't freak out. I just want to know, am I okay?" I asked, trying to stay calm.
"You are okay. It's just some other stuff going on that I talked with Dr. Saunders about and it doesn't have anything to do with your health. You know I told you he is my friend and we were just talking about some things. I think you should just focus on you right now though and get a lot of rest."

I just looked at X. I didn't say anything else, but I was still panicking inside. X looked at me and put his head down.

"Alright, some shit happened. I got a phone call while you were sleeping about an hour ago. I shouldn't be telling you this right now, because the last thing you need to be doing is worrying," X paused. "Deja, it's Liz. She's in the hospital too."
"What? In this hospital? I need to go see her. What happened?" I said, trying to get up, but X stopped me.
"Listen, you can't go see her. Her family is here and I don't know what Randy told them exactly but they think you are bad news too."
"What? I didn't do anything to Liz," I started to worry.
"What I know is, Liz's boyfriend Eddie Maze came to New York last night. I guess Liz has been ignoring his calls since she's been here. So, he came to New York sometime yesterday. He asked around and found out she was at Club Essence with Tammy last night so he went there. He pulled her out of the club, well, dragged her out and took her somewhere. I don't know where. But word has it he beat her up pretty bad, and drugged her with heroin. She made it back home and her family immediately brought her to the hospital this morning."
"Oh, my God," I said, shocked. I was lost for words. I wanted to see her.
"That look right there is why I didn't want to say anything." X said, acknowledging my tears.

We sat in silence for a while as I wiped away my tears. I still loved her no matter the situation going on right now. And hearing that just made me feel horrible again. I never thought Eddie would be that brutal. It bothered me that her family was mad at me and I wouldn't be able to see her. That really hurt my soul. I just wanted to hug her.

I Am A Survivor: Sex, Lies, and Abuse

I fell back to sleep and woke up again to Dr. Saunders talking with X. X told him that he told me everything and he hated my reaction. He stated he felt like he just put more worrying on my plate. Dr. Saunders reassured him everything would be fine. Dr. Saunders saw I was awake.

"Well, she's awake. How are you feeling Deja?"
"I feel okay, a little sore now."
"I'm going to send you home with some pain meds, nothing too serious, just some Tylenol 3's to ease the pain at night. Soon you will start feeling a lot better. But I am going to release you in a few. Let me check in on a few things and I will be back," Dr. Saunders said before leaving the room.

Dr. Saunders came back with my discharge papers, prescriptions, and follow up instructions. X and I left the hospital and headed back to the hotel. When we got back to the hotel X handed my prescriptions to the hotel clerk and asked him to make sure they got picked up. I didn't know hotels did that. But the hotel clerk just agreed and said he would bring them up once they were picked up. We made it into the suite. I had on hospital clothes so I went to take a shower in the 2nd bathroom and put on something comfortable. I pulled out some sweat pants and a t-shirt. I came back into the living room. I slowly walked over to the couch and propped up some pillows behind me to sit down comfortably. I turned the TV on hoping to find something good to watch. I figured at this point I was stuck in this hotel with X for at least a few days, before I could figure out my next move. But for now, I didn't want to think about anything really, I just wanted to watch some TV. Besides, X seemed a little bothered himself. He didn't say much once we got in the suite. He just went to the owner's suite and I heard him turn the shower on and close the door. I found some crime documentaries to watch and just chilled.

About an hour later I heard the elevator. I was still watching TV and X never came out of the room. I figured he must have gone to sleep. The hotel clerk asked if he could come inside. I said yes. He handed me the prescription pills and he asked if I needed anything else. I said no and thanked him. I started to tip him, but he said no Mr. Thomas has already taken care of all of his tips. I just said okay, and he left.

A couple of hours went by, I thought I better get up and check on X. He hasn't said anything to me since we got here and he's been in the room the whole time even after his shower. I was starting to get hungry and figured I was going to have to do something for food. I opened the door to the owner's suite to see him passed out on the bed still in the towel he obviously put on after his shower. He looked like he just dropped from being worn out, but he did look sexy laying there. No Deja chill with your thoughts, besides I don't even think I had the

I Am A Survivor: Sex, Lies, and Abuse

energy for sex right now. I tried to help him out a little and picked his legs up and placed him correctly in the bed. That hurt a little but not too bad. I covered him with the blanket and kissed his cheek.

I went back in the living room heading to the kitchen hoping there was food to cook in the fridge. I happened to see the fridge was actually stocked with food. I pulled out some chicken and seasoning to go with it. I saw there were some macaroni noodles in the cabinet. I figured I was going to make some fried chicken with mac and cheese. I turned some music on, from my phone not too loud so I wouldn't wake X. I always liked cooking with music on, it gets the vibe going. I started singing and frying my chicken. The mac and cheese was done. I just had a few pieces of chicken left to cook. I finished those and cut the fryer off. I jumped back when I turned around and saw X standing in the kitchen.

"SHIT! You scared me. Ouch," I screamed. I felt sharp pain on my side when I jumped back.
"You okay."
"Yea, I'm fine. You almost gave me a heart attack."
"You cooked?"
"I did. I started to get hungry, you were sleeping, and I didn't want to wake you. You looked really tired. So, I figured I would see what was in this kitchen."
"Hmmm,"
"What?"
"I guess I didn't know you could cook."
"Well, not downing my cooking or anything, but you haven't tried it yet either," I said jokingly.
"I guess I'll order a pizza if it's horrible."
"Hey," I said, frowning my face.

X laughed. I made our plates and he placed them on the table for me.
"You know you really shouldn't be standing for too long," X said.
"Are you going to be that strict about this? I feel fine."
"Okay, if you feel fine. I will leave it alone."
"Thank you, try the food," I said sitting down at the table with X.

He took the first bite of his chicken. It crunched so; I knew I made it good. His face said it all.

"Damn, that's some good fried chicken right there."
I smiled at his reaction. "Good, I'm glad you like it."

We ate and talked. He kept complimenting the food so I knew I did good. He also seemed in better spirits, but I also felt better too. I guess it just felt good to do something normal again. I mean I feel like since I came to New York nothing felt normal. So, this felt good. X cleaned up the kitchen once we were done. I tried to help but he just kept pushing me away and then he told me to go find a movie to watch. So, I went into the living room to find a movie on the streaming channels. He joined me once he finished the kitchen. We watched a movie and when it went off, I started to look for another one but X grabbed the remote. I looked at him.

"Why did you leave when Randy called you?" he said, a little frustrated.
I looked at X and then I looked down. I felt a little guilty. "He said he had to tell me something about you and that you were dangerous?"
"And you believed him."
"I don't know if I actually believed him."
"But you snuck out of here, didn't say nothing to me, and you went."
"I did," I paused. I felt horrible again. "I went because I felt like I owed it to Randy. I hurt him and I thought if I could just tell him I'm sorry and talk it out maybe I would feel better about what I was doing."
"And what were you doing?"
"I'm with you X. Even though I was talking to Randy first. A part of me felt like I should at least give him the benefit of the doubt, because I didn't even try to make it right. I just stayed with you."
"So, were you planning to fuck him?"
"X, no I was not planning to fuck him," I said irritated.
"Then what were you expecting from him?"
"I don't know. I was scared. He called me saying you were dangerous. I didn't know if I should believe him, but I didn't know if I should ignore it either. I thought about it the whole ride there. I even just thought about going to the airport, because I didn't know why I was still here. My mind was just going crazy and I didn't know what was the right thing to do," I said, about to cry.
"You know I was super worried about you when I got up and you weren't here," X said, calming his tone.
"How did you find me?"
"I tracked you."
"I thought you said you took the app off my phone."
"I took the app off your phone, not the tracker."
"Thank you," I said feeling guilty. "If you didn't show up, I don't know if I would still be alive."
"I want you to trust me, Deja." X said, grabbing my wrist.

Shit! The feelings were coming back and I could feel the chills shooting through my body. I don't even know if I had strength to do anything, but my body was yearning for him. He stood up and pulled me up. He walked me to the owner's suite. He pulled me in front of him facing the bed.

I Am A Survivor: Sex, Lies, and Abuse

He whispered in my ear. "I'll go slow and if you trust me, I won't hurt you."

I felt my pussy get wet. He was doing it again. My body was reacting to his words, his touch, every breath he took I could feel it. He pulled my jogging pants off and gently laid me on the bed. He took my panties off. He lifted my right leg up and bit my thigh. I laughed a little. His face went in my pussy massaging away with his tongue. I screamed in ecstasy as I started to cum. My body was covered in chills and sensations were flowing through me. I was feeling every movement and my body was screaming in joy. I couldn't control myself as I started cumming back-to-back. He made me feel so amazing. My legs began to shake and my pussy was super wet. I whispered "fuck me X" I was ready to feel him inside me. He wouldn't stop eating me out. I couldn't stop cumming either. He had me screaming in ecstasy. Shit he was working his mouth on me and I was yearning for his penis inside me. Fuck, he was making me want him bad. "Please, X fuck me" I cried as my pussy was getting hotter and wetter.

I just wanted to feel him inside me. I cried out again as I was cumming again "I trust you, X, I trust you." He lifted up and slid his penis inside me. He went so deep my pussy started pulsating immediately as I was cumming again. I cried in ecstasy as the feeling was what I wanted, what I was yearning for. He began to glide back and forth going deep. I was over flowing in juices. My pussy missed him. I came so many times my legs couldn't stop shaking. He put his hands on my legs and pushed all his weight on my pelvic. I immediately came as I felt him going deeper inside me. I screamed out "fuck me X". He began pounding harder and harder, I couldn't keep quiet, my moans got louder. I was overwhelmed with chills when I felt myself about to cum again, he was taking me to my highest highs with the way he fucked me. I was enjoying every minute of it. I could feel we were both about to climax. I couldn't stop the words I whispered "I love you X" as I felt my body shaking and I came at the same time as him. He leaned down to kiss me hard and I wrapped my legs and arms around him. Damn, I was falling for this man.

I don't know what time we passed out but it wasn't too long after we finished having sex. I woke up to see that it was 5am. I looked over at X. He was still sleeping. I slowly got up to go to the bathroom. I already felt like the pain was getting better, because it was not hard to move. I stopped at the mirror again to view my bruises. The swelling went down in my face and I could just see a dark bruise on my cheek and the cut was healing on my lip. My arms didn't look so bad. But I lifted up my shirt to see my stomach. It was some improvement but I was still black and blue all over my stomach. I touched it again to see if it still hurt. It was sore, but not as bad as before. I went to the bathroom. I finished in the bathroom and came back to the room. X was still sleeping. I went into the living room to watch TV, because I wasn't sleepy and didn't want to wake X cutting on the room TV.

I walked in the living room to someone standing in the kitchen. I cut the light on and realized who it was.

"Tammy, what are you doing here?" I said, nervous.
"Oh, what, like you're the only one that knows this place. X brought me here many times, you ain't special. Where the hell is he anyway, bitch," Tammy said, leaning on the kitchen counter.
"He's asleep," I said annoyed.
"Well, did he do that to your face?" Tammy said laughing. "Hmm, he started early with you. What the hell you do, to piss him off so quickly."
"Excuse me," I said confused.
"I mean at least he gave me a whole year of the lavish life, before he showed me his true colors. I guess that's what you get for fucking him when he was still mine, bitch."
"Tammy, I think you need to leave. How did you even get up here?" I said, pissed now.
"Oh, don't mind me. I was just coming to collect my money from X and then I will be long gone. Hell, I don't want him and I don't care what he's doing to you. Hell, you probably would have been better off with Randy anyway. But that's just my opinion. They're both assholes, you just picked the worst one." Tammy continued on. "And, I hope you don't think you're the only one."
"That's enough Tammy," X said, coming out of the room. "Deja, go back in the room."
I stood there for a minute frustrated.
"Deja, go back in the room," X said again. I went back into the owner's suite and X closed the door.

I was furious. What the hell was she talking about? How did she even get up here? I tried to listen at the door. I could hear Tammy say she used the code to the elevator. She mentioned him giving her the money he promised her. I heard X tell her she needed to leave and he was going to make sure he changed the code. He also said something about if she had a problem with the money she was to receive she needed to take that up with his assistant. X yelled for her to get the fuck out and Tammy yelled fuck you when I heard the elevator. I stepped away from the door. I sat on the bed with my arms crossed waiting for X to explain this shit. This shit just keeps getting better and better.

Chapter Six: Home
"It's comfortable here."

X came into the room and closed the door. I just stared at him waiting for him to say something.

"What do you want to say Deja?" X said, with an attitude.
"I figured you had something to say. I don't have nothing to say," I said, trying to watch my tone just in case what Tammy said about him being abusive is true.
"Okay, well she's been here before. Yes, she knows the code to the elevator without the key. I will get that changed asap. The bullshit she said about me having other females well that's what she always assumed and that's why we weren't working out. We argued a lot and sometimes I had to restrain her, because she would get physical with me not the other way around. And yes, I did promise her money but she needs to talk with my assistant about that, not me. I'm true to my word and she will get what she was promised," X said, standing against the door. "Do you have any questions?"
"Were you friends with Randy before all of this?" I said, thinking about what Randy mentioned and what Tammy said.
"Yes," X said, sighing.
"Why didn't you tell me that?"
"I didn't think it would matter at this point. He wants nothing to do with me or you obviously."
"But it kind of matters X. You said you knew I was talking to Randy and if he was your friend and you still went for me. Your loyalty is a little weary."
"My relationship with Tammy and my friendship with Randy wasn't that strong. Honestly, I was on the verge of calling it quits with Tammy and Randy had a few bullshit stunts he pulled on me. I wasn't loyal to them, because I was close to being done with them. Like I said before when I laid eyes on you for the first time, I wanted you and I was in a vulnerable state too. So, I saw an opportunity and I took it."
"Did you first lay eyes on me at the club or at Tammy's house?"
X looked at me. "At the club. How did you know about that?"
"Randy, showed me a video of you checking me out from a distance."
"Damn, that dude was trying it wasn't he," X put his head down and laughed to himself. "Does this make you think differently of me?"
"It's definitely making me think. But my feelings haven't changed as far as how I feel about you. That doesn't change easily X."
"Oh yea, how do you feel about me?" X said, walking towards me.
"I told you last night X," I said, trying not to smile. I wanted to be mad right now.
"I want to hear it again," X said, leaning down in my face to kiss me.

I gave in, because he was just turning me on. "I love you," I said, kissing him back.
"You what?"
"I love you, X," I said as I wrapped my arms around him and we began kissing again.
"Well, get dressed and pack your things," X said.
"Wait, why?"
"I may be a day late, but like I said I'm true to my word. We are going to Paris."

I smiled ear to ear when he said that. Okay call me crazy, but this man stuck to his word. We flew to Paris, we went to Venice, and Rome. He showered me with the lavish life and made the rest of my vacation fun. We stayed at the fanciest of hotels. We explored everything we possibly could while we were there. We ate, laughed, we had lots of sex, and I loved every bit of it. He had me on cloud nine. I didn't want to end the vacation, but I had to come home. We vacationed for a week and then we did come back to Manhattan, before I went home, because X was big on me following up with Dr. Saunders. Dr. Saunders cleared me and said my wounds were healing good. And they were. My face was pretty much good, but for the bruises that still remained I wore a little makeup to hide those. I knew my parents would want to see me once I made it to Columbus so I didn't want to worry them. X tried to convince me to stay in Manhattan, but I knew I had to get back to reality. I still wanted to work and I would eventually have to figure out what I was going to do about staying with Liz. I still worried about her, but I was hoping she was doing okay. And maybe I would see her at the apartment. Who knows. But since X couldn't get me to stay in Manhattan, he sure did fly back to Columbus with me.

We got off the airplane and headed through the airport of Columbus.

"So, where is your first stop?" X said.
"Home, I want to shower, eat, and then rest. I told my parents I will see them tomorrow, because I don't have to go back to work until Tuesday," I said, happy to be back in Columbus.
"Okay, well home it is," X said, playing along.

I got us a rideshare and headed to the apartment. I walked into the apartment in shock.

"What the hell?" I said, confused. I ran to my room. The whole apartment was empty like nothing was left. They didn't leave anything. It looked like it had been cleaned out literally. I started to panic.

"Deja, calm down," X said as he saw me panicking. "I moved you."

"What?" I said, confused. "What do you mean you moved me?"
"I moved you to another place."
"X, what the fuck?"
"Chill Deja, it was going to happen regardless. Now that I'm with you in Columbus we needed a bigger place."
"X, I don't like this."
"You will have to get used to it. I found a nice high-rise apartment in downtown Columbus close to your job so you can walk if you want and not have to worry about driving."
"X, what's going on?"
"For one, I want you safe. And with the high-rise we are on the top floor and we are the only ones that can access the top floor. It's for your safety."
"X, really."
"Deja, chill. Come on, I will show you our new home."
"Ugh," I said, frustrated with him.

He ordered us a rideshare to take us to the new place. Once we got in the car I thought about Liz.

"So, what did you do with Liz's stuff?"
"When I had my people come to Columbus to make the arrangements for you, they said the 2nd bedroom had already been cleared out. I guess Liz or her family had already moved her back to New York. I followed up with that and she is living in New York full time."
"Is she doing, okay?"
"For the most part. I was told she is fighting a war with herself. After Eddie gave her those drugs she's still using. The family wants to put her in rehab but every time they bring it up, she threatens to leave and they don't want her on the streets."
"Oh God, I didn't know it got that serious. I wish I could help her."
"I tried Deja. I had a good friend of mine, he's a counselor, talk with her about kicking the habit, but she wasn't ready. He did say he could tell she was using before this thing with Eddie. It may not have been heroin, but she was definitely already addicted to drugs."
"How did I miss that?"
"She was probably functional, especially if it was something like cocaine. Cocaine is an upper; it just keeps you wired with energy."
"She didn't sleep much and she was full of energy, high energy. I mean she did drive us all the way to New York on no sleep and she was still not tired when we got there. I just never assumed it was drugs."

I was just shocked to hear that. Maybe I didn't really know Liz at all. We pulled up to the apartment complex downtown. I wanted to smack X. My job was literally

right down the street not even 2 blocks, maybe a block and a half. I would definitely be walking to work. But that made me think, where is my car?
"Where is my car X?" I said as we were getting out the rideshare.
"Oh yeah, this new apartment complex has a parking garage in the back. Your car is parked there."
"But how did you know what car I had?"
"I had to do some digging while you were sleeping. See I figured you had a picture of your car in your phone. The keys were in the house so I just had to let my crew know what car it was."
"250 High Apartments." I read as we walked in the building.

We went up to the top floor. X handed me the keycard and the codes for the doors, elevator, and garage. I can't believe he moved me. I was still in shock. I wanted to be mad, but we just had a really good time this last week enjoying each other. Getting to know each other more and making this madness of craziness work.

We made it to the top which was the 12th floor. The elevators opened to a small hallway with the door to our apartment. I opened the door with the key card. It was a long hallway that led right into the living room. To the left of the front door was a spacious kitchen. The hallway led you right into the open living room. The place was already furnished. The furniture was new, it didn't come from my apartment. The living room also had a wall of windows like the hotel we stayed at in Manhattan. You could see a beautiful view of the city. There was a huge balcony area furnished with patio furniture. To the left of the living room there was a small hallway that led to the offices. The room on the right of the hallway was X's office, he said. The room at the end on the left was my office area. It had the furniture from my old apartment living room in it with my computer desk and bookshelf.

On the right side of the living room was another hallway that led to the bedrooms and the bathrooms. This apartment had the owner's suite bedroom at the end of the hallway with the walk-in closet and ensuite bath. The 2nd bedroom was first, on the right side of the hallway with the 2nd bath right next to it. I looked in the 2nd bedroom; X said he just put my bed in there because he bought a king size bed for the owner suite bedroom. When I saw the owner suite bedroom I checked the walk-in closet first. My clothes were already put up in the drawers and hanging in the walk-in closet. I also saw some clothes that had tags on it. I looked at X.

"What is this?" I said showing him a pretty ass dress but nothing I bought.
"I wanted to buy you a little something."
"X, you just upgraded my whole apartment. I think that was good enough."

I Am A Survivor: Sex, Lies, and Abuse

"Just accept this is what I do. You're going to have to adjust Deja," he said laying on that big ass king bed.
"Thank you. How much did this place cost or what is the rent here?"
"You're welcome and that's not for you to worry about. I'm covering the expenses."
"All the expenses?"
"Yes, all the expenses. You don't have to work if you don't want to."
"No, I want to work. But this is a lot X. I mean I don't know."
"What are you worried about?"
"What if we don't work out? Can I even afford this place?"
X smirked. "I ain't going nowhere Deja. Why are you trying to sabotage us?"
"Okay hear me out," I said sitting on the bed next to him. "You know I like to think reasonably right. I mean people break up all the time and I know we are doing good and I'm not trying to jinx anything but I know I can't afford this X."
"What if I told you I own the apartments and even if we break up you can stay here rent free."
"What?" I said, shocked. "Are you playing?"
"I'm not playing Deja."
I pulled out my phone. "250 High Apartments in Columbus, Ohio were recently sold to Xavier Thomas who is 36 years old, the owner of the top marketing firm in Brooklyn, New York called the X Factor. Mr. Thomas also partners with local businesses around New York to continue growing his wealth. He continues to work on ventures outside of New York as he has been in contract with some new partnerships in the state of New Jersey," I paused. "Oh my God. I never googled you before, you really are a big deal."
X smiled. "Kiss me."
I kissed him.

I continued to admire the room. I saw the closet door had a hook but it was far up. I would have to stand on my tippy toes to reach it. That seemed pretty high for a coat hanger. I also noticed a similar hook attached to the middle of the head board.

"X, what is the hook on the head board for?" I said, curious.
"You want to find out?"
"What is it for?" I said hoping he would tell me.
"Alright, stand up," X said, getting up from the bed.
"Why?" I said standing up anyway.

X didn't say nothing, he just lifted my shirt up over my head and then he took off my bra. I was confused. He walked over to the dresser and went in one of the top drawers and pulled out some handcuffs.

I Am A Survivor: Sex, Lies, and Abuse

"Hold your arms out."
"X, what is this?"
"You asked, now hold your arms out? You trust me, right?"
"Yes," I said, a little worried about what he was doing.

I held my arms out in front of me. He put the handcuffs on me. He grabbed the chain on the handcuffs and pulled me to the side of the bed. Still holding the chain, he sat me on the bed and laid me back. He climbed on top of me to place the chain of the handcuffs on the hook so that my hands were above my head and I was unable to free myself from the hook. Why the hell did I ask what the hook was for? He then lifted me up to position me in the center of the bed. He pulled off my shoes, pants, and underwear. He walked out of the room and left me in the middle of the bed, handcuffed to the hook on the head board. I called his name and he didn't even turn around. I tried seeing if I could at least unhook myself. But I couldn't, because the hook on the head board had a latch which locked it. This dude really left me on the bed naked, unable to get free.

I waited for 5 minutes and X did not return. I lifted myself up so that I wasn't lying down but sitting instead. I kept trying to figure out if there was a way to unlock this hook, but I couldn't see anything. I was starting to get cold so I slid my feet under the covers to warm up some. 10 minutes passed and still no X. I was trying not to panic, but he was making me worry. I called his name again and nothing. My arms were getting tired. I laid my head back on the head board and closed my eyes hoping he would walk in soon. I fell asleep.

I woke up maybe 30 minutes later and my arms were sore now. It was getting dark outside. And the room was pretty dark.

"X, where are you? My arms are getting tired," I spoke loudly, hoping he was still in the apartment at this point.

I looked at the clock by the bed. It was 6pm. I was also getting hungry as I realized I hadn't eaten anything since the plane ride. Where the hell is X? Finally, it sounded like he was coming back to the room.

X stood at the door. "You had enough?"
"Yes, where did you go? Why did you leave me?" I said, so frustrated.
"You giving me lip? I don't think you had enough?" X said, turning back around.
"X, no please don't leave me like this please," I said, begging.

X walked to the side of the bed and bent down coming close to me.

"I like when you beg," he said whispering in my ear.

I Am A Survivor: Sex, Lies, and Abuse

"X, please," I begged again, entertaining his nonsense hoping he would free me.

He reached up and took the handcuffs off of me and I was relieved to be able to put my arms down. I hurried up and got off the bed and ran to the bathroom, because I had to pee. I don't know why he did that and I hope that was not going to happen again. Next time don't ask about shit Deja. I cut the shower on and closed the door. I figured since I was already naked, I would take a shower and I locked the door, because that shit kind of pissed me off. And I just needed to not be bothered with him for a minute. I took my time in the shower as it felt good and warm. Plus, there were multiple shower heads in this shower and it felt like a full body massage. I heard X knock on the door, but I didn't care at this point. I just wanted to be alone and not tied up.

But I should have known this man had a damn key. He unlocked the door and stood at the shower door.

"What the fuck you locking doors for?" he said, agitated.
"X, I just wanted to take a shower and clear my head," I said, still enjoying the water hitting me.

X opened the shower door and cut the water off. Whatever, I thought to myself. I was so annoyed. Like I just didn't understand what that was all about. I stepped out of the shower and slid past X not even looking at him. I grabbed a towel to wrap around me.

"You mad now?" X said.
"No, X I'm annoyed. You left me tied up on the bed naked. My arms are sore, I was cold, and hungry. I called you multiple times and you said nothing. Like what was that for?"
X wrapped his arms around my waist. "I like to use that to keep you in line. See when you're mine, you do what I say. I'm in charge of this household and that pussy belongs to me now," X said, grabbing me down there.

I didn't even know what to say. My mood was so off I just couldn't and didn't want to start any arguments or find myself tied up again. I just put my head down and let him bask in his control issues.

"Well, when you get dressed there is food in the kitchen for you to eat," X said, smacking my ass before he walked out the bathroom. "Oh, and don't lock the door anymore."

I don't know what was happening, but I felt like I wanted to cry. I went into the bedroom and found some pajama pants and a tank top to put on. I went into the kitchen to see what X had for me to eat. X was in his office. He must have left the apartment while I was tied up, because there was Chinese food on the kitchen counter. I opened the containers to see what he had bought. He had some fried rice, a couple of egg rolls, and beef and broccoli. I put some fried rice, beef and broccoli on a plate and sat at the kitchen bar to eat.

After I ate, I washed the dishes and closed up the food. X was still in his office so I figured I would just go in the room and lay down. I cut the TV on and found a good movie to watch. I dozed off around 9pm.

I was startled awake to X on top of me placing the handcuffs back on me. I screamed "No, please don't do this again." I tried to push him away and turn to my side so he couldn't get my other hand. He was obviously stronger than me. He turned me back over and grabbed my other hand. I was still trying to pull away. I didn't want to do this again. He handcuffed my other hand and placed them back on the hook. I started to cry, because I just felt defeated. I screamed as loud as I could. I couldn't take it anymore. I didn't like this.

"Deja, Deja," X said, shaking me awake.

It was just a dream. I looked at X and I just started crying. He wrapped his arms around me and held me tight. I was balling and I couldn't stop. I cried until I felt myself getting sleepy again. X continued to hold me as I fell back to sleep.

I woke up to chills all over my body as I could feel X massaging my pussy. I couldn't hold back as I began to moan. My body was shaking inside from his touch. I could feel the intensity rising and I was about to cum. My body was getting hot. X whispered "Cum baby". Shit, my whole body exploded with his words and I came so hard I could feel my pussy dripping wet. I grabbed the pillow and squeezed as I was feeling like I was losing control of my body. X slid his penis in my pussy and I heard him moan. "Damn that shit is crazy wet." He whispered in my ear. He kissed me and began to fuck me hard. I screamed out a loud moan as I felt myself cumming. The feeling was pure ecstasy. I just couldn't understand how every time we had sex it just felt like it was better than before.

When we finished, I looked at the clock. It was 9am. I figured I would get up and get in the shower. I wanted to get my day started early. I had to go to the store for some necessities and get food to make for my lunch. Since I will be going back to work tomorrow. I also had a nail appointment scheduled for today. I would end the day with going to my parents, because they will call me by tonight if they don't see me today.

"Where are you going?" X said as he saw me getting up.

I Am A Survivor: Sex, Lies, and Abuse

"I'm going to take a shower. I only have today to run some errands and get back on track for work tomorrow. I have a nail appointment at 1pm then I will go see my parents around 4pm today."
"What errands do you have to run?"
"I need to go grocery shopping and get some necessities like toothpaste, mouth wash, deodorant, and so on. I have a list I wrote up on my phone."
"Where is your phone?"
"It's on the nightstand, why?"
"I'll send your list to my assistant and she will get whatever you need."
"X, that's cool but I don't mind getting out of the house and doing it myself. It's supposed to be a nice spring day today and I just want to get out and enjoy it."
"You're really trying me," X said, agitated.
"X, I just want to get out of the house and go to the store. I'm not trying to try you."

X got out of the bed and walked towards me. I got nervous, because all I could think was, he's about to put me back on the hook. X towered over me pushing me back until I was pinned against the wall.

"Why do you always gotta be defiant?" X said in a stern voice.
"X, that's not fair. I'm just expressing how I feel."
"Well, you're out of line. Put your hands out."
"Okay X you win. I won't go nowhere. I will cancel my nail appointment and tell my parents I will see them after work tomorrow. Just please don't tie me up."
"Put your hands out, Deja," X said, backing up so I can put my hands out.

I shook my head no. Not sure what to do next at this point. I figured if I tried to run, he would grab me, because he was still close to me. He grabbed my wrist, and even though I was nervous about what he might do, my body still got chills. He pulled out the handcuffs and I began to cry.

"You need to learn a lesson, Deja," he said, putting the cuffs on me. "You're mine and you need to understand what I say goes."
"Please X don't do this," I begged. I put my arms over his head and tried to kiss him hoping he would change his mind.

He kissed me, and pulled me over to the closet door. He put my back to the door and lifted my hands up on the hook. I could barely touch the ground I was standing on my tip toes. This was not comfortable.

"X, please don't do this," I begged again.

I Am A Survivor: Sex, Lies, and Abuse

X pulled my pants and underwear off. He walked over to the dresser and he pulled out some keys to unlock the top drawer on the dresser. I didn't even know the drawers locked. I watched as he pulled out some adult toys. He had a vibrator, anal beads, a strap of some sort, and a tube of some type of oil. He turned me around so now I was facing the door. I couldn't see what he was doing but I felt him put the oil on my ass. He pushed the anal beads inside my ass. I screeched a little from the pressure and pain. My body immediately reacted and I could feel the beads causing my pussy to get wet. The chills were overflowing and the sensations were ridiculous. He then put the vibrator in my pussy and I felt me getting wetter. He took the strap and put it on me so that it was holding the vibrator in place. He cut the vibrator on and I instantly felt myself about to cum. There was sensation everywhere and my whole body was pulsating. I screamed in moans as I kept feeling closer to cumming. X turned me back around so I was facing the bed. X sat on the bed and watched as I continued to moan and shake. The feeling was out of this world, but it was driving me crazy at the same time. It was like I was stuck at the feeling of cumming but I couldn't cum. I began yearning for X to come fuck me. The intensity of the vibrator and the beads in my ass were making me want to feel him inside me and I wanted to cum so bad.

"X, I'm sorry baby please stop this and come fuck me," I begged. I could feel the intensity of me getting close to cumming but I couldn't cum.

It was making me sweat as I could feel it right there at the tip, but I couldn't get myself to cum. The vibrator was hitting the tip of my spot, but not close enough for me to release. I was screaming in ecstasy and moaning like crazy but I couldn't cum. My body was shaking, I was getting hot, and my pussy was dripping wet. The shit was making me insane. I just wanted for X to fuck me. I looked at X and he was just lying on the bed watching me and smiling. Fuck I just wanted him to come fuck me until I came all over his dick. This shit was heating me up and not allowing me to cum. The sensations were overflowing, but I couldn't cum.

"X, what are you trying to do to me. I just want to fuck you please," I begged. "My body can't take no more please X."
"Apologize for speaking out of line and being defiant," X finally spoke.
"I apologize X, ahhh shit, X please," I said as the sensations startled me.
"You apologize for what?"
"Fuck, X I want to cum. Oh shit this is driving me crazy. I apologize for speaking, oh my-, out of line and shit!! Shit! being defiant," I said struggling to get the words out.

I Am A Survivor: Sex, Lies, and Abuse

X stood up and walked towards me. He took the strap off, cut the vibrator off, and took it out of my pussy. My legs were shaking. He pulled the beads out too. I could still feel a crazy sensation in my pussy. X turned me back around to face the door. He slid the vibrator in my ass and cut it on. I instantly felt the intensity of cumming again. X slid his penis in my pussy and within seconds I was cumming. I screamed in moans as the intensity of the moment was sensational. I kept cumming with every stroke of his penis inside me pounding harder and harder. I was losing my mind, but it felt worth it. He was fucking me crazy and I was wanting him more and more. My eyes rolled back in my head as I felt myself cum one last time while X finished too.

He unhooked me and took the handcuffs off. He had to catch me as I lost my balance, because my legs were weak. He walked me to the bed to sit me down.

"You're going to learn what I say goes." X said in a stern voice. "Now my assistant will take care of your errands. You can go jump in the shower and I will take you to your nail appointment when it's time. I will also drop you off at your parents around 4pm and pick you up later. But you need to understand from now on when I say I'll handle it I will handle it. Understood?"

I didn't say anything at first. I just didn't understand why he was doing this. I guess my mind was still trying to figure out what was going on. I was thinking to myself what the hell did I get myself into. One minute he was making me feel like I was on cloud nine and then next he was telling me I was defying him for speaking my mind. Don't get me wrong, the tactics he was using was erotic, but also irritating. I didn't know if I should like this or be thinking about leaving.

"Deja, I'm speaking to you."

He snapped his fingers to get my attention as I was staring into space.

"Yes, I understand," I said, irritated.
"Good, then lose the fucking attitude," he said walking out of the room.

I sat on the bed for 20 minutes just going over everything that seemed to have happened since I went to New York. I was full of overwhelming emotions and not sure if I was even thinking clearly anymore. I couldn't understand for the life of me why I was dealing with this man. I mean the bond was great between us and I was starting to believe that's what was holding me from leaving. Is this what relationships consist of? Or was I too wrapped up in the moment of it all that I wasn't thinking clearly to see that I should walk away. My emotions were so lost in him and how he got me to this point. I didn't even know who I was anymore.

I Am A Survivor: Sex, Lies, and Abuse

I went to the closet to pick out something to wear. I guess I will get ready for this nail appointment and collect my thoughts later. I found some jeans, and pulled out a black t-shirt to go with them. I figured I would wear some flip flops today since I would be getting my toes done too. I put my braids up in a bun and jumped in the shower. I got dressed and I heard a female voice in the living room talking to X.

"Yeah, I got everything she asked for on the list, X. Plus I got the stuff you wanted. The maid should be coming tomorrow and she will clean once a week. I also talked with Mike. He finished the last deal in New Jersey and you should be all good. I will be setting up the payouts and it will be directly deposited into your accounts. I also wanted to ask you about setting up a bank account for Deja. I know you mentioned it, but should she go to the bank with me to set up this account or will you send me everything I need to set it up?"

I walked into the living room. Some woman was standing by the kitchen bar with X. She looked to be in her early 30's late 20's. She looked biracial, long pretty curly hair. Very slim, no shape, but still a beautiful young lady. She saw me and waved.

"Deja, I want you to meet Alicia, my assistant," X said, inviting me to come closer.
"Hello Alicia, nice to meet you."
"Hello, I was just talking to X about some business. I got everything from your list and put the groceries up for you. Here's the other stuff. I would have put it up, but X said you were in the back getting dressed," Alicia said, handing me a bag.
"Thank you. So, you live in Columbus too?" I said, trying to make conversation.
"No, not exactly. I am wherever X is when he needs me. I'm just getting some things squared away for X while he is getting settled in Columbus. I actually live in Chicago, but I will probably be in and out of Columbus for the next month or two. I am staying in the same building on the 5th floor. X, likes me close," Alicia said smiling.
"Oh, okay well thank you for shopping for me," I said being nice.
"You know if it's cool with you, can I get your phone number? I mean not like that, but I know with X he likes me to keep close with you as well so I can get things setup for you too. And if you ever need me to run errands or anything I'm like your assistant too," Alicia said being friendly.
"Oh, okay well my phone number is 614-555-6786."
"Deja, I was thinking since Alicia's here and we were just talking about setting up your bank account. Maybe you can ride with her to the bank and then she can drop you at the nail salon. I actually have to run out myself for a little bit to handle some business so I won't be able to take you," X said. "But I trust you will be in good hands."

I Am A Survivor: Sex, Lies, and Abuse

"Yeah, sounds okay with me. Can I ask what the bank account is for though?" I said hesitant, not sure if that is something I could ask about.
"Well, I want to set you up with a bank account to cover your expenses. Like I promised I will cover all of your expenses," X said, leaning in to kiss me. "I have to run though I will see you later tonight. Have a good time at your parents' house too."
"See you later, X." I said as X left.

Once again, I was emotionally confused. First, he said he was taking me everywhere now I am on my own. I left with Alicia to go to the bank. We went to Ace bank. Alicia said I could choose whatever bank I wanted, but it should be separate from my normal bank. She explained X liked to keep track of the money he gives. Alicia tried to explain it was a trust thing with setting up a new account so I wouldn't think he was trying to have access to my personal money. Alicia also said what X puts in your account is yours and he never takes it back. She said he just likes to keep you happy financially and she hinted I would be very happy.

Alicia did most of the talking. I just gave the banker my information when they asked for it. The banker gave me the account information and Alicia wrote the account number in her phone. Alicia also told the banker to link my account to X's account and she requested that a deposit of $20,000 would go in my account today. The banker completed the setup and gave me the receipt of the balance. I read the receipt for $20,000 deposited. What in the world?? Alicia saw my face and smiled. The banker handed me my temporary card and said the new one would come in the mail. It was around 11:30am when we finished at the bank. I couldn't believe it. Alicia mentioned that she had to go take care of some other stuff, but she already ordered a driver to come take me wherever I wanted to go. She said I had the driver for the day and she informed X so he was aware. She also mentioned X would probably not be back until late tonight, because he was working on a new project in Columbus as he was trying to establish some businesses here, but he would be texting me to check in.

I thanked Alicia. She seemed pretty cool and she even reassured me, not that I was worried, but X was not messing with her, she liked women. She said she felt the need to tell me that, because she wanted us to be cool and X would never mix business with pleasure. I thanked her for that information. We talked for a little bit while she waited with me for the car. I told her she didn't have to wait, but she said X would be pissed if she left me without the car arriving. She told me a little about herself. She said she's been working with X for 5 years. They met when he was at a conference in Chicago for his marketing firm. She was the event coordinator for the conference and he stepped to her to inform her that he admired her dedication, work ethic, and passion for what she did. She said she didn't jump at working for him right away, but when he promised her, she would make a lot of money and travel she said she couldn't say no. She stated she loves what she does and X is a good man to work for. She loves traveling and X always gives her a lot of time off too, to be with her family. She said she will do this until she has kids. She did let me know she is 28 years old. She has a girlfriend in Chicago and they are planning on getting married soon. They don't want to rush kids, because they haven't decided if they want to adopt or who will carry.

Alicia then switched the topic to how I felt about X. I didn't want to give her all my feelings about X as I know she is loyal to him not me. I just let her know that I loved him even though I felt like I said that too early, but I didn't tell her that part. I told her that he seemed like a good man and I was going with the flow.

She went on about how he is good to the women he dates and began to praise him on how he treats his woman. She talked about how he is loyal to the woman he is dating at the time. She mentioned he doesn't cheat, but his exes in the past never lasted long because they always thought he was cheating. She explained that him being a businessman he would go on long business trips, and this would cause his exes to leave him or cause problems in the relationship. I just let her rant about him and nodded in agreement. The car showed up and Alicia hugged me like we were best friends. She left and I got in the car. I gave the driver the address to my nail salon. It was now 12pm. I figured I would go get some coffee at the coffee shop next to my nail salon while I waited for my appointment time.

The driver parked right in front of the nail salon and stated he would just wait outside until I was finished to take me wherever I needed to go next. I got out of the car and walked into the coffee shop. I ordered my favorite caramel latte with extra caramel and sat down at a table. I really didn't know what to think about now, because I was focused on the fact that I had $20,000 in my new bank account. Alicia also helped me set up the app to the bank account and I just kept opening it to see if the money was really there and it was.

I sat in the coffee shop sipping my drink for about 20 minutes just looking outside and watching people.

"Excuse me, I know this will sound corny. But I just wanted to let you know that you are beautiful," I heard a voice say.

I looked up to make sure he wasn't talking to someone else. He looked to be around my height, maybe an inch taller. He had a pretty smile as he smiled at me. Dark skin, dreads, very clean cut, and slim.

"Thank you," I said.
"Is it okay if I sit with you?"
"I'm not sure that's a good idea. I might disappoint you, because I am seeing someone."
"Damn, the good ones are always taken," he said sitting anyway.
"How can I help you?"
"Well, you just said you are seeing someone. So, I'm thinking you must not have a title yet with this person and maybe I still have a chance."
"Excuse me, I misspoke. I have a man and I live with him so you don't have a chance," I said, a little irritated.
"Ohh, okay my bad. But my name is David."
"Good to know, but excuse me I have to go now. Nice meeting you," I said, getting up and leaving.

Like, really the bullshit I have already dealt with I don't need nothing else added to my plate, dude was kind of rude carrying on like that. I went into my nail salon and waited my turn. The salon seemed to be busy for a Monday, but I got right in and out within an hour. I figured I had the key to my parents' house. I would just head over there and chill until they got home. I told the driver where to take me.

I made it to my parents around 2:45pm. I told the driver he didn't have to wait, because I would be here for a while. He gave me his phone number and said I could just call when I needed him to pick me up. I said okay. I didn't see my parents' cars in the garage so I just went in the house. Home, I thought to myself. It's comfortable here.

Chapter Seven: Controlling
"What X says goes."

I laid around in my parents' house watching TV. I raided their fridge since I didn't eat nothing all day. My mom showed up around 4pm.

"What are you doing here and where is your car? I was starting to think I was being robbed," My mom said coming into the house.
"Hi mom," I said, jumping up to hug her. "I missed you."
"Hey baby, I missed you too. Where is your car?"
"I didn't feel like driving so I took a rideshare here," I said, telling a lie. I really hated lying to my mom but it was a little lie.
"Oh, okay you were getting used to that foreign lifestyle huh? Did you enjoy yourself?"
"Yes ma'am, I had a blast."
"How is Liz and her family?"
"They're doing good, mom. Her family is so sweet," I said, thinking about Liz.
"Yeah, that's good to hear. You and Liz must have been worn out. You didn't come see us yesterday."
"Yeah, worn out was not the word."
"I figured Liz would have come with you. She said she would come see us when you guys got back."
What was I going to say I thought. I can't lie to my mom. "You know actually, Liz was home sick so she decided to move back home."
"What? What do you mean? You are in that apartment by yourself now? Why wouldn't Liz at least stay until the lease was up? Can you afford it, by yourself?"

Fuck now what do I say? Oh, well I guess I better tell the truth.

"Mom, come sit down, we have to talk."
"Oh, Lord, this is never good. Should we wait for your father?"

No, I was thinking that will be worse, but of course I would have to deal with him eventually.

"Yes, maybe we should so I can tell you both everything at once."
"Okay, well did you eat. I'm going to get us some dinner together, before your dad gets home."
"Yes, I had some snacks, but I can definitely eat again."
"You're not pregnant, are you?"
"Mom, why would you say that?" I said thinking about that myself now.

I Am A Survivor: Sex, Lies, and Abuse

Is my period late? SHIT! Not something else I need to worry about. No wait, it's only Monday. I have a few days left. I checked my period tracker on my phone. But I better get on something hell it didn't cross my mind being that I was a virgin for so long.

My dad walked in the house while my mom was finishing up cooking. I was in the kitchen with my mom telling her about my trip to Paris. I just didn't tell her I didn't go with Liz. I just talked about all that I got to see and do.

"Well, I'll be, my baby girl is home."
"Daddy!" I said running into his arms hugging him.
"How was your trip?"
"It was amazing dad I did so much it was crazy."
"Yeah, and your daughter has something she needs to talk about so grab the food we will eat in the dining room tonight."
"Thanks mom," I said, nervous. She just had to bring it back up.
"What's going on baby girl?" Dad said helping us grab food to take to the dining room.
"Let's get everything in the dining room first and get settled."
"Oh, this must be serious," my dad said.

We all sat down at the table and prayed over our food. I was shaking inside but I knew I had to tell them something, maybe not everything.

"So, get to talking," my dad said, sounding serious.
"Liz, moved back home. I don't live in the apartment anymore. I actually moved to a different place," I started with that.
"What happened? Are you two still friends?" my dad said.

I couldn't lie to my dad either. "No, I don't think we are friends anymore. Something happened that I don't really want to talk about, but Liz stopped talking to me during the trip. I met this guy and he is a good guy, a businessman. He owns his own marketing firm and other businesses. We've been talking and I moved in with him here in Columbus," I said as fast as I could.
"Deja, what the hell is going on?" my dad said.

Same thing I was thinking.

"I know dad this sounds like it's too fast, too soon but I really like him."
"You had sex with him?"
"Oh God dad, not the conversation I want to have right now, but yes I did."
"And you went to Paris with this man?" my mom chimed in.
"Yeah, we went to Paris, Venice, and Rome," I said, nervous looking at my dad.

I Am A Survivor: Sex, Lies, and Abuse

"I want to meet him. What's his name?"
"Xavier Thomas."
"What? The guy that just bought the 250 High Apartments here?" my dad said shocked.
"Yeah, how did you know? That's the apartment complex we moved into."
"I just met him this afternoon. He is contracting with my company to make improvements to the apartment complex," my dad said, taking a bite of his food.
"What?"
"Yeah, he seems like a pretty cool guy. Very rich. He just paid me double what I normally quote for my contracts," my dad said smiling.
"Well, Deja, you seem to have chosen someone your dad already likes," my mom said, a little relieved.

This was some bullshit. Did I tell X my dad was a contractor. How the hell did he know? Or was this just a random move? I can't believe this.

"Well, wait. Now that I know he is dating my daughter I may have to do some more digging, but for now he seems okay. And I'm still upset with you moving quickly with this man. I thought I taught you better."
"I know dad. I'm sorry. I just really like him. He offered to move with me and wanted us to figure this out as we go."
"I mean cut her some slack Harold. It's not like she was going to be single forever or a virgin. It does seem a little fast but we were her age before. I guess we'll just wait it out and see how things go. But if it doesn't work out Deja, you know you can always come home," my mom said.
"Thank you, mom. Dad, I'm really sorry," I said feeling guilty.
"You're grown. Like your mother said. And I knew I was going to have to prepare for this moment one day. I guess it's happening now. I'm not mad at you. I'm just afraid to see you get hurt, that's all and I'm a little worried," my dad said, grabbing my hand. "But I will be keeping a close eye on him."
"Invite him over for Sunday dinner. I would like to meet him too," my mom said.
"Okay, I will."

Well, the conversation went better than I thought. I was so nervous. I still left a lot out, but my parents don't need to know everything. We finished eating and I helped my mom clean up. I watched a few movies with my parents. I checked my phone a few times. I didn't receive any text from X. I texted him just to let him know I was still with my parents. I couldn't wait until I saw him though because I had so many questions. What was he really doing? I was getting frustrated, but I stopped thinking about it to enjoy my time with my parents. I was so excited that they weren't ready to throw me out about me moving so quickly with X. Of course, my dad being a dad still tried to do his relationship talk and told me to be safe. I listened to him and told him I would come back home if I ever needed to.

I Am A Survivor: Sex, Lies, and Abuse

He said that made him feel better knowing I knew I could always come home where I would be safe.

It was probably around 8pm when I called the driver to come get me. I hugged and kissed my parents. My dad told me to call him for anything he didn't care what it was about or what time of day. He said if I ever felt unsafe, I better call him. I agreed and reassured him I was fine.

I made it back to the apartment around 8:30pm. I thanked the driver and tried to tip him, but he said his tips were already covered. I went inside the apartment and it was pretty dark. I guess X was not home yet. I looked in the fridge and saw that Alicia did buy everything I had on my list. I prepared a salad for lunch tomorrow. I picked out the clothes I was going to wear to work. I jumped in the shower and put on my pj's just a tank and some shorts. I laid down in the bed and turned the TV on to watch me, because I was already getting sleepy. I set my alarms on my phone so I would get up in the morning. It was 9:30pm when I looked at the clock. Not too soon after I went to sleep.

"Deja," X said, waking me up.
I looked at the clock. It was 2am. "I'm up X. What's going on?"
"We need to talk."
"Right now?"
"Get up, girl."
"Shit! Okay," I said, sitting up and trying to wake up.
"What did you do today?"
"Really X. You woke me up knowing I have to go to work, to ask me what I did today? Is this real?"
X put his hand to my head like he was checking my temperature. "Are you sick or something? We just talked about you giving me lip."
"I'm sorry X, I'm tired and I have to go to work in a couple of hours," I said, calm and trying to not have an attitude.
"Answer my question"
"I went with Alicia to the bank. We talked while we waited for the driver to take me to the nail salon. I got my nails done and then I went to my parents."
"You're lying," X said, looking me in the eyes.
"What? I'm not lying."
"You forgot to mention you met some dude at the coffee shop."
"No, I went to the coffee shop by my nail salon while I waited. I didn't think to mention it, because I just got coffee and I didn't purposely meet anyone. He started talking to me and he invited himself to sit down. You're following me now?"
"No, the driver told me."

I Am A Survivor: Sex, Lies, and Abuse

"X, I didn't say much to him but that I had a man and when he sat down, I politely walked away."

"Did you stay at your parents' house until 8pm or did you send the driver away to sneak away?"

"X," I paused and put my head down and back up irritated again. "I had the driver leave, because I knew I was going to be at my parents' house for a while. Do you not trust me?"

"I trust you when you do what I expect you to do."

"And what do you expect of me, X? I didn't think I did anything wrong."

"I expect for my driver to wait on you and not leave. I expect you know to tell me everything when I ask you the first time," X said, angry.

"I'm sorry X. I didn't know these were your expectations, and I wasn't trying to hide anything or sneak around," I said, trying to keep my eyes open.

X grabbed my face and kissed me hard. He pulled my shorts down, and pushed me down on the bed. Within seconds he was inside of me fucking me hard as hell. It actually hurt at first. I screamed out, but then it started to feel good. I was getting wet and the sensations were pulsating through my body. He had me cumming in no time. I was overwhelmed with chills and sensations. My pussy was throbbing and I was cumming like clockwork every 5 minutes. My legs started shaking. X was going in and pounding harder with each stroke. He flipped me over and started fucking me doggy style. I cried out in moans as my body couldn't stop cumming. His penis was so hard I didn't know if he was ever going to stop. He fucked me for hours. My body was exploding in excitement. I had tears coming down my face as I couldn't control the sensations, the shakes, the pulsation. I was cumming over and over until he finally released too.

I covered my head when my alarm went off. X had me up until 5am. I didn't want to move. I turned the alarm off. I looked over and X was still sleeping. It was 6:35am when I looked at the clock. I had to talk myself into moving. Get up Deja you have to go to work. I stood up only to sit back down. My damn legs were still a little shaky. I waited a minute and finally got up and headed to the bathroom. I took a shower and got ready for work. I was super tired but I kept telling myself I will get through the day. I still had to talk to X, but I was so tired last night I wasn't trying to prolong the unwanted conversation we already had and then the hours of sex just wore me out.

I put on the clothes I had picked out last night. I wore a baby blue skirt that was one of the new purchases X provided for me in the closet, with a flowery navy-blue tank top blouse. I put on the baby blue blazer that went with the skirt. I also found some navy-blue sandals I figured they must have been picked out to wear with this outfit, because it matched well. I did a once over in the mirror. I was cute. I styled my braids half up in a bun with the back down. I checked to see if X was up, but his ass was still asleep. I was so mad at him. He was sleeping in and my ass was tired. But to be nice I kissed him on the cheek and whispered have a good day baby. I grabbed my lunch out of the fridge and headed to work. I just walked to work since I was so close. I also texted X to be nice letting him know I left.

Hey Baby,

I am at work until 3:30pm. I hope you have a good day. Love you!

Deja

I walked into work and Stacy, one of Liz's co-workers met me at the door. She worked in Liz's old department but she always chatted with me too.

"Girl, what the hell happened to Liz?" Stacy said, curious. "I have been waiting for you to get back. Liz came in here last week looking horrible. She grabbed her shit and told our boss she was going home. She had enough of Ohio."
"Liz, was here? She came to Ohio? I didn't even know. So much happened Stacy. I don't know if I have time to tell you everything now."
"Well, we can do lunch and girl you are glowing. I think we have a lot to talk about. A new man??"
"We will talk later Stacy," I said smiling.
"I knew it," Stacy said, going the other way.

I went to my department and my team welcomed me back. We talked about work stuff and the normal work drama. I got caught up with my emails because I had over 100. I also got caught up on some other things. I was thinking about X and him working with my father. I couldn't get over the fact that he checked in with my driver to spy on me. But my pussy was thinking about his sexy ass fucking me like that this morning too. I had way too many thoughts going on. Get focused back on your work Deja. It was getting close to lunch time and I knew Stacy would meet me at the park in the back where we always sat to eat lunch. I checked my phone and saw that X texted me about 5 minutes ago.

Deja,

Have a good day at work baby. I love you too!

X

What? Did he just say he loved me? That was the first time he said that. I was smiling ear to ear. He said he loves me. I must have read that text 20 times. My body was covered in chills. I was in shock. He said he loves me. I sent a happy smiling emoji and a heart emoji. He sent me back the heart emoji. Damn, he was doing something to me, because I was all in again.

I finished up what I was working on and headed to the park. It was lunch time. Stacy was already at our table.

"Girl, I am so glad you are back. So where do you want to start with the new man or what's going on with Liz?" Stacy said so interested.

I talked with Stacy. Again, I didn't go into too much detail about the whole 2 weeks. But I told her enough to know that I was dating X. She already knew about Liz and Eddie. She said it was on the news, because Eddie got arrested and was charged with assaulting Liz. She told me Liz came into work last Wednesday looking rough. She said Liz had on oversized clothes. She looked frail and looked like she hadn't done her hair in days. She tried to talk with her but Liz just grabbed her things and left. I did tell her, me and Liz fell out, because her friend Tammy didn't get along with me too well. Again, I didn't think she needed to know everything. But I did tell her that X took me to Paris instead and we have been just having a lot of fun together.

"Girl, you better keep that man. He sounds like a winner. And he's getting paid. You just hit the jackpot," Stacy said.
"Yeah, I know I really like him."
"Shit, you better be hoping you get pregnant by that man."
"Oh, that reminds me. I need to call my doctor and make an appointment."
"Why? Are you pregnant?"
"No, I need to get on birth control so I don't get pregnant."
"Girl, please have his baby you will be set for life."
"Hell No. I'm not ready for kids and we haven't even been talking that long."
"So, you already live with him."
"I know but I don't need no kids right now."
"Well, here then. I guess if you don't want to get pregnant, I have plenty of birth control. My doctor gives me samples. I keep birth control packs on me, because I ain't lucky enough to have a man like yours," Stacy said, pulling packs of birth control out of her bag. "Just don't start them until your period and take the last week first, that's the ones for your period."
"Wow, you are serious about having packs."
"Yes girl, I do not want to get pregnant by these broke ass dudes I mess with," Stacy said, handing me 4 packs. "You can have these that should hold you until you get an appointment with your doctor. Even though I think you should get pregnant."
"Well, I will start my period on Thursday so I will start them then."

I Am A Survivor: Sex, Lies, and Abuse

"And take a pregnancy test first, because you've been doing a lot without protection."
"You just want me to be pregnant. But I'll grab one on the way home. There is a pharmacy just down the street."
"Oh, and because you have a good ass man and I know this sex stuff is new to you; make sure while you are on your period you are still keeping him happy."
"What do you mean? I'm not having sex on my period."
"Girl, not sex. You better be sucking his dick as many times as you need to. That man should not want to stray from you."

I laughed at Stacy. But I started thinking I never even did that with X. That's something I needed to do. He is always pleasing me and I should be pleasing him too.

Lunch was over. I went back to work to finish up some stuff. I thought about what Stacy said and couldn't wait to get home. I wanted to make sure I was taking care of X too. I didn't want to give him any reason to stray like Stacy said.

I finished early, playing catch up. I left work around 3:15pm. I stopped by the pharmacy on my way home and got a pregnancy test. I put it in my purse, and headed home.

I made it to our apartment and opened the door. X was talking to some guys in the living room. I walked in and it was the guys that helped X when Randy beat me up.

"Hey baby," I said, giving X a kiss on the cheek.
"Hey," he said, not really acknowledging me.

I went to the room and closed the door. I figured he was busy talking to them dudes so I would leave him alone. I also thought this would be a good time to take this damn test. Stacy had me worried and honestly, I was thinking about it ever since my mom mentioned it. I peed on the stick and waited. I took the birth control out of my purse and put it in the bathroom cabinet. I left one in my purse just to make sure I started them on Thursday as long as I wasn't pregnant. 3 minutes passed so it was time to check the test. I was a little nervous. I read the test and thank God; I was not pregnant. I wrapped up the test and put it in the trash can. I made sure to throw some paper towels on top of it to cover it up. X didn't need to know I took a test.

I took off my sandals and put them back in the closet. I also noticed our bed had been changed. The dirty clothes had also been washed and put up. The maid must have come today. I remember hearing Alicia say something about a maid coming once a week. I wasn't sure I cared about having a maid I could clean up just fine, but I remembered "what X says goes". I took my blazer off and sat on the bed. I turned the TV on to see what was on. I turned to my favorite crime documentaries. I called my doctor to schedule an appointment as well. She got me in, pretty quick too. I will be seeing her in two weeks.

I heard X telling the dudes he would catch up with them later. I was ready to please my man. I had been thinking about it since Stacy mentioned it. I wanted to take control and show him how much he meant to me. I waited to see if he would come to the room.

"Deja," X said as he opened the door.

He looked so sexy to me. I was so ready to show him what I could do to him. I walked towards him and kissed him. I kissed him on his neck and started taking his shirt off. I unbuckled his pants.

"Damn, did you miss me?" he said, not stopping me.

I shook my head yes and kissed him again. I put my hands down his boxers and began to massage his penis. I wanted to please him, that was my mission. He grabbed my ass. I moved his hands and interlocked my fingers with his.

I whispered "Let me take care of you this time."

I kissed his neck, and his chest. I started kissing him all over making my way down.

"Damn girl," he whispered.

I pulled his pants down. I put my mouth on his penis and went as far as I could and closed my mouth around his penis. I sucked hard while I massaged his balls.

"Shit," he moaned.

Yes, I thought to myself I'm working this. The more he reacted the more I felt myself getting wet with excitement of doing it right. I began moving back and forth slowly with my mouth sucking hard each time. I twirled my tongue in the process and moaned on his penis. "Fuck, baby," he moaned again. I started moving a little faster, getting excited that he was feeling good. I continued massaging his balls and I could feel his penis jerking. I wanted to make him cum. I kept going as deep as I could with my mouth sucking him gently and at a steady pace. I moaned again on his penis. "Shit, baby I'm about to cum," he moaned. I got excited and felt myself getting wetter, but I kept the same pace so I could make him cum. "What the fuck baby you really must have missed me," he whispered. I said "Mmmh hmmm," still sucking his penis. "Fuck, Deja," he moaned and he came in my mouth. I leaned back after finishing him off and smiled in excitement for making him cum.

I stood up and he grabbed me. He pulled me close to him and kissed me. I wrapped my arms around him.

"Damn, that was good." He said, kissing my neck. "We need to talk. Shit, hold on."

X answered his phone and walked into the bathroom. What did we need to talk about? I was a little worried but I guess I had to wait until he got off the phone. I sat on the bed waiting for him.

"What the fuck is this Deja," X said holding the birth control pills.
"They're birth control pills."
"Why do you have them?"
"To be safe X. We don't use condoms and I haven't been on anything. We didn't talk about kids and besides it's too soon for that right?"
"This is the shit that we should talk about first. Are you taking the pills now?"
"No, I haven't started them yet. I'm supposed to start them when I start my period on Thursday."

X walked back in the bathroom and came back out with all the birth control pills.

"Do you have any more?"
"I have a pack in my purse. X don't you think we should be safe?"
"Give me the pack in your purse."
"X," I said, frustrated.
"Deja,"

I got up and got the pack out of my purse and gave it to him. He went back to the bathroom and I watched from the door as he opened each pack and flushed them down the toilet.

"You're not doing birth control. And if you get pregnant, we will deal with that when it happens. Understood?"
"Understood," I sighed.
"Hey," X said, grabbing my face. "You're my girl. I told you I will take care of you. What I say goes."

I Am A Survivor: Sex, Lies, and Abuse

X kissed me and grabbed me by my wrist. He led me to the bed. The chills were already racing though me. He took my clothes off and leaned me over the bed. I was already secreting. He touched my pussy and massaged my clitoris. I moaned as his touch was sending sensations through me. He entered me hard and I screamed in ecstasy. "That pussy stays ready for me," he laughed. He fucked me pounding harder and harder with each stroke. My legs were already shaking and my pussy was throbbing. I was cumming before I knew it. I screamed in moans as my body began to shake. His sex was something else and I just couldn't get enough of it. Damn, he knew what he was doing and I just continued to yearn for his touch, his sex, the intimacy, and everything about him. I closed my eyes to take in all that I was feeling. I was amazed by him. I cried tears of joy with how much I loved this feeling. I loved him. My body began to pulsate, shake, and tremble. I was cumming over and over. Damn, he had me wrapped up in him.

Once we finished, we laid down. He cuddled with me. He rubbed my back and played with my braids. It just felt good to be in his arms. It was getting more and more comfortable for me to be with him.

"Deja, we need to talk." X said, reminding me he mentioned that.
"What's wrong X?"
"So, some business stuff has come up and I have to leave Columbus for a little bit."
I lifted my head up to look at him. "What's a little bit?"
"Maybe 2 or 3 months I don't know yet."
"X, like 2 months straight no coming back on the weekends?" I said, worried.
"Like, 2 months straight."
I sat all the way up at this point. "X, seriously? Like why so long? I mean what am I supposed to do? Like, I'm trying not to be upset but that's a long time X."
"Deja, I am a businessman and sometimes I have to be in certain places to handle shit. Everything here will be good. Alicia will still be in Columbus and she can assist with anything you need."
"Fine, whatever," I said, upset.
"Come here,"
"No," I said, pouting.
"You mad now? Talk to me," X said, grabbing my wrist.
"X, that's not fair," I said as the chills were coming back. He knew what he was doing trying to get me in the mood to get his way.
"Talk to me Deja."
"X, there are like so many thoughts going through my head right now. I haven't been without you since I met you. I don't know how I will feel 2 maybe 3 months and you're not here at all. I mean-," I paused.
"Say what you feel Deja,"

I Am A Survivor: Sex, Lies, and Abuse

"X, I've fallen super hard for you, super-fast. And we have been together every day and though I didn't know how I felt at first, I know now I don't want to be without you. I love you X. And I just feel like you have been spoiling me with your time and attention. I don't know how I am going to feel with you being gone so long. I mean, I get it. I know you would eventually leave for business trips, but I was thinking, a week or two not months."
"Deja, you can be cute at times." X said smiling. "I love that about you. How you share your feelings with me. But me not being here physically is not going to stop what we got going on. And if I find time to get away, I will definitely be back when I can. I want nothing more but to be right here with you. I love you, Deja."
"I love you too," I said, leaning down to kiss him.

He pulled me back down to lay with him.

"Don't worry the time will fly by. I will be back soon." X said, rubbing my back.
"When do you leave?"
"Tonight."
"X, really?" I said trying to push away from him, but he held me to his chest.
"Deja, let's not argue. I just want this moment with you, before I have to leave."
"X, I don't like this."
"I know Deja, but it won't always be like this. There are just some things I have to take care of."
"Well, I was going to tell you that my parents wanted you to come over for dinner this weekend. I forgot to mention that yesterday."
"Oh yeah, I will meet them when I get back. Let them know I had to go handle some business. But I would like to meet them."
"Well, you already met my dad," I said, seeing if X knew that.
"Who's your dad Deja?"
"Harold Anderson. My dad said he is in contract with you on fixing up this apartment complex."
"What a small world. I didn't know Mr. Anderson was your dad. But now thinking about it, you look like him."
"You really didn't know that was my dad?" I asked, confused.
"No, Deja I didn't know," X said, looking at me. "What, do you think I scoped him out on purpose huh?"
"I mean, it crossed my mind."
"No, I didn't, but I'm glad to be working with him, now I know he is your dad. That means he's good people."
"Yeah, he is pretty amazing," I said smiling.

We laid there talking for hours cuddled up. I didn't want him to leave. It just felt so peaceful, and comfortable. He wasn't being controlling. He was actually being very open and vulnerable with me. It felt good to be laying with him and just

I Am A Survivor: Sex, Lies, and Abuse

knowing he would be leaving soon made me sad. But I also felt so good in his arms. He told me he would call me when he touched down in New York. He said he was going to New York first for a few weeks and then he had to go to New Jersey. He said Alicia would be calling to check on me and he would always be in contact too. He mentioned that he would also have security for my safety. I told him I didn't need that, but you know, "What X says goes".

Chapter Eight: Devilish Smile
"Payback is a bitch, right?"

I woke up the next morning alone. X left around 11pm last night to go to the airport. He didn't leave without me feeling him inside me one more time of course. We had sex until he got up to take his shower around 10pm. I missed him already. I looked at the clock, it was 6am. I had a text from X.

I know I said I would call, but I figured you would still be sleeping. But I am in New York. Remember to reach out to Alicia if you need anything. I will call you before you leave for work Deja.

Love you,

X

I texted back.

I love you too and be safe. And I will talk to you soon!

Deja

That was my man and I was in love with him. I hurried up and got dressed hoping he would call soon. I was going crazy like he didn't just leave last night. But it was just weird he was not here with me. As soon as I got out of the shower, he was video calling me.

"Hey baby," I said, excited that he called.
"Damn, sexy. I'm missing out already," X said, being flirty as he could see I was naked.
"Well, I just got out of the shower and you were calling."
"I like what I see too, sexy."
"Don't, you are not here to start something you can't finish."
"Oh, I will finish for sure."
"Oh, yeah,"
"Yeah, what are you wearing to work?"
"I picked out this orange body con dress with a brown cardigan and my brown flat sandals," I said, showing him the outfit.
"Deja, you are not wearing that," X said agitated.
"What why?"
"Pick something else to wear."
"Why X?"

I Am A Survivor: Sex, Lies, and Abuse

"Deja, don't start. I'm not there and you damn sure are not wearing that while I'm not there," X said, getting upset.
"Okay, X. I will wear this instead," I hurried to show him my black blouse tank top shirt with some red dress pants.
"That looks good," X said smiling.

Even from a distance he can still be annoying. X watched me put my outfit on and told me how sexy I was. He stayed on the phone with me until I left the house. He said he would call me during lunch and then after work.

When I opened the door to the apartment, I saw a man standing at the door.

"Hello," I said, confused at what he was doing there.
"Hello, my name is Cash. I work for X. I'm your security. He told you about me right," he said.
"Oh yeah, I forgot. He did mention you. Well nice to meet you."
"I will stay close behind you and try not to be too obvious and check the surroundings for your safety."
"I'm sorry so you will be following me? I thought you were just, you know, watching the door when I'm in the apartment."
"No, I go wherever you go ma'am."
"Oh, okay. So, you will come with me to work?"
"Yes, but I will just position myself somewhere outside. I will not go into work with you. Alicia should have sent you my phone number to call if you need me to come in for any safety reasons."
"Yep, it looks like Alicia sent me your number." I said looking at my phone.
"Great, I guess we should get going now."

I was annoyed even more. I couldn't help but to keep turning around while I walked to work to see if he was following me. I didn't understand why I needed security. I texted X.

This is really awkward by the way. Thanks for the detail.

Deja

X texted back quickly.

You're welcome baby!

X

I Am A Survivor: Sex, Lies, and Abuse

Asshole, I thought to myself but I smiled at his response. He was really annoying, but cute at the same time. I made it into work and looked back. I saw Cash get comfortable on a bench right in front of my job. I thought to myself he is going to sit there all day. I walked into my job and Stacy was at the front waiting on me.

"Hey girl, so how is the love life?" Stacy said.
"Annoying. He left last night and won't be back for 3 months on a business trip."
"Damn, that's messed up."
"Yeah, that's what I was thinking," I said annoyed.
"Why so long?"
"I have no idea, but it's whatever. I guess I can't do nothing about it."
"Yeah, I know, but he's a good one."
"Oh, and the birth control he was not a fan of. He flushed them down the toilet, sorry about that."
"Oh girl, I don't care, I have plenty. But that means someone will be pregnant soon."
"I hope not. I took the pregnancy test and I wasn't pregnant."
"Did he see the test?"
"No, I hid that."
"Oh okay. Well, I won't see you for lunch today. It's an early day for me."
"Oh okay. Well, have fun, see you tomorrow then."

I went to my department and started working. Alicia texted me around 11am and informed me Cash was leaving. She said that Greg would be taking over and would be my security for the rest of the day. She sent me a picture of Greg so I would know who to look for and his phone number. She stated Cash, Greg, and Micah would be switching off to detail me every day. She said I would probably meet Micah tomorrow morning, and she sent me a picture of him with his phone number as well.

I went to my table outside at the park for lunch and video called X. He was at the X Factor. He showed me around his office. He also showed me he had a picture of me from when we were in Paris on his desk. We talked until my lunch was over and then I went back to work to finish off my day.

I left work and greeted Greg outside and we headed to the apartment. I told him when I got close to the apartment, I wanted to go up the street to get some food. I didn't want to cook so I figured I better grab some dinner. There was a restaurant up the way called The Goat River South not too far from the apartments. Greg walked with me. I went inside and ordered my food to go. I ordered the goat burrito, with hot chicken dip, and a salad. The host brought my order and I left the restaurant.

When I got outside Greg gave me this look and signaled for me to go back inside the restaurant so I did. I watched as 2 guys approached Greg. He said something to them and then they left. Greg watched as they got into the car down the street and pulled off. He then signaled for me to hurry up. I came outside and we hurried down the street. We didn't go in the front door to the apartment. He walked me around the back to the garage entrance.

"What's going on? Who were those guys?" I said, nervous at this point.
Greg pushed the elevator button. "I can't say. You will have to talk to X."
"Right," I said agitated.

Greg got me in the apartment safely and stayed outside guarding the door. He stated for me to lock the door. I put everything down and immediately video called X.

"Deja, you calling me. You missed me already?" X said jokingly until he saw my facial expression. "What's with the face?"
"You tell me X. Why did you make sure I had security, before you left?"

I could see X must have received a text. He was looking at the phone like he was reading something.

"What happened Deja?"
"I went down the street to get some dinner and when I was coming out. Greg scared me, signaling me to go back in the restaurant. He said something to these two guys that walked up and then he waited for them to leave before he signaled for me to come out. Then he rushed me down the street and we had to go in the back way to the apartment like something was wrong."
"Deja, I'm sorry."
"What's going on X?"
"I'm handling it. You are safe. I trust my crew and you are safe."
"X,"
"Deja," X paused. "I need you to trust me on this. You are safe. I will not let anything happen to you. And I am handling everything. I will tell you everything when you need to know."
"X, that doesn't make me feel good."
"Do you trust me?"
"Yes, X I trust you."
"Then let me handle this. I'll call you back in a little bit."
"X,"
"Deja, I love you. You're safe okay."
"I love you too. Please call me back."
"I will," X said, hanging up the phone.

I Am A Survivor: Sex, Lies, and Abuse

What was going on? I did not feel comfortable. And now I was worried. I was getting nervous sitting in the house by myself waiting for X to call me back. I couldn't even eat at this point. I know X said I was safe, but he was in a different state. I didn't know his security crew to think I was safe with them. I wanted X to call me back or be here. I heard a knock on the door. I got nervous. I know Greg was out there, but I didn't want to open the door. Then I saw a text come through. It was Alicia she was at the door. I hurried up to open the door. I didn't know Alicia well but I was happy to see her standing there.

"Hey Deja. X told me what was going on. I just thought I would check on you," Alicia said, after I let her in.

I saw Greg standing out there on his phone. I figured he must have been talking to X.

"Hey Alicia. Yeah, I'm not sure what is actually going on," I said, relieved to not be alone in my thoughts.

We sat down on the couch.

"X told me he thinks it was the two guys he just recently fired. They were working on the apartments but they weren't doing what they needed to do. They were taking the money but not completing the work. X fired them when he saw they weren't doing anything. He said they were pretty upset and made some threatening remarks to him and one of the managers on the project. Greg said he recognized them and when they saw Greg, they made some threatening remarks about X," Alicia said. "You know sometimes this comes with the business. People think they can get off doing a half ass job and still get paid. Then they want to cause trouble when they get caught."
"Yeah, well it definitely scared me. They seemed pretty upset talking to Greg."
"Did they notice you?"
"No, I was inside the restaurant. Greg saw them coming and signaled for me to stay in the restaurant."
"Oh good. You never know what people might do nowadays. Especially when they lose out on money."
"Yeah, you can say that again."

Alicia made me feel a little better. I liked that she came over to calm my nerves. After I felt better, I shared my food with her and we watched some movies to take my focus off of being worried. We talked about any and everything. She really was a cool person to hang with. It was around 8pm when I saw X was calling me.

"Deja, you good?" X said.

I Am A Survivor: Sex, Lies, and Abuse

"Yes X, I'm good. Alicia's here," I said, turning the phone so X could see Alicia.
"Hey Alicia, thank you for checking on my baby."
"No problem. I like hanging with Deja. She's pretty cool. But I'm going to get out of here it's getting late," Alicia said, getting up to leave.
"Thanks again Alicia," I said walking her to the door. She left and I locked the door.

I talked with X until around 9:30pm. I felt a little better. He told me the same thing Alicia did and said I had nothing to worry about. I got ready for bed and went to sleep.

I woke up at 6:15am. X was already calling me. I talked to him for a little bit, before getting in the shower. I got dressed. X was calling me again.

"Hey baby you missed me already," I said jokingly.
"I did. What are you wearing today?"
I rolled my eyes. "That's why you called back?"
"Deja, show me your outfit," X said, sounding serious.
I showed him my outfit. I just had on a red button-down shirt, some jeans, and red sandals. "See, this is my outfit."
"You look cute, but I'm not feeling the attitude," X said, satisfied with my outfit.
"You called me back to check my outfit X. Why?"
"Deja, you keep giving me lip," X said, irritated. I could see him biting down and tightening his jaw. I was obviously making him upset.
"X, you say you trust me, but you keep checking my outfits like I'm out here trying to find my next man or something. I'm not," I said frustrated.
I saw X getting more irritated with my replies. "Deja, I trust you. I just don't trust who might be checking you out. And I need to know you only dress sexy for me," X said, trying to lighten up.
I smiled. "I love you baby. I only want to dress sexy for you."
"I love you too and I like that response, stop giving me lip all the time," X said smiling.

I talked with X until I left the house to go to work. I met Micah at the door and he followed close behind me while I walked to work.

I went inside my work building and watched as Micah got comfortable on the bench outside. I didn't see Stacy this morning so I wasn't sure if she came into work today. I went to my station and started my day. The morning flew by as I had a few meetings and before I knew it, it was lunch time. I went to my normal spot to eat lunch. I saw one of Stacy's co-workers and she told me Stacy called off today. I looked at my phone to see if X called or texted me but he didn't. I was getting ready to call him when I saw Liz sitting at the table I always sit at. I was shocked to see her. I walked over to her.

"Liz, how are you?" I said, not sure what to say. She seemed to be a little skinnier than before, but she looked good.
"Deja, I'm good, how are you?"
"I'm good."
"You're still with X?"
"Yeah, I am," I sighed, worried about what she had to say.
"He's treating you good?"
"Yeah, why do you ask that?"
"Just checking. You know Tammy told me he beat you up?"
"X, didn't beat me up, that was your brother who did that."
"Hmmm, that's crazy. I didn't know. I'm sorry my brother did that. I haven't seen my brother since everything went down with you and X. I was coming to see if maybe you heard from him, or seen him."
"I haven't seen your brother Liz, not since he tried to kill me."
"Has X seen him?"
"I don't know. He hasn't mentioned it."
"You know so much has happened in such a short time. I miss you, Deja. I really miss our friendship," Liz said, beginning to cry.
"I miss you too Liz. I was so worried about you. I heard what happened with you and Eddie. I'm so sorry that happened to you."
"I'm okay. I'm still trying to recover from it, but baby steps, that's all I can do. I really just wanted to see you. I know this is probably not the place, but I don't know where you live now. And I didn't want to call you."
"It's okay. I'm glad you're okay and I'm happy to see you too. How long will you be in Columbus?"
"I'm here until Monday. I'm staying with Michaela. She asked me to come see her. I kind of needed to get away. My family has been on me about everything. I'm just trying to stay focused on my sobriety. But they are worried about Randy. They are worried about me staying sober. And my dad hasn't stopped gambling. My mom is just losing her mind worrying about us all. So, I needed a break."
"Oh man, so much has been going on. I hope it gets better for you," I said, worried.

I didn't know Randy was missing. I worried if X's crew had something to do with this. But I was happy to hear Liz was working on her sobriety.

"It will. Right now, it's just a slow process. I worry more about Randy and where he is at. He has never just left like this. I hope he's okay," Liz paused. "Michaela was talking about you yesterday and how she hasn't heard from you. It made me want to check on you, because Tammy had me worried when she said she saw

you all bruised up. She thought X did it, but I guess it was my brother. So much has happened I just didn't know if it would be appropriate to just call you. I figured it would be better to see you in person."
"I know a lot has happened, but I'm glad to see you. I know I need to call Michaela so much has been going on. I haven't talked to many people since I've been home."
I looked at my phone X was calling. I didn't want to answer it, because Liz was here.
"I won't hold you, Deja. I just wanted to talk with you and see you. Maybe we can have dinner tomorrow night or this weekend?"
"Yeah, I would like that."
"Okay, I will call you tomorrow," Liz said, getting up to give me a hug.

I hugged Liz and once she left, I called X back. He was a little upset I didn't answer, but I just told him I didn't see it, because my phone was on vibrate and I was talking to my co-worker. I wasn't sure I wanted to tell him I ran into Liz yet. I figured that would be a conversation for later since I didn't have much time left on my lunch. I talked with X until my lunch was over. We didn't talk about much because he was still in New York handling business. I went back to work to finish off my day. I couldn't help but to think if maybe X's crew did something to Randy. I didn't want to think that. But Liz saying Randy was missing really worried me.

I left work at my normal time and met Cash outside. I guess they switched security again to give Micah a break. Cash followed me home. This time I went straight to the apartment and figured I would eat leftovers from yesterday. Cash stood at the door as I went into the apartment and locked it.

I went straight to the back to get comfortable. I decided to take a nice long bath to soak and deal with these emotions from seeing Liz today. I wanted to tell X I saw her. But I didn't know if I wanted to have that conversation with him. I guess I was worried if he had anything to do with Randy missing. I don't know why I would even think that, but it definitely kept crossing my mind. I laid back in the tub and closed my eyes. It just felt good to soak in the warm water. I thought I should just tell X when he calls, I talked to Liz today, because if I go to dinner with her his security would be there too, I'm sure of it. I didn't know if I could find a way to get away from them. Even if I did, X would flip for sure. It was nice that he wasn't here to punish me, but if I kept being defiant, I'm sure I would get it when he did come back.

I got out of the tub after 30 minutes and put on my pj's. I wasn't going anywhere else today so I figured I would eat dinner and watch some movies until I got sleepy. I ate dinner. My mom called me and I told her that X wouldn't be coming over this Sunday for dinner. He was gone on a business trip. She seemed disappointed. She said she really wanted to meet him, but she would see him when he came back. I talked to her for a little bit and then went back to watching my movie. I fell asleep early. I think it was around 7:50pm when I last looked at the clock.

I was startled awake as I felt someone touching me. I jumped up as I saw someone standing over my bed. It was dark in the room. I looked up and it was X. He cut the light on by the bed. I looked at the clock and it was 3am.

"X," I said, surprised and put my arms around him to hug him.
"Deja," he said, upset. "I've been calling you since 8pm."
"I'm sorry X. I was tired and went to sleep early. Are you back now? Or do you have to leave again," I said, hoping he didn't have to leave again.
"I took a flight out to see you, but I have to go back tomorrow."
"Wishful thinking," I said disappointed.
"You need to keep your phone on loud. I kept calling and when I couldn't get you, I figured something was wrong," he said, upset again.
"X, you flew here, because I didn't answer my phone?"
"What did you do today to make you so tired Deja?"
"You're not going to answer my question?"
"Deja, what did you do today?" X said, grabbing my wrist.
"You don't play fair X. I've missed you," I said, trying to lighten the mood as I felt the chills starting to flow.
"Deja," X said, grabbing my waist and then pulling my pants down.
"Fuck me X," I said ready for him. I wanted him so bad I didn't care what he was going to make me do. I was being defiant on purpose now. I was trembling inside with excitement of him being here.

I wrapped my arms around him and kissed him. I climbed on him and I could feel immediately his penis was already hard. He missed me too; I thought to myself. I wanted to feel him inside me so bad. I didn't want to talk. I wanted him. X stood up with me wrapped around him. He carried me and sat me on the dresser. He opened the drawer with the handcuffs, and adult toys. I knew where this was going but I didn't care as long as he fucked me.

"Deja, put your hands out," X said, holding the cuffs.

I put my hands out. X handcuffed me and led me to the closet where he put my hands over my head to the hook on the door. I was standing on my tip toes. He pulled out the anal beads and oil. I was beginning to regret my thought process, but I wanted X. "X, I'm sorry baby," I said hoping it would make him go easy. X turned me to face the door and put the oil on my ass. He immediately stuck the beads in my ass. I screamed as that was painful, but my pussy still began to get wet. I could feel the chills, and pulsations flowing through me. X turned me back around. I could see he was already naked and his penis was hard. My body was trembling in excitement. "X, fuck me please baby," I moaned. X came close to me and pushed his body up against mine. I could feel his penis touching my pussy, but he didn't enter me. "X, please baby," I begged. X lifted up my shirt and started kissing and sucking on my nipples. My body was going crazy for him. I was getting wetter and wetter. I was pulsating throughout my whole body. I could feel his penis right there, but he wouldn't enter me. He was driving me crazy. "X, I will tell you about my day please fuck me," I said begging. Tears started to fall. He licked my tears and began to kiss me. I wrapped my legs around him hoping he would enter me. He grabbed my legs and pushed them open smashing my ass to the door. I felt a crazy sensation hit me from behind. I screamed out a loud moan. My legs were shaking and I started to feel like I was about to cum.

The intensity of the moment, the trembles, the shaking, and the secretion was making me sweat. I wanted X to fuck me so bad. I started crying and begging him to please fuck me. He continued to push my legs into the door for what felt like forever, but may have been 20 minutes. The sensations were overflowing, I was so ready to cum. I wanted him inside me. "You're done being defiant," X finally spoke. "YES, X," I yelled out. He put my legs down and he turned me around to face the door again. He lifted my ass and entered my pussy hard. I felt so many sensations, I screamed out in moans. I was trembling as he fucked me hard. It felt amazing, but I could only still feel like I was close to cumming as he didn't take the beads out. I cried out to X begging to cum. He felt so good, but it was only driving me crazy. Without even stopping X pulled the beads out and I immediately came screaming in ecstasy as I felt my body shaking. I continued to cum repeatedly. "Oh fuck," I cried out as the sensations were throbbing through my whole body. What the hell was he doing to me? His sex was a crazy high. When X finished, he unhooked me and uncuffed me. My legs were super weak. He had to carry me to the bed.

We laid down and I could still feel my body shaking and my pussy pulsating. I thought I would close my eyes and try to get some sleep since it was now 5:00am.

"Deja," X said, making me open my eyes back up to look at him.
"Yes X," I said, calm and sweet, trying not to get him upset.
"What did you do to make yourself so tired and ignore my calls?"
"It wasn't like I was ignoring your calls on purpose. I came home just drained from my work day and I took a long warm bath. I talked to my mom for a little bit and I watched a movie and fell asleep."

I Am A Survivor: Sex, Lies, and Abuse

I wasn't sure I wanted to mention that I saw Liz. But I started to think what if Micah or Cash was watching and that is why he wanted to know about my day. I started to think if I didn't tell him, I might find myself handcuffed again.

"I also saw Liz," I quickly said, before he could say anything.
"You saw Liz? When did you see her?"
"At lunch she came to my job."
"So that's why you didn't answer my phone call at lunch?" X said, catching me in a lie. I forgot I told him I was talking to a coworker.
"Yeah, X. I just didn't want to say anything at that moment. Not that I was trying to hide it but it was close to the end of my lunch so I didn't want to have to go through all those emotions again on the phone with you. I was going to tell you though."
"What did you talk about with her?"

I truly hated when X did that. He would just move on to the next question instead of addressing that I wasn't trying to keep secrets or be defiant. It always made me feel so guilty, because I know he was leading up to getting mad that I kept something from him.

"We talked about her being sober, her brother is missing, and her dad is still gambling. She said her mom is driving herself crazy over all that has been happening. She asked if I was still with you and if I saw her brother. I told her I haven't seen him since he tried to kill me. And she mentioned that Tammy told her I was bruised up and you did it, but I let her know it was her brother who bruised me up," I said, trying to go over everything. "She said she missed our friendship and wanted to have dinner while she was in town. She said she is staying with our friend Michaela and is only here until Monday."
"What did you tell her about me?"
"I told her I was still with you. She asked if you saw Randy. I told her I didn't know you never mentioned anything to me about seeing him."
"Did you talk about anything else?"
"No, not really X, I was just happy to see she was doing okay. And a lot of emotions were going through my head at the moment that I was just glad to know she still cares about me and I miss her."
"Hmm, I told you she would come back around. But I don't like when you hide things from me Deja. I can always tell when you're hiding shit," X said, irritated.
"X, it wasn't like that. I wasn't trying to hide anything. I just wasn't in the right place to talk about it. I mean my emotions were already wacky from seeing her. And I probably would have just broken down if I started talking about it with you at that moment," I said, wiping away a tear as I felt myself getting emotional.

I Am A Survivor: Sex, Lies, and Abuse

X wiped my tears away as I started to cry and he kissed my cheek. I closed my eyes and fell asleep.

I woke up to my body shaking and chills all over. X was fucking me and I was cumming when I realized what was happening. The sensations were overflowing. Damn he was good at this shit. I looked at the clock and realized I slept in. It was 7:30am. "Shit!" I moaned as I didn't want X to stop, but I was late for work. "X baby what are you doing to me, I'm so late," I moaned as I was starting to cum again. "Shh, I called off for you baby," X said fucking me harder. Fuck he felt so damn good. I couldn't even be mad. I was feeling every stroke hit my pussy so right. I was overflowing with wetness and I missed him. I damn sure missed him.

After we finished X got up and took a shower. I laid there thinking to myself how the hell did he call off for me and what did he say. I checked my phone. It was Friday and the time read 8:45am. I looked at my messages. I could see X just texted my boss from my phone saying I was sick. I guess that worked. That's normally what I would do when I called off anyway.

X came out of the bathroom with his towel wrapped around him. He looked so damn sexy. I really must have missed him, because I could feel myself getting wet just looking at how sexy he was. He leaned in to kiss me.

"Get up and get dressed. I'm taking you to breakfast," X said walking to the closet to pick out some clothes.

I got up and jumped in the shower. My legs were feeling sore, but that shower helped me feel a little better. I got out of the shower and picked out some clothes. X was in the living room while I was getting dressed. I figured since X was here, I could wear something sexier since I couldn't do it while he was away. I pulled out this slim fitting blue dress with a white, blue, and orange cardigan to match the dress. I put on my white heel sandals with the toes out. X came into the room. He looked at me and smiled. He was in agreement with my outfit. He came up to me and grabbed me by the waist. He kissed me and whispered "good girl". I just smiled at him.

We left to go get breakfast. I noticed when we left the apartment X's security was gone. I guess since X was here, we didn't need security. We went to a restaurant called Hyde Out Kitchen for breakfast. The food looked pretty good of course X ordered for us. We ate, talked, and enjoyed each other's company. I really hated that he had to leave. X said he would be leaving around 1pm today so he wanted to spend some time with me. We went to the mall afterwards. X said he had to get some suits, because he had a few conferences to attend. It was kind of fun helping him pick out suits and watching how good he looked when he tried them on. He let me pick three of the suits he chose. He looked good in all of them. We went to a few stores, for me. I didn't really need anything but he insisted I get something. So, I picked out a few outfits and a really nice designer purse from Louis Vuitton.

We got back to the apartment around 11:30am. We didn't even make it two steps inside the house when I felt X grabbing me. He picked me up and sat me on the kitchen counter. He raised my dress up and started taking his pants off. He pulled off my panties and he was inside me. I didn't want him to stop or leave me. I know it was getting close to his time to leave. I also made sure I pleased him too. We pleasured each other until it was time for him to get ready to go.

"I will try to sneak away again if I can, baby," X said, giving me a kiss.
"You better. I miss you already."
"I miss you more. And I love you."
"I love you too, be safe, and text me when you get there."
"I will," he said, opening the door. I saw Greg was outside so they knew what time to return. X left and I locked the door.

I was alone again. I turned the TV on to watch some shows. I thought it's the weekend and I should do something fun tonight. I started scrolling through my contacts to see who I could hang out with. I know X wasn't going to be here so I might as well get out and do something. I also thought I should catch up with some friends since all I've been around is X since I've been home. I called my home girl Cassie to see what she was up to.

"Hey Cassie,"
"Omg, Deja. Where the hell have you been? I saw what went down with Liz and her dude on the news. I wanted to call you but I didn't know if you came back to Ohio yet."
"Yeah, a lot went down girl. But I came home on Sunday. I just went back to working and staying out the way. But I wanted to call my boo and see what you were doing tonight?"
"Oh, don't try to call me your boo and leave out the juicy details. You know I talked to Michaela and she told me you got a new boo honey. She told me everything that Liz told her."
I rolled my eyes and thought oh shit how much did Liz say? "What did Micheala say?"
"Girl, you went to New York talking to Liz's brother and lost your virginity to Tammy's man," Cassie said laughing.
Damn, Liz told it all. I put my hand over my face. "You think I'm a horrible person?"

"No girl, you were a drunk, and horny virgin. And he obviously put it down right, because I heard you live with him."
"I am living with him. You don't hate me, Cassie?"
"Girl, no you are grown. You just had some hell, good ass dick and it just happened to be Liz's friend's man. Not my problem. You weren't loyal to Tammy nor did you have to be. Hell, she obviously wasn't doing something right. He ended up in your room."

This is why I loved Cassie; she didn't see me as being horrible. Even though, I felt horrible.

"Thank you, Cassie. I felt so horrible after everything went down. Liz wouldn't talk to me at all afterwards."
"Girl, because that was Liz's friend. I mean I get Liz being mad, but if I was Liz, I wouldn't have left you stranded like that. I probably would have laughed it off with you once I wasn't around Tammy. So, I get why you continued to talk to him hell, he was all you had when Liz bailed on you. Plus, that sex must have been everything, right? And it was your first time."
"It was everything. I didn't even know it would be like that. Cassie I'm all in."
"Look, I can tell you are blushing right now through the phone. Is he there?"
"No, he's back in New York on a business trip."
"Oh okay, well what you want to get into tonight, Ms. Thing. My boo got a boo on me now."
"Shut up. I don't know. I was thinking something laid back but fun."
"Oh well let's go to Jarred's crib. He's throwing a house party up in Dublin. It will be pretty laid back. But I don't know if Liz and Michaela will be there. They were talking about it yesterday but they didn't confirm if they were going."
"We can do that. I think me and Liz are okay for now. I saw her yesterday and we talked for a minute."
"Okay, well do you want me to pick you up or are you coming to me?"
"I'll come to you."
"Okay, see you in a little while then."
"Okay," I said, hanging up.

I had to figure out how I was going to get away from the security. I didn't want to have them come, but how was I going to deal with X. I wasn't trying to be defiant, I just wanted to hang out without him questioning me. Maybe I could just ask him about it and see what he says. But what if he says he doesn't want me to go then what. I really will be defiant if I go. Fine I will just let the security come with me and I will just explain it to Cassie. That way X won't be mad right? I mean I would probably have a few drinks and chill but nothing too crazy.

I Am A Survivor: Sex, Lies, and Abuse

I continued to watch TV until around 7pm. X never texted me saying he made it to New York. I texted him to see if he made it. I waited for him to text me back but he didn't. I figured he must have gotten busy. I went to go pick out an outfit. I thought I would just keep it simple, nothing sexy since X wasn't here. I put on a slim fitting black t-shirt and some ripped skinny jeans that were only ripped at the knee. I figured I would just do some black flip flops, something simple but cute. I jumped in the shower. I checked my phone when I got out. I saw that X called me. I called him back, but he didn't answer. Hmm, well he called me so I guess he made it.

I put my clothes on and called Cassie to let her know I would be on my way soon. It was around 8:45pm when I left the apartment. Greg was standing outside.

"Are we going somewhere tonight?" Greg said, confused.
"Yeah, actually I am going out with a friend tonight. It's the weekend and I want to see my friends," I said, trying to explain myself to the security. X really had me tripping.
"Okay, I will get us a driver," Greg said with no hesitation.
"It's okay I can drive. I do have a car."
"Look, you're leaving this late at night. I assume X doesn't know, the last thing I would hate for X to say is I let you drive on top of sneaking out. At least he will know you were being safe if I call a driver for us. I mean I don't know if you will be drinking tonight. I don't want to be at fault for driving your car and not keeping my eyes on you at all cost. I'm security, not your designated driver too," Greg said, with an attitude.
"Hmm, well okay," I smirked. "Call the driver."

We waited outside for the driver and he arrived within 20 minutes. I saw Greg texting someone so I assumed he was informing X. I told the driver where Cassie lived and we headed to her house. I knew I was going to regret this but I just really wanted to have some fun tonight. I wanted to kick it with my girl. And maybe see some friends I haven't seen in a long time. Jarred was one of my college friends so I knew a lot of my college friends would be here tonight. I just wanted to join the world of socializing again at least for one night. I kept checking my phone though, because I was worried X would be calling me soon. But so far nothing.

We made it to Cassie's place. I walked to her apartment with Greg and knocked on the door. Greg stood back.

"Oooh, is this your man?"
"Hell, no," I said going inside the apartment. Greg stood outside and guarded the door.

"Who is that then?"
"That's my security. I'm sorry I guess I should have mentioned that on the phone. X, while he is out of town, provided me with security."
"Oh, that's cute,"
"Whatever,"
"No, for real, he worries about you."
"Cassie,"
"I mean, you know. I'm just over here getting lit before the party," Cassie said, holding up some 1800.
"Let me get some."
"Here girl, I already had a glass for you."

We sat playing catch up and drinking until about 11pm. I kept checking my phone but nothing from X. We were definitely feeling it. We got up ready to go. I was definitely buzzed. My head was spinning. Good thing Greg called for the driver. We left out. Cassie talked about how fancy I was, because X had a driver for me. We laughed and danced to the music the whole way there. We were definitely drunk, but it felt good to be out having fun.

We got to the party and went inside. Greg didn't stay outside this time he came in. He tried to stay his distance, but he was definitely scoping the place out. Cassie grabbed us some more drinks and I stopped paying attention to Greg and walked around the house with Cassie saying hi to everyone. I saw people I hadn't seen in years. We danced, drank, and laughed about the good old college days with friends. I saw Michaela was there, but I didn't see Liz. I went to go say hi to Michaela.

"Hey Michaela," I said.
"Oh Deja, hi," Micheala said like she was shocked to see me.
"Is everything okay?" I said, confused.
"Yeah, everything is good. Oh shit!" Michaela said, looking behind me and then looking down.

I turned around to see Liz and X coming out of the room behind me. What the fuck? Liz just gave me this devilish smile. I couldn't even look at X. That's what I get for thinking everything was good. Payback is a bitch, right?

Chapter Nine: Lies
"I think I'm done."

I didn't even look in X's direction. I walked out the house furious. Michaela followed behind me.

"Deja, wait. I don't know what is happening but I swear this has nothing to do with me. Liz said she had something she had to handle and when I heard her call his name, I knew it was your X she was talking about. I don't know what they were doing. I was just shocked when I saw you and I knew X was here too," Michaela said, trying to sound apologetic.
"Hey, what's going on?" Cassie said coming outside.
"Payback is a bitch. That was X coming out of that room with Liz," I said pissed off waving my hands, because I was so pissed.

I saw X walking towards my direction and Greg was behind him. I started to walk away, but I had nowhere to go.

"Deja," X said.

I couldn't stand the sound of his voice right now. I just kept walking trying to ignore him.

"Deja, stop," X said, catching up to me and grabbing my wrist. I pulled my wrist away, because that was not going to work this time.
"What the fuck were you doing X?" I said, disgusted.
"Deja, it's not what you think. And why the fuck are you here?"
"Don't question me when you were coming out of the room with that BITCH," I screamed.
"Deja, you're drunk. Let me take you home."
"Don't touch me," I said, walking away from X.

I started to cry but I was trying my best to hold back the tears, because I didn't want him to see me cry not like this. I started to feel queasy.

"Deja, can we go home and talk about this?" X said, walking towards me.

I turned away from him and began to throw up. I wasn't feeling so good. I lost my balance and X grabbed me. I couldn't even push him away because I was dizzy. He picked me up and carried me to the car. He had a driver waiting for him. He put me in the car and got in the back with me. He laid my head in his lap and rubbed on my back. I was still mad but I was so sick I couldn't do anything.

I Am A Survivor: Sex, Lies, and Abuse

"I can't leave Cassie," I said, barely getting the words out.
"Greg knows what to do. He will make sure she gets home," X said.

The driver got us back to the apartment. I must have fallen asleep, because I don't even remember the drive home. X carried me to the elevators and in the apartment. He sat me down on the couch.

"Did you fuck her X?" the words came out without me even knowing I was speaking it.
"No Deja,"
"Then why were you there? You said you were going to New York?"
"That was the original plan. I postponed the flight when Liz called and said she needed to speak with me, it was urgent. She had some family trouble. I didn't think it would hurt to see what she needed. I was pretty close to her family and wanted to know if I could assist in any way. I agreed to meet Liz for dinner. She said she wanted to talk to me about some family matters and she discussed working for me to help pay back any money she needed for her family. I was going to give her a loan up front to cover some expenses and she would come work for me."
"So, how did you end up at the party with her?"
"We didn't meet for dinner. I got another call about a business matter here in Columbus and I asked if I could meet her after I was done with that. She said yeah and gave me the address where she would be. I didn't get done with the business matter until around 10pm. I called Liz and she told me she was out in Dublin if I still wanted to meet up with her. So, I drove out to Dublin to meet with her. But nothing happened. We just found a quiet room to talk in and when we came out the room there you were."
"Right,"
"Why were you there and why didn't you tell me you were leaving the house?"
"I didn't feel like telling you, because I knew you would tell me no. And now I see why. I did try to call you back, but you didn't answer," I said knowing the liquor was making me speak the truth.
"I tried calling you, to tell you that I was still in Columbus. But when you didn't answer I handled my business matters. I couldn't answer when you called me back."
"What is this business matter you keep talking about?"
"I had to take care of some things, nothing that concerns you."
"Hmmm,"
"What Deja?"
"Nothing. So, when do you go back to New York?"
"Once I know everything is good between us."
I just looked at him. "I'm sleeping in the 2nd bedroom tonight alone."
"Deja,"

I Am A Survivor: Sex, Lies, and Abuse

I got up and walked to the 2nd bedroom and closed the door. I laid down. I was still pissed, but I did believe him. Liz pissed me off. If you would have seen Liz's devilish smile, she made it seem like something happened. I cried myself to sleep. I mean I cried. I'm sure X heard me because it was the loud cry.

I rolled over and looked at the clock. It was 5am. I felt sick to my stomach again. Shit! I hurried and ran to the bathroom. I threw up. My stomach felt so horrible. I should never drink again, I thought to myself. I laid my head on the toilet. I didn't want to go lay back down just yet, because my stomach still felt sick.

"Deja, are you okay?" X said, coming to my rescue.
I couldn't even look at him. "I'm fine."

He grabbed a washcloth and ran water on it. He sat down next to me and wiped my face. He rubbed my back trying to make me feel better. I wanted to be so mad at him, but he was just so gentle with me. I just wanted to put my arms around him, but I didn't want to give in so easily. Whether he slept with her or not Liz made me feel so disgusted with her facial expression. I hated that she even got an opportunity to make me think they did something. Like this girl was trying to find a way to get back at me no matter what. She didn't care about me at all.

"Deja come lay with me. Let me take care of you," X said, very tempting.
"No, I'll be fine."
"Deja, how long are you going to do this?"
"X, I don't know. It just doesn't feel right. I don't like it."
"What can I do?"
"Go back to New York. I need time to think this over. I don't want to keep you here if you have business elsewhere."
"I'll back off if you want me to, but I'm not leaving until I know we are okay. I will have Alicia cover for me in New York."
"You don't have to do that. Go back to New York things will be okay," I said, trying to convince myself, I guess. I didn't know for sure.
"Deja," X paused. "Fine, have it your way."

X got up and left the bathroom. I laid there for a minute but eventually I got up to go lay back down in the 2nd bedroom. I went back to sleep but I woke up a few hours later when I heard the front door shut. I got up to check our bedroom. X was gone. Damn, he didn't even say goodbye. I guess I pissed him off. My stomach felt horrible. I went to the kitchen to drink some milk. I know milk helps to coat your stomach. I drank some milk and immediately I threw up in the kitchen sink. This was horrible.

I Am A Survivor: Sex, Lies, and Abuse

I laid on the couch after cleaning up. I was hoping this would pass soon. I started thinking to myself, oh shit, I didn't start my period Thursday. It was now Saturday. I was only two days late but my period is always on time. Shit. I need to get dressed and go to the pharmacy. I made myself get up and go take a shower. I just threw on a t-shirt and some jogging pants. I left the apartment. I realized there was no security. Oh well, maybe he's done with me all the way, I thought. I didn't care right now. I was more worried about if I was pregnant, that was more concerning. I went to the pharmacy and picked up 3 pregnancy tests this time. I was going to keep checking until my period started. I was so nervous; I could feel myself getting sick to my stomach again. Please just don't be pregnant. Not now.

I ran back home to hurry up and take the test. I went straight to the bathroom when I got in the apartment. I waited sitting on the toilet. I was so scared I kept wiping to see if maybe I was bleeding a little bit. I got nothing. I didn't even feel like I would be starting my period soon. 3 minutes passed and it was time to check the stick. I was breathing super hard, and I felt panicky like I just knew something was not right this time. I looked at the pregnancy test and it read pregnant. SHIT!!! I screamed to myself. I will wait a few hours and take another one. It could be wrong, right?

I got up from the toilet and washed my hands. I kept staring at the test. I didn't even notice X walked in the bathroom. He looked at the test and then looked at me. I was already in panic mode so I know he could tell.

"Deja," X said smiling.
"It could be false. Right? I mean I am going to wait and take another one," I said, shaking at this point.

X put his arms around me and held me tight. I started to cry immediately. I was shaking in fear. Was I ready to be a mom? What the hell? Why was everything happening so fast? I couldn't catch a break.

"Everything is going to be okay, Deja. I'm going to make sure of it," X said, trying to reassure me.

I sat down on the bed still in my thoughts. I saw X pick up the test again and smile. He started calling someone. He put it on speaker and walked into the bedroom. I heard a familiar voice say hello.

"Liz, tell Deja nothing happened between us," X said in his stern voice.
"X, seriously why are you calling me?" Liz said with an attitude.
"Stop playing and clear this shit up right now."

I Am A Survivor: Sex, Lies, and Abuse

"Fine, nothing happened Deja. I just wanted to piss you off, because you pissed off my friend," Liz said, mad.
"Thank you," X said, hanging up the phone.

I just looked at X. I knew nothing happened but it just pissed me off that Liz looked like something did happen. I believed X when he said it the first time, I just hated Liz did that.

"Deja, can we work through this please."
"Where did you go this morning?"
"I went for a walk. I had to clear my head. I never meant to put you in a situation like that Deja. I know it looked bad, but I swear I didn't do nothing with that girl."
"I believe you, X."

X walked up to me and leaned over to kiss me. X was still smiling. He was excited about this pregnancy test. I was just hoping it was false. I was still planning to retest.

"We need to get a doctor's appointment scheduled soon," X said.
"I actually have one scheduled for Tuesday at 8am the following week," I said remembering I scheduled it for birth control.
"You do? I will go with you," X said, still smiling.

X went to his office to do some work. He said he would try to do some zoom meetings and take care of things that way so he didn't have to go back to New York. He said Alicia was already on her way there so he would have her handle a lot of the work, as well. I laid in the bed and went back to sleep lost in my thoughts I didn't want to think anymore.

My phone rang a few hours later. I looked at the clock. It was almost 12pm.

"Hello," I said, clearing my throat.
"Girl, are you okay?" Cassie said.
"Yeah, I'm good."
"I was not expecting that to happen last night. Liz was foul but just so you know she said nothing happened. She just wanted you to think that something happened. I guess I messed up telling Michaela you were coming to the party, because Liz took full advantage of setting that up so you could see it."
"So, Liz knew I was coming to the party?"
"Yeah, that's my fault. I texted Michaela after you confirmed you were coming to my house. But I didn't know Liz was going to do that bullshit."
"It's cool girl. I don't blame you."
"But are you okay though?"

"Yeah, everything is good over here."
"You and X cool too?"
"Yeah, we're cool."
"Good, because I just want to say your man is fine, girl," Cassie said laughing.
"You better not lose him."
"You stupid Cassie," I said laughing.
"No, I'm serious. He's tall, dark, and built nicely. But I'm not drooling."
"What am I going to do with you?"
"Girl, I'm just saying. But hey your security guard wasn't too bad looking either. I got his number."
"Cassie,"
"What? He was cute."
"I can't take you nowhere."
"Oh, whatever girl. I gotta go. I just wanted to check on you. Love you girl."
"Love you too, talk to you later." I said hanging up the phone.

Cassie was hilarious. I was glad to know Liz told her the truth too. It's just crazy how I really thought we were getting to be cool again and she goes and does that bullshit. I was truly over trying to be her friend again.

I also saw I had a text from Michaela.

Hey Deja,

I'm so sorry for what Liz did. I didn't know she was still mad at you like that. I thought she was trying to work things out with you. Please don't be mad at me for her nonsense. I really didn't know she was going to do that. But she said she didn't do nothing with X. She said he didn't even budge when she tried to make a move, he just brushed her off. You got a good man for real.

Love you,

Michaela

I texted Michaela back.

Hi Michaela,

Thank you for this. I'm not mad at you. I get it Liz wanted to get her revenge, I guess. But I'm over her.
Love you,

Deja

I Am A Survivor: Sex, Lies, and Abuse

I got up and went to the bathroom. I took another pregnancy test hoping the first one was a false positive. I wiped and still didn't see any blood either. I got up and washed my hands as I waited for the results. The damn test still said pregnant.

I went to lay back down in the bed. I started to think I never asked X if he even had kids. I mean he was 36 years old, he had to have kids, right? I mean he was fucking me without a condom he had to be like that with all his exes. I was thinking I should ask him. I know he didn't talk about kids, but does he have any? Maybe I should Google him again. I pulled out my phone and Googled Xavier Thomas. I saw a lot about his businesses. I saw one article that read "Xavier Thomas single, black entrepreneur, with no kids, and never married." Why the hell was I googling him? I clicked off of the page and put my phone down. I should just talk to him, I thought to myself. I started watching TV to get my mind off of foolish things.

I got up around 2pm to go to the kitchen. My stomach was feeling much better and I was starting to get hungry. I saw X standing in the kitchen.

"Hey," I said, coming to see what he was doing.
"Hey baby. You hungry?" X said cooking.
"You cook?" I said, smiling thinking about when he said that to me.
"Yeah, I can cook," X said, sounding cocky.
"Hmmm, what are you cooking?"
"Something that will make that baby happy and healthy."
"Oh yeah, it smells good, what is it?"
"I'm cooking some beef stew. It's meaty, lots of vegetables, and healthy for you and the baby."
"That sounds good. I'm starving."

I sat down at the kitchen bar and X made our bowls of stew. He came and sat next to me.

"Mmmmh, that is really good," I said, complimenting his cooking.
"I'm glad you like it," X said smiling. "You know we should probably eat at home more now that you're pregnant. I don't trust all these restaurants and how they handle the food. I want to make sure you are getting the best supplements and nutrition. We definitely got to get you on some vitamins as well."
"X, you're going to be that guy?"
"What do you mean?"
"Now that you know I'm pregnant, I'm going to have to watch everything I eat and do?"
"It's what's best for the baby, Deja. I want you to be healthy and happy so that you carry the baby full term with no complications. You know I was reading up on

pregnancies and if you're stressed and not eating right it can affect you having a healthy baby."
"X, I'm scared," I said, trying to hold back my tears. Just talking about there being a baby was freaking me out.
"What are you afraid of? I'm going to make sure everything is good. I'm going to take care of you and I'm not going to leave your side."
"I know that, but don't you think everything is just happening so fast? I mean we are making a big step with a baby on the way and only knowing each other for such a short time. I don't even know a lot about you X."
"What do you want to know, Deja?"
"I know you never talked about kids, but did you ever want to have kids with your exes or do you have kids?"
"I don't have any kids. This will be my first. And I always wanted kids, but I believe things happen the way they are supposed to happen with the right person. I got someone pregnant in the past, but they chose to abort the child without me knowing. That also ended our relationship," X said, sounding upset.
"Do you worry about if we will make it?"
"I don't, but why do you ask that?"
"X, I just can't get over how we met, and we are moving like we've known each other for years. That doesn't make you think maybe we are rushing things?"
"Deja, I honestly don't think we are rushing anything. I knew when I first saw you, I wanted you, and when I want something, I go after it. I don't take my time, because time is short. And when you know something is worth it, time shouldn't matter."

I sat quiet for a minute. His response was cute. I guess I was just taken back on how he views things.

"What are you thinking, Deja?"
"The way you think just amazes me. I've never met nobody like you, X."
X smiled. "Yeah, well I never met no one like you either. You're submissive in some ways, but you like to challenge my authority at times. And that mouth of yours pisses me off, but arouses me at the same time. And I think you know that. That's why you be trying me. But I love that you're vulnerable with me too. That's why I don't think that we are rushing things. We are just figuring each other out as we go. But I'm still figuring out how to tame that mouth of yours, because nobody has ever challenged my authority like you do," X said in his stern voice.
"Why do you get to be the only one in charge?"
"Deja, there you go," X paused, I could see he was biting down, tightening his jaw. "That shouldn't be a question. I told you plenty of times what I say goes."
"I was just testing you," I said jokingly.
"Not funny, Deja."

I Am A Survivor: Sex, Lies, and Abuse

"What about your parents? Are they still living? Did you come from a single parent home or two parents in the household?"

"I was adopted into a two-parent household. My birth mother was a crack whore. I don't know who my bio father is. I was told he was the pimp my mother ran with, but she was a whore so I could have been anyone's child. When I was 6 years old children services was called on my mother, because she had me in abandoned houses while she was fucking whoever she could to make a dollar. My mother's sister was called when children services took custody of me and I went to stay with her and her husband. So, I was raised and adopted by my aunt and uncle. It was a good Christian home. They had two kids older than me; we grew up as siblings. My brother Mike, also my business partner. He's the oldest and the 2nd oldest is my brother James. He manages X Factor for me when I can't be there. But my uncle/father passed away a year ago from cancer. My aunt/mom is retired living in New Jersey. I normally go see her when I go up there for business."

"I'm sorry to hear about your father's passing. Do you have any relationship with your bio mother?"

"Not at all. I was told she is still living. I guess she tried to come see me a few times when I was younger, but she would really only stop in to ask her sister for money. My father wouldn't even let her get close to me if he thought she was high and she was always high. I would just watch from the window as they would ask her to leave. I didn't care to have a relationship with her. I was being raised good so I didn't need her." X said with sadness in his voice.
"Sorry, I didn't mean to bring up bad memories."
"Nah, it's okay. I want to be open with you and you can ask me anything," X said, sounding sincere.
"Oh man, this food was so good, X. I am stuffed," I said, laying back on the chair and patting my belly.
"Yeah, I'm glad you enjoyed it. Pretty soon that belly is going to be poking out," X said, touching my stomach.
"Oh God, am I even going to be attractive to you by then?" I said, thinking about my pregnant belly.
"Deja, you will always be attractive to me. You are sexy as hell, with or without a belly," X said, making me feel good.
"So, can I ask another question?"
"Ask away, Deja."
"So, how did you and Randy become friends?"
"I met Randy through the construction company he works for about 3 years ago. The company he works for did some work on one of my businesses. He was a good worker. He did some side jobs for me and I was putting him into learning how to start his own company. I got close with his family and friends and I met Tammy through him. So, when I started dating her, I learned that Liz was

Randy's sister and Tammy's high school friend. I only met Liz a few times, because she was living in Columbus with you at that time. Why'd you ask that?"
"I just wanted to know how you met them. You seem very willing to help Liz and her family with stuff. I just wanted to know how close you guys were, before me."
"What are you thinking, Deja? You messed up my friendships?"
"I mean I still feel bad knowing you were friends and you seem like you do a lot for Liz's family. I feel like I'm at fault for the distance. And with Randy missing I think Liz is mad at me for that too."
"Deja, you're not at fault. Like I said before I was ending my ties with Randy anyway. He did some foul business shit, behind my back and we were already distant. I still respect his family and I don't mind helping them, but I don't regret nothing that's happened between us. Liz's mind is clouded, because she's fighting her own demons right now and she just needs someone to blame. It just happens to be you she wants to blame right now."
"I'm trying to see it differently, it's just hard. I keep thinking about how my actions caused hurt to Tammy and Randy. Don't get me wrong X, I love being with you. I just wish we met differently. You know, I just don't want to feel like I wrecked things."
"Deja, I knew what I was doing when I walked in your room that night. I take the blame for my own actions. I wrecked my friendship and relationship with them. I don't regret nothing, because I love what we got going on. You are all I worry about now and I'm over the past."
"Okay, one more question."
"Deja, just ask me."
"You say I'm different and I challenge you. Tammy didn't do that?"
"Nah, Tammy was very submissive. She did what I told her to do. She only acted out if she thought I was cheating on her, because I was gone a lot for business trips. She was very jealous and clingy so she always did what I told her too. Like when I told her she didn't have to work she quit her job immediately," X said, trying to hint towards me.
"X, I don't want to stop working. I like what I do."
"You will stop working once you have this baby, Deja. I'm not going to allow that."
"Why?"
"Deja, why you gotta be so damn defiant on this?" X said, irritated.
"I'm not trying to be defiant, X. I just don't understand why I have to quit working. I like having my own money. I went to school for what I do and it makes me feel happy to know that I can work in my field. I can continue to work towards something, maybe even advance in my career."
X was tightening his jaw again. "Deja, I can take care of you and give you whatever you want. You want me to put more money in your account? Will that make you feel more secure?"
"No X, you don't have to do that. What will be different with me working or not working?"

I Am A Survivor: Sex, Lies, and Abuse

X grabbed my wrist. I tried to pull away but he was holding tight. "Deja, if you were not working, I could take you with me on some of my business trips. You and the baby could be with me all the time. I didn't fight you on staying in Columbus, I just moved here with you. When are you going to stop being so defiant and compromise with me?"
"Let me think about it. Maybe after having the baby, I can see about quitting, maybe," I said, not so sure.
X let my wrist go. "It's a start. I guess we will discuss it then," X said standing up. "I have to get back to work. I'll be in my office if you need me."

X went back in his office to work. I cleaned up the kitchen and put the leftovers in the fridge. It was 4:15pm when I looked at the clock. I saw a notification come through on my phone. I thought someone texted me, but it was a notification from ACE Bank saying $50,000 was deposited into my account. My balance was now $70,000. What the fuck? X, was going to do everything he could to make me stop working. I just wasn't ready to give up working though. I was going to go to his office and say something, but I didn't want to start an argument. I just sat on the couch and turned the TV on instead to watch my favorite crime documentaries. Man, what should I do with this money? I could probably pay off my student loans. I only owe about $58,000 now. I had been working on getting that paid off for a while now. I was happy to see I only owed $58,000. I covered a lot of my college with scholarships but I still ended up owing $75,000 total out of pocket. I worked hard trying to bring that number down. But thanks to X I was about to pay that off.

I logged into my student loan account to check the balance. I was tripping. I looked at the last payment history. It showed that I paid the balance in full on Monday. I downloaded the receipt to my phone to look at it. It said my balance was $0 and showed that my last payment was Monday. I started thinking about my other bills. I logged on to my car loan account. It showed the last payment was Monday and I had a $0 balance. There was a message stating my paperwork for my title was in the mail. I checked my phone bill. I had a credit of $2000 on my bill to cover my phone bill for a while. My car insurance also had a credit on it to cover my insurance for the remainder of this year. I checked my credit card account. I put my ticket to Paris on when I planned to go with Liz and Tammy. My credit card balance was $0. I didn't have any bills to pay. Everything was covered or paid off.

I went to X's office. I stood at the door.

"Come in Deja," X said.
I sat in the recliner X had in his office. "You paid off all my bills?"
"I told you I would cover all your expenses."

I Am A Survivor: Sex, Lies, and Abuse

"Thank you, X."
"You're welcome."

I stood up and went over to X and kissed him. I began to straddle him and unbuckle his pants. X stopped me.

"I can't right now Deja. I have to get some paperwork done," X said, turning me down.

I was shocked. Hurt actually. I didn't say nothing I just left his office so he could finish his work. I was feeling a little emotional after he turned me away for the first time, that really hurt. I tried to brush it off and went back to watching my crime documentary. I know he had to focus on his work since he wasn't out of town handling it. My phone started ringing.

"Hello," I said.
"Deja, we need to talk," Cassie said.
I walked to the bedroom. "What's going on?"
"Liz is over Michaela's house going through it. Micheala called me and asked me, well begged me to call you. She said she thinks Liz is high and all she is asking for is you. Michaela said she keeps rocking back and forth, crying, and screaming for Deja."
"Cassie, you know I don't want to deal with Liz."
"That's what I told Michaela, but she is begging for you to come over."
"I can't go over there," I said, knowing X would not allow it.
"Look, I know Liz was saying something about X probably wouldn't let you come anyway. Maybe if you tell X you're coming to my house and then from my house we can go to Michaela's together."
"I don't want to come whether X says yes or no."
"Deja, look Liz did some fuck up shit yesterday and I'm not asking you to look past that, but she's going through the motions and she wants to see you and only you. She said she will let Michaela call the ambulance if she can see you first. Michaela is freaking out. Do it for Michaela please."
"Fine, I'll be on my way in a little bit."
"Okay see you soon," Cassie said, hanging up.

I didn't want to go, but I get it Michaela didn't know what else to do. I put my shoes on. I figured I would just keep on my t-shirt and jogging pants.

"Hey X, I'm going to Cassie's for a little bit. Is that cool?" I said standing at X's office door.
"What are you going over there for?"
"Just to have some girl time. You're busy and I'm tired of watching TV."

I Am A Survivor: Sex, Lies, and Abuse

"I get it. Just call my driver. I feel safe knowing you're with him."
"Okay," I said.

I left the apartment and called X's driver. He came to pick me up. I figured I would just have him drop me off at Cassie's and then I would ride with Cassie to Michaela's house. I arrived at Cassie's house and told the driver he didn't have to wait. He left after I went inside.

"Girl, I'm sorry to put you through all of this, but Liz is not sober like she stated. I have been listening to her since I got off the phone with you. I have the phone on mute, but Michaela called me so I can just listen to everything Liz is saying. She is tripping Deja."

Cassie put the phone to my ear. I could hear Liz mumbling words.

"She's my best friend. I should have protected her. She doesn't know what's next? She doesn't. I want Deja. Deja is my best friend. I love Deja. Deja. I should have helped her. Why didn't I help her?" I heard Liz say as she started to cry.

Cassie and I got in her car to head over there. I kept listening on the phone. Liz would say something really clear and then she would start mumbling and crying. I was worried for Liz. I didn't know why Michaela didn't just call the ambulance. I started to call 911 on my phone. Cassie stopped me and said Liz has a knife to her wrist and if she hears the sirens, she told Michaela she was going to slit her own wrist. I hung up the phone. Cassie didn't say that over the phone to me. We made it to the house and Michaela opened the door for us.

"DEJA," Liz yelled.
I could see she had the knife to her wrist.
"Hi Liz, what are you doing?" I said, staying calm.
"I was hoping you would come see me. I missed you. I'm so sorry I didn't protect you. You are my best friend and I should have protected you, Deja," Liz said crying.
"You did protect me, Liz. I'm safe, see," I said playing along.
"No, I knew what Randy was doing. He was prepping you for X the whole time. And I didn't tell you. Sweet and innocent, that's what he wanted," Liz paused.
"Oops, I wasn't supposed to tell you that," Liz started laughing.
"Liz, honey can we call the ambulance. You need to get checked."
"NOOOO, I'm not sick or crazy. If you call them, I will kill myself," Liz said holding the knife up to her wrist.
"Okay, we won't call. I just wanted to check to make sure you are okay."
"I'm okay. You're not okay. When I told Randy you were a virgin. X came to Columbus to scope you out. He wanted you, Deja. Randy was grooming you for

I Am A Survivor: Sex, Lies, and Abuse

X. I knew everything, because X was paying me and Randy to get you. Everything was an act. We all played our part to get paid. Tammy was fucking X, and she loved X, but she helped because she wanted to please him. She didn't really think he would be able to get you. We did good, didn't we? I told X you wouldn't fall for it. But I was wrong, because you did. And I should have protected you. I really liked our friendship, but my family needed the money. Because my fucking dad couldn't stop gambling. He blew every penny. And I had to go back and ask X for more money. The humility of it all. And Randy ran off with his trifling ass. He took his cut and just left us. It was my money who paid off my mom's house and cleaned up my dad's debt just for him to put us back in the FUCKING HOLE," Liz screamed.

"Liz, so you're telling me that from day one you were helping to get me to New York so that I could meet X?" I said with tears in my eyes. I couldn't believe what I was hearing.

"No, we were friends first. I didn't tell Randy about you being a virgin until a year before we came to New York. And then I told Tammy that's when X wanted me to hook you up with Randy to get you to come to New York. X planned the whole scenario. I would introduce you to my brother 2 weeks before the trip to New York, because X said you would be comfortable talking to someone I trusted, my brother. And then when you met Randy, Randy would get you hot and ready for X. And you played right into it," Liz paused. "But I didn't know Randy beat you up. I guess he really liked you too. He was hoping you didn't fall for it either. Hell, we were all shocked that it worked. Tammy knew X was good, but she had her doubts too. But he won. It really hurt us all to see you fall for his bullshit."

I couldn't say anything, my whole body was trembling as I listened to what Liz was saying. I powered my phone down as I thought X could track my location. I wasn't going back this time. The lies were hitting me right in my face. I couldn't believe what Liz was saying. I would have to have Cassie take me to a hotel or something, but I would have to pay cash so he couldn't find me. I know I couldn't stay with Cassie. His driver and Greg knew where she lived. I had nothing else to say. I think I'm done.

Chapter Ten: Stuck
"I couldn't run if I tried."

Michaela finally called 911. She told them if Liz heard the sirens, she would slit her wrist. She went outside to call while I was talking with Liz. The cops and the ambulance showed up with the lights and sirens off. An officer came in from the back and snuck up on Liz grabbing the knife before she could hurt herself. They took her to the hospital.

"Deja, I know Liz said a lot of fuck up shit. You don't believe her, do you?" Cassie said.
"I don't know Cassie. I don't know," I said, holding back my tears. I believed her. I remembered hearing the hallway conversations at Liz's parents' house. That was Randy telling X about me. And X even commented to me that I was "sweet and innocent." I don't know why I didn't put that together until now.
"You can stay here if you want Deja. You don't have to go to a hotel," Michaela said.
"I don't know if he knows where you live, but I really don't want to find out. I just need to be away from him tonight until I can clear my head."

Cassie took me to the bank so I could get cash. I found a hotel in Upper Arlington far from Downtown that took cash payments. Cassie dropped me off at the hotel and I asked her to please not tell X where I was if he showed up. Cassie promised.

I checked into the hotel and went to my room. I locked and latched the door. I sat on the bed and began to cry.

This shit was beyond crazy. I didn't know what to think. I just knew I was done with X. I tried to lay down and watch some TV. I closed my eyes and went to sleep.

I woke up the next morning around 9am. I couldn't cut my phone on, because I knew X would probably track my phone. I called Cassie from the hotel room phone.

"Deja, girl, are you okay?" Cassie said with fear in her voice.
"Cassie, what happened?" I said, nervous.
"They came over here and they went to Michaela's house too. She called me crying. It was X, Greg, and 6 other dudes. X was pissed. He scared me," Cassie said, nervous.
"Did you tell X where I was?"

"No, I told him you took a cab from Michaela's house. But Deja I'm worried he was calling people and I think he got everybody looking for you. I'm sure he will find you soon."
"Cassie, did you tell him where I was?" I said, nervous now.
"No, Deja I promise. I didn't say nothing. But he's pissed off."
"Are you okay he didn't hurt you, did he?"
"No, he just scared me, that's all."
"Okay, I will call a cab and go to my parents' house."
"Deja be safe. I love you."
"I love you too and I will," I said, hanging up.

Shit. I knew he would be mad; I didn't think he would have everyone looking for me. I had to get out of this hotel safely. I got up and put my shoes on. I called for a cab. I looked out the window to see if I could see any cars out front. I didn't see anything. I unlatched the door and opened it. Fuck, X was at the door. I tried to close it but he was already halfway in the room when he pushed the door back open.

"Deja, seriously what the fuck are you doing?" X said, pissed.
"X, I just needed some space," I said, backing away from X.
"Space for what Deja? What the fuck is going on?" He said, pushing me down on the bed.

I crawled up to the head board scared he was going to hit me. I couldn't say anything, I was just watching him.

"WHAT THE FUCK IS GOING ON, DEJA?" X yelled. He climbed on the bed and grabbed my leg. I screamed. He pulled me toward him. I covered my face afraid he would swing on me. He grabbed my wrists and pulled my hands away from my face. I was so scared, but chills still ran through me. "DEJA, WHY ARE YOU DOING THIS?"
I had to say something. "Liz, told me everything. How you had Randy grooming me. How I was your plan from jump. How you paid everybody," I said, crying at this point.

X let me go and backed up. He put his head down and sat in the chair next to the bed. I sat up. He looked puzzled.

"Is it true?" I said breaking the silence.
"You know Tammy showed me a picture of you and Liz. She was trying to show me Liz, but you were in the picture too. She was showing me that her and Liz had the same taste and wore similar styles even when they were in different states. She was trying to tell me Liz was like her twin sister. They dressed alike

and thought alike. But when I saw you. You were all I saw," X paused and looked at me. "I wanted you, Deja."
"But you paid Randy to groom me. And Liz to get me to New York."
"I just needed you to be ready for me. Tammy told me Liz said you never experienced sex before and I wanted you to be ready."
"You lied to me X," I said, as the tears started to fall.
"I can't lose you, Deja. Not now."
"I can't be with you, X."
"Deja," X paused. "Please don't do this."

I didn't have anything else to say. The hotel phone rang. It was my cab.

"I'm going to my parents' house. I'll come get my things later."
"No, I'll leave. You can stay in the apartment like I promised. I at least still want to go to the Dr. appointment with you. Please. I don't want to miss anything."
"I guess that's okay."
"Thank you, Deja."

I left and got in the cab. I turned my phone back on now that he already found me. I would just go to my parents for now and go back to the apartment later. I wouldn't tell my parents anything right now. I still had time to hold off on sharing the news.

I got to my parents' house. They were shocked to see me so early, but they were pleased. I told them I stayed out with Cassie last night and needed to go take a shower. I had clothes at my parents' house so I knew they wouldn't care.

After my shower I ate breakfast with my parents and we talked. We watched TV and talked about my relationship. I didn't tell them it was over. I just talked about how well it was going. I looked at my phone and saw X texted me.

Hey Deja,

I am leaving now going back to New York. I will be back next Monday for the Dr. appt on Tuesday. I'm really sorry baby. I really hope you can forgive me. Everything I feel about you is the truth.

I love you

X

I Am A Survivor: Sex, Lies, and Abuse

I didn't reply back. I just continued hanging with my parents. I stayed with them pretty much all day. It was around 7pm I placed an order for a rideshare. I kissed my mom and dad. I told them I loved them and left to go back to the apartment.

I called Cassie and Michaela on 3-way on the ride home. Michaela told me Liz was doing okay. She had been apologizing for everything she said. Michaela said she was okay; X and his crew just scared her. They both asked if I was okay. I told them yeah. I told them X left to go back to New York. I told them I would be staying at the apartment until I found something else. Cassie insisted I come live with her, but I wasn't ready to share that I was pregnant, so I just told her I wanted my own space. They talked to me until I made it inside the apartment. I hung up with them and locked the door.

I walked in the apartment. It was quiet. I went into the bedroom. I saw a bouquet of roses and a letter on the bed. I checked the closet and the drawers. It looked like X took his clothes and stuff with him. I went to the bed to grab the letter.

Deja,

I know nothing I say right now will change how you feel. But I want you to know I love you and I may have done some fucked up shit to get you, but my feelings for you were genuine. I didn't mean to hurt you. Like I said before, I go after what I want and I wanted you and still do. I will find my way back to you no matter what. I love you too much to give up easily. I hope you understand it's me and you forever.

I love you
X

I moved the roses off the bed and saw a box underneath the roses. I put the roses on the dresser and opened the box. It was a beautiful silver sparkling diamond heart necklace with matching earrings. I loved it, but I just didn't know how to feel right now. I got ready for bed and went to sleep.

****

The week flew by. It was weird not having X around or him calling me every day. He still texted to check on me of course, but his reasoning was for the baby. It was already the Monday before my Dr. appointment. X said he would be in later tonight. He asked to stay with me. He said he would sleep in the 2nd bedroom. I figured he was paying for everything he could stay. I was still looking to move though just to get my own space. I know it had only been a week since I found out I was pregnant. But looking in the mirror I feel like my stomach was already

I Am A Survivor: Sex, Lies, and Abuse

poking out. It wasn't super noticeable, but I could see it while I stood naked in the mirror. I still didn't tell anyone yet. I figured this Dr. appointment would make it official. I scheduled PTO time for today through Wednesday, because I didn't know how I would feel after this appointment. Besides, I had been sick to my stomach every day since last week and I just wanted to rest.

I looked at the clock. It was 4pm. I had just got out of the shower from being lazy all day. I figured I would get dressed before X showed up. But I was stuck looking at my stomach in the mirror now.

"Damn, you're still so sexy," X said. I jumped out of my skin. I grabbed my towel to cover up.
"Shit, you scared me. I thought you weren't coming until later."
"I got in a little earlier than I thought. Don't stop admiring yourself on my behalf," X said smiling.
"Whatever, X. I need to get dressed. Can you go back in the living room?"
"Deja, you act like I haven't seen you naked before," X said, walking towards me.
"X, we are no longer together, things are different now."
"It won't last too much longer. I've missed you," X said, grabbing my wrist and pinning me to the wall.
"X," I paused. My breathing was getting heavy. Damn, I did miss him, but I had to fight this. "X, I can't."
"But you want to," X said, leaning in to kiss me. His hands slid under my towel. "Your pussy says you want to."
"X," I paused again. I was going to lose this fight. It's been a while since I felt him so close like this. My body was reacting to him.

X kissed me hard and I wrapped my arms around him, dropping my towel. He picked me up and carried me to the bed. Damn, I couldn't hold it in. I wanted him. He laid me down on the bed. He sucked my nipples and kissed on my belly. He lifted my legs on his shoulder and he put his mouth on my clitoris. I moaned. He still felt so amazing. My body began to tremble, the chills were flowing, and my pussy was super wet. I've missed him. I moaned as I began to cum. X ate my pussy for an hour, not even coming up for a breath. He was sending chills through my whole body. I was crying out in moans. I was cumming back-to-back. X got up and turned me over on my stomach. He lifted my ass up and slid inside my pussy from behind quickly. I came immediately. My pussy was pulsating, and my legs were shaking. I just kept thinking damn, I've missed this, I've missed him. He began pounding harder and harder with every stroke. He whispered "I've missed you Deja" as he released.

X laid beside me on the bed.

"Deja, I'm over this bullshit. You got your break and I want you back now."
"So, you're just going to demand your way back in?"

X lifted up and climbed on top of me. I could feel his penis touching the tip of my pussy. He was getting hard and I could feel it. "I'm going to fuck you until you tell me you're over this shit," X said, now sticking his dick inside me. "X," I moaned. "Tell me you want me, Deja," X said slowly stroking me. I was really bad at this. My body was already trembling. My pussy was getting wetter. X started moving faster and going deep. He pushed my legs back to go deeper. I moaned as the feeling was amazing. I was about to cum. X stopped when he saw my eyes roll back. I screamed out "X, don't stop". "Tell me you want me, Deja," X said again. Fuck, I wanted to cum. I tried to grind on him and he stopped me by grabbing my waist. "Deja, why are you torturing yourself?" X said. X kissed me. "I know you want me. Why are you so defiant?" X said. X still wouldn't move. I was starting to shake. "You don't play fair X. We should talk about this first." I said as my body was beginning to get hot. "Okay then let's talk about it." X said. "Fuck, X I want to cum," I said, getting frustrated. My body was trembling with excitement and he was stopping me from cumming. "You want to talk, because you're not ready to tell me you want me. So, we need to talk first," X said, still not moving. My pussy was pulsating. I was getting frustrated. Deja, just take him back you are already fucking him. "I want you, X. Please fuck me," I cried out. X started fucking me. I moaned so loud as my body exploded. He kept going and I kept cumming. Shit he felt so good. I cried out "I've missed you, X." X pounded harder and we climaxed together.

X stayed on top of me kissing me.

"Why do you always make things so difficult?" X said, kissing my cheek.
"X, I just don't think this is how we should have conversations. You know what you do to me and how you make me feel. It's never fair game when we are having sex."
"It is to me. The chemistry speaks the truth. You missed me just as much as I missed you. But you pretend like you're mad, because of how things happened. But you know I was genuine with you."
"But you lied X about how we met. You planned it to be that way. And then you used your friend to groom me. That hurt to hear that."
"Deja, it was stupid I know. But I knew you would be open and ready for me, because I knew I wanted to fuck you as soon as I saw you. And I get what I want," X said. Fuck, I could feel him getting hard again.
"X," I moaned as I was getting wet again as he was still inside me.

I Am A Survivor: Sex, Lies, and Abuse

X fucked me the rest of the night. He said he was just catching up on the days he missed with me. I was going to go to the doctors with a sore body messing with him. But stupid or not I really did miss him and I did want him back.

As I thought, I woke up the next morning sore as hell. It was 6:30am. I got up and jumped in the shower. I know the pregnancy test said I was pregnant, but I was still hoping the doctor would say no it was false. X got in the shower with me.

He took my washcloth and washed me up. I washed him too. I guess I was all in again. The roller coaster of this relationship was driving me crazy.

We got dressed and headed out around 7:15am. The driver pulled up to take us to the dr. appointment. We arrived at the doctors at 7:45am.

"Good morning, my name is Deja Anderson. I have an appointment with Dr. Chang at 8am."
"Yes, I just need you to sign these papers here and your insurance is still the same?" The receptionist asked.
"Yes,"
"Actually, she has two insurances," X chimed in.
"I do," I said confused.
"This is her primary one and the one you have on file is her secondary," X said, handing her an insurance card.
"When did you do that?"
"Deja, I told you I'm going to take care of you."

The receptionist took the card and made copies. And she handed the card back to X and he gave it to me.

"Well, Ms. Anderson, with the new card you don't have any co-pay, you are all set," the receptionist said.

We sat down and waited to be called.

"Is there anything else I need to know that you did?" I said, curious.
"I can't think of anything right now. But if it crosses my mind, I will let you know," X said.
"Ms. Anderson, we are ready for you," the nurse said, coming out to greet us.

We walked back to the room. The nurse took my weight and blood pressure. She checked my pulse.

"So, what brings you in today?" the nurse said.

"I took a pregnancy test. Two of them and they both said I was pregnant."
"Oh okay. Have you had any symptoms?"
"I have been experiencing morning sickness. It normally goes away by noon. Sometimes I throw up, sometimes I just feel queasy."
"Well, it sounds like morning sickness. I will go get your doctor. She should be in soon."
"Thanks."
"So, you've been having symptoms. Why didn't you tell me?" X said.
"I guess it just slipped my mind. I'm normally sick in the morning but it's done by lunch time. And it hasn't been every day."
"Well, hello Deja this is exciting. Oh, and who are you?" Dr. Chang said, coming in the room.
"Hi Dr. Chang," I said smiling.
"Hello, my name is Xavier Thomas. I am Deja's partner."
"Well, glad to meet you. And Ms. Deja, when did you lose your virginity?"

I put my head down. I forgot Dr. Chang has been my doctor for a while now and she knew I was a virgin.

"Dr. Chang, it's a long story, but probably 4 weeks ago," I said, embarrassed.
"Wow, okay and you are here because you're pregnant," Dr. Chang said.
"Yep," I said, ashamed.
"Well, let's take a look here," Dr. Chang said.

Dr. Chang took some blood work. I had to step out to pee in a cup. And she did an ultrasound.

"Well, it looks like there is a baby. Congratulations," Dr. Chang said. "It looks like you are still pretty early in the pregnancy, but I will prescribe you some prenatal vitamins. Also, schedule with the front desk to see me in a month, but don't hesitate to come in sooner if you feel anything seems off. Since this is your first pregnancy if anything feels weird or seems uncomfortable just come back and see me. But I'm sure it will be just fine."
"Thank you, doc," I said, disappointed.
"No problem and it was nice to meet you Mr. Thomas," Dr. Chang said leaving.

I scheduled for a month with the receptionist. She scheduled me for another Tuesday in the morning.

We made it back to the apartment. The maid was there when we arrived. She came every Tuesday.

I Am A Survivor: Sex, Lies, and Abuse

"Hello Mr. Thomas and Ms. Anderson. Mr. Thomas, I put all your clothes and shoes back in the closet and drawers. Ms. Alicia stopped by and with movers to drop everything off for you."
"Thank you, Ms. Laura," X said. I looked at X, but I didn't say anything.

I guess he didn't take his time moving right back in, but why would he. He already had it planned that I would be back with him. He plans everything. I was a little annoyed with his tactics, but he was right he knew I would be back with him. It's like I can't tell him no for long. This man had a hold on me.

I didn't do much the rest of the day. X was in his office working. I slept off and on, watching TV. When I woke up, I looked at my phone. It was 5:05pm. I saw I had another notification from ACE Bank. I opened it up. X replaced the money I used for the hotel so my balance was $70,000 again.

I got up and went to X's office.

"Hey Deja," X said, when he saw me standing at his office door.
"Hey," I paused. "I want to go shopping."
"What do you need? I can tell Alicia to pick it up."
"No, I want to go shopping myself, X. I really want to paint and do some arts and craft projects."
"Deja, I got a lot of work to finish up and I don't want you out there by yourself."
"Cassie will go with me, she is off today."
"Hell no. The last time you went with Cassie you didn't come back."
"So, I can't hang, with my friends now? I will come back."
"Deja, there you go with that mouth again," X said, tightening his jaw.
"X, I'm bored and I just want to go get something to keep me busy that I like to do. Please."
"I'll take you, just give me an hour," X said.
"Really X, I can't go to the store without you? Like what the fuck. I am so irritated. You said you have to work, just let me go to the store," I said, walking out of the room.
"WHAT THE FUCK IS YOUR PROBLEM?" X yelled following behind me. He pushed me against the wall and put his hands around my neck.
"Ouch, X that hurts" I cried out.

X backed up away from me throwing his hands up like he had enough. "Damn, Deja. I am trying my hardest with you, but you are really testing me."
I held my sore neck. He really grabbed me tight around my neck. "I'm sorry," I said, scared to say much else.

I Am A Survivor: Sex, Lies, and Abuse

X walked back into his office and I went into the bedroom. I figured I wasn't going to the store. I laid down and watched TV. X came in the room around 6:30pm.

"You ready to go?" X said.
I sat up and looked at him. "It's okay X. I don't want to go anymore."
"You're mad now?" X said coming to sit next to me.
I tensed up a little nervous of what he might do. "I'm not mad. I just don't want to go anymore."
X put his hand up to rub my shoulder, but I jumped thinking he was going to grab me again.

"I'm sorry, Deja. I shouldn't have scared you like that. You don't have to be afraid I'm not going to hurt you," X said, noticing my fear.

X grabbed my wrist. I felt the chills, but I also felt fear too. He was different now. I didn't know how I should feel anymore. He kissed me hard and immediately my body reacted. I still wanted him, but I was also scared. I was really going to have to work on listening to him and not talking back. He put his hands down my pants and started massaging my clitoris. I moaned as the tears ran down my face. It felt good, but I was having mixed emotions at the same time. He pulled my pants down and had me turn over. He fucked me doggy style. He fucked me hard and fast. I came quickly and continuously. But I also noticed I was crying. The feeling of him inside me fucking me was still amazing, but the mixed emotions was making me feel lost. Once he finished, I laid down with my back facing him, because I was trying to wipe my tears. But I knew he knew I was crying. He turned me around and wiped my face. He held me tight. I cried even harder. He whispered "Deja, I'm sorry baby." I cried myself to sleep while X held me.

I woke up the next morning super sick. I ran to the bathroom to throw up. Ugh I felt horrible. I washed my hands and brushed my teeth once I was done. I had to jump in the shower after I noticed I peed on myself a little too. I cleaned up the floor and jumped in the shower. Once I got out of the shower, I wrapped the towel around me and walked into the bedroom. I didn't even notice X was gone. There was a new bouquet of roses on the dresser with another box and a letter. I picked up the letter to read first.

Deja,

A lot has happened in these last weeks and I noticed with so much on my plate with my businesses I have been frustrated a lot more. I didn't mean to hurt you Deja and I don't want to hurt you, but your defiance takes me there sometimes. I love you and until I get over this hurdle with my business projects, I think we need just a little space. I know I upset you yesterday and maybe those baby hormones are kicking in too, but I really want to keep my promise of making you happy. So, I am going to go back to New York for a few months just to get on track with everything here and in New Jersey. So that when I come back, we can get focused on preparing for this new addition to the family. I love you girl. Alicia will be checking in on you while I'm away and I will call you every day. Please forgive me Deja. Also, go shopping for whatever you need, just please make sure to use my driver and have my security with you.

I love you,

X

I agree I think space is needed. I opened the box on the dresser. X bought me a silver diamond bracelet that matched the necklace and earrings he bought me earlier. It was beautiful and sparkly too.

****

I was in my office painting when my dad video called me.

"Hi daddy,"
"Hey baby girl. What are you doing?"
"Just painting. I'm running out of wall space. I have been painting a lot these last couple of months. And I'm running out of space to put things. I don't know if it's the baby making me so artsy again, but I just want to paint all the time," I said, rubbing my belly. I was 3 months almost 4 months in this pregnancy now and I definitely had a belly.

"Oh yeah, and your face is getting chunkier. Your mom has been buying baby stuff like crazy. She was so excited to see that you're showing now since the last time you visited. She said you looked like you blew up overnight," my dad said, laughing.

I told my parents I was pregnant a week after my first dr. appointment. My dad was a little worried at first, but my mom was so excited. My mom still hasn't met X yet, because he has been back and forth from New York, New Jersey, and Ohio the last couple of months. He has been to every dr. appointment I had so far though. And things have been going well with us. He's been letting me go places with my friends a lot more too. I mean of course he still has his security with me, and his driver takes me everywhere but at least I am doing more with Cassie and Michaela. I even hung out with Stacy who was super excited when I told her I was pregnant. She is still all in with me and X's relationship. Cassie and Michaela were hesitant at first that I was still talking to X, but when I told them everything he had been doing, they were okay with it again. They were excited about my pregnancy. They are planning my baby shower for me. I told them I wanted to wait until I was 7 or 8 months for the baby shower. They already picked the place and have the date set. My mom has been going crazy with baby shopping. She also has a room in her house setup for the baby, because she wants to be my baby sitter. Her and my dad already worked it out that my mom would just work from home while she watched the baby for me. Everybody I told so far is super excited about my pregnancy. I was getting excited too. Just feeling him or her moving around in my stomach was a feeling I couldn't even explain, but I was happy.

I would talk to my belly, and X when he was here, would do the same. X got me headphones to place on my belly so the baby could listen to music too. We were really enjoying the excitement of this little Peanut growing inside me. I felt like it was bringing us even closer together. I know he was busy with his business and not here every day, but when he was here with me, he gave me and the baby all of his attention. And even while he was gone, he still called me every day.

"You know Deja, I was thinking why don't you sell your paintings. I keep thinking about when you used to paint and you let your mom hang them up in our house. You know we still get compliments on your paintings when we have people over," my dad said.
"You know I didn't think about that. Maybe I will start looking into that," I said, thinking that could be a good idea.
"Well, baby girl, I don't want to hold you up. I just wanted to check on you. I know you are by yourself a lot with X being gone. When is X coming home for good?" my dad, said always worrying.
"Daddy, I'm doing okay, but I think he's finishing all his big projects soon and will be home for good in another month. But you know work, mom, and my friends have been keeping me busy too."
"I know baby girl, but I just don't like you being alone in the house at night while you're pregnant. I always made sure I was home every night with your mom when she was pregnant with you."
"Daddy, I'm okay. But thank you for worrying about me. I love you daddy," I said, reassuring him that everything was good.
"I love you too, baby girl," my dad said, hanging up.

"Well, Peanut the whole world is worried about you." I said as I rubbed my belly.

I continued painting until I finished the piece. I left it on the easel to dry. I went and washed my hands and cleaned up my mess. I started going to the parks after work and on the weekends to start a walking routine. I figured I would head to the park now that I was finished painting. It was good to start walking and getting fresh air for the baby. I threw on a t-shirt and some leggings. My t-shirt was fitting tight now. I was going to have to go buy new clothes soon. I've been wearing loose fitting stuff now that I was poking out. But maybe it was time to buy some maternity clothes.

I headed out once I was dressed. Greg was on duty today so he followed me out. "How's it going Greg?" I said, talking to him while we were going down the elevator.
"Everything is good, Ms. Deja. How are you?"
"I'm good. Just hoping it's not too hot out here now that it's July. The heat has been kicking my but with an extra load on me," I laughed while making small talk. Greg chuckled. "Well, it's supposed to be 80 degrees by noon on this beautiful Saturday."
I looked at my watch. "Well, it's 10:30am hopefully it's okay outside or we will have a short walk today."

It actually felt nice once we made it outside. We walked to the park a few blocks away. I talked to my peanut as Greg trailed behind. I figured I would do maybe two laps around the track and then head home. It was nice feeling like I could do more again. X was allowing me to have more freedom which I feel made things easier between us. Of course, I was never alone, but at least with security, they weren't all up in my face. I started trying to make conversations and get to know them too, since they were always around. It would help me be more comfortable with them being there. And they really seemed like cool people too. Cassie was actually dating Greg. She decided to give him a chance even after that run in with X. She said Greg was a pretty genuine guy and she liked him. They have been dating for 3 months now.

I was almost done with my walk. I had just made it halfway around the track for the 2nd time. So, I would be heading back home once I made it fully back around. I heard Greg call my name and I turned around.

I saw Randy standing close to Greg with a gun pointed at his side. Shit, I was stuck. I couldn't move, I was frozen. Randy had on a jacket and once he knew I saw the gun he hid it inside his jacket still pointing it at Greg. I didn't know what to do. I couldn't run if I tried.

Chapter Eleven: Loved
"I want to give you the world."

"Deja here's what is going to happen. You will walk to that black truck up there and get in the back seat. If you don't, I will shoot this dude and you," Randy said.
"Deja don't listen to him," Greg said.
"SHUT THE FUCK UP," Randy yelled.
I jumped trying to come back to reality.
"MOVE DEJA," Randy yelled.
"Okay, Randy I will do whatever you say just don't hurt us," I said, turning back around to walk to the truck.

I had my phone in my pants close to my belly. I slowly pulled it out trying not to make too much movement so Randy couldn't see what I was doing. I pretended like I was holding my belly. Randy and Greg were behind me. I called X, and put my phone close to my belly. I heard X say Hello. I was hoping he wouldn't hang up.

"Randy, I don't know what you want but please don't hurt us," I said hoping X could hear me.
"SHUT THE FUCK UP, DEJA. JUST DO WHAT I SAID AND NOBODY WILL GET HURT," Randy yelled.

I was praying X could hear everything. I put my phone back in my pants as we were getting close to the truck. We reached the truck and I opened the back door like Randy said to do. I paused.

"Get in the fucking truck, Deja," Randy said.
"Okay, I'm getting in," I said. I was scared. I didn't know what was going to happen.

Randy closed my door and walked with Greg to the driver's side. I tried to see if I could open the door and get out, but it was child locked. He held the gun out while he got in the truck pointing it at Greg. He started the car still pointing the gun at Greg. Randy rolled the window down to keep the gun on Greg so he didn't try anything. He closed his door still holding the gun on Greg. He pulled off leaving Greg standing in the street. I turned around as I saw Greg running behind the car and hit the car with his hand, before Randy sped off. I was panicking at this point.

"Where the fuck is your phone, Deja?" Randy said.

I Am A Survivor: Sex, Lies, and Abuse

Shit, I forgot I called X. Randy pointed the gun at me. I hurried up and pulled my phone from my pants and gave it to Randy.

"Fuck, you called X," Randy said as X was still on the phone. "Well, well nigga guess who got your girl. I'm going to have a hell of a time too," Randy said, hanging up and throwing my phone out the window.

Fuck. How was X going to find me now? I held on to my peanut. I was so scared for us. The last time I was with Randy he tried to kill me. I didn't want nothing to happen to my peanut. Please God, help me. I didn't want to die.

I saw Randy hit the highway. I figured I could just watch and see where he was taking me. Randy wasn't saying nothing to me. He was just playing his music super loud and speeding down the highway. After a couple of hours, I was assuming we were going back to New York because we were headed in that direction as I saw we were passing through Cleveland, Ohio. I had to pee. I didn't know if I should say anything, but I really had to go to the bathroom.

"Randy, I have to pee," I said, nervous.
Randy cut his music down. "Here, you can use this cup, and napkins, because I'm not stopping."

Fuck was he serious? He handed me the cup and some napkins. He was serious. Shit I pulled my pants down. I could see Randy was watching me from the rear-view mirror. I peed and used the napkins. I put the cup in the center cup holder. I hurried up and pulled my pants back up. He watched the whole time.

6 hours passed. I was getting hungry. We were in New York now only 3 hours from Manhattan. I kept using the cup and napkins since Randy said he wasn't stopping. But now I was getting hungry and I needed to make sure I ate something for my Peanut.

"Randy, I need to eat something," I said.
"We almost to our destination. You can eat once we get there."

I sat quietly the rest of the way rubbing my belly hoping my peanut was okay. I didn't know what was going to happen. I just hoped X was going to find me somehow. I was scared out of my mind, but I was trying to stay calm for my peanut.

We pulled up to some suburban neighborhood right outside the city of Manhattan. Randy pulled in the driveway of some house. It was not the house he first took me to, but it was similar in style. Randy got out of the car and came to open my door. I got out of the car and Randy grabbed my arm pulling me in the house. When I walked in the house, I noticed two guys that looked familiar. They were the guys that confronted Greg outside when I was inside the restaurant down the street from the apartment.

X said those were employees he fired, but they weren't. It was starting to make sense the whole reason for the security. X knew Randy was looking for me this whole time. Randy kept pulling me through the house. I saw a few females who looked strung out on something in another room lying lifeless on the couch. There were a few more guys in the kitchen, but I'd never seen any of them before. I saw money and drugs spread out on the kitchen table. Randy walked me in the back of the house and pushed me into a room with a dirty half made bed that was on the floor. He shut the door and locked it. I banged on the door, screaming, and trying to open it. I was freaking out. I burst out in tears. I was so scared. What was he going to do?

Hours went by and my stomach was hurting now from the hunger pains. I needed to eat, but this house was so dirty I wouldn't eat nothing he gave me even if he tried to feed me. I sat in a corner close to the door, too afraid to even touch that bed or anything in that room. Everything looked dirty and disgusting. I could see it was getting dark outside. My watch said it was 8:45pm. The windows in the room were too high for me to reach. I closed my eyes and dozed off trying not to think about being hungry.

I woke up quickly as I heard someone at the door. I stood up.

"We need to go. Your dumb ass security put a tracker on my truck. I'm sure X is on his way," Randy said, grabbing my arm.

He dragged me through the house and he put me in the backseat of a car. He sped off. We were headed to the city now. I was starving at this point.

"Randy, please can we get some food," I begged.
"You think I give a fuck that you're pregnant and hungry," Randy said with anger in his voice. "I'm going to fuck you up so good you're going to lose that baby."

I started to cry. Please don't let nothing happen to my peanut. I promise if you get me out of this God, I will never leave the house again. I will quit my job and do whatever X tells me to do. I started thinking if I wasn't defiant and I didn't want to be able to do more things this would have never happened.

Randy was flying down the street. The light was turning red and Randy went through it. Instantly, I heard a loud bang and I felt the impact as another car ran right into us. We went spinning in circles and I heard another loud bang as we hit something else. Luckily, I had my seat belt on. But my head was spinning and it hurt. I looked and saw that Randy was pinned in by the light pole. The driver side hit the light pole. His face was in the airbag. He was bleeding from his head and he looked like he was dead. I saw people everywhere and could hear sirens.

I took my seat belt off and tried to open my door. There was a man outside trying to open my door too, it was stuck.

"I'm going to bust the window. Sit on the other side. And cover your face," the man said, grabbing something to bust the window.

I moved to the other side and covered my face. He busted the window. He reached his arms in to grab me. I slid back over wrapping my arms around him. He started to pull me out, but Randy grabbed my legs. I screamed. He tried to pull me back in the car. I held tight to the guy. I heard some commotion, Randy let go, and the guy finally pulled me out. I fell right on top of him. I got up quickly ready to run as I thought Randy might be after me. I ran right into X.

"Deja, are you okay?" X said. I jumped in his arms and just started crying. I was so happy to see him. "Did he hurt you?"
I just shook my head no.
"I want to go home, X." It was the only words I could get out.
"Okay, let's go," X said.

X carried me to his car. I couldn't see Randy but I saw some of X's crew standing by the car that hit us. It looked like it was X's crew who hit us. X went over towards the car. He looked like he had a pole or something in his hand. X was furious. One of the guys told X he would handle everything, and took the weapon from X. X was determined to get to Randy. But his crew said they would take care of it and X just needed to get me out of here. X got in the car and drove off.

We didn't go home of course we were in New York, but X took me to the Haven Hotel we stayed at when I was in New York with him before. We went to the tenth floor in the same suite. The elevator doors opened and I ran to the bathroom. I threw up. It was only water coming out. I really needed food.

"Deja, damn baby," X said as he came to the bathroom door.
I just started crying. My head was hurting. I was starving, and my emotions were everywhere.
"I need to eat something," I cried, holding my stomach.
"Okay, baby," X picked me up and carried me to the kitchen.

I Am A Survivor: Sex, Lies, and Abuse

He must have been staying here while he was in New York on his business trip, because he already had food on the kitchen counter. He brought me the food on the counter and placed it in front of me at the table. I opened it up. He had Chinese food. I didn't care what it was I needed to eat. I scarfed down the chicken fried rice and ate some egg rolls he had. I ate so fast I think I was making myself sick again.

"Deja, slow down baby. You are going to get sick again," X said, grabbing my hand.
I stopped and started crying again. X hugged me.
"I was so scared, X. I thought he was going to hurt Peanut. I thought I was going to die," I said, frantic at this point.
"Deja, you're safe now. I am going to call Dr. Saunders since we are in New York to check on you and the baby though."

I shook my head in agreement.

After I finished eating at a slower pace now, I went to jump in the shower to calm myself. I stayed in that shower for an hour. I was feeling a lot better, but I felt heavy with emotions. By the time I got out of the shower. X had already had some clothes waiting for me. He must have had the hotel staff shop for me again. I put the clothes on which was just something simple: a t-shirt, some jogging pants, and under clothes. I went back in the bathroom to brush my teeth as I saw he also got me a toothbrush and some hygiene necessities.

I went out into the living room and X was talking to Dr. Saunders. I thought he meant he would come in the morning. I didn't realize he would be here so late. I looked at my watch and it was 11pm.

"Ms. Deja, how are you feeling?" Dr. Saunders said.
"Hello, Dr. Saunders, I feel okay. My head was hurting but it feels better now."
"It was probably from the impact. Have a seat on the couch. I just want to check your vitals and listen to the baby. To make sure everything is good."

I sat down on the couch while Dr. Saunders ran my vitals and listened to the baby.

"Everything checks out to be good. The baby sounds good. So, no worries there. Just keep up with your normal appointments with your doctor."
"We will, thank you doc," X chimed in.

Dr. Saunders left. I sat on the couch with X. I was a little calmer, but my emotions were still heavy.

I Am A Survivor: Sex, Lies, and Abuse

"How did you find me, X?"
X grabbed my hand and touched my bracelet that he bought me.
"I put trackers in your jewelry."
I smiled. He was crazy, but I was thankful he did that. "Thank you, X."
"Did he touch you?"
"No, I was afraid he was going to, but he didn't."
"What happened?"
"He had a gun to Greg when I turned around. He threatened to shoot Greg and me if I didn't get in his truck. We drove from Ohio to New York no stopping. And he took me to this nasty, trap house in a suburban neighborhood. He dragged me inside and locked me in this dirty room. I was so scared. I just knew I wasn't going to leave alive. Randy came back to the room and said we had to leave, because Greg put a tracker on his car and he said you were probably on your way. That's when we were headed into the city and the car hit us," I said, wiping away my tears.
"Deja, I don't even know what to say," X said, lost.
"You don't have to say nothing X. You saved me once again and I am indebted to you. You saved me and Peanut. I made a promise to God that if I lived through this, I won't be defiant or leave the house unless you're with me. I will put my two weeks in when I get home too. I don't have to work. I just want to be safe and keep Peanut safe too."
"You're serious," X said, shocked.
"Yes, I know now you were just trying to keep me safe and I was being selfish. I'm so sorry."
"Deja, I love you."
"I love you too baby," I said, kissing X.

X held me while we laid on the couch. We talked about how things would be different when we got home. I told him I could set up my own business selling my paintings instead of working. I really didn't care if I made any money since X was covering everything, but I figured it would be a fun hobby and it would keep me busy. I told him I just wanted to do everything right and not get myself caught up in crazy situations anymore. X said he would get me a treadmill so I could still walk since that was also my new hobby. We talked until we both fell asleep.

I woke up around 7am still laying on the couch X was gone. I checked the bedroom just to make sure, but I was in the suite alone. I went into the kitchen to fix something to eat. I saw a small box on the kitchen table. I didn't know if I should open it. I didn't see a card or a letter next to it. I ate some cereal standing in the kitchen looking at the box. It was a jewelry box, like the size of an earring or ring box.

"Open it," X said, coming off the elevator, watching me stare at the box.

"What is it?" I said, curious.
"Open it, Deja."

I put my cereal down and walked over to the kitchen table. I looked at X and then picked up the box. I opened it. I gasped. I turned to look at X and he was on one knee.

"Will you marry me?" X said.
"Yes," I said without hesitation. X picked me up and kissed me. He put the ring on my finger. Wow that ring was beautiful. It was a princess cut 14k white gold 10 carats diamond ring.

****

"X," I moaned as he was fucking the shit out of me. He was pounding harder with every stroke. My pussy was throbbing. I was wetter than wet. It felt ten times better than it ever felt. He was going deep fucking me from the back. "Shit, X, I'm about to cum," I moaned as I could feel myself about to explode. "Cum for me Deja," X moaned. I came as he released too. "Damn that pussy is good." X said pulling out of me. He kissed my back as he stood up. My legs were shaking as I tried to lay on my back.

I rubbed my belly. I was huge now. I was just hitting 7 months. I feel like the treadmill was helping though, because I was all belly. My legs were toned and I had recently been working on lifting weights so my arms would be toned too. My ass was a little bigger and X loved that. My breasts were bigger too and X was pleased with that too.

Everything was good between us. X was keeping up with his businesses from Columbus and didn't have to leave my side for anything. I was no longer working, besides painting. I was actually making decent money online from my paintings too. X never said what happened with Randy. But I Googled the car accident in New York. Randy suffered some severe injuries from the crash. The report stated he was shot by his own gun during the crash and can no longer walk. I remember hearing a gun go off when the man was pulling me out of the car. So, I don't think that was accidental. But I hope he was no longer a concern for us.

I was focused on getting ready for this baby shower my girls were planning. Cassie told me that they had to change the location, but she wouldn't tell me the new location. She and Michaela were actually in cahoots with X and my mom on the planning of this baby shower. My mom finally met X and she has been adoring him ever since. I didn't know it, but X actually asked my dad for my hand in marriage before he proposed. My dad told me, once we announced that we

I Am A Survivor: Sex, Lies, and Abuse

were engaged. We were working on planning the wedding, but I told X I really wanted to wait until after I had the baby so I wouldn't be so huge in my dress. He was okay with that.

X bought me a dress to wear for the baby shower. It was baby blue with a hint of pink in it. It was knee height at the bottom in the front, it was longer in the back, and it had two layers. The dress looked ridged and flowy at the bottom. It had thin straps at the top so I had a pink sweater that went over it, because it was October now so it was a little chilly outside. He bought me some baby blue flats to wear to match the dress. I had to do flats, because this baby was making it hard to wear heels for too long. My feet would definitely swell up. I jumped in the shower as it was now 12pm and the party started at 2pm. I got out of the shower and started getting dressed. X jumped in the shower to get ready too.

I was kind of excited, because X's family was going to be there too. His mom and brothers were here. This would be my first time meeting them so I hoped I was going to make a good impression. X said they knew about me and from what he told them they already loved me. I was still nervous though, because I'd never met them before.

I looked at my phone. Cassie was calling me. I had a newer phone now since my other phone was thrown out the window. X quickly replaced that before we left New York.

"Hey Cassie," I said, answering the phone.
"Hey Deja boo. Are you ready for your big day?"
"Where is it at, Cassie?" I said, trying to get her to tell me the location.
"X, knows where it is. You will see soon enough."
"Whatever Cassie, I want to know."
"You will soon. How's my baby doing?"
"Kicking my ass like crazy. Peanut is vicious with those kicks' girl."
"Awe my baby ready to meet the world."
"Yeah, I'm still getting dressed so I will see you in a few hours."
"Okay, cool. I was hoping you were getting ready. I am heading over there now. I think Michaela and your mom are already there setting up."
"Where is it at?"
"See you when you get there Deja," Cassie said, rushing me off the phone so she didn't tell me the location.

"You're still trying to get the location," X said coming out of the bathroom.
"I was trying, but it didn't work. You got my friends going against me now."
"I don't recall anything," X said, pretending he wasn't in on it.
"Go ahead, keep your secrets. It's cool," I said, jokingly.

I Am A Survivor: Sex, Lies, and Abuse

I looked in the mirror after I got dressed. I loved the dress, but I looked so big in it.

"You look beautiful," X said, noticing my facial expressions.
"I look like a cow."
"A beautiful one if that's what you want to call yourself," X said, kissing my cheek.
"I'm so ready for Peanut to come out so I can work on losing this belly."
"Peanut will be here soon. You're still sexy, Deja."

I stopped looking in the mirror and put my shoes on. We were ready to head out by 1pm. X drove my car to the place, instead of calling his driver. We were going into Dublin. I really wanted to know where this place was. I kept watching and saw all these beautiful homes we were passing. We pulled up to this gated entry. The gates were open so we just drove right in. It was a long driveway. We were pulling up to this huge house. It was beautiful. It had to be expensive to rent this place.

"You rented a house for my baby shower X. This looks expensive."
"Don't worry. I told you I will cover all the expenses."

We got out of the car and walked to the door. The landscaping was immaculate. There were flowers on both sides of the doorway. The door had a double door entrance like you were walking into a palace. X opened the door and it truly was a grand entrance walking in. I could see straight to the back of the house. It had a lot of windows and I noticed there was a pool in the backyard. There were two sets of stairs on each side of the front hall. If you walked straight through you could see a sitting area that was in the center and the kitchen was on the left side. The kitchen was huge. It had an island with barstools and a dining room on the other side. There was also a half bath in between the kitchen and dining room. On the right side of the sitting room there was a bigger living room area. And two other rooms off to the side with another bathroom. Everyone was in the living room.

"SURPRISE!" Everyone yelled when they saw us walking in the living room.

There were so many people. Cassie, Michaela, and my mom did a great job decorating. I saw the balloons and the boy or girl signs all setup in the front of the living room with chairs and a table for me and X to sit in front. They had a table full of gifts like we needed anything else. My mom had tons of stuff already at her house. It looked so elegant and fancy in there.

Everyone hugged us as we came in. I saw Stacy was there. My dad was there. Some of my mom's friends, some of my college friends, and old coworkers were there. X's brothers Mike and James hugged me and welcomed me to the family. X's mom Clara hugged me.

"You have a lovely family. Your mom Patty has been talking about you nonstop," Clara said. "I just love how she adores you. I'm so glad to finally meet you, Deja."
"I'm happy to meet you too Mrs. Thomas. X has told me a lot about you too."
"Honey, you can call me Clara or mom. I know you are family now that you got my baby putting a ring on it. I thought I would never see that day," Clara said, laughing. "Now when we get some alone time together, I can tell you some stories about X when he was younger. He was always a playa."
"Now mom, that's enough sharing for today," X said, cutting in on our conversation.
"Hey X, I want to hear the stories," I said, laughing.
"Don't worry Deja, I will share them," Clara said, winking her eye.

We were enjoying ourselves and everyone was having a good time playing the baby shower games and guessing if we were having a boy or a girl. We went outside in the back to do the gender reveal. X had a reveal cannon and I had a reveal cannon. Michaela counted down for us.

"ONE, TWO, THREE," Michala yelled.

We popped the cannons and the color pink flew out everywhere. Everybody screamed. We were having a girl. X hugged me so tight and kissed me. Everybody was yelling "I knew it was a girl". Oh, it was a great feeling to finally know my peanut was a girl. We had a ball. We opened all the gifts and had plenty of baby stuff and diapers to last for at least a year.

The party was coming to an end, but I really enjoyed myself. I loved the environment. I saw Cassie talking to X. I thought it was cool that Michaela and Cassie were cool with X again. Cassie started walking towards me.

"Hey Deja,"
"Hey Cassie,"
"Let's walk."
"What's going on?" I said, nervous.
"Girl, just walk with me. I love this house X rented. I just want to explore it."
"I know this is beautiful. And I can't believe you actually didn't tell me he rented a house. You know you can't keep secrets."
"It was hard, but I can keep secrets sometimes," Cassie said, as we went up the stairs.
"Don't go so fast you know this baby takes my breath," I said, struggling up the steps.

Cassie laughed. We walked down the right side of the hall first looking in each room. From the balcony you could look down and see the center sitting area. There were two offices in the first two rooms. Then there was a bathroom next to the offices. The rooms were huge and spacious. All the rooms had stuff in it so someone was living here. They had two other bedrooms and another bathroom on the right side of the house. When we walked to the left side of the hall there was a baby room, a bathroom, and then the owner's suite. Cassie wanted to go into the owner's suite first. The owner's suite was huge. It had a king size bed, 60' inch flat screen TV on the wall. The closet was a walk-in with a center dresser in the middle of the floor. The closet was separated with men's clothing on the left side and men's shoes. And the right side had women's clothing with dresses, shoes, and designer purses on the shelves. On top of the center dresser there were jewelry boxes with men's and women's jewelry. Everything was so neat and organized and looked brand new.

"Cassie, I don't know if the people that own this house want us in the closet. I mean they got everything in here. They didn't lock up nothing."
"Girl, this closet is dope though. Let's go see the ensuite bath."

We walked into the massive bathroom. It was huge too. The shower took up one side of the room. It had shower heads hitting from every angle with one of those big circle shower heads right at the top in the center. The tub was a jacuzzi tub you had to step down in. The sink took up a whole wall with his and her sinks. It was a pretty big house. Cassie and I started walking back to head down stairs. X was standing by the baby's room. Cassie left me to go back downstairs.

"X, this house is huge. Do you know the people that live here?"
"Yeah, actually I do."
"I thought so, because they had to trust you to leave everything so out in the open. Me and Cassie saw that closet and they probably have over $50,000 dollars or more of jewelry and designer wear in there."
X laughed. "Do you like the house, Deja?"
"Yeah, it's big, and it's beautiful," I paused and looked at X. "What's going on, X?"

X pulled me into the baby room. I looked around. The colors were pink, yellow, and green. The crib was wooden, and it looked like it was handmade. There was a bookshelf made out of wood, and a toy box made out of wood. There was even a cute wooden changing table for the baby. They had a rocking chair in the corner by the bookshelf. I looked at the bookshelf again and noticed a picture of me and X on the gondola when we were in Venice. No way. I also saw our 4D ultrasound in a frame.

"X, are you serious?" I said, shocked.

"Welcome home baby."
"AHHHH," I screamed. I didn't know if I should cry, dance, or what. I hugged X.
"Thank you baby. Thank you."
"You're welcome, Deja."
"Is this real, like for real? This is our house?" I said, still in shock.
"It's our house, Deja, do you want to see the deed?"
"Shut up X for real?" I was so shocked.

X walked into the owner's suite and opened the dresser drawer. He came back with some papers in his hand. He handed them to me. I read congratulations to Mr. Xavier Thomas and Mrs. Deja Thomas. You are the owners of this lovely new home. I didn't even read the rest. I couldn't believe my eyes. We owned this house.

"Let me show you the best part," X said, grabbing my hand.

We went back down stairs to the living room. Everyone congratulated us on the house as they all knew. X opened the first door in the living room. It was a gym. I had my own personal gym. It had a treadmill, a weight station, and a lift bench. That must have been for X. But it also had a yoga space with a TV to watch yoga videos. I told X I wanted to get into yoga. He opened the other door in the living room and I was stunned. I had my own painting area. It had two painting easels, a desk stocked with painting supplies and a shelf with paint. It was so cute and spacious. I was in awe. I felt so loved.

"All of this for me X?" I paused. "Wow, thank you baby."
"You're the best thing that ever happened to me, Deja. I want to give you the world."

Chapter Twelve: Marriage
"It's not what I thought it would be."

"So how many kids do you want, X?"
"As many as I can."
"Um, what's that mean?"
"I'm open to as many kids as you can give me."
"Really?"
"Yeah really," X said, being serious.
"Well, I'm good with two, maybe three."
"How about six?"
"X, six kids?" I said looking at him crazy.
"What's wrong with six?"
"That's a lot."
"We can handle it."
"Maybe you can sir not me."
"Deja, you're not going to have my six kids?" X said, grabbing my wrist.
"Not fair X. Six is a lot. Let's see how I feel with this one first."

X kissed the back of my head while we were cuddled up on the couch. We were officially living in our new house. We didn't have to bring much over from the apartment but the things we really wanted to keep like valuables and my paintings. X donated all of our clothes and furniture we didn't keep. I was nine months. I was ready for my little Amara Rae Thomas to make her way into this world. We scheduled the wedding to be February 14th so that was going to give me almost 2 months after having Amara to get this belly gone.

Cassie was my maid of honor, Stacy, and Michaela were my bridesmaids. X's best man was his older brother Mike and his groomsmen were his brother James and his friend/security Greg. X got closer to Greg after the incident with Randy. X was in awe of how Greg was quick thinking, placing the tracker on Randy's car. Greg has been hanging out with X more and X promoted him to head of security.

"Deja, what do you think about going to Bora Bora for our honeymoon?" X said, rubbing my belly.
"Wow, Bora Bora sounds good. I think between your mom and mine we don't have to worry about Amara."
"So, I will have Alicia set it up."
"Okay, I like that idea."

I got up from the couch to go to the bathroom. I walked to the bathroom and I felt like I peed on myself.

I Am A Survivor: Sex, Lies, and Abuse

"Uh X," I yelled from the bathroom.
X came to the bathroom. "Yeah, oh shit."
"I think the baby is coming."
"Okay, I will grab the go bag. Hold on Deja."

X ran to get the bag we packed for the hospital and some clothes for me to change into. He helped me to the car and we headed to the hospital. I felt the contractions coming and they were painful. I was trying to deal with it but I was holding on to X's arm every time they hit. We were at the hospital within 30 minutes. X had called Dr. Chang on the way. She told him she would call the hospital so they knew we were coming. They took us straight back to get us prepared.

After 10 hours of labor, me screaming at the top of my lungs, and pushing a life out of me; I birthed my beautiful baby girl Amara Rae Thomas. X shed a few tears when he saw her. He tried to hide it, but I saw him wipe his eyes a few times. He held her in his arms and it was such a beautiful sight. She smiled at him like she already knew who he was. Amara was so beautiful. When I finally got to hold her, my heart just melted. We are parents now.

****

It was hours before our wedding. My mom and mama Clara insisted I had to stay at my parents' house the night before, because X couldn't see me until the wedding. Me and Amara stayed at my parents' house. Well, I should say Amara stayed at my parents' house. I came back from the bachelorette party at 5am, that Cassie planned. We had drinks and food at Cassie's house and then went to a nightclub called Gage's. I had a blast. Cassie also took us to a male review. Man, we had so much fun. Cassie told me I better not tell X, because she left that part out when she told Greg where we were going for the night. I figured X and his boys did the same. It was the last night of being Ms. Anderson so, why not make the best of it right.

It was now 10am and though I was sleepy my mom was waking me up.

"Deja, the hair stylist will be here in 30 minutes. Go get in the shower."
"Yes, ma'am I'm going."

I went to check on Amara. Mama Clara was holding her. I gave her a kiss on her cheek and went to get in the shower. I cleaned up and got dressed. I admired myself in the mirror a little bit. I made my goal weight so I was super excited about putting on my dress later. It took some hard work and X hired me, a personal trainer, but I succeeded in losing that weight before the wedding.

I Am A Survivor: Sex, Lies, and Abuse

"Okay you're going to have to breastfeed Amara. She is ready to eat, girl," Mama Clara said, giving me the baby.
"I will feed her, but I have some already made bottles in the fridge. I drank alcohol last night or early this morning so I will have to dump any milk that comes out when I pump."
"Oh, okay well I can feed her then."
"No, it's okay. I can feed her before the hair stylist gets here. I don't mind mama Clara."

I kissed Amara and headed down stairs to get her milk.

"Hey, Ms. Amara. You are so loved I can barely hold you when I'm around your grandmas' girl," I said, getting Amara's bottle ready.

I sat in the living room feeding Amara when the hair stylist, Kim, showed up. My mom took Amara from me when the hairstylist was ready to start my hair. She brought everything with her. She washed my hair in the sink and then blow dried it out. My hair was to the middle of my back. Those braids I rocked for 2 months really grew my hair out, and I think those prenatal vitamins definitely helped.

The hair stylist flat ironed my hair and then did some loose curls. It was 11:30am and we were ready to head to the venue to get ready for my big day. Cassie had my dress and was on her way to the venue. The wedding would take place at 1pm. But I still had to get my dress on and makeup done once I got there. My mom, dad, and mama Clara were ready to go. X got us a limo. Amara would be staying at the house with the babysitter. I kissed Amara and headed to the car. We got to the venue at 11:50am. I had to go straight to the dressing room to start getting my dress on so the makeup artist could do my makeup. My parents and mama Clara went to make sure everything was in line for the wedding.

The venue was huge. We would have our wedding ceremony and the reception here. The wedding would be in the chapel section of the venue and the reception would be in the dance hall. I was getting excited. I couldn't believe this was it. I was getting married to X. I never thought things would ever happen like this, but I was all in. Right after the wedding X said we would go see Amara, before we left for Bora Bora for a week. My mom and mama Clara would take turns watching Amara while we were on our honeymoon.

I was finally ready for the wedding. I did a once over in the mirror. My dress was stunning. It was all white slim fit with a long train. It had a bell shape at the bottom and a strap around my neck at the top. My breast sat just right in this dress. It had a deep v neck in the front making my breast stand out. I loved the dress and my makeup looked good too.

I Am A Survivor: Sex, Lies, and Abuse

It was almost time to walk down the aisle. I was getting nervous. I hadn't seen X at all yet. I couldn't wait to see him. I just wanted to wrap my arms around him and kiss him already. The wedding was beginning. My mom and mama Clara walked down the aisle. They closed the curtain on me when it was time for X to walk down the aisle, because I couldn't see him yet. I had to wait for it to be my turn. They opened the curtain back up as the maid of honor and the best man walked down the aisle. And now it was my turn.

I grabbed my dad's arm and we walked to the door. I gasped when I saw X. He looked so handsome. Oh, how I wanted to run to him. I made it down the aisle and realized I was crying. My dad wiped away my tears and told the preacher he was honored to give me away to Xavier Thomas. I kissed my dad and X grabbed my hand as I stood in front of him now.

The preacher read 1 Corinthians 13 and we said our vows.

"Xavier, do you take this woman to be your lawfully wedded wife, to live together in holy matrimony, to love her, to honor her, to comfort her, and to keep her in sickness and in health, forsaking all others, for as long as you both shall live?" the preacher said to X.
"I do," X said, smiling at me.
"Deja, do you take this man to be your lawfully wedded husband, to live together in holy matrimony, to love him, to honor him, to comfort him, and to keep him in sickness and in health, forsaking all others, for as long as you both shall live?" the preacher said.
"I do," I said.

The preacher then asked us to repeat after him starting with X.

"I Xavier Thomas, take you Deja Anderson, to be my wife, to have and to hold from this day forward, for better, for worse, for richer, for poorer, in sickness and in health, to love and to cherish, till death do us part," X said.
"I, Deja Anderson, take you Xavier Thomas, to be my husband, to have and to hold from this day forward, for better, for worse, for richer, for poorer, in sickness and in health, to love and to cherish, till death do us part."
"I give you this ring as a token and pledge of our constant faith and abiding love," X said, while placing the ring on my finger.
"I give you this ring as a token and pledge of our constant faith and abiding love," I said, placing the ring on X's finger.
"By the power vested in me by the State of Ohio, I now pronounce you husband and wife. You may kiss your bride," the preacher said.

I Am A Survivor: Sex, Lies, and Abuse

X picked me up and kissed me. I wrapped my arms around him and kissed him back hard. He whispered in my ear "I told you; you would be mine." He was right, I was all his now.

"Family and friends, it is my pleasure to present to you Mr. and Mrs. Thomas," the preacher ended with.

Everyone stood up, clapped and hollered. We walked down the aisle together as we exited the chapel.

The reception was beautiful. We danced, laughed, and had so much fun. I was now Mrs. Deja Thomas and I loved it. I smiled the whole night as we partied like we were in the club. I danced with my father and X danced with his mom. X's brother Mike gave a phenomenal speech and Cassie did too. It felt good to be married to X. I was ready for our honeymoon.

The wedding reception ended at 7pm. X and I left in the limo saying goodbye to everyone. We stopped by my parents' house to give Amara kisses and spend some time with her before we caught our flight. We both changed into comfortable clothes. We didn't pack anything, because X said Alicia bought us new clothes already in our bungalow in Bora, Bora. X always had to do the most, but I loved him. We left around 9pm to leave for our trip to Bora Bora.

When we made it into Bora Bora it was 6am in the morning. We had to stay in Los Angeles for a day and then take our flight to Tahiti to get to Bora Bora. We traveled about 30 hours total. I was done with the traveling but excited to see Bora Bora which was beautiful. Our bungalow was so cute. They had rose petals in the shape of a heart on our bed with a card that said congratulations Mr. and Mrs. Thomas. The bungalow was pretty open and spacious. We had our own pool and entrance to swim in the ocean. The tub was right next to the bedroom and there was a shower outside on the private deck area. We could pretty much just relax in the bungalow all week if we didn't want to explore the beach and area. But I knew I wanted to explore too.

X wasted no time once we were inside the bungalow. He started taking my clothes off and pushed me on the bed. He turned me on my stomach and before I could even position myself in the doggy style position, he was already pushing himself inside me. "X," I moaned as I felt him deep inside me. "I missed being in this pussy," X moaned as he began to stroke faster and go deeper. I screamed out in moans as it felt so good and my pussy was super wet. I could feel the chills rising and my body pulsating with excitement. I was about to cum. I screamed "Fuck me X." I came so hard. It had been a few days since we had sex and it felt

I Am A Survivor: Sex, Lies, and Abuse

amazing. After X came, he kissed me on the back of my head, calling me "Mrs. Thomas." That sounded so good. It felt good to call him my husband too.

I jumped in the shower. It felt weird showering outside but it was a private area so no one could see me. X came and joined me in the shower. And without a doubt he was going for round 2. He must have really missed me. But I was loving every minute of his touch. After we got out of the shower and got dressed. X called for room service and I video called my mom to see Amara. X and I talked with Amara as she smiled and cooed at us. I missed her already, but I was enjoying my time with my husband too. Once the food arrived, we got off the phone and ate our food.

X was staring at me like he was ready for round 3. I don't know what got into him, but he was making this a great honeymoon already. I was thinking he was trying to make baby number 2 happen real soon.

"Mrs. Thomas, come here," X said, sounding sexy.
"Yes, husband," I said, coming closer to him.
"I like how you said that wife," X said smiling.

I stood in front of him while he sat at the end of the bed. He kissed my stomach and slid his hands up my dress. I wasn't wearing any panties so he started massaging my clitoris. I moaned as I felt the chills and my pussy getting wet. X stood up and lifted my dress off. I slid down to kiss his chest, kissing down to his stomach, and pulled his pants down. "Deja," he moaned as I put my mouth on his penis. I sucked and licked listening to him moan. He got super hard. I kept sucking and twirling my tongue as he continued to enjoy me. "Fuck, Deja that feels so good baby," he moaned. I started to massage his balls, but X pulled me up and laid me on the bed. He spread my legs and pushed them back. He started eating my pussy, and sucking on my clitoris. I cried out in moans as his mouth was amazing. "X, I'm cumming," I moaned. X immediately pushed his penis inside me and started pounding deep, hard, and fast. I screamed as my body started shaking and I came again. Every time felt better than the next. X was fucking me good and I was cumming for him. We both released. X laid down with me until we fell asleep.

I woke up around 2pm. X was still sleeping. I got up and took a shower. I thought X would wake up if he heard me, but he was still asleep even after I got dressed. I just threw on a swim suit that Alicia had picked out. It was a bikini. I put the swim cover over it and figured I would go walk the beach. I left a note by the bed for X so I didn't wake him. He looked like he was still in a deep sleep.

I Am A Survivor: Sex, Lies, and Abuse

The weather was amazing, hot, but a cool breeze. I walked the beach for a little bit and then found a lawn chair to lay on. I took my swim cover off and laid down to feel the sun on my body. I put my sunglasses on to shade the bright sun. I laid there thinking about everything that has happened within a year. I couldn't even believe I was married now. It just felt crazy how this whole year went. But I was happy, I had my little Amara, and now my husband X. I closed my eyes for a little bit, but opened them when I felt someone standing over me.

"Deja," X said, angry.
"Hey, husband, is everything okay?" I said, sounding flirty.
"Get up, let's go."
"X, what's wrong?" I said, nervous.
"Put your cover up on, and let's go now," X said, heated at this point.
"Okay," I said, putting the swim cover back on and following X back to the bungalow.

He was walking fast. I could barely keep up. He turned around and saw I was not right behind him. He walked towards me and grabbed my wrist really tight.

"X, is everything okay?" I said trying to keep up with his pace.

He didn't say nothing. We got to the bungalow and as soon as we got inside, he pushed me against the wall and put his hands tightly around my neck.

"X, that hurts. I can't breathe," I said, trying to pull his hands from my neck.
"Deja, you are so fucking hard headed," X said, still choking me. "Why the fuck would you go outside like that and I am not with you. Are you purposely trying to piss me off."
"X, I'm sorry please, you are hurting me," I said, still trying to get him to stop.

X let go. I grabbed my neck. I started to cry. I started to walk to the bathroom, but X grabbed me by the waist and pushed me back against the wall.

"Did I tell you to fucking move?" X said, scaring me.
"X, why are you doing this? I didn't mean to upset you. I just wanted to go to the beach. And you were sleep-," I said as X cut me off.
"Deja, you straight disrespected me leaving here and showing off your ass to the world," X said frustrated.
"X, I'm sorry," I said, not sure why this was happening.

X walked towards me and I flinched.

I Am A Survivor: Sex, Lies, and Abuse

"I'll give you something to flinch about," X said as he grabbed my wrist pulling me from the wall. He then raised his hand and hit me across my face. I fell on the floor. I screamed. I tried to move away from him, but he bent down and grabbed me by my waist and held me there.

"X, please I'M SORRY," I screamed. "Please don't hit me, X."
"SHUT THE FUCK UP DEJA. I'M SICK OF YOUR BULLSHIT," X yelled.

I was balling in tears, scared to move, not sure what he would do next. What the fuck was happening? I didn't expect this. X took the swim cover off of me, and ripped the bikini bra off. He also ripped the bottoms off of me. He stood up and walked in the bathroom area. I was afraid to move so I stayed on the floor naked. He came back and I began to cry when I saw he had the handcuffs in his hands. Why? Is all I could think. I curled up in a ball trying to keep my hands covered so he couldn't get to them. X walked up and bent down in front of me.

"Deja, give me your hands," X said sternly.

I shook my head "no", still crying. X grabbed my arm trying to pull my hands from underneath me. I screamed "NO". He punched me on my side and slapped my ass really hard. I was trying my hardest to not give him my hands, but then he pinched my leg. I screamed and grabbed his hand where he was pinching me and he put the handcuff on my wrist. I cried out and tried to hide my other wrist but he already grabbed it and put the handcuffs on me. I felt defeated.

"Damn, Deja why you gotta be so defiant? Damn, now you're going to have bruises."

I couldn't say anything, I was just crying. X put my hands over my head and lifted the dresser next to me to put the chain of the handcuffs under the post, so I wouldn't be able to get up. He left me lying on the floor as he walked back into the bathroom. He came back within 5 minutes with something in his hands. I couldn't see what he had. He came and bent down next to me and I saw he had the anal beads, oil, the strap, and the vibrator. The tears just rolled down my face.

"Deja, you will learn not to fuck up. You're mine and you need to understand what I say goes," X paused. "Now I'm going to go get us some dinner. I know you will be hungry by the time I return."

X put the oil on my ass and pushed the beads in my ass. He put the vibrator in my pussy and cut it on. He put the strap on to hold the vibrator in place. I cried, moaned, and screamed at the same time.

I Am A Survivor: Sex, Lies, and Abuse

"X, please don't do this," I cried.
"I'll be back," X said, standing up to leave.
"X, NOOOO," I yelled.

X left. I couldn't stop the feeling. My legs were shaking. I kept feeling like I was about to cum. I wanted it to stop. I felt the chills shooting through my body, and my pussy was getting wetter. I was shaking uncontrollably. I know it hadn't been that long but I was going crazy. I was moaning from the vibrating and the intensity of the feeling. I wanted to cum and X left me like this. The vibrator literally sat at the tip of my spot and I couldn't move it deeper so I could cum. My legs were shaking and I was trying to move to see if I could push the vibrator out. I just wanted it to stop, because I couldn't cum. And the feeling was driving me crazy, because I couldn't get my body to release. The strap would not move and every time I moved, I just felt more like cumming. I tried to see if I could lift the dresser but it was too heavy for me to move laying down. I had to endured the torture, because I was not making any solutions. I kept crying, moaning, and feeling the need to cum. This shit was driving me crazy. X had been gone 30 minutes now and I was screaming in moans as the intensity was killing me. I finally heard the door open.

"You had enough?" X said coming in the door with bags of food in his hands.
"Yes, X please. I'm sorry," I cried.

He sat the food down on the dresser and bent down beside me.

"I don't think you did," X said smiling.
"X, please stop this. I'm so sorry please," I begged.
"What are you sorry for?"
"X, please. I'm sorry for leaving without you and only having on a swimsuit, please X."
"Damn, you look so sexy when you beg."

X leaned down and kissed me. He rubbed my breast only making the intensity heighten. "X, please just fuck me," I cried. X took the beads out first and I immediately started to cum as the vibrator was still on and it shifted to hit my spot. I moaned so loud. X just watched as my body was shaking. "Cum again Deja," X said as he started to massage my clitoris. I screamed as my pussy was pulsating. I cried out "I'm cumming," X pulled the strap off and pulled out the vibrator. He turned me over and went inside me fast and hard. I cried out as I felt myself cumming again. He started pounding hard and deep. The chills rushed through me as I felt myself cuming back-to-back. I couldn't stop it. X was fucking me faster and my body was reacting. I couldn't control my body from shaking,

I Am A Survivor: Sex, Lies, and Abuse

pulsating, and throbbing. "Cum for me Deja," X said. I closed my eyes and I felt my whole body explode. "Good girl," X said, as he released with me.

X took the handcuffs off of me.

"Go clean yourself up. I got us some dinner," X said, smacking my ass.

I got up slowly as my legs were shaky and walked to the bathroom. I went outside to the shower and got in. I cried. I didn't know what was happening. I can't believe he hit me and choked me. My leg was also hurting from him pinching me. I cleaned myself up, but I didn't want to get out of the shower, because I would have to face him.

"Deja, are you going to come eat?" X said as he came outside.

I cut the shower off and grabbed a towel. X grabbed my waist as I walked by him. He kissed me on my cheek. I felt so disgusted.

"How long are we going to do this, Deja? You're not talking to me now?" X paused. "You know if you just stop disobeying me this wouldn't have had to happen."
"I didn't know I was disobeying you," I said frustrated.
X grabbed my face. "You giving me lip?"
"No, X," I said quickly.

X kissed my lips and let me go. I went inside and put on a tank and shorts. X came inside and showed me what he got us to eat. I ate some of my food. I really wasn't hungry after all of that. I guess I was just trying to figure out what was going on.

"You need to eat more than that Deja," X said, still eating his food.

I took a few more bites to appease him. I just wanted to go to sleep. I just felt like I was in a bad dream and needed to go to sleep to wake up again. X finished eating and he put our food on the counter. I laid down in the bed hoping to fall asleep soon. I felt like crying but I was trying to hold it in. X laid down and wrapped his arms around me. I felt the tears falling, but I tried to stay quiet. I closed my eyes and fell asleep.

I woke up the next morning around 8am. I turned over to see if X was still asleep. He was not even in the room. I saw on his side of the bed he left a bouquet of roses. I sat up. My side and leg were still hurting and my face also felt sore. I saw X ordered breakfast as it was on the table with a card.

I Am A Survivor: Sex, Lies, and Abuse

Mrs. Thomas,

I went out for a little bit to get some fresh air. I didn't mean to hurt you, but I didn't like that you were out there almost naked and men were staring. I need you to obey me and not wander around like that without me.

I love you,

Your Husband, X

I was disgusted. He couldn't even apologize. He really pissed me off, but what was I going to do or even could do? I tried to suck it up and let it go. I ate breakfast and got in the shower. I put on a blue flower tank slim fitting dress that only showed my arms and it was long so I didn't show my legs. I didn't know when X would be back, but I was afraid to leave the bungalow without him. So, I sat on the deck and put my feet in the pool and looked out into the ocean. I was ready to go home.

"Deja," X said standing at the door. I didn't even hear him come in.
"Yeah,"
"I see you're already dressed. I went to the store and got some cream for your bruises. I was thinking we can go out today and explore," X said, handing me the cream.
"Yeah, sounds fun." I said, trying to sound enthused.

X walked towards me. I stood up. He grabbed my face.

"Your face and neck look good. Did you have bruises on your leg or side?"
"There is a bruise on my leg and side," I said, pulling away.
"You still mad?"
"I'm good, X."
"Give me a kiss."

I looked at X and then gave him a kiss.

We left out and walked the beach to a bar close by. They were playing some good music and the people were friendly. X bought us some drinks and I got us a table.

"Hello beautiful," some guy said, talking to me.
"Hello," I said, looking at X watching me.
"Are you here alone?"
"No, I'm married, my husband is over there," I said pointing at X.

I Am A Survivor: Sex, Lies, and Abuse

"Oh, excuse me. He's a lucky man."
"I sure am," X said, walking up with our drinks.
"My bad. I will leave you two alone."
"Thanks," X said, giving me my drink. "And that's the bullshit I'm talking about."
"I told him I was married X," I said, worried about what he might do.
"That's why you walking around here half naked bothers me. Hell, that dress is obviously too damn tight too."

I didn't respond, I just took a sip of my drink. I was thinking to myself I don't even know how to respond anymore. I feel like anything I say would have X putting me back in those handcuffs. I wasn't sure what was happening anymore.

"Deja, dance with me," X said, trying to lighten the mood.
"What?"
"Come on, let's have a little fun. It's still our honeymoon."

X grabbed my hand and took me to the dance floor. We danced and it started to feel okay. As we were laughing and enjoying ourselves. X got us another round of drinks and I started to ease up. Bora Bora was welcoming being around the people. I was starting to feel good as we danced and kept drinking. I was really feeling the music and the alcohol was making me feel good too. I was grinding on X and beginning to feel the chills running through me. X grabbed my wrist and I gasped as I felt my pussy getting wet. He kissed me and it felt amazing. He wrapped his arms around me and squeezed my ass. I felt like everything was going to be okay again. He was loving on me and not trying to correct me. I was ready to go back to the bungalow with my husband.

"You ready to leave?" X said, still holding me.
"Yes, X I'm ready."

We walked the trail headed back to the bungalows. We walked past the little shops on the beach. It was around 9pm and dark outside most of the shops were closed or closing. X pulled me into an alleyway behind the shops.

"X, what are you doing?" I said nervously.
"I can't wait. I want you now," X said, leaning me against the brick wall.

X pulled my dress up and took my panties off. I was nervous, but excited at the same time. He kissed me hard as he unbuckled his pants. He lifted my leg and went inside me. I tried not to moan too loud. He felt amazing. My adrenaline was rushing doing something I never did before, and it was making me super wet. X went deep and slow and I could feel the intensity rising. It felt so good. My pussy was already throbbing and pulsating. I was about to cum. X whispered "Deja, cum for me". I came immediately. I couldn't believe we were having sex outside behind the stores in an alley. The nervousness and excitement of it all was driving me wild. X turned me around and started pounding me hard from the back. I was cumming again and X also released. Damn, that was amazing I thought to myself. X kissed me and after we got ourselves together, we started walking back to the bungalow. I kept looking at X, and smiling. That was crazy. I couldn't believe we just did that.

The rest of our honeymoon was great. X was back to giving me all his attention and loving on me. We went hiking, snorkeling, and partied at the bars. We took a few boat rides to see the views of the island and we also saw some dolphins. We explored as much as we could and we had a lot of fun. We were ready to go home, we missed Amara. Even though we video called her everyday it only made me miss her more. We were flying to New Jersey first, because mama Clara had Amara now, and then we would head home.

We made it to mama Clara's house at 6:15pm. I was so excited to see Amara. X grabbed our things since we were staying overnight. I went inside. Mama Clara was in the living room.

"Well, you made it back," Mama Clara said, standing up to hug me.
"Yes, we did. How are you doing mama?"
"I'm doing good, did you have fun?"
"Yes, lots of fun. Bora Bora is beautiful."
"Oh, I'm so glad you guys had fun. Mike is around here somewhere he came over to help with Amara. Not that I needed any help. I think he just wanted to see his niece. He is feeding Amara."
"Oh, okay I will go find him."

I walked to the bedroom and Mike was sitting in the rocking chair feeding Amara.

"Hey, you're back. How was the honeymoon?"
"It was good. I missed my baby though."
"Oh, I bet you did. Here she's not sleep yet but I think she was going," Mike said, giving her to me.
"Hi, Amara. I missed you baby," I said, giving her a kiss.
"Oh, here you might want her bottle. I just started feeding her so she might be grumpy without this. I will go talk with X. We got some business to talk about," Mike said.
"Okay," I said as Mike left the room.

I Am A Survivor: Sex, Lies, and Abuse

I just kept kissing on Amara. I didn't know how much I missed her until I saw her. She grew a little on me. She was just smiling. I talked with her and fed her until she fell asleep.

"You put her to sleep already," X said, coming in the room.
"Yeah, I think she got tired of me kissing her," I said laughing.
X leaned down to kiss her. "Deja, we might be in New Jersey a little longer than I expected."
"Why? What's going on?"
"One of my local shops here caught on fire. Mike has been handling it, but I just want to follow up on the investigation and get some contractors in to rebuild asap."
"Is mama okay with us staying here? I know she doesn't have a lot of space here."
"Mama doesn't care she will make room for us, but we are not going to stay here. Alicia already set up a hotel for the week. So, we will head over there after dinner. Mama wants us to stay for dinner."
"A week X?"
"Well, it may be sooner than that but she secured it for a week for now."
"Okay, I guess."
"Deja," X grabbed my wrist. "This is important and I will finish up as soon as I can."
"It's fine, X, it's not a big deal," I said calmly, trying not to change X's mood too much.
"I'm going to run out with Mike for a minute and I should be back before mama's done cooking."
"Okay."

X kissed Amara and me then left with Mike. I put Amara in the crib that mama Clara bought for her and went to help mama in the kitchen.

"Hey, mama I was seeing if you needed any help. I put Amara to sleep."
"Yeah, baby you can knead the bread for me. The boys left to do their business stuff. They probably won't be back for dinner, even though they said they would. But they always say that. I'll just make them to-go plates."
"Okay,"
"My business men are always busy with the business, but they are doing well."
"Yeah, I know X said we might be here for a week."
"I know he told me. You know he will probably be in and out. So, if you and Amara want to come over, you're welcome anytime. I told X it would be okay if you all stayed here, but he didn't want to intrude. He's always been such a gentleman."
"That's X."

I Am A Survivor: Sex, Lies, and Abuse

"What's on your mind, Deja? You seem bothered."
"I'm okay, probably just tired from the travel."
"Mmmmh hmmm,"
"Mama, can I ask you a serious question?" I said, unsure if I wanted to say anything.
"You can ask me anything."
"Does X ever get angry to the point where he can hit someone?"
"X, has a temper. I think he gets that from his father."
"Your husband?"
"No, his real father."
"Wait, you know his real father?"
"Well, X denies it, because I'm pretty sure he's told you his mom was a prostitute and drug addict. He never wanted to admit it, but her Pimp Anthony was his father. And he was a mean son of bitch. X looks like him, but X always said any of his mom's johns could have been his father. He never accepted Anthony as his father."
"Is his father still alive?"
"Yeah, he is in prison for murder serving 30 years. He tried to establish a relationship with X when he was 12 years old. X wasn't having it and Anthony didn't fight to have a relationship once he knew how X felt. They both are very strong, stubborn, and proud men. So, I didn't stop the relationship, but I didn't force it either, because X was old enough to make up his own mind. But back to the real question. Did X hit you?"
"I was just asking. He gets really upset sometimes."
"Deja, that's not what I asked you."
"Well, he got mad at me for wearing a bikini on the beach when he wasn't with me, and he got really mad and hit me," I said, trying to hold my tears back.
"Oh Deja, I'm sorry honey. X loves you like crazy. You know he would go crazy if someone tried to flirt with you or come at you. He's a protector and X doesn't play about who he loves. He was probably just upset that he wasn't there to protect you. I'm sure his anger just got the best of him. I will talk to him."
"No, mama, please don't say nothing. I don't want to upset him or make things worse. I just hope it doesn't happen again."
"Deja, X is a good man. He can be demanding about some of the things you do, but he means well and wants the best for you. The best way to explain it is X likes a woman who is submissive. He loves you. He is trying to teach you his ways. And as a wife you should want to follow your husband's lead. You're still young baby, you have a lot to learn, but you're the one he fell for. And he plans to give you the world, Deja. He told me that."
"Thanks, mama. Maybe I am just overthinking this," I said, giving mama a hug.

I felt better talking to mama. I guess I will have to learn how to be more submissive for X. I believe he didn't mean to hit me and mama made sense. I left the bungalow without him. Someone could have stepped to me. I should want to be more respectful in my dress around others or when X is not with me. I will work on being better for my husband, because I do know he loves me. I have to look at this differently. Now that I am in a marriage. I may not agree with everything he does, but he is in charge and he will not lead me down the wrong path. He wants the best for our family. I have to remember it's not about me alone anymore. I have to think about how he feels about things I do too. I guess I just have to really think about being married. And I have to understand I am no longer just one person in this life trying to make it. I have to think about my husband when I make decisions. I have to prepare for the arguments, and disagreements, but I also have to learn to compromise. We will have good moments and bad, but we will make it work. He loves me, even if it feels like I'm talking myself into this marriage. X just seems scary when he's mad, and I don't know if I can ever get used to that. I'm just a little worried. It's not what I thought it would be.

Chapter Thirteen: Scared
"I have to get away."

Me and mama ate dinner and cleaned up the kitchen. I also helped her make plates for the boys, because they did not come back. I checked on Amara and she was still asleep. It was now 9pm. I was getting tired. Mama got me a blanket and I laid on the couch in Amara's room while mama went to her room. It was about 10:15pm when I heard someone coming in the house. I could hear mama talking to someone. I was half awake so I closed my eyes again.

"Deja," I heard X say. "Get up, we are going to the hotel."
"Okay," I said sitting up. I grabbed Amara's car seat.
"No, Deja it's late mama said Amara can stay here. We will get her in the morning," X said, taking the car seat from me.
"X, we just got back. I want to be with Amara."
"Deja, she's sleeping. You're tired. You really want to wake her?" X said upset.
"No, you're right. I'll come back in the morning," I said, trying to appease X.

I felt defeated again. I wanted to take Amara with me. I knew she would be safe, but I missed her. I wanted her to be with me. I felt really emotional, but I sucked it up. Mama Clara gave me a kiss and hug. I think she could tell I was hurt as she whispered "Everything will be okay. Amara is safe with me". I felt my eyes watering, so I hurried up and got in the car. X stood outside and talked with mama and Mike for a little bit. I wiped my tears, before he got in the car. The driver took off to take us to the hotel.

"What did you tell my mama?" X said, staring at me.
"What do you mean?"
"Deja, don't play stupid. You told her I hit you? Did you?"
"X," I paused, trying not to cry. Fuck he was mad. "It kind of came up in conversation. But she assured me everything would be okay."
"Deja," X paused. I could see he was tightening his jaw. "Why the fuck would that come up in conversation?"
"X, I'm sorry. I just needed help understanding what I did wrong." I said, crying.

I was scared this is why he wanted to leave Amara at his mama's house. He was going to hit me again.

"Deja, you talk to me, not my mama. Understood?" X said, pissed.
"Yes, X, I'm sorry," I said, terrified.

I Am A Survivor: Sex, Lies, and Abuse

I messed up. I should have never told mama. He was going to hurt me now. I didn't know if I should try to run when we got out of the car. Where was I going to go? I was scared to go in the room with him though. What can I do right now? The car stopped in front of the hotel. I hurried to open the door. X grabbed my wrist.

"Deja, don't do nothing stupid. If you think you're going to leave me. I swear you will never see Amara again," X said, looking me dead in my eyes. He let my wrist go.

I got out of the car and followed X into the hotel. I couldn't take the risk of not seeing Amara again. I will take whatever is coming. I just want to see my daughter again. X checked in with the front desk and we headed up to the hotel suite. We walked on the elevator and X hit the 12th floor. He grabbed my wrist and stood in front of me. I was shaking in fear. I knew this was not going to go well.

"Deja, look at me," X said. I looked him in the eyes. "You're mine and I need you to understand what we do is between us. When you disobey me, you piss me off. And though I don't like hitting you, I need you to understand, I mean what I say, and you need to obey."
"But why do you have to hurt me? Can we just talk about it and compromise?" I said, not sure I should have said anything. X tightened his grip around my wrist. "I don't compromise. What I say goes, Deja, and you know that," X said, tightening his jaw again.

The elevator doors opened to the suite we were staying in. X pulled me into the suite. I was shaking. I already pissed X off. I knew I wasn't going to get out of this. X walked me to the couch and pushed me down. He went back to the door as the hotel staff was bringing up our luggage. He thanked the staff and took our luggage to the owner's suite. I was afraid to move from the couch. I didn't know what X was doing as he was still in the room. I was hoping he didn't have the handcuffs, but I'm sure that's what he was getting. I tried not to cry as I thought about what he could be doing.

X came back to the living room with a black bag in his hand. I just watched, afraid of what was going to happen next. He put the bag on the table and stood in front of me. He leaned down and pulled my jacket and shirt off. He took my bra off. He took my shoes off. He pulled my pants and panties off. I was completely naked and scared. He grabbed my wrist, pulled me up to stand, and grabbed the black bag. He walked me to the bathroom.

"X, please understand I was not trying to upset you. I love you and I am sorry," I said, nervous.

X didn't say nothing. He opened the black bag and pulled out the handcuffs. Tears were already falling. He grabbed my wrist and I didn't even fight it. He handcuffed me to the handle in the shower. X left the room. I was panicking thinking what was he doing now. 20 minutes went by and X didn't come back. I sat down in the shower. I was getting sleepy. It had to be almost midnight if not midnight. My arms were getting tired from holding them above me. Another 20 minutes went by and I figured I must be sleeping here tonight. I closed my eyes, because they were getting heavy. I woke up when I heard X taking the handcuffs off. He picked me up and carried me into the bedroom. He laid me in the bed and covered me up with the blanket and kissed my forehead. He laid down next to me and I went to sleep.

X woke me up. It was 7am when I looked at the clock.

"Deja, get up," X said, taking the covers off of me. "Get in the doggy style position."
"X, my arms are sore from holding them up in the shower."
"Deja, what did I say?"
"X, please I'm sorry for everything I did wrong. When are you going to stop punishing me?"
"DEJA," X said, pissed now.
"Okay X," I said, getting in the position. "Ouch, my arms hurt."
"Stay like that and don't you dare lay down."

X got up and went to get the black bag. He pulled out the vibrator, the oil, and the anal beads. He put the oil on my ass and put the beads inside my ass. He put the vibrator in my pussy and cut it on. I couldn't control my moans. My arms hurt so bad I wanted to lay down but I tried to keep my pose. The intensity was rising and I was getting warm all over as the chills started. I felt like I was going to cum, but I just couldn't. My legs started shaking and my pussy was throbbing. X started moving the vibrator in and out and it was making me want to cum. I cried out in moans. "X, please baby I'm sorry". X moved the vibrator faster. I could feel it. I was so ready to cum. My arms were getting weak and I almost went down.

"Deja, don't you dare lay down."
"X, please fuck me," I cried out.
"You need to learn to obey me."
"I will X, I will please, I want to cum baby."

I Am A Survivor: Sex, Lies, and Abuse

X continued to move the vibrator. My body was shaking. The intensity was driving me crazy. I didn't know what to do he wouldn't fuck me and I just wanted to explode. I could feel myself reaching the peak again, but I couldn't climax. The torture was horrible I just wanted to cum. Why did he have to do this to me? "X, please," I cried. X took the vibrator out and then removed the beads. He then put the vibrator in my ass. I gasped as the vibrator hurt going in. He cut the vibrator on. He moved it in and out. I could feel the pressure in my pussy. I started moaning. I was about to cum. X immediately stuck his penis inside my pussy and again I couldn't cum. I cried as I was so close. X fucked me hard but I could only feel the sensations, the chills, and the intensity. I couldn't cum. "X, please I want to cum," I cried. X kept fucking me until he released. I cried. He pulled out and took the vibrator out. He went to the bathroom.

"You can lay down now Deja."
"X, seriously?" I questioned him as my pussy was still throbbing.
"I got to get ready for my meeting," X said, cutting on the shower.
"Why are you doing this?"
"Don't question me. And if you masturbate it will only be worse later," X said getting in the shower.

I laid on the bed. I was so frustrated. I didn't know what to do. I was over this. X came out of the shower naked. I was certain he did that on purpose. I got up and grabbed his penis. I started massaging him. I was about to go down and he pushed me off him.

"X, please baby. Why are you doing this?"
"Deja, I told you I have a meeting."

I wrapped my arms around him and kissed him.

"X, please don't leave me like this."
"Deja, you need to chill," X pushed me away.

I sat on the bed frustrated. He really was making me feel like I did something horrible. I felt so hurt. X got dressed.

"I gotta go. I will have a driver coming to get you in an hour to take you to mama's so you might want to get dressed. And stop pouting."

I didn't say nothing. X leaned down to kiss me and I turned my head. X grabbed my face and kissed me.

I Am A Survivor: Sex, Lies, and Abuse

"I'll have the driver pick you up at 6pm tonight to bring you back to the hotel. I have a Business Gala to attend and you're coming with me. So, mama will keep Amara tonight too. I'll see you later, Deja," X said, leaving.
I was pissed. Once again, I couldn't bring my baby back with me and now, I was horny as hell and couldn't do shit about it. I was so frustrated.

I took a shower and got dressed. The driver called my phone around 9am and said he was outside. I grabbed my coat and headed downstairs. The driver dropped me off at mama's house. I went inside.

"Hey, mama," I said, trying to sound happy.
"Hey, Deja. Amara is in the playpen in the living room. I have to run to the store. So, I will be back."
"Okay, mama."

I went to get Amara and kiss all over her. She was awake and smiling. I talked to her and sang to her. She was making me feel better, being with her. I just missed seeing her little face.

Mama came back and we made breakfast together while Amara slept. I didn't say anything to mama about telling on me. I just figured I wouldn't say anything else about what X does. We watched some TV, and talked about normal daily life stuff. When Amara woke up, we played with her and gave her all the love. Before I knew it the day was gone and it was 6pm. X's driver was outside. I kissed Amara and hugged mama and left.

I made it back to the hotel and went to our suite. X was sitting in the living room.

"Did you have fun?" X said.
"I always have fun with Amara and mama."
"So, you don't have fun with me?"
"I didn't say that, X," I said feeling frustrated again.
"Come here," X said.

I walked over to him and stood in front of him. X grabbed my wrist and pulled me down to straddle him. He grabbed my ass and pulled me close to kiss him.

"I've missed you today," X said, holding me.
"I-," I paused.
"Say how you feel Deja."
"I'm frustrated," I said, not sure if I should have said anything.
"I know you are. And I apologize. But I hate when you disobey me."

I Am A Survivor: Sex, Lies, and Abuse

"X, sometimes I don't even know I'm disobeying you. It's not like you gave me a rule book. And sometimes I fee-," I paused again and took a deep breath. "I feel like I can't speak my own opinions or feelings because that's disobeying you."
"You're right and I apologize. I should be considerate to your feelings and opinions. I will work on that," X said, sounding sincere.
"Now, can we please have sex without teasing me?" I said, smiling.
"Not yet. We have to get ready," X said, pushing me off him.
"X, seriously I want you so bad," I whined.
"Later, Deja," X said, leaning over to kiss my forehead before walking to the bedroom.
"Ugh," I said, laying back on the couch.

X jumped in the shower. I went to the room. I saw he had a red long slim fitting dress on the bed with some red heels that matched the dress perfectly. I also saw a long black peacoat to pair with the dress, because it was cold outside. It was beautiful. I jumped in the shower with X and kissed him. "Thank you, baby, that dress is beautiful," I said, rubbing on his chest. "You're welcome," X said, kissing me back. He got out of the shower. He was really annoying me, but I just cleaned myself and got out of the shower. We both got dressed and X looked sexy as hell in his all-black suit with a red tie to match my dress. I wanted him so bad and I know he knew it.

"You look beautiful, Deja. You ready?" X said.
"I'm ready."

We went to the lobby and the driver was waiting for us. We headed to X's Business Gala. We arrived and the place was crowded. Everyone was dressed up in fancy attire. They had a few photographers taking pictures like they were paparazzi. I was a little nervous to get out of the car with so many people here. X came and opened my door as I stared in amazement. I got out of the car and the photographers were going crazy taking pictures of X.

"X, they really love you," I whispered to him.
"No, they love you. They're shocked I brought someone to this event. I normally come alone when I do attend," X whispered back. "You better be on your best behavior here and I will reward you later."

I was really nervous now. I had to make a good impression. X said we would probably be in the gossip magazines tomorrow, now that he was making it known he had a woman. It felt kind of exciting knowing I was the first woman he took to these types of events. But I was nervous for sure. We stopped at the banner that said New Jersey's Entrepreneurs Gala and had our picture taken. It felt like how you see celebrities on the red carpet getting their pictures taken.

I Am A Survivor: Sex, Lies, and Abuse

We went inside and were seated at our assigned table. Mike and his girlfriend were there. Mike introduced me to his girlfriend. Her name was Whitney. We talked for a little bit. Whitney mentioned we would be best friends tonight, because she was new to these events too and didn't know anyone. She said if Mike and X wandered off, we would stick together so we don't have to feel awkward. I was happy to know she felt the same way I did.

It was a pretty nice event. They had some speakers come up and talk about how New Jersey's entrepreneurs were rising and showed data that businesses were making great progress. They gave awards to the most successful rising entrepreneurs and X received a few awards. He won the award for most successful, giving back to the community, and making a difference in business. It was really interesting and exciting to see X in this light. He had a great reputation in the business world. Mike also received a few awards.

They brought out dinner and we ate. Afterwards we went into this big show room. Where the people were just walking around and mingling with each other. And like Whitney said Mike and X were pulled away and we were left standing drinking our champagne by ourselves. We laughed about it and walked around looking at the art on the walls and sculptures. I kept looking around for X and Mike. They were talking with everyone. Whitney started telling me how she met Mike. She said they have been dating for 8 months now. She said she is madly in love with him. He treats her like a queen. She said she hopes to get as lucky as me and marry Mike. I didn't say anything bad about my relationship with X, but I wanted to tell her it's not what I thought it would be. But I chose to listen to the voice in my head and just hyped our marriage up. I talked about Amara. She said she wanted kids with Mike. She did mention she already had a son, but she wanted more kids.

We kept walking around and talking. I looked for X again. I saw Mike talking to a group of people, but I didn't see X with him anymore. I searched around the room and saw X talking to some woman. They looked like they knew each other as she kept touching his shoulder and she was being flirty with him. X didn't seem to be interested, but I did notice he grabbed her wrist when she touched his hand. I felt something inside me get irritated. I turned away, because I didn't want to seem like I was staring too hard. I knew I had to be on my best behavior and I did not want to cause a scene when X was well respected in his business. I still watched, turning away to make sure he didn't see me. But she was irritating me as she kept finding reasons to touch him.

Whitney caught me watching.

"Let's go introduce ourselves Deja," Whitney said, grabbing my arm.

I Am A Survivor: Sex, Lies, and Abuse

"X, you just amaze me with all your intelligence. You are just doing so much for the community, and small businesses to help them grow. I love it," the lady talking to X said as we interrupted the conversation.
"I know, don't you just adore, X. He is such a good man and too bad he is spoken for," Whitney said.

I put my face behind my champagne glass embarrassed.

"Oh, hello I'm Senator Grace and you must be the lucky woman," Senator Grace said, talking to Whitney.
"Actually, Deja is my wife," X said, grabbing my hand.

Whitney looked at me and smiled then walked away to go find Mike.

"Hello, Senator, nice to meet you," I said, squeezing X's hand.

I felt so embarrassed.

"Hello Deja, you are beautiful. X, looks like you're pretty lucky yourself."
"I am lucky," X said, smiling.
"Thank you, we didn't mean to intrude. I will let you get back to talking," I said, being nice.
"No, actually Senator, it was nice talking with you, but I think we are going to head home. It's getting late," X said, still holding my hand.
"No worries. You have my number X. When you are ready to talk about some business ventures, please call me. I am interested in seeing what we can do to continue to grow, New Jersey. And nice meeting you Deja."
"Yes, I will be calling you. Have a good night," X said.
"Nice meeting you, have a good night," I said.

X squeezed my hand. We let Mike and Whitney know we were leaving. We headed outside. It was close to midnight. We were there for a long time. The driver showed up and we headed to the hotel.

"You looked so beautiful tonight," X said.
"Thank you. You looked very sexy and handsome tonight," I said, being flirty.
"You really turned me on, watching me from a distance, Deja. I think I sensed some jealousy too," X said, smirking.
"I was just, you know, checking on my man," I said, being coy.
"Come here,"

I moved closer to X. He kissed me. It felt so good I could feel myself getting wet. I was hoping he was going to be nice tonight. We made it to the hotel. We got on the elevator. X unzipped my dress on the elevator and stuck his hand in my dress down my back and began to massage my clitoris. My whole body shook as his touch felt so good. "Damn, baby you are super wet," X whispered in my ear. I kissed him hard. I wanted him so bad. The elevator doors opened to our suite and X picked me up and carried me to the living room. He put me down and pulled my dress off. He started kissing me and I took my bra off. He squeezed my breast and I moaned instantly. He pulled my panties off and took his clothes off. He had me lean on the couch as he entered me from behind. I moaned as it felt so good feeling him inside me. I was already ready to cum. I had been waiting for this all day. X was going deep, fast, and hard. I could feel the chills, the intensity rising, and I was about to fucking explode. My whole body was screaming in excitement. It felt so exhilarating. I was crying happy tears as I was cumming and I was cumming back-to-back. It felt so amazing. X fucked me for hours and it was the best feeling in the world. I was so relieved and loving the feeling. I moaned "X, I love you." As we both released. X kissed me and said "I love you too."

****

It was December 12th, and it was my baby Amara's 1st birthday. And I was 6 months pregnant with our 2nd child. X and I were still having some ups and downs, but being pregnant again I knew I was going to try to keep my family together. I will say being pregnant was a plus as I learned X hasn't hit me since I've been pregnant. He still was working on his temper and I was trying to be more submissive, but every now and then we would have some disagreements.

The last time he actually hit me was the same day I found out I was pregnant. I had taken a pregnancy test when I returned home from my parents. I was late starting my period and stopped to get a pregnancy test on my way home. I had put Amara to bed before going back to check the test. I guess while I was at my parents' house my phone died and I didn't check my phone. It was around 8pm when X called my mom. My mom gave me the phone and X sounded pissed. That's when I looked at my phone and realized it was dead. I tried to apologize and I came home right after I stopped at the store to get the pregnancy test. X of course waited until I put Amara to bed before he decided to lash out at me.

I didn't get a chance to look at the test, because X was waiting for me as soon as I came out of Amara's room. He slapped me and pulled me by my hair dragging me to our bedroom. He threw me on the bed and started yelling at me. He went into the bathroom to get his black bag and that's when he saw I took a pregnancy test. He came back to the bedroom apologizing saying he was stressed about some business deals. He showed me the test, and it read I was pregnant. He immediately had makeup sex with me, bought me roses, and jewelry the next day. I thought about leaving many times, but I also thought about how X said he would make sure I never saw Amara again. I guess I was just trying to manage and hope that he would get better, because I didn't want to break up our family. And I was scared to leave and not be able to take Amara with me. And now being pregnant with our 2nd child there is no way I would leave my kids.

I never shared that X hits me with anyone after telling mama that one time. I know Cassie always knew when I wasn't myself, but I would just make something up like I was tired or feeling sick just to brush it off. I didn't want to give X any more reasons to punish me. I figured we were going to get past this somehow. Because when we are doing good, we are doing really good.

But for Amara's party we decided we would just have a small family gathering. I invited Cassie and Greg to come. They were still together and engaged now. My parents were coming, mama Clara, James, Mike and his now finance Whitney. They would be arriving soon. The party was being held at our house and it was starting at 12pm. It was 11:30am now. I just finished decorating the living room and putting Amara's gifts on the table.

"Mom," Amara said, coming in the living room.
"Yes baby,"
"Oooh, so pewty,"
"You like it, Mara?"
"Yea, bawoons."
"Yes, baby those are balloons."
"Bawoons," Amara said again.

I laughed at her words. She was learning but she was just adorable.

"Deja,"
"Yeah X,"
"The caterer is here, do you have a special place for them to set up?" X said, coming into the living room. "It looks good in here."
"Thanks. I will let them know where to put everything," I said walking in the kitchen to show the caterer where they could set up.

The caterer brought in all the food and set up the table. Cassie and Greg made it to our house first, I noticed them walking in as I was talking to the caterer.

"Well, there is my baby mama," Cassie said, coming in and hugging me.
"Hey Cassie, so glad you are here."
"Yes, and how's my baby doing?" Cassie said, rubbing my stomach.
"Girl, kicking my ass like crazy."
"Don't be talking about my little bug."

I Am A Survivor: Sex, Lies, and Abuse

"Yeah, yeah,"
"Where's my daughter?"
"She's in the living room. She is in love with the "bawoons". She's just staring at them."
"Let me go give my baby some love," Cassie said, going to the living room.
"Hi Greg, how are you doing?"
"I'm good Deja. Where's X?"
"He's in the living room too."
"Okay, I'm going to go catch up with him."
"Okay."

Mama Clara, James, Mike, and Whitney showed up next. I hugged everybody and pointed them to the living room where everyone was. My parents showed up last. They came in and I hugged them. We all went into the living room. We all talked for a little bit and then we ate. We had music playing so we danced with Amara. After everyone got done eating, we sang happy birthday and Amara opened her presents. She loved all the gifts. She got new clothes and baby dolls from Greg and Cassie. Mama Clara brought tons of toys. My parents went overboard with clothes and toys. James bought her a cute little purse. Mike and Whitney got her some toys, and shoes. Me and X got her a doll house and some toys. Amara's 1st birthday was a success. She loved it all.

Everyone stayed until about 4pm just talking and playing catch up. It was good to have everyone over, it had been a minute since I saw them. Mama Clara, James, Mike, and Whitney all lived in New Jersey so I rarely saw them. I normally would talk to them on the phone. It was nice they could come into town to see us. And I know Mama Clara was missing Amara. Cassie and Greg, they lived in Columbus, but I still didn't see them a lot either. Having Amara and trying to follow X's rules I could barely even see my parents. So, it was nice to see everyone and get to hang with them.

After everyone left, I carried all of Amara's toys to her playroom and put up her new clothes. X cleaned up the food and put the leftovers in the fridge. I cleaned up the living room. Once everything was clean. I sat on the couch and rocked Amara to sleep, she was tired trying to stay woke to play with her new stuff. Once she went to sleep X took her from me and put her in her bed.

I laid on the couch and watched TV. I was a little tired myself. X stated he had some work to finish up so he would be in his office. I fell asleep watching my favorite crime documentaries.

I woke up when I thought I heard a soft knock on the door. X must have left the entrance gate open after everyone left. He always left our gate open. I figured I

I Am A Survivor: Sex, Lies, and Abuse

would get up and look out the window. I did hear a knock on the door. Someone was standing outside. But I couldn't make out who it was. I slowly opened the door leaving only a crack to see the person.

"I was hoping you would answer," a familiar voice said. She was frail looking, almost sickly, but I recognized her.
"Tammy, what are you doing here?"
"I want to talk to you."

I stepped outside. I don't think X heard the door.

"Tammy, it's probably not a good idea for you to be here. If X sees you, I don't know what he will do."
"I don't care. I hope he does see me or better yet I want you to tell him I was here. Maybe I can catch a deal like Liz."
"What are you talking about?"
"Wow, I had to come see if it was true."
"What?"
"I heard X married you and you had his child. And I can see you're pregnant again. I thought that man wasn't made to settle down. But I guess he was right when he said he wanted you. I know Liz told you how he had us all playing the field to set you up. Hmm, Liz and Randy thought you wouldn't fall for it, but I knew you would. Hell, X wooed the shit out of me. I knew he would get you. And X was right, he got exactly what he wanted. I guess the fucked-up shit about it was how he played us."
"What do you mean, Tammy?"
"Oh, you didn't hear. X paid Eddie to inject Liz with heroin. So she would be so fucked up that she would be out of the picture and no longer your friend. And the day you left my house he paid Randy to do the same to me. X played us. He promised to pay all our debts and give us enough money to live off, but he never told us he was going to drug us to spend all the money as quickly as we got it. He wanted to get rid of us so we wouldn't fuck up his perfect world. Well, I'm here to catch a deal like Liz did."
"Tammy, what are you talking about? What deal did Liz take?"
"Oh, you didn't know. Well, you probably don't know, being all wrapped up in X. I know he wasn't going to tell you. After Liz aired out all the plans to you about how X pursued you, Liz was found in an abandoned house with a needle in her arm. Coroner states she overdosed. But I know X did that shit to get rid of her. X would do anything to keep you from leaving him. And when he thought you weren't coming back to him, he took it out on Liz. He paid someone to kill her and make it look like an overdose."
"What? Liz is dead??" I said, shocked and hurt.

"Yeah, and I am hoping to catch the same deal. X got me out here fucked-up on these damn drugs and I want to be done with this life. I can't seem to kill myself so maybe if he knows I was here telling you more details I can get the same deal."

"Tammy no, I won't tell him you were here. Let me see if I can get you into a rehab or something."

"Hell no, Deja, I have nothing to live for. I have nothing, you hear me. Tell him I was here or he'll find out and probably hurt you for not saying anything. X is a dangerous and powerful man. Married or not if he finds out I was here and you didn't tell him you will pay for being disobedient or defiant is what he always used to say to me. X always gets his way, and he knows everything. Even when you think he doesn't."

"Tammy, I don't feel comfortable telling him, if what you are saying is true. I don't want to be responsible for your death. I don't even like what I am hearing right now. I need to leave."

"Deja, for your own safety, I don't think leaving is an option. Even if you get away X is good for finding you. He knows a lot of people in high places. You think he didn't know about Randy coming to Columbus to kidnap you. Deja, he set that shit up to play hero, so you would feel like you were indebted to him. Him and Randy have been playing you from the jump. It was all part of the plan. X only called Randy in to bring you closer to him, because he knows that hero shit works. Randy was paid for that shit, even if he ended up in a wheelchair, he is set for life financially. So, don't worry about me. Continue to play X's game, because you're stuck now. So, make sure you tell him I was here. Because it's too late for me, please save yourself and tell him everything I told you," Tammy paused, with tears in her eyes. "Please, tell him Deja."

Tammy left and ran down our driveway. I don't know how she got here or if maybe she parked on the street. I was freaking out at this point. Tammy said a lot and I didn't know what to think or do. Should I tell X and risk Tammy ending up dead somewhere. But I was afraid to not say anything and X finds out. Would he try to kill me? I thought I was going to try to stick this marriage out, but after hearing that I don't know if I want to. But she could have been lying to freak me out. What do I do now?

I walked back in the house and locked the door. It was quiet and I didn't see X anywhere. I was thinking about telling him I was going to go to my parents. But I know they just left, since they were here for Amara's party, he might question that. Maybe I will just go see if he is still working and if he says anything about who was at the door. I turned off the TV in the living room and headed upstairs.

I Am A Survivor: Sex, Lies, and Abuse

I checked on Amara and she was still sleeping. I would wake her up soon. I didn't want her to sleep too long or she wouldn't sleep tonight. I walked to X's office a little nervous. He was sitting at his desk still working.

"Deja, what's going on?"
"Nothing, I was just seeing if you were still working."
"Yeah, I'm almost finished."
"Oh, okay I'm going to get Amara up and change her diaper. I don't want her to sleep too long or she won't sleep tonight. I'll leave you alone."
"Okay, baby," X said, continuing to work.

Everything seemed okay. He didn't mention anything about hearing the door. Hopefully that meant he didn't hear anything. I went to get Amara up. She was grumpy. I changed her diaper and made her a bottle. She played with her toys and I sat in her room and just watched her. She was a busy body. I watched as she would play with the baby doll and then go play with her doll house. Then she would come climb on me and go back to playing with a toy. She was just so cute. Being with Amara made me feel safe. I didn't think much about Tammy, but it did cross my mind a few times. I was still worried if X knew and if he was just waiting for me to say something.

I let Amara run around her room and play with her toys. It was now 7pm. I went downstairs to get her some dinner. I got her some fruit and mashed potatoes from the food we had from her party. I put it on her little dinner plate she got from my mom a while back.

"Deja,"
"Oh, shit, X. You scared me," I said, nervously I didn't even hear him come in the kitchen.
"I didn't mean to scare you. You seem different, is everything okay?"
"Yeah, I mean besides you sneaking in the kitchen and scaring me. I'm fine. I'm just making Amara her dinner."

X walked behind me and placed his hands on my belly and kissed my neck.

"You know you are so good with Amara. I was thinking about how worried you were about having her. And now we are about to have baby number 2," X said, rubbing my belly.

I eased up a little as the conversation was going well.

"That little girl and this bug in my belly means the world to me now. I guess I didn't know I would be good at this, but I love it. Just like I love you," I said, giving X a kiss.
"I love you too baby," X said, getting some water out of the fridge. "Who was at the door earlier?"

Fuck! I said to myself. He did hear the door. What was I going to say? I didn't want to lie if he may have known. Shit! Shit! Think of something Deja quick. I couldn't risk lying.

"X, you probably don't want to know," I said, nervous.

X slammed the fridge door. I jumped startled by him.

"Deja, who was it?"
"It was Tammy," I said, feeling so guilty.
"Why the fuck didn't you say anything?" X said, upset.
"Because I knew you would get upset."
"What did she say?"
"A lot, some fucked up shit. Did you know Liz was dead?"
"I heard about it."
"And you didn't think to tell me. I know we weren't friends anymore but I would have wanted to know."
"I didn't think you needed to know. Like you said you weren't friends anymore. What else did she say?"
"X, I think that's something you should have told me."
"But I didn't so what else did she say Deja?"
"X, she looked frail and sick. She said she was on drugs, because of you."
"Hmm," X paused. "And what else did she say?"
"X, that's it," I paused, a little confused on how he was questioning me. "She talked about how she was fucked up because of you and she wanted to end her life."
"Deja, I don't think you're giving me the full story," X said, grabbing my wrist.

I was getting super nervous. I already said enough.

"X, she was just talking nonsense. I didn't believe her so I stopped listening. I did offer her help. She turned it down," I said as X pushed up against me pinning me to the counter.
"Deja, you're pissing me off right now," X said, squeezing my wrist.
"Ouch, X that hurts. Can I please go feed our daughter?"
"Yeah, go ahead, we will finish this conversation when Amara goes to bed," X said, letting me go and walking away.

I Am A Survivor: Sex, Lies, and Abuse

I said too much, but what else could I do? I knew he already knew when he asked me who came to the door. I was freaking out. I tried to not say everything, but I know he already knows everything. This was not going to go well. I will try to hold off as long as I can and let Amara stay up late tonight. I was super nervous now.

Amara ate her dinner and I cleaned up her plate. I came back upstairs and my plan was ruined. X was already holding Amara and rocking her to sleep. Shit!

"Hey, Amara, give mommy kisses," I said, trying to see if Amara would lift up.

Amara gave me kisses, but she was tired because she laid right back on X. Damn, I went to the bedroom and sat on the bed. Amara would be asleep soon and X was going to beat me.

"Deja," X said, standing at the bedroom door. "You ready to talk?"
"X, does it matter what she said? I don't believe her."
"I want to know word for word what she said to you."

I couldn't hold it in any longer. I told him everything she said. I even mentioned she said she wanted me to tell him, because she knew she would end up dead.

"Why the fuck didn't you say this to me immediately, Deja," X said, standing over me.
"She's already sick X, like I said I didn't believe her."
"I don't understand why you have to be so secretive about shit. You just want to piss me off, don't you?"
"That was not my intention."
"But that's what you did," X said. "Stand up Deja."

I stood up holding my belly. I was hoping he wasn't going to hit me. X started taking my clothes off. Once I was naked, he grabbed my wrist and pulled me to the bathroom. He told me to get into the shower. I did and he pulled out the black bag from the counter drawer. He put the handcuffs on me and attached it to the handle in the shower. I was so nervous I couldn't even cry anymore. He cut the shower on and I immediately started to scream, the water was freezing cold. I couldn't even catch my breath because it was so cold.

"If you wake up Amara. I'm going to punch you," X said.

I was shivering and I tried not to scream but it was so cold. I started to beg him to cut the water off.

I Am A Survivor: Sex, Lies, and Abuse

"I'm sorry X, please, please cut the water off," I said, shaking.
"Deja, I'm sick of your defiance. You really pissed me off."
"I'm sorry X, please," I said defeated.

X cut the water off. I could hear Amara crying. Fuck, she woke up. X looked at me and walked out of the bathroom. I was still shaking as I was soaking wet, naked, and cold. I sat down in the shower trying to ball myself up to find a way to warm myself. It wasn't working as my arms were hanging above me on the handle of the shower. X was gone for a good 30 minutes. I was so cold and my arms were getting tired.

X came back in the bathroom and I could tell he was angry. He grabbed me and pulled me up. He punched me across my face. I tried not to scream so Amara wouldn't wake up again. He pulled off his belt and started hitting my leg. It hurt so bad; I couldn't help but to scream. He wouldn't stop, he just kept hitting me. This is the worst he ever did. It was burning and it hurt so bad. I begged him to stop, but he was enraged. He just kept hitting me. He hit my legs, my arms, and my ass over and over nonstop. I was screaming at this point and crying. He did that for a good 5 minutes and then finally he stopped. I fell to the floor. I was balling in tears, and hurting so bad. I couldn't believe he did that. I had to leave now. I couldn't stay with him.

He stood there looking at me for a minute. He then took off his pants and stood me up. He entered me from behind putting his dick in my pussy. I cried as I was in so much pain it didn't feel good. He started fucking me fast and hard and I just wanted him to stop. I couldn't stop crying. I kept screaming ouch and he just kept fucking me. Everything felt so painful. I just needed him to stop touching me, but he didn't stop. I cried the whole time. I couldn't take the pain. "Stop fighting it and fucking cum Deja," X said fucking me harder. I closed my eyes and tried not to think about the pain. I felt the chills starting to run through me and my pussy started to get wet. "That's right Deja cum for me," X said, going harder. I felt the pulsating in my pussy, and I started to moan. The intensity was rising and I finally exploded. "That's my baby," X said as he released too.

He took the handcuffs off. He tried to kiss me. I turned my head, but he grabbed my face and kissed me anyway.

"Stop being defiant Deja," X said, still holding my face.

He let me go and grabbed a towel to dry me off. I screamed as he started to dry me off. My whole body was hurting.

"Let me go get the cream for your marks," X said, going into the bedroom.

I Am A Survivor: Sex, Lies, and Abuse

I got out of the shower and looked in the mirror. I had belt marks all on my legs, arms, and ass. My face was also reddish purple. X came back in the bathroom.

"Here let me put this cream on you," he said, opening the bottle.

I backed up as he tried to touch my skin.

"Deja, if you don't want these marks to stay, let me put the cream on it," he said.
"It hurts," I said, barely getting the words out.
"Maybe next time you won't keep shit from me," X said, with an attitude.

I sat on the counter while he rubbed the cream on me. I tried not to scream but it hurt. After he was done. I went to the bedroom to lay down. It hurt getting in the bed. I got in the bed naked, because I knew putting on clothes would hurt too. X got in the bed with me. I closed my eyes and just forced myself to go to sleep.

I woke up as I felt X move the covers off of me.

"Ouch," I screamed as X hit my ass.

He pulled me to the edge of the bed and pushed my legs up to my stomach. He jammed his dick into my pussy. I screamed again. He started fucking me hard squeezing my already sore legs. I tried to ignore the pain so I could get wet. X just kept pounding. "Deja, I'm going to fuck you until you cum hard baby," X said, moving faster. I felt the chills and my pussy started to get wet. I was about to cum. I closed my eyes. I felt the tears fall. I began to moan and X got excited and started going deeper. My legs started shaking. My whole body was covered in chills. I was cumming. I moaned so loud as I felt like I was exploding over and over. "That's right, keep cumming baby," X moaned. My pussy was super wet and I just kept cumming.

X stopped and flipped me over. He jammed his dick in my pussy from behind sending my whole body into convulsions. His movement got faster. I was cumming again hard. I felt like I couldn't stop cumming. He started massaging my clitoris as he was fucking me, causing me to shake and moan louder. X was fucking me hard and I was cumming again. I cried out in moans as I didn't understand why my body was reacting like this. I was so wet. Every stroke was taking me over the top. It felt so good. "Tell me you like it, Deja," X moaned. I couldn't deny it felt amazing. "I love it, X," I moaned. "I'm going to wear that ass out," X said. I felt X putting oil on my ass as he was still fucking me. He stuck the vibrator in my ass and cut it on. I screamed in moans as I felt the intensity of the vibrator making me want to cum. "I want you to beg, Deja," X said as he kept fucking me. "X, please, oh shit," I moaned as I kept feeling the intensity of cumming. "Beg better, Deja," X said, moving the vibrator up and down. "Fuck, X please I want to cum, baby," I moaned. "Not good enough," X said. Fuck I was getting hot and I wanted to cum so bad. He was driving me crazy. "X, please baby let me cum," I begged. X took the vibrator out of my ass and placed it on my clitoris. I was screaming in moans as I started to cum and X was fucking me harder. My body was shaking like crazy. What the fuck was he doing to me? I was cumming back-to-back. I couldn't stop. X went deeper and I exploded as he released.

"Shit, baby that was good," X said, pulling out of me.

I didn't say anything. I didn't know how I felt right now. The sex was amazing, but I was frustrated with X. I got up and went to the bathroom. I looked at my belt marks and face. My face still looked a little purple, but the belt marks looked like they were going away. X walked in the bathroom.

"I have to go handle some business today," X said, getting in the shower. "Your scars look like they're healing pretty good."

X touched me and I jerked a little as I was still sore. He just gave me a look. He jumped in the shower. I put on a robe as I went to check on Amara. Amara was not in the crib. I checked the playroom. I was panicking. I ran downstairs to check the door. It was locked. I checked the whole house. I came back upstairs and X was still in the shower.

"X, Amara is not here," I said, freaking out.
"I know she left this morning," X said, getting out of the shower.
"What, where is she?"
"I figured you needed a break today. She's safe."
"X, where is my daughter?"
"She's safe Deja. What, you think I'm going to hurt my own child?"
"X, please just tell me where she is?"
"You don't need to know. You need to stay here and heal and think about the selfish shit you did."
"X, why are you doing this? I want to see my daughter."
"You will see her when I get back. This way I know you ain't going nowhere."
"Jesus, X don't do this please. I won't go nowhere just please let me see my daughter."
"You will see her later. Maybe this will teach you not to defy me."

I started to cry. I can't believe he would do this. That's my baby. I had to find my baby. He was not going to keep her from me.

"Deja, she's safe. Stop stressing yourself. You need to think about what you could be doing to the baby in your belly stressing like this."
"I just want to see Amara please X."
"You will see her later, now move, I need to get dressed," X said, pushing me out of his way.

I was shaking now. I didn't know what to do. X got dressed and came back in the bathroom. I was standing next to the counter looking lost.

"Deja, you trust me?" X said, putting his hands between my legs.

I gasped as he began to massage my clitoris.

"I trust you X. Please can I see my daughter."
"Not right now, Deja. I need to know you will be here when I return," X said, kissing me.

I grabbed on to the counter as X was about to make me cum again. I was feeling so many different emotions, but my body was still reacting to his touch. X started moving his fingers in a circular motion on my clitoris. I was about to cum. I moaned. "Cum for me baby," X said. Fuck, my body was listening to his every word. I came so fast my legs started shaking and I moaned loud. X kissed my cheek. And wiped away my tears.

"Now that's my baby. I will be back Deja to fuck you like crazy again," X said, leaving.

I hurried up and jumped in the shower. I was not staying here. I had to make some calls and see where Amara was. As soon as I got out of the shower. I called mama Clara to see if she would say anything about X dropping off Amara to their hotel. I didn't want to sound suspicious or give her a reason to worry. But she asked me how Amara was doing so I knew she couldn't have her. I called Whitney, and Cassie, they didn't have her as they also asked me about Amara. I was afraid to call Mike or James as I know they would tell X I called. I jumped in my car and headed to my parent's house. I sped over there hoping X would have just let them take her.

I pulled up barely remembering to put my car in park but I did. I ran in the house.

"Well, hey baby. I wasn't expecting to see you today. X called us early this morning saying you were tired and needed a break and he had to go do some work."
"Is Amara here?"

I Am A Survivor: Sex, Lies, and Abuse

Before my mom could answer that question, my dad was walking in the house holding Amara. I ran to her. I took her from my dad and kissed all over her.

"Well, I missed you too, baby girl," my dad said joking.
"Hey, dad," I said, hugging him.
"Deja, is everything alright?" my dad said, grabbing my face and noticing the bruise.
"Yeah, everything is fine dad," I said, walking away holding Amara.
"Deja, what's going on?" my dad said.
"It's nothing."
"It's nothing but you came running to me and grabbing Amara like I stole her and don't act like I can't see that bruise on your face," my dad said, getting upset.
"Bruise, what bruise?" my mom said, coming to look at me. "Oh, my lord, Deja, what is going on in that house?"

I tried to hold back my tears.

"Everything will be okay. I'm not going back."
"You damn right you're not going back," my dad, said upset.
"Dad, please don't do nothing crazy."
"Like hell, he put his hands on my daughter. I'll be damned if I don't go beat his ass."
"Dad, just leave it be. I have enough money to leave. I can't stay here, but I will let you know when I'm safe."
"Where are you going Deja?" my mom chimed in.
"I don't know but even if I did, I can't tell you right now, because X probably has my phone bugged. I will get another phone when I get to my destination."
"Deja, this is crazy. Why didn't you say something?"
"I thought I could handle it. But we will talk later. I have to go before he gets here. And dad please don't do nothing. X is dangerous and he knows all the right people. I don't want nothing to happen to you or mom."
"For you and Amara's safety I won't do anything. I love you baby girl," my dad said.
"I love you both."

My mom and dad hugged and kissed me and Amara. My mom gave me Amara's diaper bag and car seat. I drove to the bank to withdraw money first. I took all of it out. I had over $100,000 in the account X gave me. I transferred most of it to my personal account that X didn't have control over and I took $5000 in cash. I left the bank and headed to the bus station. I figured I would take a bus out of Ohio and then fly out of a different state. I needed to go far away for me and my baby's safety. I got to the bus station and parked my car in the lot and left my phone in the car. I figured if he was tracking my phone, he would just find my car. I bought a bus ticket to Memphis, Tennessee. It was the bus leaving right now.

I got on the bus and we took off headed to Memphis. I checked the diaper bag for bottles. My mom was awesome. She had bottles and food in the bag for Amara. I fed her and watched as we left Ohio. I didn't really know my next move, but I knew I had to get away, far away. I was scared. All I was thinking was "I have to get away."

Chapter Fourteen: Hurt
"I understand. And I will do right by Deja."

We made it to Memphis, Tennessee. I decided to pay cash for a hotel for the night. It was 10pm and I didn't quite know where I wanted to go next so I would check flights tomorrow. I took a cab to the closest hotel and checked in with the front desk to see if they had availability. Luckily, they did and they accepted my cash. I saw there was a shopping mall across the street. I would go there in the morning to see if I could buy a phone.

Amara was already sleeping so I put her in the bed and secured her with some pillows around her so she wouldn't fall out of the bed. I figured I would call my parents from the hotel phone and not tell them where I was, but let them know I was safe.

"Hey dad,"
"Deja, oh thank God I didn't know if we would hear from you tonight. Are you safe?"
"Yes, I am safe."
"I put you on speaker. Your mom was worried."
"Hi mom,"
"Hey baby, how are you and Amara?" my mom said, sounding worried.
"We are okay. Amara is sleeping right now. We will be traveling again tomorrow so I wanted to check in before I went to sleep."
"We love you baby girl," my dad said.
"I love you both so much," I said, wiping away my tears.
"If you need anything Deja, please let us know," my dad said.
"I will. Did X call or come by?"
"Yeah, he stopped by and I told him where he could go. He said he would be filing kidnapping charges, Deja."
"What why?"
"Technically, by law you're married and you disappeared with his child. You share 50% custody and he has rights to Amara too."
"That's bullshit. If I return, he will make sure I never see Amara again. How is that fair?" I said, frustrated.
"I looked into it and I talked with a few attorney friends and he would have a good case. You skipped town and if you don't return, he could gain full custody."
"Oh my God. I can't come back dad. I just can't."
"I know, baby girl. Look, one of the attorneys told me he will check in with me every week to see if anything was filed. And we will all know if they do an amber alert. But he said you need to call the police and file a report for your record on what he did to you. He said if X tries to do anything legally your report will also be

I Am A Survivor: Sex, Lies, and Abuse

documented for court records. Once you get a phone, I will get you the attorney's information. His name is Tremond Deetz and he wants to help you."
"Thank you, dad. I will get a phone tomorrow."
"He did say for now. If X doesn't file anything you don't have to return, but if he does you have to get back here immediately. Or they will have a warrant for your arrest and they will take Amara and return her to X immediately."
"Okay dad. I have to go. I love you both so much," I said, trying to hold back my tears.
"We love you too Deja," my parents said before they hung up.

I couldn't go back no matter what. If I ever went back X would never let me out of his site again. I couldn't do that and I damn sure didn't want him to take my kids from me. I would go to California and make my way to Mexico if needed. I would fly to Cuba from there. I would leave the U.S. before I let him take my kids.

I laid next to Amara as she slept. I played with her hair and rubbed her back. I touched her little fingers and wrist. Shit! It just caught my attention Amara had a bracelet like mine. I left all my jewelry at home, because I knew X put trackers in them. X probably already knew where I was. I jumped up and put my shoes on. I grabbed Amara's bag and picked Amara up. I took her bracelet off and left the room. I went to the front desk and gave them back their key card and asked them to call for me a cab.

"Deja," I heard X's voice.
Fuck! "Excuse me sir, can you call the police," I whispered, to the front desk clerk.
"Yes, ma'am," the front desk clerk said, picking up the phone.
"No need for all of that sir. My name is Xavier Thomas and that's my wife," X said as he was standing close to me.
"Wow, Xavier Thomas the business mogul. I saw you on Fortune's 100 list this month. It's an honor to meet you," the front desk clerk said, putting the phone down.
"Nice to meet you," X said, shaking the man's hand. "I apologize for my wife, she's been off her medication since she's been pregnant. She's paranoid that someone is after her," X said, trying to make an excuse for me.
"I'm not crazy," I said with an attitude.
"Let's go home, Deja," X said, pushing me to the door. "Greg's outside, he will take Amara for the night. I already booked us a hotel down the way. We will go home in the morning," X said, pushing me outside.
"No, Amara goes with us. I'm not leaving her with no one," I said, stern.
"Deja, you have no idea what the fuck I want to do to you right now. Give Greg Amara so we can go now," X said, pissed.

"Deja, I will be in the same hotel as you. Amara will be safe," Greg said, trying to calm me.

I was already shaking and panicking. X pulled Amara out of my arms and my heart dropped. I burst out in tears. X handed Amara to Greg and he pushed me into the car. X got in the car and the driver drove off.

"What the fuck were you thinking Deja?" X said, punching my arm.
"Aaaahh," I screamed.
"Have you lost your damn mind? You came all the way to Memphis. You really pissed me off with this shit. You told your parents and now they fucking hate me. Deja you really fucked up," X said, angry.

I stared out the window holding my arm. I really did fuck up. Why didn't I check Amara? Now I was also without a phone and I couldn't call anyone. The driver pulled up to the hotel and we got out of the car. X grabbed my wrist and pulled me inside. X checked in with the front desk and got our key. We went up the elevator to the 18th floor. X smacked me as soon as the elevator doors closed.

"You fucking bitch. Deja, I swear if you weren't pregnant, I would fuck you up worse than ever."

I grabbed my face. It was throbbing. I just kept thinking he would probably kill me if I wasn't pregnant. I didn't know what to do, X was beyond angry and I don't think I was ever going to make this better. I don't think I would ever get another chance to run either.

The elevator opened to the hotel suite. X pushed me in the suite. I almost fell, he pushed me so hard. I tried to walk away from him, but he grabbed my hair and dragged me to the owner's suite. I screamed and cried. X put me in the shower and he took off all of my clothes. He took his t-shirt off and twisted it up. I guess because X didn't have his black bag, he used his shirt to tie my hands up to the shower handle. He tied it so tight I couldn't move my hands at all.

"You disobeyed me when I told your ass to stay at home. You lied and said you trusted me. Why the fuck would you think I would do anything to our daughter, Deja? And then you skip town with my child. Like I wasn't going to find you," X said, standing close to my face.
"X, please I was scared you made it sound like I would never see Amara again."
"So, you thought you would do it to me instead?" X said, smacking my ass hard. I screamed. "X, please don't hurt me."
"Well, from now on you are going to have to earn your time with my kids," X said, smacking my ass hard again.

I Am A Survivor: Sex, Lies, and Abuse

I cried out. "X, no what does that mean?"
"Deja, you don't deserve to see my kids until you are doing everything, I told you to do, and you're being obedient."
"X, please don't do this. I made a stupid decision. Punish me but don't take my babies please," I cried.

X walked out of the bathroom and went into the owner's suite. He walked back in the bathroom holding a belt. I tensed up.

"Deja," X paused as he walked up close to me, I flinched. He grabbed my face and kissed me hard. "I fucking missed you baby. I thought I lost you for good."

X got naked and stood behind me. He rubbed his dick on me and I could feel him getting hard. He squeezed my ass. And then he jammed his dick inside of me pounding fast. I couldn't control the feeling. I was already wet and had chills going through my whole body. I was moaning now as the intensity, heat, and shakes were starting to rise. I was about to cum. "Tell me when you cum baby," X moaned. "Shit, I'm cumming," I moaned. X immediately stopped and hit me with the belt on my ass hitting my pussy too. I screamed in pain. "X, what the fuck?" I cried out. It was the craziest, most painful, and most sensitive feeling I ever felt.

X jammed his dick in my pussy again pounding fast. My body was reacting but I didn't know how to feel emotionally. "Tell me when you're cumming, Deja," X said again. I was about to cum. I was scared to say anything, but it could be worse if I don't. I felt the intensity rising again. "I'm cumming, X," I said. X stopped again and hit me harder with the belt. "Oh, my God, X," I cried out as my body was stinging and shaking at the same time. Fuck what the hell was he doing? I couldn't control it. I was cumming, and hurting at the same damn time. Fuck, this shit was crazy. X did it again he jammed his dick in my pussy and started pounding again hard and fast. "Don't hold back Deja, tell me when you're cumming?" X said, entertained by this. The shit was getting crazy. My body was shaking, tingling, and pulsating. I was about to cum again. "Fuck, X I'm cumming," I said trying to prepare for the hit. X stopped and hit me right in my pussy this time.

"Shit! Fuck! X, what are you doing to me?" I cried out as my body was shaking like crazy, I was cumming, and feeling a really stinging pain all at the same time. X jammed his dick in me again. "Tell me you love me Deja when you start to cum," X said, pounding faster. Fuck I was already about to cum. It's like the intensity of it all was coming faster and I was about to cum now. "I love you, X," I moaned as my body was covered in chills and I was about to explode. X stopped and hit my pussy harder with the belt and I cried out loud as hell as my legs went weak, while I was exploding inside, and the pain was excruciating at the same time. "I can't take no more please. I'm sorry X. You are driving me crazy right now. I will do whatever you want, just stop." I cried out, weakened by the pain.

"Get up, Deja," X said, standing over me.
"I can't X my legs are weak, please."
"Deja, get the fuck up."

I couldn't move. I instantly put his dick in my mouth to suck him off. I couldn't bear him hitting me again like that. So, I thought if I just made him cum, we could end this. "Fuck, Deja," X moaned. I sucked hard, twirling my tongue, and moving at a fast pace. I wasn't going to stop until he came. "Damn, baby. Fuck that shit feels good." I massaged his balls with my mouth and I think that took him over the edge. "Damn, Deja. Shit!" X said as he released. I was relieved.

X untied me and helped me to stand. My legs were shaking, my whole body felt weak, and my pussy was sore. I walked to the bed slowly. I looked at the clock. It was now 2am. I just wanted to lay down. I pulled the covers back to get in the bed.

"I ain't fucking done with you, Deja," X said as he took the belt and hit my ass.

I screamed in pain. He continued to hit me as I fell on the bed. I tried to curl up as much as I could. But I couldn't stop him from hitting me. I tried to grab for the blanket but he pulled it away. He kept hitting me with the belt. I cried out for him to stop, but he didn't. I couldn't move, the pain was unbearable. I just screamed and cried hoping he would stop soon. He just kept hitting me.

"X, please I can't breathe. It hurts so bad," I cried.

After a few more hits X finally stopped. My whole body was on fire. I tried to catch my breath. I literally felt like I was stinging all over. X left the room. I tried to get comfortable on the bed slowly moving, because it hurt. I put the covers over me and cried until I fell asleep.

I woke up the next morning around 9am. X was not in the room. I was so sore. I could barely get up but I forced myself up. I went to the bathroom. My whole body was black and purple. It hurt to touch anything. I threw on my clothes I had on yesterday even though it hurt. I walked in the living room. X was not in the suite at all. I grabbed my purse and went to the lobby. I asked the front desk clerk what room Greg was in. He said Greg checked out around 7am. I tried not to panic, but I knew X left with Amara and Greg. He was paying me back. I had to go back home. I told myself Amara was okay. I would see her again.

I Am A Survivor: Sex, Lies, and Abuse

I went and purchased a phone. I called my parents to let them know X found me and he had Amara. They left me in Memphis and he took Amara home. My dad was pissed, and my mom was freaking out. I told them I would get on the next plane home. I made it to the airport. I was walking slowly as I was in so much pain. I just knew I had to get home to see my baby.

My plane landed in Columbus at 2pm. I was so upset with myself for not checking Amara. I should have known he would have something to track her. I didn't even think about her bracelet. Now I was going to have to fight to get my daughter back. I went straight to my parents' house first. I wanted to make a police report since I had bruises to show.

My dad and mom freaked out when they saw me. My face was bruised and I showed them my arms and legs. They called the Columbus Police. The police came out and took a report. They took pictures of my bruises and stated they would follow up with me once they talked with X. They also told me they couldn't take Amara from him. I would have to take that to court, but they stated they would do a wellness check. They did say a detective would follow up with me.

I waited for hours to hear back from the police. They finally called and stated that they talked with X and he denied hitting me. He called me crazy and delusional. They did say Amara was good and they didn't have any concerns. I didn't want to be without Amara, but I knew I couldn't go over there until I was healed. I was in too much pain to try and do anything.

I went upstairs and took a shower. I cried. I laid down and rested as I tried to keep thinking I will see Amara again. I fell asleep.

I woke up to yelling. I jumped up and headed downstairs.

"Get the fuck off my property X," I heard my dad say.
"She's my wife and I want her home now," X said.
"What's going on?" I said going to the door.
"Deja, let's go home," X said, when he saw me.
"No, X. You took my daughter and left me."
"I was just paying you back for how you made me feel."
"You need help X, and I can't help you."
"I messed up Deja. I'm sorry. I want you to come home."
"X, you scare me. It's different now. I can't go home with you."
"Deja, you got to understand. I didn't mean none of it. I love you."
"I want to see Amara."
"Okay, I will bring her to you," X said, sounding sad.

I Am A Survivor: Sex, Lies, and Abuse

X left. I hoped he was telling the truth. I just wanted to see Amara. My dad was pissed but he knew I was trying to get Amara so he backed off. X came back within an hour and knocked on the door. He had Amara. I grabbed her so fast and kissed her I forgot I was hurting.

"I'm sorry Deja. I will get help. The police gave me some groups I can attend. I will go to the groups and do whatever I need to do. I don't want to lose my family," X said, sounding sincere.
"I hope you take them seriously. But for now, I will be staying with my parents."
"Deja, don't do this please."
"If we can be civil about this, I will keep Amara until Friday. You can come back and get her then. We will exchange again next Friday. I don't know exactly what's going to happen X. But I know I don't want you ever hitting me again."
"Deja, I'm done. I just want you baby."
"I need a break X. Are you okay with my plan for Amara?"
"Yeah, that's fine. I love you, Deja."
"I'll see you on Friday, X."

I closed the door and took a deep breath. I was so happy to see Amara, but hurt because I loved him.

****

It had been two months. Me and X had been keeping to the visitation arrangement for Amara. I was still staying with my parents. They didn't mind as they got to see me and Amara. X was telling me he was doing the anger management groups and he was learning new things. He asked me to go to one with him, but I wasn't ready to go anywhere with him. I was now 8 months so I was close to having this baby. X kept buying me stuff for the baby, Amara, and me. He also put more money in my bank account. He actually put it back to $100,000. He was trying his best to be sweet to me. I just wasn't sure I was ready. I missed him like crazy, but I was scared he would just go back to being controlling and mean.

I didn't want to lose my family, but I didn't want Amara and this one in my belly to grow up thinking it was okay to hit people or be hit. I didn't go through with the charges though. A detective James Moon from the Columbus Police Dept did call me. He gave me a hard time about the report and made me feel like he was trying to say I was lying. He talked about what X told them about me being crazy. I really didn't feel supported at all. He then said I had enough to press charges. I was so done with Detective Moon. I dropped the charges and he said he would close the case. Besides, I didn't want to ruin X's reputation or put him in jail. I just wanted him to change. My parents were pretty much staying out of it. They

I Am A Survivor: Sex, Lies, and Abuse

stated it was my decision whatever I decided, but they hoped I would make the right choice. I know they wanted me to divorce him and move on. But that just didn't seem right.

I did eventually look up Liz's death though. She did pass away and they have it listed as an overdose. I also looked up Tammy to see if anything happened to her, but she was still alive. She recently received a DUI charge in New York. So that put me at ease to see she didn't end up dead too. I knew Tammy wasn't being completely truthful with me. But I wasn't trying to excuse X's behavior at all. I still was not going back until I felt it was okay too. If I would go back at all.

I was finally starting to get out more after not being with X. I was going to the mall and shopping on my own. I was getting back to getting my nails done at my favorite nail salon. I actually had an appointment today. My mom was going to watch Amara for me while I went and had a pamper day. It was 12pm when I left the house to go get my nails done. I went to my favorite coffee shop right next to the nail salon. I grabbed some coffee and sat at the table while I waited for my appointment.

"Deja Thomas, right?" a lady's voice said, from behind me.
I turned around to see who knew me. "Oh, wow Senator Grace. Good to see you. What are you doing in Columbus?"
"Good to see you," Senator Grace said, sitting down at my table. "I actually came in town to meet with your husband. It's funny I ran into you. I just told X about some business stuff I wanted to do and he told me you paint. One of the business ventures I want to do is an art gallery in New Jersey. I was wondering if you would be interested in setting this up with your paintings?"
"Oh, wow really that sounds awesome. I would love to do that."
"Oh great, what's your number? I will give you a call to get this started. I know you are close to having the baby so I was thinking maybe April or early May to give you some time with the new baby."
"Yes, that should work out fine. I will get to creating some new artwork for the gallery. Thank you for this opportunity," I said, giving her my number.
"Great, I will keep in touch with you. Oh, and start working on a theme or name you would like the event to be called. It was great running into you," Senator Grace said, getting up to leave.
"Yes, thanks again!" I said, excited.

Wow, I didn't expect that to happen. I was excited about the new opportunity. Of course, I would have to go to the house to get my paintings and art stuff. I don't know if I was ready for that. But I wanted to start working on it as soon as I could and X had the perfect art room he made for me. Man, I didn't know if I should even risk that.

I Am A Survivor: Sex, Lies, and Abuse

I went to my nail appointment. I thought about stopping by the house when I was done. I mean X could be at work. I knew with his new businesses in Columbus he has been working outside of the house. I still had a key and I doubt he changed the locks. I finished my appointment and decided I would try to go to the house. If he was there, I would leave. I pulled up to the house. I got out of the car and walked up to the door. I unlocked the door. It sounded quiet in the house. I actually missed being in this house. It was my home too. I walked upstairs to see if X was in his office. I didn't see him. I went into our bedroom. He wasn't in there. I checked the drawers and closet. He didn't get rid of my stuff so that was good. I checked the bathroom and no one was home. I went back downstairs to the art room. I took my coat off and sat down to see if I even felt comfortable painting.

I wasted no time getting right back in the groove. I was painting and already had a theme for the art gallery, "Distracted Love". It had a catchy ring to it. I wrote that down and continued painting. I was so into my zone I didn't even hear X come in the room.

"Deja," X said, standing behind me.
"Oh shit!" I gasped. "You scared me. I didn't even hear you come in."
"That painting is beautiful."
"Thank you,"
"What made you come over here? You wanted to paint?"
"Well, not exactly. I mean I ran into Senator Grace at the coffee shop. She said she was in town because she was meeting with you. She said my name came up for her art gallery idea in New Jersey and she wanted me to do the paintings. I told her yeah, so I thought I would come over here to see if I even still had the painting vibe. It's been so long since I painted."
"I think that's a great idea Deja."
"You think so? I've never done something like this before."
"But you will be great at it. You love painting and you can host an art gallery," X said, leaning down to kiss me.
"X, wait I don't know about this yet."
"Deja, I miss you. It's been two months."
"X, I'm just not ready yet. What happened between us last time really scared me."
"Okay, fine. Let me take you out tonight."
"What?" I said, confused.
"We start over the right way this time. I will take you out and we will get to know each other again."
"X, I don't know," I said, smiling.

X grabbed my wrist.

I Am A Survivor: Sex, Lies, and Abuse

"Deja, I've missed you baby. Let me take care of you again."

I took a deep breath, as I felt myself giving in.

"Okay, we can go out tonight."

X kissed my forehead.

"Okay Deja, I'll let you get back to painting."

I called my mom. I had to let her know what was going on. She was not happy about it, but she understood I had to see if this marriage could be saved. She didn't mind watching Amara, she was just worried about me. I told her I would call if anything happened.

I finished my painting and headed upstairs. It was now 5pm so I wanted to find something to wear. I heard X in the shower. I walked in our bedroom and saw a dress already laying on the bed with tags on it. X was already planning this to happen. The dress was gorgeous though it was a shimmery pinkish rose gold color. It was a long sleeve off the shoulder right above the knee in length. He had some rose gold flats to match. X got out of the shower and came in the room naked. Damn, I couldn't help but to look. It's been 2 months like X said. It's a big difference when you were used to having sex almost every day. Shit, I was missing that for sure.

"Deja, you're really staring," X said.
"Whatever, you could have put a towel around you," I smirked.
"What for, you're still my wife," X said, coming close.

I was so, not going to win this fight if he tried anything.

"X," I sighed. "I need to get in the shower if we are going out right?"
"Mmmhhh, I guess so," X said, stepping back.

I went to the bathroom to take a shower. Man, the physical chemistry between us was still on fire. I wanted him even if I knew I shouldn't want him. I stayed in the shower a little longer just trying to recollect my thoughts so I would at least make it to dinner first. I got out of the shower. And came into the bedroom. X was sitting on the bed watching me. I dried off with my towel. I put lotion on my body while X continued to watch me. I looked at him and smiled. He smiled back. I don't know if we were going to dinner at this point. X got up and walked towards me. He kissed me and it felt so amazing the chills were already starting. He put his fingers on my clitoris and my pussy was already getting wet. I wanted him so

I Am A Survivor: Sex, Lies, and Abuse

bad. I began to moan as I felt like I was ready to cum. X just knew how to touch me and my body just spoke his language. He whispered "Cum for me Deja." I moaned and came so hard just from X massaging my clitoris. Shit he was good. X had me in a doggy style position on the bed and he entered me. I fucking came immediately. Fuck he didn't even do nothing yet. "Damn, girl did you miss me?" X laughed. "Shut up, X," I said, laughing. X starting fucking me deep and slow. It felt so good. I was already shaking, and my pussy was throbbing. "Fuck, Deja that pussy feels good," X moaned. X began to speed up and pound harder. I could feel it, the intensity was rising and my pussy was soaking wet. I was going to explode. "Oh, shit X, I'm about to cum," I moaned. X went faster and I moaned so loud as we both climaxed together.

X and I laid in the bed. X was rubbing my belly and kissing it.

"Deja," X paused. "I'm sorry for everything. I want my family back. I know the shit I did was fucked up, but I don't want to lose you. I am working on my anger and trying to understand my emotions. I'm just used to getting my way and you can be a challenge at times. But I'm trying to understand and accept that I need to learn to compromise even if things are not going to go the way I want it. I really want you to come home, Deja. And I will do whatever that takes. I love you."
"I love you too, X. And I want to come home, but I want to take my time on making that decision. X, you hurt me really bad, and it scared me. And I'm sorry for running off, but I was so afraid you were trying to control me by keeping me away from Amara. The only thing that I could think was to get far away from you, because I didn't know who you were anymore. When you're angry X, you are a different person," I said, a little nervous being so open with him.
"I know Deja. I know. I was wrong. And I truly am sorry for that." X said, sounding sincere.
"Stay with me tonight," X said, starting to massage my clitoris.
"X," I moaned. "Fuck, okay."

It felt so good to feel his touch again. I couldn't say no. This moment was everything to me. X was being X again and I loved it. X positioned himself between my legs. X pushed my legs up and entered me. I moaned. He shifted all his weight on my pelvic and went deep inside me. He kept pushing deeper. My pussy was pulsating. His touch, his strokes, and his moans were sending me over the top. My body reacted to him every time. X started massaging my clitoris. I started to shake as the feeling was about to make me cum. I moaned "X, I'm about to cum." "Come on this dick, Deja," X moaned as he stopped moving and focused on massaging my clitoris. Feeling his dick inside me as he massaged my clitoris felt exhilarating. I came so hard. X started fucking me hard and fast after I came. The intensity was insane. X grabbed my wrists as he pounded faster holding my wrists tight. I felt my pussy jerk. I didn't know this feeling, but it felt good. I cried out in moans as the sensation was insane. "Fuck, Deja this pussy is so good. I'm about to cum," X moaned. X pounded harder. I came one more time and he released right after me.

"Shit, baby. That pussy be doing something to me," X said, kissing me.
"No, you be doing something to me. You're making me crazy for you, X," I said, smiling.
"Oh, really that's how you feel."
"Yeah, that's how I feel."
"Get up, we still need to go eat. You have to eat something for the baby."

It was 7:30pm. X and I got in the shower together. We were dressed and ready by 8pm. X's driver was outside. We got in the car and headed to the restaurant. We pulled up to the back of the airport; this was not a restaurant. I looked at X.

"X, what's going on?" I said, confused.
"You'll see Deja," X said smiling.

I watched as the driver stopped by a private jet. X got out of the car before I could ask what we were doing. X came and opened my door.

"X, where are we going?"
"You will see Deja. You trust me?"
"Yes," I said with hesitation.

X just smiled. I got on the plane and saw there were roses all over the seats. There was a small table setup with strawberries, a bottle of champagne, and glasses.

"Happy one year anniversary, Deja," X said. I turned around to look at him.
"Oh my God, it's our anniversary," I felt so stupid it was Valentine's Day.
"I wanted to surprise you."
"Wait so you had all of this planned. You set up Senator Grace meeting with me?" I said, taken aback.
"Yeah, I couldn't track you by your phone since you got a new one. But I had Greg put a tracker on your car so I could know where you would be. I told Grace where you were and she met with you. I was hoping the art gallery idea would make you come to the house to start looking at your paintings and see what you wanted to do for the art gallery. And luckily it did. I wanted to make today special for us. I would have had Grace call you, but my wife got a new phone and I don't have that number," X said, reminding me that I never gave him my new number.
"Wait, so the whole art gallery thing is fake?"

I Am A Survivor: Sex, Lies, and Abuse

"No, Grace really wants to set that up. We did talk about you doing the art gallery, but I saw it as a perfect opportunity to get you home."
"And if I didn't come home, how were you going to set this up?" I said, curious.
"Hmmm, I thought about that. I was going to come to your parents' house or find you myself. I know your parents don't like me now, but I was going to take the risk of trying to convince you to come home or spend the day with me. In hopes that you would say yes."
I smiled at the thought of his plans. "X, where are you taking me?"
"It's a surprise."

We sat down and X poured us some champagne. I ate some strawberries as the plane took off. I wanted to know where we were going, but X wouldn't tell me. I can't believe I forgot it was our anniversary. I apologized to X. He didn't care, he said he was happy he could spend the day with me. I couldn't believe everything he did so far. I was in awe. I felt like I was falling in love all over again. I hoped this time it would be better.

The plane landed. The pilot didn't say where we were so I was still confused on where he had taken me, but we didn't fly for too long. So, I was thinking we were still in the U.S. We got off the plane and there was a limo waiting for us. The driver opened the door for me. X pulled out a silky black scarf.

"Deja, wait," X said, holding the scarf. "I'm going to blindfold you so the surprise is not ruined."
"X," I said, nervous.
"You trust me, right?"
"Yes, X," I said.

X put the blindfold on me and helped me in the car. I could feel the car moving, but I couldn't see anything. My heartbeat was racing and I was breathing heavily. It felt uncomfortable not being able to see. X grabbed my wrist and I gasped as I felt my body reacting to his touch. It was getting hot in here. "Deja, I kind of like this," X whispered in my ear. I felt his hand touch my thigh and my pussy was getting wet. I felt him squeeze my thigh and his hand went up my dress. He pulled my panties to the side and started massaging my clitoris. I moaned from the excitement of the unknown and his touch. He began to kiss me. My body was covered in chills and I was shaking. "Cum for me Deja," X whispered. I laid my head back and came moaning really loud. I hope the driver wasn't watching but I couldn't see. "That's my girl," X whispered. He kissed me again, covering my body in chills. The sensation was mesmerizing.

The car stopped and I heard the door open. X grabbed my hand and guided me out. I heard him open a door and he guided me inside. Wherever we were it was colder than Columbus. I felt the cold hit my legs when we got out of the car. It felt warmer once we went inside.

"X, are you going to take this off now?" I said, curious.
"Deja, have patience. Just a few more steps," X said, still guiding me.

X walked with me a few more steps and finally he took the blindfold off. I looked around the room amazed. We were in a house. I think I was in the living room. The view in front of me was beautiful. It was a wall of windows looking out into the ocean. It was dark so I couldn't see the water but I could see the waves hit the rocks from the light outside in the yard. I looked around the room and it had a huge electric fireplace. It made the room look orange. The place was furnished with a cream-colored living room set. When I turned to my left, I could see the kitchen. The kitchen was open and had an island with barstools. The dining area separated the two rooms. I saw the table was already set for two. There was a bouquet of roses in the middle. Food was on the table. I looked at X. This place was beautiful and the inside décor gave cozy vibes.

"I think we should eat before the food gets cold," X said.
"Was it just prepared?" I asked.
"Yeah, the chef just left before we pulled up."
"Whose place is this X?"
"Let's eat Deja, I'm starving," X said, not answering my question.

We sat down and began to eat. The food tasted amazing. We had steak, shrimp, mashed potatoes, and greens.

"Wow, this food is good," I said to X.
"Yeah, the chef did good."
"So, are you going to at least tell me where we are?"
"Is my wife going to give me her new phone number?" X said, being sarcastic.
"X, you can have my phone number where are we?" I said, calling his phone to give him my number.
"We are in New Jersey," X said, storing my number.
"And whose place is this?"
"Are you done eating?" X said, ignoring my question.
"Yes, I'm full."
"Come on, I want to show you something," X said, grabbing my hand.

X, walked me to the other side of the living room where there was a door. He opened the door and I gasped. The room was beautiful. It had a wall of windows. In the daytime this room would be lit up by the sun. It was an art room. I saw the easels and the painting materials. I knew then this was for me. I didn't know what to think.

"Deja, this is our house," X said, confirming what I thought.
"We're moving to New Jersey?" I said, a little worried.
"You don't want to move here?" X said, upset.
"This house is beautiful. And it's not that I don't want to live here. It's just-," I paused.
"What is it, Deja?"
"Don't you think this is too fast? I mean I haven't even said if I was coming back home yet. And now you're trying to move me out of Columbus."
"Well, I'm not giving the house up in Columbus. We will still have that house too. I just figured while you're working on this art gallery deal with Grace, we can be here so you don't have to travel back and forth. I mean when I talked with Grace, she was talking like this is going to be an ongoing thing here in New Jersey. This is something Grace wants to do with you more than once," X said, trying to convince me this was a good idea.
"I don't know X. This is a big move for me. I like Columbus," I said, not sure about this.

X wrapped his arms around me and started rubbing my belly.

"Deja, do you want to see the rest of the house?" X said, kissing the back of my head.

I knew what he was doing. He was trying to sell me on this house. X grabbed my wrist and walked me to the front of the house. On the right side of the house by the front door X showed me his office. He showed me the kids' playroom which was next to his office. He already had new toys in the playroom. On the left side of the house was a long hallway. He walked me down to show me the room he had furnished as a guest room. Right across from the guest room was our gym. There was also a bathroom next to the guest room. Coming back up the hallway he showed me Amara's room which was already furnished. And she had a bathroom across from her room. Then he showed me the baby's room that was next to Amara's room. The house was ranch style.

We walked back to the owner's suite which he wanted to show me last. I walked in the room and it was huge. It had a king size bed that had a bench at the foot of the bed. The headboard was attached to the wall and was cushioned. The room was decorated with some of my paintings on the walls. There was a bookcase and two sofa chairs with a table in one of the corners. Like a reading space which I thought was cute. He showed me the walk-in closet where he had the dressers custom built on the wall. There were clothes for me and him in the closet. And he had the center dresser in the middle with our jewelry on top of the dresser and in the drawers. X walked me to the bathroom next where I saw we had a long counter with his and her sinks. He had a shelf on his side and I had a shelf on my side for our necessities. The mirror was as long as the counter with the vanity lights at the top. The shower was huge with the tub inside the shower. And the shower part had multiple shower heads that hit from every direction.

If I wasn't sold on this house I was now. It was beautiful. I loved the layout and how it was furnished.

"This house is beautiful, X," I said, admiring the bedroom.
"So, you like it enough to move here?" X said, still trying to convince me.

I sat on the bench at the end of the bed and looked up at X.

"Yes," I paused. "But can we stay in Columbus just until I know that things are better between us."
"Does that mean you will be with me; I mean living with me when we go back to Columbus?"
"Yes, X. I want to try to make this work, but I just don't want you to hurt me again," I said, a little nervous.
"I know Deja, I love you."
"I love you too, X," I said, as X leaned down to kiss me.

We spent the rest of the night making love and got up the next morning to return back to Columbus. I went to my parents' house once we got back home so I could have a conversation with them about moving back home. I didn't know how this would go.

"Hey, mom. Where's Amara?" I said, coming into the house.
"She's with your dad upstairs playing."
"I heard someone come in. I was hoping it was you," my dad said coming downstairs. "Amara just went to sleep."
"Hey dad," I said, giving him a hug.
"Well, I don't see any bruises. I take it, everything went well?" my dad said, inspecting my face.
"Actually, it went really well. I forgot it was our anniversary and X took me out. I really enjoyed it. He apologized and he bought us a house in New Jersey," I said, quickly as I knew their response would be upsetting.
"DEJA," my parents said together.
"I know, it doesn't sound good. But X has been doing his anger management classes and he is different. I mean he is learning to compromise and he is being

really patient with me. We won't move to New Jersey until I feel I'm ready," I said, trying to convince them.

"Deja, I can't believe this. So, you're moving back in with him?" my dad said, upset.

"Yeah, I am," I said, feeling guilty.

"Deja, I was hoping you would do better," my mom said, frustrated.

"He's my husband. I have to give it a try before I just throw in the towel."

"The man put his hands on you. And you don't think he won't do it again when he finds some reason to get upset with you. I hope you don't think that's love, Deja." my dad said.

"We have been talking about that dad and he knows if it happens again. I will not go back."

"I can't believe this, Deja. You deserve better than him," my mom said.

"Look, I can't make you like him after what happened and I get that. But I love him and I want to see if it will be better. I have to at least give him a chance to prove to me he can be different for the sake of my family."

"Or you just want him to teach your daughter it's okay for a man to hit her," my dad said, pissed.

"Dad, please. Understand that I want nothing but the best for my daughter and X is good with her. He will not teach her that and neither will I. I want to go home and see if I can make this work."

"I can't stop you. You are grown but if he puts his hands on you again and you come running back here you better be ready to divorce him," my dad said, stern.

"And if that happens, I will divorce him," I said, reassuring my dad.

"Oh Deja, I thought we taught you better than this," my mom said, sounding disappointed.

"Thanks, mom," I said, upset.

"I'm just saying I'm not sure you are thinking clearly right now. He just wooed you and now everything is all good. But like your dad I don't believe it will last," my mom said.

"Well, I'm willing to give it another chance to see if that is the truth."

"Fine Deja. When are you going back?" my dad said.

"Today," I said.

"Great, so you're not even going to think about it overnight?" my dad said.

"No, X will be here soon. He wants to talk with you both and apologize."

"HELL NO, THAT MAN WILL NOT COME IN THIS HOUSE," my dad yelled.

"Dad, please just let him explain himself for me. He's trying and he wants to make things right."

"I can't believe this shit! You really think he has changed?" my dad said, frustrated.

"Please dad at least hear him out," I begged.

"Fine Deja, but I don't like this at all," my dad said, walking away.

I Am A Survivor: Sex, Lies, and Abuse

"You know Deja I don't like this either, but we will listen to what he has to say," my mom said.

X showed up a few minutes later. I let him in the house and we all sat in the living room. I sat by X holding his hand.

"I just want to say when I asked you for your daughter's hand in marriage and we said our vows. I knew I wanted to cherish her with all my heart. My intentions were never to hurt her. But I realized I hadn't dealt with all my demons in the past and I let my anger get the best of me. I should have never taken my anger out on Deja. I messed up and I did exactly what I didn't want to do. Hurt her and you both. I know I don't expect to be forgiven, and I can't change what I did, but I hope that from what I've been learning I can make things better for my family. And I wanted you both to know that I truly am sorry for my actions and for hurting Deja. I love Deja with all my heart and I don't want to lose her. She is my world and I know now even a day without her kills me inside. I have never experienced the love that she shows me every day. I will admit I took that for granted, because I didn't know how to love her like she loves me. I don't know if Deja ever shared with you my family history and I know I didn't tell Deja everything, but I am willing to talk about it now. I hated my birth mother because she was a drug addict and prostitute. She had me in places I should have never been, seeing things I should have never seen. I can't forget the things I've seen. My mother exposed me to so much in the time she had me. I was raped and she allowed it for a small bag of crack," X paused.

I could see he was tearing up. I rubbed his back. He never told me that. I didn't know how to feel. I was hurting for him.

"Excuse me," X cleared his throat. "I was angry with her and I didn't realize it still affected me today. I was happy to get away from her when children services got involved and placed me with my aunt and uncle. They adopted me with no hesitation when they realized my mother wasn't giving up her lifestyle for me. I am forever grateful for my aunt and uncle. But I now know I have a lot to work on. I know taking these anger management classes have been helping me to see a lot of my past trauma and how the hurt has affected me. But no matter what I am dealing with, I'm not trying to make excuses for my actions. I just hope Deja knows I will do right by her. And I want that chance to prove it to her."

The room was quiet for a minute.

"I appreciate you sharing your story and explaining yourself. I truly love my daughter and want the best for her. I know I can't make decisions for her and she is grown. But it really hurt us to know what you did to her. And you're right, I'm not sure I'm ready to forgive you. But for my daughter I will watch and see if your actions say differently. I'm sorry to hear what you had to go through as a child and I hope you continue to work on healing from that. But for now, and for my daughter, I will accept that she wants to continue her marriage with you. But as her father I will always be looking out for her safety," my dad said being stern with X.

X stood up to shake my dad's hand and said, "I understand. And I will do right by Deja."

Chapter Fifteen: Shocked
"X has lost his damn mind."

Everything was getting better. We were planning to move to New Jersey tomorrow. My parents were happy to know things were working out and going good since our anniversary. It was now March 20th and Xavier Emmanuel Thomas Jr. was born on March 8th. My little Manny was just a character already at 12 days old. X was in love all over again having a junior. X couldn't wait to get to New Jersey and show off Manny. Mama Clara and his brothers weren't able to come down when I gave birth so they would be seeing Manny for the first time tomorrow. My parents were already in love and sad that we were leaving, but I told them we would be back to visit often. X promised them we would have Amara and Manny stay with them the week of my art show so they could have grandparent time. My art show was going to be on April 10th so that was only a few weeks away.

Cassie, Stacy, and Michaela were sad about me moving. I had been talking and hanging with them more so they were really upset with me leaving. But they understood I had to do what was good for my family, and besides Cassie wasn't too upset, because with her engagement to Greg they would be moving to New Jersey in April. Greg was head of security for X, so he was going to have to be wherever X was. Greg would be traveling back and forth for a couple of weeks, but Cassie would be moving to New Jersey in April so that Greg wouldn't have to travel so much. It was kind of nice to know I would still have Cassie to hang with and I know Whitney was excited I was coming to New Jersey too. When I really sat back and looked at things, it was really going well. And it was good to see Cassie and Greg were still going strong. They had plans to get married in May of this year. Cassie wasn't sharing the good news with me yet, but X told me she just found out she was pregnant. Greg told X but Cassie was waiting to share. She wanted to be further along before she said anything. Which I understood, because I waited to tell everyone I was pregnant with Amara. I figured I would just wait for her to tell me and act surprised even though X already told me.

But everything was really good with X and I right now. I never shared with any of my friends what we went through. I was thankful that Greg was loyal to X, because Cassie didn't seem to portray, she knew anything about the last incident. As far as I knew my friends adored our relationship, because I only shared with them the good moments. I wanted to keep it that way, because I knew X was a good man and I didn't want him to be seen as anything else. I know telling my parents tainted their relationship, but at least they were trying to see him as good still. But hopefully things were going to stay good.

I Am A Survivor: Sex, Lies, and Abuse

I just got done packing up some of the things I wanted to take to New Jersey with us. Amara and Manny were at my parents' house for the day since we are leaving tomorrow afternoon. My mom really wanted to spend the day with them so we let her. Alicia arranged for some movers to take the things I packed. We were not taking a lot since we still would be coming back every now and then. We were only taking what X and I really needed so we had a few boxes for the movers. They came and got everything. X was out finishing up some business, before we left Columbus.

I pretty much had the house to myself for a minute. X didn't say when he would be back so I was alone for now. I knew we would be picking up the kids in the morning. I didn't have to clean the house, because the maid had already come through yesterday and would be checking in while we were gone. X also already found a maid to clean the new house too.

I decided to fix myself some lunch and watch a movie since I didn't have anything else to do. I made some pasta salad and fried chicken. I found a good movie to watch and curled up on the couch. It was 1pm. I figured I would finish the movie and take a nap.

I woke up around 2pm, because I heard someone knocking at the door. I got up and checked. I looked out the window. It was some older white man with a beard. He was wearing a suit. I opened the door.

"Hello, how can I help you?"
"Are you Mrs. Deja Thomas?" the man said.
"Who is asking?" I said, nervous.
"Hello, I think I talked with you a while back on the phone. I am Detective James Moon. I was looking to speak with Mr. Xavier Thomas."
"He is not home right now. May I ask what this is concerning?" I said, curious.
"I am inquiring for the NYPD about a death and Mr. Thomas is listed as a suspect."
"Who's dead?" I said, nervous.
"Tammy Clay was found dead a few weeks ago in New York. It looks like it could have been an overdose, but there was a letter found next to her that read Xavier Thomas was responsible for my death. And the NYPD would like for me to interview Mr. Thomas."

X was standing behind Detective Moon at this point.

"Excuse me, what did you say your name was?" X said, interrupting.
"Oh, I am Detective James Moon from the Columbus Police Department. Are you Mr. Xavier Thomas?"

I Am A Survivor: Sex, Lies, and Abuse

"Yes, I am," X said, with confidence.
"I was just telling your wife-," Detective Moon was interrupted by X.
"I heard what you told my wife. I don't know what happened to Tammy and why that letter was left, but it has nothing to do with me. If you have any further questions, you can reach out to my attorney," X said, handing Detective Moon his attorney's card.
"Thank you, as of right now you are being considered as a suspect so please don't leave town. I will contact your attorney to set up an interview," Detective Moon said holding the attorney's card.
"I run businesses outside of Columbus, I will not be able to stay in town, but when you set up a meeting with my attorney, I'm sure he will let me know where I need to be. Thank you for stopping by," X said, walking in the house and closing the door.

Detective Moon left the premises. X didn't even say anything to me. He immediately made a phone call and went to his office. I think I was in shock that Tammy was dead. And she wrote a note or someone wrote a note saying X did it. This didn't look good. I was nervous and scared.

I wanted to talk with X, but he was in his office with the door closed. I went to our bedroom hoping he would come out soon. I waited a few minutes and I saw he opened the office door. He was off the phone but he didn't come out of the office. I walked to his office door. X was sitting in his chair with his head down. He was crying. That's when I realized he loved Tammy. I think X was being set up.

"X," I said calmly.

X wiped away his tears and looked up at me.

"Yeah, Deja."
"You don't have to be strong for me. I know you loved her and it's okay to cry X."
"Deja, come here," X said, as I walked closer to him.

He grabbed me and sat me on his lap. He began to ball. I held him tight. My baby was hurt. I just wanted to make him feel better. I kissed him on his head and he squeezed me tightly. I've never seen him so vulnerable. I just wanted to comfort him and make it better somehow.

I walked X to our bedroom. I laid down with him and held him as he held on to me. We didn't say anything, we just held each other for a while. X finally said something.

"I'm sorry Deja,"

I Am A Survivor: Sex, Lies, and Abuse

"For what X?"
"For this, I mean my wife is consoling me over my ex-girlfriend."
"X, you're human. You have a heart and you loved her who wouldn't feel hurt about someone they loved dying."
"Thank you for understanding baby. I love you," X paused. "I know I never corrected you when you told me what Tammy said. But I hope you don't think I had something to do with her death or Liz's death. I did love Tammy; I was with her for 3 years. I loved her, but we were not working out like I hoped. When I saw you, I knew I would be ending my relationship with Tammy soon. What she told you about me seeking you out was the truth. I told Tammy I was done with her and I gave her and Liz an offer to help me get you. I know it sounds fucked up having my ex help me get with you. But I am a man who will do whatever to get what he wants. But I am not a murderer. I get what I want with money. And I wanted you and needed for you to be ready for what I wanted to do to you. That's why I chose to do things the way I did. But I didn't murder no one I just paid them money. I may have my flaws, but I am not evil," X said.
"Thank you, X for being honest with me," I said, giving him a kiss.
"I love you, Deja, you are my world."
"I love you too, X."

We laid in silence again. I really appreciated X being real with me. It was a fucked-up way to seek me out, but I was his now and obviously he got me that way. X fell asleep. I just laid there listening to him sleep. I didn't want to leave his side. X's phone went off. He jumped up. I sat up. He put the phone on speaker. It was his attorney.

"Hey X," his attorney said. "I talked with Detective Moon and Detective Schultz at the NYPD. After hearing the reason why they wanted to talk with you. I denied the meeting. They have no evidence to pursue you as a suspect, besides a letter that anyone could have written, because they don't like you. If anything else comes of this I will keep you informed, but they stated they will keep investigating for now and if they need to speak with you, they will let me know."
"Thank you, Eric," X said, hanging up the phone.

I could still feel X's sadness. I wrapped my arms around him and kissed his shoulder. I laid my head on him. X picked his phone back up. I could tell he was biting down on his jaw and tightening it. He texted Greg. I could see him texting. He texted Greg saying have Micah look into Tammy's death I want to know what happened to her. He threw his phone on the bed and turned around and started kissing me hard. X was angry I could tell. He pulled my pants and panties off and he put my legs on his shoulder. He started sucking on my clitoris hard. It hurt a little, but chills were running through my whole body. I closed my eyes. X was not stopping or slowing down. He was massaging my clitoris with his mouth fast and hard. I was moaning loudly as the feeling felt amazing, but X was relentless. I came multiple times and X was still going in. I was ready for him to fuck me, but he wasn't stopping. I started shaking, and my pussy was throbbing. X put his finger in my pussy and started moving in and out of me fast and rough. I was about to explode. "X, baby I'm about to cum hard," I moaned. X stopped and flipped me over. He jammed his dick in my pussy from behind and I fucking exploded while he was pounding hard. I screamed in ecstasy as the feeling was crazy good. X kept moving faster and faster. He grabbed my hair and gripped it hard. He was fucking me so hard; my body was reacting like crazy and I was soaking wet. X pushed his finger in my ass. I screamed out in moans as I felt a little pain, but it was sending me over the top as I could feel the pressure in my pussy too. X continued to stroke faster and harder. He was being rough as hell, but I was enjoying it. I came a few more times and finally X released letting out a loud sigh. He kissed my back and went to the bathroom and closed the door.

He never fucked me like that before with so much force he was definitely angry. I heard X turn the shower on. I was going to leave him alone, but something told me to check on him. I opened the bathroom door and X was standing in the shower just letting the water hit him. He looked defeated. He was taking Tammy's death harder than I thought. I took my shirt and bra off and got in the shower with him. I soaped up his washcloth and started washing his chest. He grabbed me by my waist and pushed me towards him. He kissed and hugged me so tight.

"Let me take care of you, X," I said, washing his back while he held me.

I washed his whole body and mine. I let the water rinse the soap off of us. I held him as he just felt like he wasn't really there. I turned the water off and dried him off. I dried myself off and helped him to lay down. I went to get him some water; I was about to cook, but he said he wasn't hungry. I came back up with the water and placed it on the nightstand. X was already sleeping.

I went downstairs and cleaned the kitchen. I didn't realize it but I was crying. I noticed when I saw the tear fall on the kitchen counter. It hurt to see X so down. It hurt to know he loved her that much too. But I understood it and it just hurt a little. I finished the kitchen and straightened up the living room. I wasn't sleepy. I just had so much on my mind right now. I decided to sit in the living room and watch my favorite crime documentaries. I actually dozed off after an hour.

I was startled awake when I saw a man standing over me. I jumped up when I realized it was Randy. He was not in a wheelchair, he was standing. I started to panic. I screamed. Randy came towards me. I tried to run, but he grabbed me. He had a gun. I screamed again and he covered my mouth. I was trying to break

I Am A Survivor: Sex, Lies, and Abuse

free. I was shaking and panicking at this point. He was going to kill me. I screamed "NO" really loud.

"Deja, Deja," X said, waking me. I jumped up.
"Shit!" I said, realizing it was a dream.
"You, okay?"
"Yeah, I just had a really bad dream."
"Tell me what it was about?"
"Randy was standing in this room. Trying to kill me. It felt so real X."
"It was a dream. It's just me and you, Deja. Nobody else is here," X said, hugging me. "Damn, Deja you are shaking. Come on, let's go to bed."

X grabbed my hand and we headed towards the stairs. X made sure all the doors were locked. He checked the front door and it was unlocked. He locked it. X set the alarm at the front door. I turned around and saw something in the hallway near the kitchen.

"X," I screamed as I pushed him when I saw the gun.

The alarm sounded when the gun went off. I fell to the floor. I felt a sharp pain in my side. I think I was shot. I heard the back door glass break as another shot fired. I saw X run past me trying to see where the person went. X ran out the door. My side started to feel like it was on fire. I screamed. Oh God, all I could think was thank God my babies weren't here. I was breathing fast and I couldn't catch my breath. I heard the sirens, but they sounded so far away. X came back and took his shirt off. He held it to my side and it hurt, but I know he had to apply pressure. I was shaking and scared.

"Deja, I'm right by your side baby. Hold on, the ambulance is almost here. Shit, Deja, hold on baby," X's voice felt like it was fading away as everything went black.

I woke up in the hospital. My parents, Cassie, and Greg were in the room with me. I was looking for X, but I didn't see him anywhere.

"Deja baby. Hey you're awake," my dad said, coming to my side.
"Where's my kids?"
"Mama Clara, James, Mike, and Whitney are at our house with the babies," my mom said, grabbing my hand.

I could see she was crying.

"Where is X?"

I Am A Survivor: Sex, Lies, and Abuse

"He's at the police station trying to figure out what happened and who did this," Greg said, chiming in.
"Hi Deja, I'm so happy to see you're awake," Cassie said.

I could see she was crying too.

"I will get the doctor. He wanted to know when you woke up," Greg said.
"What happened?" I said, as I couldn't recall.
"You were at the house with X. He said you saw someone in the house and pushed him out of the way when the intruder fired and you were shot," my dad said.
"He said he tried to go after them, but he couldn't see them once he got outside. But he said he had cameras around the house and he's trying to see now if the police can see anything on the cameras," my mom said.
"He's so worried about you Deja. He has been calling and texting every 20 minutes. I am going to call him now so you can talk to him," Cassie said.

Cassie called X's phone.

"Hello, is Deja awake?" I heard X say.
"Yes, she is awake X," Cassie said.

X called Cassie on video call. Cassie answered and turn the phone towards me.

"Oh God, Deja, baby it's so good to see your face. I love you," X said, smiling.
"I love you too, X," I said, with tears coming down.
"Baby, I'll be there in a little bit. I was just finishing up with the police. I will be there soon, Deja," X said.
"Okay, baby I will see you soon," I said, and then X hung up.

I couldn't feel any pain right now. The doctor walked in the room.

"Mrs. Thomas, how are you feeling? I am Dr. Drum. I just wanted to check on you and see what your pain level is right now."
"Hello, Dr. Drum, I am feeling okay. Right now, I can't feel any pain."
"Well, that's probably the medication. We had to do an emergency surgery and we were able to get the bullet out. Nothing was damaged and all major organs were missed. So, right now it's just going to be monitoring how well you heal. I do want to run a few more tests and maybe if everything is looking good, we can have you out of here by Saturday morning," Dr. Drum said. He left the room.
"What's today?" I said, thinking I have to stay until Saturday.
"Today is Friday, Deja," my mom said.
"Wait what? I've been in the hospital for two days," I said, confused.

I Am A Survivor: Sex, Lies, and Abuse

"Baby girl you were out of it. You lost a lot of blood. The doctor was hoping you would wake up today, but he didn't know for sure," my dad said.

I couldn't believe it. I was in the hospital for two days. I wanted to see X. I needed to know he was okay. 30 minutes passed and I saw Greg standing at the door talking to someone, but I couldn't see who he was talking to. Greg looked upset about whatever was being said. Greg walked in the room and I saw X behind him. I was so relieved to see X.

"Hey baby," X said, coming to kiss me.
"X, are you okay?" I said, so worried.
"I'm fine Deja. I was worried about you more than anything."
"What did the police say?"
"We will talk about that later. Right now, I want you to focus on getting better. I talked with the doc. He said everything looks good."
"X, what happened at the police station?" I said again.
"Not here Deja. I promise I will tell you everything," X kissed my hands and sat next to me.

My parents, Cassie, and Greg went home. They had been up here since Wednesday night. X said he would stay with me tonight. He talked about the house being worked on and he was going to make sure the place was secured. He was changing the locks to automatic locks and adding more security features around the house to make it safer.

X wouldn't tell me about what happened at the police station. So, we just started watching TV and X made himself comfortable on the couch. I went to sleep after the nurse came in and checked on me.

Dr. Drum came in the next morning and said all my tests came back good and he was okay with releasing me. He gave X instructions on how to take care of my wound and change the bandages. And then we headed to my parents' house. X said everyone was at my parents' house and we would be staying in a hotel tonight, but he said the family wanted to see me first.

We made it to my parents' house. And everyone was happy to see us. Mama Clara started crying. Whitney was crying. James and Mike said they were worried about me. My mom had been crying since yesterday so she was still crying. My dad was worried, but he was tough. I got to see my babies and kiss on them. I couldn't really hold Manny yet and that upset me, but X held him and let me kiss on Manny. Amara was just all over the place, but she let me get some kisses. X didn't have us stay too long, maybe two hours. He said I needed to go rest and lay down and of course everyone agreed. I was just happy to be out of the

I Am A Survivor: Sex, Lies, and Abuse

hospital. I hugged everyone and my parents said they would keep my babies for me. Mama Clara said she was staying with my parents so she would help too.

Mike, Whitney, and James were staying at the same hotel as us. And X said Micah and Cash would be monitoring the hotel tonight for safety.

We made it to the hotel and X checked us in. We were on the 14th floor. The whole floor was our suite. We got off the elevator and walked into the suite. My side was starting to hurt. I sat down on the couch holding my side.

"Deja, what's wrong?"
"Ugh, it hurts. I was fine until right now," I said, still holding my side.
"I think the medication may have worn off; you had it about 4 hours ago. You may need some more. Hold on, I will get you something to drink," X said, going to the kitchen.

I laid back on the couch. X brought me some water and my medication. I took it.

"So, can we talk about what happened now?" I said, not forgetting.
"Deja," X paused.

I could see he was tightening his jaw again as he sat on the table in front of me.

"It was Randy. He is walking again. I was told he did intensive physical therapy and he learned how to walk again."

X looked so upset.

"He disappeared after the last incident. I had my people tracking him for the longest, but he left town and we lost all contact with him. I didn't know he was off training to get better so he could come back to fuck with us," X said, punching his fist into the table. "The cops are also looking at him for Tammy's death. He was the one who drugged her after I left the apartment to meet up with you that day."

"That day after Tammy got upset and kicked me and Liz out of the house. When Randy went upstairs, he drugged Tammy?" I said, trying to figure it out.
"Yeah, Tammy was drugged by Randy. After you left, I was coming outside to meet you at the hotel, your car was pulling out of the driveway of Tammy's apartment when I left. I saw Randy in passing, but I had no idea what his plans were."
"Randy has been behind all of this?"

I Am A Survivor: Sex, Lies, and Abuse

"When you told me what Tammy said about me getting Eddie to drug Liz and I had Randy drug Tammy. That shit pissed me off, because I would never do that to anyone, especially not Tammy. And I told Tammy that."
"Wait, you told Tammy when?" I said, confused.
"After I left the house and told you not to leave, but you skipped town on me. Greg let me know where Tammy was and I went to go talk to her."
"So, that was the business you had to go take care of?" I said, a little upset.

"Yeah, Deja it was. I went to see Tammy. I wanted to make things right between us. I wanted her to know I didn't have Randy drug her and I didn't do anything to Liz. The only thing I did was give her money for doing her part for helping me get you. What Randy did, had nothing to do with me. I just wanted her to know that I cared about her and would never hurt her like that. I loved her. I saw how frail and sick she looked. I wanted to help her, but she told me no. I was pissed that Randy did that shit. Tammy was a good girl; she didn't deserve that," X said angry.

"Where's Randy now?"
"We don't know. He went back in hiding," X said frustrated.
"Hmmm," I said, thinking.
"Deja, talk to me. What's bothering you?"

I looked at X. I wiped away my tears. I didn't want to cry.

"Talk to me Deja," X said, again.
"I know Tammy was before me and I know you loved her. But I can't help to think you were still in love with her. The way you cried for her and talked about her like she meant so much more. I don't know, I guess I feel a little jealous. Or maybe I'm just emotional right now. So much has happened," I said, wiping my tears.
"No, Deja, I love you and you are my world. I just don't do well with death at all. I did love Tammy, but like I told you before she was not the one for me. You are my everything and I am happy I got you, baby," X said, kissing my hands.
"Why me though? You didn't know me. What was it about me?"

"Deja, you were more than beautiful to me when I saw you. When I came to Columbus, I saw how you carried yourself. You were sweet and innocent. You had class and seemed very well mannered. You were what I wanted instantly and I knew you would be everything to me. I didn't see that in Tammy. Tammy was wild, loud, and sometimes feisty. She knew how to be submissive but she also had a wild jealousy side to her. I didn't see her as someone I could marry. I needed someone like you. I wanted you. I knew it when I first saw you."

"So, what do we do now? Randy hasn't been caught?"

I Am A Survivor: Sex, Lies, and Abuse

"We go to New Jersey. He thinks we are in Columbus so we leave like we were planning too anyway," X said.
"Okay," I said, shaking my head yes.
"I think me and you will go to New Jersey first. I will send for the kids later. Micah and Cash will come with us to New Jersey. Then Greg and Cassie will bring our kids once we know everything is safe."

I started to cry again, but I shook my head yes. I really think my emotions were all over the place.

"Deja, everything will be fine."
"I know, but I hate this."
"I know Deja me too. But I will find him and end this," X said, serious.

****

We have been in New Jersey for a week now. Our kids were still in Ohio. X said he wanted the kids to stay with my parents until after my event so they would be in Ohio for another two weeks. I hated that, but I wanted them to be safe. So far everything seemed okay in New Jersey, but X wanted to wait to bring them here. Cassie would be coming to New Jersey next week to help me with the event and then her and Greg would go back to Ohio to pick up our kids. I wanted to see my kids, but I guess video calls were all I could do for now.

Senator Grace was keeping me busy with planning the event for this art gallery. We finally found the right venue and as far as the guest list we had a lot of important people already registered to attend. X was busy with his businesses, but he was very supportive with my event. I was super excited. I was trying to be okay with everything. I was preparing for this event, but I was worried Randy wasn't done with us. I was hoping he didn't know we were in New Jersey and things would be okay. But keeping busy with Senator Grace was keeping me focused.

"X, baby," I said, going into X's office.
"Yea, Deja."
"Hey baby, I am going to the venue today with Senator Grace. I just wanted to let you know. Can you help me with my bandage, before I get in the shower?"
"Yea, I'll be in there in a minute," X said.

I went to the bathroom to turn the shower on. I brushed my teeth and took my clothes off. X came in a few minutes later and pulled the bandage off.

"OUCH," I yelled.

I Am A Survivor: Sex, Lies, and Abuse

"Sorry Deja," X said, kissing me.
"That hurt, X,"
"I didn't mean to hurt you. I just know going slow hurts more."

I looked at my wound in the mirror and it was healing pretty good. I jumped in the shower. X jumped in the shower with me. We hadn't had sex since I was shot. I know I was ready for some action and I could tell X was ready too. He has been frustrated all week. X didn't waste no time as he began to kiss me hard. He turned me around and pushed my chest into the shower wall and lifted my ass to slide inside me. He immediately started pounding hard and fast. X moaned "Damn, Deja I missed this pussy." He felt so good inside me. I could feel myself about to cum. The chills started and my body was shaking. I moaned "Damn, X I'm about to cum." X moved deeper and harder. I was cumming hard. He released too.

We finished washing up and got out of the shower. X helped me put on a fresh bandage. X got dressed and went back to his office after kissing me and telling me to have a good day. I finished getting dressed and headed out. Micah was my security for the day so he was waiting outside for me by the car. He opened the door for me. The driver took us to the venue to meet Senator Grace. We pulled up and Senator Grace was waiting at the door. We got out of the car and Micah stayed outside while me and Senator Grace went inside the venue.

"Well, here we are finalizing the plans for the big event. Deja, it's almost sold out too," Senator Grace said, so excited.
"I can't believe this is even happening. I thank you Senator Grace for this opportunity," I said, in awe.
"Call me Grace and yes this is going to be such a great event," Grace said, grabbing my wrist.

I pulled away feeling a little awkward at her grabbing my wrist. I crossed my arms in front of me so she didn't try to grab me again.

"Grace I really appreciate everything you did and I like working with you. This whole event is exciting to me," I said, ignoring the fact she tried to grab my wrist.
"Deja, it is a pleasure to work with you. When X told me you were an artist, I wanted to work with you and when he showed me some of your work. I fell in love with your art," Grace said, walking close to me.

I stepped away from her.

"X, showed you, my art?"

I Am A Survivor: Sex, Lies, and Abuse

"Yes, when I was in Columbus, I met X at your home and he showed me your artwork," Grace smiled. "You know X, speaks so highly of you, you are all he talks about. His love for you is mesmerizing," Grace said, coming closer again.

I didn't know if she was interested in me or X at this point, but she was making me uncomfortable.

"Yes, I love my husband just the same. He is my everything," I said, reassuring her.
"Well, I can see that too," Grace said, walking away from me.

I sighed in relief; she was catching on.

"So, I will have Cassie bring the paintings next week and help get things prepared. I know you have the caterer set up, and the decorations. I just have to pick up the brochures for the event, they have already been ordered. And X of course wants us to have security at the event so he is setting that up."
"Okay, well it looks like everything is ready to go for the big day. This is going to be amazing. I am thrilled to be doing this with you, Deja. I have to admit you are on top of this, and I have to say I see exactly why X keeps you protected," Grace said, looking me up and down, and making reference to X wanting security.
"Well, so are we done here for today?" I said, ready to go.
"Yes, I think we will meet again the day before to go over final details," Grace said, walking towards me brushing against me as she passed.
"Okay, Grace, well I will see you later," I said, walking out the door.

I can't believe she was really hitting on me. I thought she was more into X than me, but I guess I was wrong. I couldn't wait to tell X when I got home. X was in the kitchen washing dishes. I shared with him how Senator Grace was acting.

"Hmmm, so Grace has a thing for my wife. I don't know if I should be jealous or turned on," X said, being sarcastic.
"X, it's not funny. I don't like girls like that."

X picked me up and sat me on the counter and stood between my legs.

"Hmmm, it sounds kind of sexy to me," X said, kissing my neck.
"Well, I thought she was into you at the Gala, but she made me very uncomfortable today."
"Oh, so you weren't into it?"
"X, hell no."
"Deja," X paused and put his hand up my shirt to squeeze my breast. "You didn't feel turned on by it?"

I Am A Survivor: Sex, Lies, and Abuse

"No, X. It's nothing I want to experience," I said, taking a deep breath as X was turning me on.
"You seem like you are turned on now," X said as he put his hands down my pants and felt my wetness.
"I'm turned on by you, X. Not her."
"You're turned on by me?" X said, kissing my breast as he had my shirt off now.
"Yes, X only you," I said as I felt the chills.
"Hmmm," X said, massaging my clitoris now.
"X," I moaned as he was making me feel so good.
"Deja," X said, as he lifted me up to take my pants and panties off.

X unbuckled his pants and I could see he was hard. X bent down and put my leg on his shoulder. I leaned back on the counter as X put his mouth on my clitoris. I moaned as it felt good. X massaged my clitoris twirling his tongue. I was getting super wet. My breathing was increasing. I could feel myself close to cumming. My legs were beginning to shake and X was massaging faster. I moaned as the intensity was rising. "X, I'm about to cum," I moaned loudly. X put his fingers in my pussy moving in and out I exploded. X got up and kissed me. He buckled his pants up. I could see he was still hard. I was confused why he stopped. X walked out of the kitchen leaving me on the counter. I jumped down and grabbed my clothes.

"X, what are you doing? We were not done," I said, following behind him.

X didn't say anything. I followed him to the bedroom.

"X, why are you ignoring me?" I said, confused about what just happened.

X turned around staring me up and down. I was naked standing in front of him. I had thrown my clothes on the floor.

"I want you Deja, but I want you, my way," X said, tightening his jaw.
"X, what does that even mean," I said, a little nervous.

X went to the drawer and pulled out his black bag. I already knew where this was going. I wasn't onboard.

"Lay on the bed, Deja," X said, stern.

I hesitated but I went to lie on the bed. X pulled out the black silky scarf. He got on the bed and tied it around my eyes so I couldn't see.

"I won't put the handcuffs on as long as you cooperate," X said.

I Am A Survivor: Sex, Lies, and Abuse

"Okay, X just don't hurt me," I said, nervous.
"You will feel some pain, but it will be a lot of pleasure," X smirked, "But keep your hands above your head or I will pull out the handcuffs."

I shook my head in agreement. I couldn't see anything. X touched my stomach and I jumped from the unexpected touch.

"Deja, the things I have been waiting to do to you," X whispered in my ear.

I let out a sigh. I was definitely nervous. Just when I thought I was figuring him out he always had something else up his sleeve. I heard X cut on the vibrator or it sounded like the vibrator. He touched my leg with it first. I could feel the vibration. He then placed it on my clitoris and my whole body jumped as I moaned.

"Deja, be still," X said.
"I can't X, it's super sensitive when you do that."

X put the vibrator on my clitoris again. I moaned so loud trying not to move. I was beginning to shake. "Deja," X said. I moaned "I'm sorry X, fuck it's hard to stay still." The chills were already running through me. My pussy was throbbing. I was losing control as the vibration was sensitive and sending me overboard. "Shit, X I'm about to cum," I moaned. X pulled the vibrator away. I screamed "NO."

"Deja, you cum when I tell you to cum," X said.
"Please, X I want to cum, baby," I begged.

X put the vibrator inside me and turned it on. I began to moan and feel the sensations again. X put his mouth on my clitoris and my legs started shaking again. I felt the intensity rising and I was about to cum. I leaned my head in the pillow as I knew I was going to cum hard. I could feel my pussy throbbing and the heat rising. I moaned as the feeling was almost there. X pulled the vibrator out and stopped again.

"Shit, X please. I just want you to fuck me now," I begged.
"Deja, you weren't going to tell me you were about to cum?" X said, a little upset.
"X, please baby this is torture."
"Stop being defiant. Tell me when you are about to cum, Deja," X said, stern.
"Baby, please don't do this. I don't like this," I said, grabbing his arm.
"Deja, did I tell you to move?" X said, putting my arm back above my head.
"X, baby I'm sorry. Please fuck me, X," I said, still begging.

I Am A Survivor: Sex, Lies, and Abuse

I felt X move off of the bed. He came back and grabbed my wrist. He put the handcuffs on me and hooked me to the head board somehow. I couldn't move. Fuck, I made him mad now and I couldn't move or see anything. X walked away again and I didn't hear or feel him anywhere close. I was getting nervous. Finally, I felt X get back on the bed. He slammed the vibrator in my ass and I screamed in pain. He cut it on immediately. Shit, that was painful, but the vibration was making me wet. I didn't know how to feel.

The intensity was rising and the sensation was crazy. I had chills running through me. I felt like I was going to cum, but I couldn't. My body was reacting and shaking. I wanted to cum so bad. I started moving my hips. I felt so close to cumming. X grabbed my hips and put his mouth on my clitoris again. I screamed in moans as the feeling was amazing. "X, baby please let me cum," I begged. X continued to eat me out and send my body into sensational chills. He was driving me crazy, but it felt so good at the same time. Why was he like this? Why did he like doing this to me? My mind was going crazy with questions as I kept begging him to fuck me and let me cum. X pulled the vibrator out still massaging my clitoris. I yelled out a loud moan as I could feel I was about to explode. X stopped and jammed his dick inside me fast and hard. I moaned as it was painful and pleasurable at the same time. I immediately exploded when I heard X say "Cum baby." I cried as I was cumming. It felt so good.

X flipped me over and starting fucking me harder, deep, and fast. I was cumming like crazy with every stroke. My whole pussy was throbbing and sensitive to his stroke. I couldn't control myself as my legs were getting weak and my body was shaking. "Fuck, X what are you doing to me? I can't stop cumming," I moaned. "Yeah, baby keep cumming for me," X moaned as he started going harder. I came as the words left his mouth. I was shaking in ecstasy as my body was reacting to X. Shit, the sensations were so heightened and it felt so good. "Fuck, Deja that pussy is pulsating. I'm about to cum hard," X whispered. I leaned my head back and felt my legs go weak as I exploded one more time as X released. X got up and uncuffed me. I couldn't move my legs and my body was weak. X took the scarf off. I just laid there staring at him. My breathing was heavy and my legs were still shaking. He leaned down and kissed me.

"Mmmmmh, that's how I like it, Deja," X said, walking to the bathroom.

I couldn't say anything. I was just so worn out and exhausted from what he just did to me. X came out of the bathroom. He laid on the bed next to me and opened my legs, they were still shaky. He took a warm rag and cleaned me up. My clitoris was so sensitive I jumped when he touched it. X smiled and kissed me.

I Am A Survivor: Sex, Lies, and Abuse

X turned the TV on and began watching it. He cuddled me and put his hand on my pussy.

"Deja, this pussy is mine and I'm going to tame it to cum when I say cum," X whispered in my ear. "Yeah, I feel that pussy getting wet for me now."

He wasn't lying, my pussy was already reacting to his touch and his words. It was like he was playing some kind of mind control game. I wasn't upset about it, but it was making me crazy for him.

"Cum for me, Deja," X whispered in my ear.

Shit, I moaned and my whole body jumped as I felt my pussy responding to his words. Fuck, I think I just came from him telling me to. Yeah, he was doing something to me.

"Good girl," X said, as he felt me jump and my pussy got wetter.

X lifted my leg to my stomach and pushed his dick inside me. I moaned as I felt how hard he was already. He pushed deep inside me. My pussy began to throb from feeling him inside me. He didn't move, he just laid inside me. My pussy was getting super wet and I had chills. I started to move on his dick as I was feeling hot and ready.

"Deja," X said as he grabbed my hips to stop me from moving. "I want to lay like this don't fucking move."
"X, you inside me like this is turning me on. I want to fuck you."
"Cum for me Deja," X said, still holding my hips.
"Fuck," I screeched as I felt my pussy jerk when he said that and I got wetter.
"Good girl," X said, kissing my neck.

Shit, he was driving me crazy with how my pussy was really reacting to his words. He laid inside me for like 2 hours just whispering every 10-20 minutes "Cum Deja," and my pussy would cum. I didn't understand how in sync my body was to his words. Finally, he fucked me hard and fast until we both exploded.

****

It was finally the day of my art gallery. Cassie, X, Greg, and I met Senator Grace at the venue at 2pm. We were doing a once over before the event tonight which started at 7:30pm. We were supposed to come yesterday, but the staff didn't have everything set up yet so we decided to come through today. We walked into the venue and Grace was already looking over everything. It looked amazing.

I Am A Survivor: Sex, Lies, and Abuse

The set up was well designed. One side was set up for the food and then the other side had the table and chairs. Grace decided she wanted to do a speech, before showing off the art. There was a curtain behind the podium where the art gallery would be. So, the idea was for the guest to come in the door to the food side, then find their seats for Grace to speak. And once everyone finished eating, they could head into the gallery to view the art, once we opened the curtains.

We all walked into the art room. It was beautiful.

"Damn, Deja this is amazing," X said, admiring the paintings.
"Thank you,"
"Distracted Love is the theme?" X asked.
"Yeah, it is," I said, in awe of how well everything looked.
"What inspired the title?" X said, grabbing my wrist.
"You did X."
"Oh yeah, how so?"
"Our whole relationship, how I met you was a distraction. You were my distraction X. You took my concentration off of the stuff around me and made me fall in love with you even when I didn't know if I should. But I did anyway, and I love you so much. So, distracted love is my theme."
X kissed me. "I love you too, Deja. Don't be too upset though," X said, holding my wrist.
"What X?"
"I'm going to miss the beginning of the event tonight. I have a business meeting I couldn't reschedule. I'm sorry."
"X, seriously," I said, upset.
"I know Deja, but I will be here right after the meeting. And Greg will record what I miss."
"Fine, what can I say."

X whispered in my ear.

"Deja, don't be defiant. I will make you cum right here."

I took a deep breath and closed my eyes as I felt the chills.

"Okay, X," I said, complying.

X kissed me and squeezed my ass. I turned around and saw Grace watching us. X looked at me and smiled.

"Don't you guys love the set up," Grace said, walking towards us.

I Am A Survivor: Sex, Lies, and Abuse

"Oh yeah, my baby did her thing on the artwork," X said, wrapping his arms around me.
"Thank you, baby," I said, holding on to X's arms around me.
"So, we are ready for tonight. I will see you all back here at 6:30pm and doors open at 7pm," Grace said.
"Sounds good Grace. Thank you for this opportunity," I smiled in awe.

We left. X left to go handle his business. I went home until it was time to come back. Cassie and Greg went home. Cassie said they would be back to get me later.

I went home and made something to eat. I had the hair stylist coming at 5pm. I ate then took a shower. I had a slim fitting black dress that was above the knee with a low open back. The V-neck front showed the crease of my breast. It was a beautiful dress. Alicia picked it out and I had to call to thank her for a great pick. I had some open toe black heels that complimented the dress. I threw on a robe. I didn't want to get dressed until after the hair stylist completed my hair.

It was 5pm and the hair stylist was at the door. Her name was Sam. Alicia recommended her. She styled my hair with some loose curls and pinned up the right side with a red rose pendant. It was beautiful. I got dressed after Sam left and Cassie and Greg were outside by 6:15pm.

"Ooh Deja, you look stunning," Cassie said, when I walked outside.
"Thank you, Cassie. You look good too," I said, admiring her short slim fitting blue dress.

We arrived at the venue a little after 6:30pm. Grace was already inside telling the caterers how to set up the food. I walked around to make sure everything else was still good. I put the brochures at the door for people to grab when they came in. I checked in with security. Greg had at least five security guards inside the venue and three outside securing the parameter.

Before I knew it, it was 7:15pm and people were coming in. Grace and I stood up front to welcome people as they came in. I was watching as the place was filling up. We definitely had maybe 100 people in the building now. I was shocked by the crowd, and there were still people coming. Cassie was shocked too and excited for me. Everyone came in, grabbed some food and took a seat.

Me, Cassie, and Greg sat in the front reserved seats as Grace stood at the podium. It was now 7:30pm and Grace started with welcoming everyone to the Distracted Love Art Gallery.

I Am A Survivor: Sex, Lies, and Abuse

"I am so excited that each and every one of you decided to grace us with your presence. As we are here for a fabulous creative experience of art. I want to say that all proceeds of this event will be donated to New Jersey's Community Project which helps to rebuild our communities by providing mentors, rec centers, and parks for every community. It also focuses on the needs of the community to help families in need. I want to thank Xavier Thomas for his support on this event and his wife Deja Thomas for the lovely artwork. I hope you all enjoy the most creative style of a beautiful work of art called Distracted Love. Thank you."

Everyone clapped as Grace stepped down from the podium. The curtains were dropped and the room for the artwork was open for people to view. I heard so many oohs and aahs as people walked into the art room. I felt so good inside. Cassie grabbed my arm in excitement from the reactions. We headed to the art room to see the paintings and listen to the reactions.

"This piece right here is a masterpiece," a male voice said behind me.
"Well, thank you," I said, admiring the compliment.
"You are the artist?" the voice said.
"Yes, I am Deja Thomas," I said, reaching out my hand to shake his.
"I am Abraham Mitchell," he said, grabbing my hand to kiss it.

I quickly moved my hand away.

"Nice to meet you, Abraham. So, what is it about this piece that makes it a masterpiece?"
"I love the sexual attraction in this piece. It's like the man and the woman in the picture are just holding each other, but you can feel the chemistry between them. I can sense the admiration of the art and how it reflects the appeal between the two. The way she looks at him, her eyes tell a lot."
"Thank you for that reflection," I said, amazed at how much he saw.
"You're welcome. You have amazing talent."
"Thank you,"
"Abraham, how are you? I see you are really admiring this piece here. Mrs. Thomas is very good at her work," Grace said, interrupting.
"Senator Grace, good to see you. And I'm doing great. I love this event you put together. I was just telling Mrs. Thomas how amazing her talent is."
"Yes, I agree. Her paintings speak volumes," Grace said, smiling at me.
"Thank you, Grace."
"Abraham, do you mind if I steal Mrs. Thomas away for a minute," Grace said, grabbing my wrist.
"Not at all. It was lovely meeting you Mrs. Thomas."
"Likewise," I said as Grace pulled me away.

I Am A Survivor: Sex, Lies, and Abuse

Grace walked me over to the far end of the room.

"Hey, Deja, you might not want to talk to Abraham like that," Grace said, sounding serious.
"We were just talking about my painting," I said, a little confused.
"Abraham is a very well-known entrepreneur here in New Jersey. And he is an Alpha male and Dom like your husband. He can see that you are a Sub. He will take advantage quickly not caring that you're married," Grace said.
"Excuse me," I said, lost.

Grace looked at me funny.

"You know your husband is a Dom, right?"
"What exactly is that?"
"Hmmm, X is into BDSM Deja," Grace said, shocked that I didn't know.
"What exactly is that?"
"Bondage, Dominance, Discipline, Submission, and Masochism."
"And how do you know this?" I said, upset.
"Deja," Grace paused, grabbing my wrist again. I pulled away from Grace. "I knew the first day I met X, he carries himself as a Dom. I am a part of the BDSM lifestyle and I knew you were a Sub the first day I saw you and how X handled you let me know too. I guess you just didn't know," Grace said, looking confused.
"So, I'm confused. Did you sleep with my husband?"
"Deja, this is probably not the time to talk about this. We still have to get through this event."
"I think you need to answer my question," I said, angry.
"Deja, I can't answer that."
"Why can't you?" I said, trying not to yell.

I felt someone grab my wrist.

"She can't, because then she would be defying me," X said.

I pulled away from X. I felt my insides on fire. I was starting to panic. What the fuck was he talking about? X grabbed my wrist again. Grace backed up.

"Grace, go ahead and mingle with the guests for now. I will come find you later."
"Yes, Sir X," Grace said, walking away from us.

I was fucking disgusted. She was submissive with X. He was fucking her? What the hell was going on?

"Deja, don't make a scene here. I need you to calm your breathing and we will talk about this later," X said, squeezing my wrist.
"Fuck you, X," I said trying to walk away, but X pulled me back grabbing my waist to position me in front of him. X smiled so no one would expect anything.

X slid his hand down the back of my dress sticking his finger inside me. I gasped as I felt the chills hit me. "Deja, you don't want me to make you cum right here. Calm your nerves."

I took a few deep breaths and calmed my breathing. X pulled his fingers out of me.

"And we are also going to talk about this fucking dress when we get home too," X said, still holding me.

I put a smile on my face as people passed by us. I saw Abraham looked over our way. He looked pissed. I felt X squeeze my wrist again. I think X was upset too. I wanted to get away from X, I was so upset, but I had to pretend to be cool right now. Cassie walked up to us with Greg.

"Deja, guess what?" Cassie said, excited.
"What?" I said, trying to be calm.
"Your artwork has been sold every last piece. We raised over $200,000 from your work girl," Cassie said, giving me a hug pulling me away from X.

I hugged Cassie back and told her we should go get a drink. I was just trying to get away from X, and it worked. I saw him tightening his jaw when I turned to look at him, but I didn't care. I was pissed right now and him holding me was making me even more angry. I drank probably 4 glasses of champagne. Me and Cassie walked around the venue talking to people so X wouldn't come near me. I was on my 6th glass of champagne when I felt someone grab my wrist again. Cassie was busy talking with some people and she didn't pay me any attention. Shit, X must have been getting frustrated with me. I turned around to say something, since I had some liquor courage. But it was Abraham. I tried to pull away, but he had a tight grip.

"Excuse me, Abraham. What are you doing?" I said, confused.
"I think you owe me a thank you for buying some of your paintings," he said, firm.
"Thank you, I didn't know it was you that bought some," I said, trying to pull away again but he did not let go. "Abraham, can you please let me go now."
"I want you to beg," Abraham whispered in my ear.

I looked at Abraham like he lost his mind.

"Abraham, let my wife go," X said, pissed off.
"Xavier, good to see you," Abraham released me. I walked behind X. "I see you don't have your Sub in line. I thought she was a free agent with that dress on."
"I'm sure you thought that, but I'm here now to inform you she's not," X said, tightening his jaw.
"Understood, I will leave you two alone," Abraham said, walking away and leaving the event.

Fuck, X is going to kill me. I could see it all over his face. It was going to be hell if I went home with him. I saw Grace watching from afar. She turned away when she noticed I saw her. X grabbed my wrist and squeezed hard. I tried to smile to not show that I was in pain.

It was now 9pm and everyone was leaving. Grace and I thanked everyone for coming. The place cleared out quickly. I saw X talking with Grace. Cassie and Greg were talking to me. Cassie and Greg congratulated me on selling all of my paintings. I kept watching X and Grace. I saw X grab Grace's wrist and he tightened his jaw. It was pissing me off to even think he was fucking her. I didn't want to go home with him. But I knew I didn't want Cassie to know what was going on. My only option would be to leave with her and Greg. I decided to just let Cassie and Greg leave. Grace left a few minutes after them. Leaving me alone with X.

"You ready to go Deja," X said, walking up on me.
"No, X," I said, stepping back.
"Deja, so you want to do this here?" X said, balling up his fist and tightening his jaw.
"I want you to answer my questions first."
"What questions do you have?" X said, angry.
"Are you fucking Grace?"
"I did years ago, before you Deja. She was my Sub and one of the rules we had was that she couldn't tell anyone she was fucking me."
"Sub? So, she was right about you being a part of BDSM?"
"Yeah, I am part of that lifestyle just like Grace."
"Why didn't you tell me that?"
"Because I knew you wouldn't understand."
"But you consider me your Sub?"
"Not exactly I was still training you, but in that world, you are my Sub."
"That world?"
"Deja, there are events, and gatherings that happen in the BDSM world. If I attend them or when I am around people who are a part of that lifestyle, then yes, they see you as my Sub. But I have not been involved in those events lately, but I have met my Subs in the past at those types of events. Like Grace, I met her at

one. And a lot of my business associates are in that lifestyle and know that I am too."
"And what if I don't want to be a part of that lifestyle."
"Deja, you married me. You are already in it. It's a part of me whether you like it or not."
"So, if I go home with you, you are going to hurt me, right?"
"Deja, I want to punish you, yes, for being defiant," X said, getting pissed as I saw him tightening his jaw.
"Why do you have to punish me?"
"Deja, you're pissing me off. Let's go home now," X said, stern.
"X, I don't want to go home with you. I'm scared of what you want to do to me."

X walked up on me. I backed up until I realized I was against the wall. X grabbed my waist and put his other hand up my dress. X kissed me. I was already shaking scared of what he might do. He started massaging my clitoris. I moaned and felt the chills, but I was also nervous. My breathing was heavy and I could feel my heart beating fast. X continued to massage my clitoris. He then whispered "Cum for me Deja." My pussy immediately responded and I felt my pussy jerk and I exploded. "Good girl," X said, smiling.

"Let's go home Deja," X said, grabbing my wrist. "You keep being defiant. I will make sure you get no sleep tonight."
"X, I don't feel comfortable going home with you," I said, scared.
"I'm done being nice, Deja."

X grabbed me by my waist and walked me to the door. I tried to pull away, but he was holding me tight. He picked me up when he felt me stopping. I tried to fight myself free, but he was stronger than me. He opened the car door and pushed me in the car, he got in and the driver drove off.

I was shaking in fear as I knew this was not going to end well. I was trying not to cry, but I was so scared this would be worse than him hitting me with the belt.

"You really pissed me off today, Deja. That dress had Abraham all over you. And you know damn well you should have changed your dress when you knew I wouldn't be at the event until later. Than you were questioning Grace about me. And you defied me by trying to pull away from me," X paused. "You will be punished for that Deja."
"X, please don't hurt me. I'm scared," I begged.

X looked at me, but he didn't say anything. The driver pulled up to the house and I was scared to move. X pulled me out of the car and carried me in the house over his shoulder. I started to cry and begged X to please not hurt me. He didn't say anything. He threw me on the bed when we got into the room. I climbed off the side of the bed trying to run out of the room, but X grabbed me.

"Deja, you're only going to make this shit worse," X said, dragging me back on the bed.

X pulled out the black bag and put the handcuffs on me as he had me pinned on the bed. He pushed me up to the headboard and pushed out the hook for the handcuffs. I tried to see if I could break free but I couldn't. X put the black silky scarf over my eyes. I cried. I was scared. He ripped my dress off. He took my panties off too. The room got quiet. X moved off the bed. I couldn't see so I couldn't tell if he was in the room anymore. Then I heard him in the room again. I felt him spread my legs. He pushed my legs up, but something didn't feel right.

"X, please let me see," I begged.
"Shut up, Deja," X said.

X sounded like he was on the side of me. I think someone else was in the room, because X wasn't on the bed.

"X, please don't do this," I cried trying to see if I could hear where he was.
"Deja, shut up," X said again, sounding like he was right by me on the side of the bed.

I then felt the person on the bed, put their mouth on my clitoris. I cried out as I knew it was not X.

"X, please who is in the room with us?" I cried.

X didn't say anything. But he then leaned on the bed as I felt him and he started kissing on my breast. I cried as my body was reacting, but I didn't want it too. I didn't know who else was in the room. I felt the chills. And X bit my nipple. I moaned. The person sucking on my clitoris started twirling their tongue and I could feel my pussy getting wetter. I hated this, but my body was still reacting. X kissed me and whispered "Cum for me Deja." I cried as my body began to cum. I moaned loudly and my legs began to shake.

"X, please stop this. I don't want this," I cried.

The person between my legs stopped and I felt them move off the bed. I then felt X position himself between my legs. He slammed his dick inside me and I screeched as it felt painful at first. X started fucking me hard and I felt the other person start kissing my breast and massaging my clitoris. I cried out as my body was shaking, but I was close to cumming. I didn't want this person touching me. But I couldn't stop my body from reacting. My pussy was throbbing and I was getting hot. "Don't you fucking cum, Deja," X said as he pounded harder. I couldn't hold it any longer. I exploded and let out a loud moan. X stopped and I felt a horrible pain hit me in my pussy. Fuck, X had the belt. I screamed. "I FUCKING TOLD YOU NOT TO CUM," X yelled. X jammed his dick inside me again and started fucking me harder. "DON'T YOU DARE CUM, DEJA," X yelled. Fuck I didn't know how to stop it I was trying to hold it. The sensations were getting intense and I could feel I was about to cum again. I tried to hold it by squeezing my pussy around X's dick. Shit, that wasn't working. "X, I can't hold it, please let me cum," I cried praying he wouldn't hit me. "No, Deja," X said.

Fuck! I came. X stopped again and hit me. I screamed in pain. "X, please I can't hold it. I don't know how to control it," I cried. X jammed his dick in me again. The person was still massaging my clitoris and sucking on my breast now. "You cum when I tell you to cum, Deja," X said. X started pounding hard and faster. I tried to focus on my breathing hoping I could get my mind off the sensations to hold off on cumming. My body was shaking. I knew I wasn't going to be able to hold off any longer. I cried as I knew X was going to hit me again, because I was about to cum. "X," I screamed as I was already cumming before I could say anything else. X stopped and hit me again. I screamed. I felt X get up and he took the scarf off of me.

I saw Grace was in our bedroom. I screamed out.

"WHAT THE FUCK? GET THE FUCK AWAY FROM ME. GET ME OUT OF THESE HANDCUFFS," I screamed.
"No, Deja," X said, standing at the end of the bed.

I watched as Grace got on her knees and began to suck X's dick. I was trying my hardest to move my hands to get the cuffs off the hook. I wanted to fuck them both up. I was so pissed. She just kept sucking him off. X started moaning. I couldn't believe what was happening. I was so shocked. I was disgusted. Grace sucked off X until he came. Grace got up and left after X released. Grace looked at me and smiled. I wanted to smack that bitch. X didn't let me out of the handcuffs until he walked Grace out. He came back and let me out of the handcuffs. I jumped up and ran to the bathroom. I slammed the door and locked it. I stood against the door.

"Deja, open the fucking door," X said, trying to open the door.
"Fuck you, X."
"Deja, open the fucking door," X said, banging on the door.

I Am A Survivor: Sex, Lies, and Abuse

I felt so disgusted. I started to feel queasy. I ran to the toilet and started throwing up. X busted open the door.

"Shit, Deja," X said, calming down once he saw me throwing up. "Are you pregnant again?"
"Fuck you, X," I mumbled as I sat over the toilet.
"Deja," X said, leaning down to rub my back.
"Don't fucking touch me. I hate you," I said, backing away from him.
"Deja, don't say that. I'm sorry baby."
"Get away from me."
"So, you think you're going to leave me now?"
"Yes," I said, pissed off.
"Deja, you ain't going nowhere. You're mine. You hear me?" X said, grabbing my neck and choking me.
"X stop," I said, trying to stop him from choking me.
"Deja, you will not leave me."

X leaned over me and I kicked him in his balls as he was still naked.

"FUCK!" X yelled as he fell to the ground.

I jumped up immediately and ran out of the bathroom. I grabbed my dress and threw it on. The straps were torn, but I just needed to throw something on. I ran out the house grabbing my purse at the door. I ran down the street looking for a neighbor to have their light on or something. I made it about 6 houses down and saw that someone had their light on. I ran to the door and banged on it.
"Yes," a woman answered the door.
"Please, I need your help. Please call the cops. My husband is trying to kill me."

A man came to the door and told her to let me in.

"What's going on?" the man said, while the lady called the police.
"My husband is trying to kill me," I said, panting as I was out of breath.
"Okay sit down," the man said, leading me to the living room.

The police showed up 20 minutes later. X was outside talking to the police. I freaked as I saw him outside. The cops looked at me while X was saying whatever bullshit he was telling them. The cops came in the house after talking with X.

"Hello Deja Thomas. Is that your name?" the Officer said.
"Yes, I am Deja."

"I am Officer Tim Lacey. I talked with your husband outside. He said there was a miscommunication between you two and you've been drinking. Is this correct?"
"No, my husband choked me and I thought he was going to kill me," I said, upset.
"Have you been drinking?" the Officer asked again.
"Yes, but only a few drinks. He is trying to kill me," I said, frustrated.
"Are you wanting to press charges?" the Officer said.
"No, I want to go home to get a change of clothes and I want an escort to the airport."
"Mrs. Thomas we can assist with that, but are you sure you don't want to press charges?"
"Look, I don't care to press charges. I want to leave this state and get away from him."
"Okay, we can take you back to the house to get you changed and escort you to the airport."

I thanked the man and woman who let me in their house. They stated their names were Breanna and Marcus. The Officer walked with me outside to their cruiser. X was gone. I figured he went back to the house. I made sure the Officer would go in the house with me. He said he would. We made it back to the house and we walked to the door. X opened the door.

"Thank you, Officer, for bringing her back home," X said.
"Well, don't thank me yet. I am just here to assist with Mrs. Deja getting some clothes and then we are escorting her out of here for the night," the Officer said.
"Sorry, Officer but I am not allowing you in my house," X said, standing at the door.
"Mrs. Deja stated she wanted to be escorted in the house," the Officer stated.
"I know my rights and this is my house. I do not want you to enter," X said.
"It's okay, it's not worth it. We can just go," I said, frustrated.
"Deja, you can come in and get some clothes," X said.
"Not alone I'm not."
"Deja, you are going to catch a cold with that ripped dress and no shoes."
"I will manage."
"Fine, I will step outside with the Officer and you can go inside," X said, walking outside.

I went inside and ran to the room to hurry up and find something. I grabbed a t-shirt, bra, jogging pants, socks, and tennis shoes. I came out of the room and X was standing at the door. I should have known he was going to pull some bullshit.

"X, I don't want to cause any trouble. Please move," I said, nervous.

I Am A Survivor: Sex, Lies, and Abuse

"Deja, you're pissing me off with this bullshit. I told you; you are not leaving me," X said, tightening his jaw.

"X, the shit you did tonight was too much. I can't be with you anymore. Let me go."

"I will never do that," X said, so serious.

"OFFICER, I AM READY TO LEAVE," I yelled.

X looked pissed, but he moved out of the way. I walked out of the door and the Officer was waiting for me. X stood in the door as the Officer pulled off. Once the Officer dropped me off at the airport. I went into the airport bathroom to change into the clothes I grabbed. I went to the desk and had the clerk find me a flight to Columbus. I was lucky one was leaving in 30 minutes. I paid for the ticket.

I made it to Columbus at 1am. I was not going to tell my parents what happened. I wasn't planning to tell anyone. I knew I could stay at me and X's house in Columbus for a little bit, before X caught a flight here. I was tired and just wanted to rest. I took a cab to the house.

I was a little nervous to stay here, but I know X changed the locks and secured the place. I made sure the house was locked up and I put a chair under the front door knob just in case. I went upstairs to the bedroom and locked the bedroom door. I laid on the bed. I couldn't even think. I was so shocked. X has lost his damn mind.

Chapter Sixteen: Dominance
"What the fuck is this shit."

I didn't even notice when I fell asleep but I woke up at 10am. I jumped up as I knew X could probably be in Columbus now. I didn't want to sleep too long. I listened at the bedroom door to see if I heard anything. I didn't hear anything. I went to use the restroom. I checked my phone. I had over 20 missed calls from X. I know he had to be in Columbus now. I would take a shower and go see my parents. I was not going to tell them anything, but I wanted to see my babies anyway.

After I was dressed, I grabbed my purse and packed a few clothes items. I knew I would not be staying here tonight. I slowly opened the bedroom door. I didn't hear anything or see anyone. I walked down stairs looking around and everything seemed okay. I moved the chair from the door and walked outside. It was all clear. I got in my car and drove to my parents' house.

I made it to my parents' house. My dad and mom's car were parked outside. They both were home. I went inside. I saw my mom in the living room holding Manny and Amara was watching TV.

"Oh my, look who's home," my mom said, turning Manny to see me.

I wanted to cry, but I held the tears back. I ran to pick up Manny. I kissed all over him. He was just smiling. It felt so good to have my baby in my hands. Amara screamed mommy and hugged my leg. I bent down to kiss her too. I missed my babies. I hugged my mom.

"I thought we weren't going to see you until Saturday," my mom said.
"I missed my babies' mom. I had to come see my babies," I said, kissing on Manny.
"Why is dad here? He didn't have to work?"
"Well, you dad is retired now. Actually, we both are," my mom said, smiling.
"Oh really, who took over the business?"
"X, bought your father's business and he gave us a nice retirement plan. We will never have to work again."
I cringed. "Wow, that's good. X sure knows how to make people happy."
"Oh, X can be a sweetheart at times. He just struggles with the trauma he has been through. But he seems to be doing better with you. Me and your dad have been making some plans to travel though. We are so excited about traveling to different countries and seeing the world. We got a travel agent last week and booked our first trip," my mom said, so excited.

I Am A Survivor: Sex, Lies, and Abuse

"Oh, okay where are you going?"
"We are going on a 2-month trip around Greece, Italy, Spain, and France."
"Wow, you're really taking a trip. I am happy for you both. I am glad that you both are retired and enjoying it. Where is dad?"
"Oh, he is upstairs. He might be asleep. He has been running around with Amara all day. He thought he was going to get her to take a nap and he took a nap instead," my mom said, laughing.
"It's good to see you so happy mom. So, when do you leave?"
"We are leaving on Monday. We knew you would be getting the kids on Saturday so we decided to leave on Monday. But you came early."
"Wow, that's real soon. I guess you and dad were serious about getting away."
"Yes, it is time," my mom said, smiling.

I was truly happy for them. I just hated X was using his money to keep people seeing him as good. But it didn't matter, because I definitely wasn't going to tell my parents anything about what happened now. I will just find a place on the cusp of Columbus to continue to make it seem like I am with X, until I make up my mind on when to tell them that I will be filing for divorce. As long as I am not anywhere in the area where they live and shop, they won't know I'm in Columbus still.

I figured once I find a place, I will make sure to set up visitation with the kids to see their dad so we don't have to go to court for that. I don't want to take nothing from my children. I just know I can't be with X anymore.

I stayed at my parents for a couple of hours. My dad woke up and I talked with him. He was also excited about traveling and being retired. He did ask me how things were going with X. I lied and said things were good. I hugged my parents and left with my kids. I will stay in a hotel tonight and look for an apartment tomorrow.

I checked into the hotel and got the kids settled. I fed Manny and bought Amara some food to eat. X was calling me. I had already ignored another 20 calls today so I knew I would have to answer soon.

"Hello," I said.
"Where are you, Deja?"
"I am safe and with my kids, X."
"So, you told your parents again?"
"Honestly, no I haven't told anyone the stupid shit you did," I said, upset.
"Deja, I want to-," X paused. I could hear him take a deep breath. "Deja, you are really pissing me off. Where are you?"

I Am A Survivor: Sex, Lies, and Abuse

"I'm safe. X, I love you and I'm not trying to hurt you, but I can't do this anymore. I don't like that you feel you need to punish me. It hurts me and scares me. But I want to be fair with you and I am not trying to keep your kids from you. I just hope we can come up with an agreement for visitation. And this time we have to learn to coparent for our kids, because I am not coming back home."

X got quiet, but I could hear him breathing.

"Deja, you will come home, but for now I will make an agreement with you for visitation. I love you too much to let you go. You will come home."
"I will talk to you tomorrow, X," I said, hanging up the phone.

I was done and I was not going to let him think for a second, I would be coming home. I would talk to him tomorrow about a plan for us to arrange pick up and drop offs for us to share custody. But I was not going to put myself in that crazy situation anymore.

The next morning, I got up and got the kids dressed. I had looked at a few places last night on my phone that I wanted to go see today for housing. I found a condo that didn't cost too much that was still in Columbus, but on the east side. I figured if I stayed away from the Dublin area and the northside of Columbus, I would be safe and my parents would never go east so I wouldn't have to worry about them finding out.

I checked out the condo first. It was actually pretty cute. It was a 3-bedroom ranch with a finished basement. I really thought this place would be perfect for me and the kids. I talked with the realtor and told them I would be paying cash. I was able to talk them down to $150,000. I needed to move in ASAP. X had been adding money to my account so I had $300,000 that I moved over to my personal bank account. I was ready to seal the deal. I know the process normally would take weeks, but the agent said they would try to make the process quick for me. I just wanted to be settled in a place before I had to make arrangements for X to have time with the kids.

The agent was able to make the closing to be on Monday. I was going to take my parents to the airport that morning and then close on the house that afternoon. So, me and the kids would have to stay in the hotel until then.

Monday came quickly. I took my parents to the airport that morning. They were happy that they got to see the kids, before they left. They gave us all kisses and hugs. I told them to enjoy themselves and then we left. X, would meet me at our house in Dublin on Thursday to take the kids. X was in Columbus now, but so far

I Am A Survivor: Sex, Lies, and Abuse

if he knew where I was, he was not saying it or showing up to find me. I felt at peace knowing I could move around with no worries of seeing him.
I went to the closing meeting and paid for the condo in cash. The agent gave me the keys and I went shopping for some things for the house. I had the furniture being delivered tomorrow and we had groceries for the house. I did buy me and the kids some clothes, shoes, and necessities. I also got Manny a playpen and me and Amara a blow-up bed until the furniture arrived tomorrow. I bought a TV too. It was nice not being in a hotel and actually in a house. I couldn't wait to cook.

I made some chicken nuggets for Amara and I just made myself a chef salad with some baked chicken. I fed Manny before I ate dinner and he fell asleep minutes after getting full. I laid him in the playpen. Amara finished her food and she went straight to the blow-up bed to lay down. She was tired too. I ate my food and cleaned up the kitchen. I laid down on my blow-up bed and turned the TV on. We were all lying in the living room until the furniture came tomorrow. My phone started to ring.

"Hello,"
"Deja, what's going on? Greg is telling me we have to come back to Columbus," Cassie said, upset.
"Cassie, I don't really want to talk about it," I said, not knowing what to say.
"You know all this moving back and forth is not good for me right now. I know I didn't tell you, but I'm pregnant. I'm 3 months," Cassie said, finally sharing the news.
"Congratulations Cassie," I said, excited. "It's just a lot going on with X's businesses and we are back in Columbus for a little bit."
"I get it. I just don't like moving around like this. But I know Greg loves what he does so I just wanted to vent. It's not a big deal. We still have our house in Columbus, but we just got the house in New Jersey."
"Girl, it comes with the men we chose," I said, making a joke.
"Yes, you're right about that. Because I know X be all over the place," Cassie said, laughing.
"Tell me about it."
"Well, I won't hold you. Kiss my babies for me."
"I will love you, girl."
"Love you too," Cassie said, before hanging up.

I just wasn't ready to tell anyone what was going on. I honestly hated this was happening, but I couldn't stay with X. My phone rang again. It was X.

"Deja, I want to see you," X said, angry.
"X, it's only been 5 days. I will see you on Thursday when I drop off the kids."

I Am A Survivor: Sex, Lies, and Abuse

"Deja this is bull shit. Why don't you just come home? I need to see you."
"X, you need to calm down. I don't want to be nowhere near you while you're angry."
"Why are you doing this, Deja? I need you here with me baby. I'm sick without you. Please come home."
"X, I can't."
"Deja, I'm done playing your stupid little game. I'm outside. Open the door."

I jumped up and hung up the phone. Was he lying? Or was he really outside. I went to the door and peaked out the blinds. There was a car outside. But I couldn't see anything. But it looked like the black cars X would order to drive him around. I wasn't going to open the door. X was calling me back.

"X, go home. I'm not letting you in."
"You don't have to Deja. I have a key."
"What?"
"You're my wife, even if you buy a house without me, you are my wife and whatever you own, I have a right to. Thank your agent she was easy to persuade in getting me a spare key when you did your closing today. I have to say the condo is cute."
Fuck, he was really outside. "X, please just leave me alone. I just want to move on and have peace."
"Deja, you're my wife. It doesn't work like that."

I hung up. I heard someone walking up to the door. I quickly called 911. I hurried and told the operator my address, before X opened the door. I heard the key in the door and I hung up the phone.

"This place is small but it's cute," X said, coming in the door.
"X, why are you here?"
"Because my family is here."
"X, I don't want you here."
"You really thought you were just going to move on and what? Find another man and live happily ever after," X said, tightening his jaw.
"It's not like that. I just needed to get away from you. You scare me X."
"Deja, baby I love you," X said, walking towards me.
"X, please. I'm tired and I just want to go to sleep."
"Who you fucking? You're tired and don't want to be bothered, who you been with Deja? Because it sure wasn't me."
"X, today was a long day. It doesn't mean I was fucking anyone."
"Oh, yeah I'll be the judge of that," X pinned me to the wall and started to take my clothes off.
"X not here, our kids are here."

I Am A Survivor: Sex, Lies, and Abuse

X pulled me to the bedroom and shut the door. He pinned me up against the wall again and finished taking my clothes off. He stuck his finger in my pussy feeling around. Then he started moving his finger in and out of me. I could feel the chills starting, but I was so upset at the same time. X leaned in to whisper in my ear "Cum for me Deja." Fuck, my pussy jerked and I came on que. I moaned as I came. "Good girl," X said, smiling. X turned me around and pressed my chest against the wall. He lifted my ass up and jammed his dick inside me. "Fuck, Deja that pussy is still good," X moaned. I cried as he started pounding hard and fast. I hated that my body was reacting to him, and I didn't want him to even be here. I moaned as the intensity was rising and I could feel myself cumming. My pussy was throbbing and I was getting hot. X whispered "Cum for me Deja." I felt the tears come down my face as I moaned loudly and came. "Damn, Deja I missed this pussy." X fucked me harder and I came two more times before he released.

X pulled up his pants and I put my clothes back on. I wiped away my tears. X grabbed my face and kissed me. I tried to pull away, but he grabbed my waist and pulled me closer to him. I heard a knock on the door. X looked at me. I looked down. X walked to the front and I walked behind him.

X opened the door. "Hello, we received a call about an intruder," the Officer said. X looked at me and then addressed the Officer. "No, that was my wife's mistake. She didn't know I was coming to town today. She thought she was being robbed." X said, putting on a fake laugh.
"Is that the case ma'am?" the Officer said.

X looked at me. I took a deep breath.

"Yeah, I'm sorry I should have called you back, but you know, once I saw it was my husband, I got excited and forgot to call back," I said trying to convince the Officer.
"Okay, what are your names?" the Officer asked.
"I am Xavier Thomas and this is my wife, Deja Thomas. Everything is good here Officer Grant," X said, reading his badge.
"I will decide that, sir," Officer Grant stated. "Mrs. Thomas, are you able to step outside and talk with me?"

I looked at X and he looked pissed. I could see he was tightening his jaw.

"Sure, let me put my shoes on,"

I grabbed my slip-on shoes and walked outside.

I Am A Survivor: Sex, Lies, and Abuse

"Mrs. Deja, I see in our records you have called the police in the past for domestic violence concerns. Now, I know with him being present he maybe persuading your answer. I just want to make sure you're, okay?"
"I really appreciate you, Officer Grant. Look, I really don't want to make a scene with my kids here, and I am not looking to file charges, but I don't feel comfortable sleeping here tonight if he doesn't leave. If you can just stay until I can get my kids in the car and I can go to my parents' house tonight."
"Yes, I can stay until you are safe and away from him."
"Thank you."

I went back inside with Officer Grant. Officer Grant walked X to the back of the house into the bedroom asking to speak with him alone. I grabbed my kids and whatever else I could grab and hurried out of the house, before they walked back up front. I will come back and change the locks tomorrow. I know X wouldn't stay if he knew I wasn't there. I got in the car and drove off.

X was calling my phone probably 20 minutes after we left. I ignored it. I made it to my parents' house. I got inside with the kids and locked the doors. I got the kids in the bed. I went to my old room in my parents' house and laid down. X called maybe 5 more times but I ignored him. I fell asleep soon after I hit the pillow.

I woke up the next morning and got in the shower and dressed before my kids woke up. I got Manny up first to feed him and get him dressed. Amara woke up and I got her dressed and made her some cereal. It was 8am. I already called the locksmith to meet me at the house around 9am. I knew the furniture would be arriving at 10am. We left the house around 8:15am and I headed to the store to also get door stoppers. I met the locksmith at 9am. X was nowhere around. The locksmith changed the locks and gave me the new keys. As he was leaving the furniture truck was arriving. The men put the beds together and brought in the living room furniture. I thanked them and gave them a tip. They left and I turned the TV on for Amara so she could watch her shows.

Manny was lying on the blanket on the floor by Amara. I watched them as Amara was so cute with her brother. She would lean down and kiss him when he would make noises. Amara would say "Shhh, baby I'm watching TV" and then give him a kiss. I watched them for like an hour. Then my phone rang.

"Hello,"
"Hey girl, I just left your house. Is everything okay? I went over there with Greg, but X said he didn't know where you and the kids were. He seemed pretty upset."
"I'm okay," I paused. I guess it was hitting me now. I started to cry.
"Oh, Deja, where are you? I want to see you girl. What's going on?" Cassie said, worried.

I Am A Survivor: Sex, Lies, and Abuse

I told her where I was. She hung up and said she was on her way. She said she was alone. Greg stayed back with X. Cassie showed up 45 minutes later. I opened the door for her and she hugged me. I started crying again.

"What's going on Deja? You got your own place?"
"I had to Cassie. I have been dealing with bullshit for a while now and I know I should have told you, but I was trying to make it work for my kids. I didn't want anyone to hate X if I was going to stay. But I can't go back. He is crazy. He choked me last week and he has been abusive on multiple occasions," I said, feeling relieved to get it out.
"Oh, Deja, why didn't you say anything? You have been dealing with this all by yourself. Girl, you don't deserve that. Did you report this to the police?"
"I called them last night and I have called in the past. But I don't want to press charges. I don't want to mess up his reputation. I just want him to leave me alone. I thought I just wanted him to stop abusing me, but I know he won't stop. So, now I just want him to let me go. We can co parent and live separately."
"Did you tell your parents?"
"No, not this time. They knew about the first time I left him. But because I went back and they were so upset about it. I didn't want to tell them it happened again. I knew that they would be upset again. And besides, they went on a 2-month vacation thanks to X providing them with an early retirement plan. I didn't want to tell them that I was leaving X when they just started liking him again. It's so crazy, like I am listening to myself protect him even though he hurts me. God, I'm so stupid."
"Deja, you're not stupid. You love him. And I get that, but what he is doing is wrong."
"Excuse me," I said, running to the bathroom. I threw up.

Cassie came to the bathroom door.

"Are you okay Deja?"
"No," I said, flushing the toilet and rinsing out my mouth. "I took a pregnancy test. I'm pregnant. I go to the doctors tomorrow to confirm it."
"Oh wow. Deja what are you going to do? Are you going to tell X?"
"I mean if the doctor confirms it, then yea I'm going to have to tell him."
"But what is that going to look like? Aren't you scared about this?"
"Of course I'm scared, Cassie. I don't want to be a single mom with 3 kids. But I can't go back. Hell, he never wants to use protection, I can't use birth control pills, because he won't allow it. I go back and I will have 4 kids before I know it, still being abused."
"I mean I was thinking have you thought about an-," I cut Cassie off before she said it.

"I will not go that route. I love my babies no matter what. And I will do whatever I have to do as a single mom to make things good for us. I can handle 3 kids. I will not kill my baby," I said, stern.
"Okay, well if you need any help, you know I am here for you," Cassie said, supporting me.
"I know. Thank you, Cassie, for being here."

We talked for hours and played with the kids. I made lunch for everyone and fed Manny. It was almost 3pm and Cassie said she had to go. I hugged her and she reassured me she was here for me. I thanked her. She opened the door to leave and X was standing at the door. Fuck! I was too tired to fight with him. I was emotionally drained and I had nothing left in me. Cassie looked at me worried.

"Don't worry, I won't hurt her," X said, coming into the house talking to Cassie.
"I'm sure she told you everything."
"I honestly don't know what you're talking about, X," Cassie said. "Deja, call me in the morning."
"I will. Thank you, Cassie, for coming to help me," I said, making it seem like Cassie just came to help me with something.
"You're welcome girl. See you later," Cassie said leaving.

I sat down on the couch next to Amara who was sleeping. Manny was in the playpen sleeping too.

"Hmmm, so you ain't running your mouth. So, what did you tell Cassie about you staying here?" X said, with a smart mouth.
"I told her we were having some disagreements and we're taking a break."
"That was some real bullshit you pulled last night with the damn police officer."
"I told you X, I don't feel safe with you anymore and you scare me."
"Deja, you're my wife. We are going to have some rough phases, but we will get through it. And when you understand that you need to be submissive, maybe you won't have to worry about being scared of me. I treat you good when you are not defiant, don't I?" X said, stern.
"X, I can't obey rules, if you don't even let me know what they are. If I think I am doing something right one day I feel like you then switch it up to say I am defiant the next day. I can't have an opinion about things sometimes, but then sometimes you let me express my opinions. I don't understand your rules. I don't know when I am doing it right or when I am not," I said, frustrated.
"Deja, you are turning me on right now," X said. "Let's go to the room baby."
"X, now you're not even being serious with me. I am so emotionally drained. I just want a break from you please," I said, fed up.
"Deja, go to the fucking room now," X said, standing over me.

I Am A Survivor: Sex, Lies, and Abuse

"Fine, can you at least put your daughter in her bed so she doesn't fall off the couch," I said standing up to go to the room.

X picked Amara up and put her in her bed. I went to the room. I had no energy to fight with him. So, I guess he was going to get what he wanted for today. I started to take my shirt off. X came behind me and helped me take it off. He took my bra off. He pulled my pants and panties off. X grabbed my wrist.

"Deja, I miss you," X wrapped his arms around me and he kissed my neck.

I wanted to believe it. Him holding me felt good, but I was so emotional I was already crying from the craziness. X laid me on my back on the bed. He pulled my legs close to the edge of the bed. He got on his knees on the floor and put my legs on his shoulders. He kissed my thighs and put his mouth on my clitoris. I moaned as it felt good. He blew his breath on my clitoris and I instantly got chills. He then started to massage my clitoris rapidly. I cried out in moans as my legs were shaking and the intensity was rising. "Fuck, X," I moaned. The feeling had me in tears. It was so sensitive and such a crazy feeling. X put his fingers in my pussy and I let out a loud moan as I came. X continued to massage my pussy with his mouth. I was cumming back-to-back at this point and I couldn't stop moaning as the intensity was on fire. I missed this and the feeling was so good. I just kept telling myself just for today, I was not going back.

I came one more time before X finally got up and flipped me over and fucked the shit out of me. He was pounding hard, and fast. He was going deep and my body was covered in chills. He was sending me over board. I was moaning with every stroke. He was making me feel so good. I was cumming again back-to-back. X, was amazing at sex. I didn't know how to deny his sex. This man was taking my body through things I didn't even know he could. My pussy was super wet and I couldn't stop cumming. I was screaming in moans. My body was shaking all over. Fuck, X was making me fall right back in. If I wasn't so weak from his touch, his dick, and the sex I could have said no. "X, shit, I'm about to explode baby," I moaned as I felt myself cumming hard. "Cum for me Deja," X moaned and I exploded within seconds moaning loudly. X was not stopping though. My body was heating up as he just kept pounding and fucking me harder. Shit he felt so good inside me. I didn't want him to stop. We fucked for 2 hours nonstop. My legs were getting weak but I continued to cum over and over. X had me soaking wet. X pounded harder and went deep and I felt my body react and I exploded as he released. X pulled out of me and I immediately ran to the bathroom. Fuck, I threw up again.

"Deja," X said, coming to the bathroom door. "Do you need to tell me something?"

I Am A Survivor: Sex, Lies, and Abuse

I looked at X. I didn't want to tell him right now.

"I took a pregnancy test. I'm pregnant. I go to the doctor tomorrow," I said, giving in.
"So, when were you planning to tell me?"
"I was going to wait until the doctor confirmed it tomorrow. You know I don't trust the test, but I'm sure I'm pregnant now. I keep throwing up."
"I'm going with you to the doctor. And then we are going back home tomorrow to New Jersey. Deja, I am not going to let you live here in this small ass place without me, knowing you are pregnant. You're coming home."
"X, if I think about going home with you. We are going to stay in our house in Columbus. But I have not made up my mind if that will happen yet."
"I am not waiting for you to make up your mind. I am your husband and I am supposed to take care of you. You want to stay in Columbus for a few months, that's fine, but we are going home tomorrow," X said, adamant.

X walked out of the bathroom before I could say anything else. I didn't have the energy to fight with him. I was just going to have to figure out how to cope until I could get him to let me go. I got up, brushed my teeth and rinsed my mouth with mouthwash. I was ready to go to sleep. I looked at the clock. It was still early but I didn't care. I was tired. It was 6pm. I went back in the room and X was drinking a bottle of water standing by the bed. He was still naked.

"You ready for another round, Deja?"

Shit, was he serious. "X, I don't know if I got it in me. I'm tired."
"Baby, we need to make up for the days we missed. I ain't done with you."

X fucked me for four more hours. He didn't stop until 10pm. I was worn out. We took little breaks in between but he just kept coming back for more. Amara and Manny woke up. And the only thing I could say I was thankful for is, X was here. He told me to lay down. He would take care of the kids. I loved that, because as soon as my head hit the pillow I was out.

The next morning, I woke up sore and running to the bathroom. I threw up again. I swear this pregnancy was different. I was never this sick feeling and tired with Amara or Manny. I saw X was not in the bed when I got up. I brushed my teeth and then went to check on the kids. I went to Amara's room and she was still sleeping. I checked in on Manny. X was holding Manny feeding him.

"Hey, you're still throwing up? I heard you running," X said.

I Am A Survivor: Sex, Lies, and Abuse

"Yeah, this is like the worst I ever felt. I have no energy, even after throwing up I still feel sick. I don't understand why this pregnancy is making me feel so horrible."
"What time is your doctor's appointment?"
"I scheduled it for 9am. I wanted to have enough time to get the kids ready."
"I actually have Greg on the way to pick up the kids while we go to the doctor's appointment. He will drop them off later when we get back to the house."
"Our house in Dublin, right?" I said, a little upset.
"Right," X paused. "Deja, it's best we just try and work this out with you being this sick you're going to need me. And I need you to understand we're married until death do us part. I will never let you leave me. You want to keep this place to get a little break every few days, fine. We will keep this place for that, but just know you will always be mine and come back to me. Understood?"

I just looked at him.

"Deja," X said.
"And what about the punishments, and choking me?"
"What about them?" X said like it was no big deal.
"Are you going to stop?"
"You still need to be punished for this bullshit you pulled. Leaving New Jersey to come buy a house in Columbus. Like we were really about to separate or get a divorce. When you defy me, you have to be punished."
"You are serious? X, you brought Grace into our bedroom without even telling me. You made me feel disgusted and then you hit me with a belt during sex, and then you choked me. That's not okay. I am not okay with your abuse," I said, upset.
"Deja, we can talk about this later. Go get dressed, you don't want to miss your appointment."
"Fuck you, X," I said walking to the bathroom.

X said something but I couldn't hear him. I went to the bathroom to take a shower. I checked the clock. It was 7:45am. I got out of the shower and was back at the toilet throwing up again. I felt miserable.

"Damn Deja, you're really sick this time," X said, coming in the bathroom.

I couldn't even say anything I was still throwing up. My stomach just felt so nauseous. I laid on the floor when I felt like I was done, because I couldn't move. X covered me up with a blanket and laid down beside me.

"Did Amara get up and eat?" I asked.

"Greg already came and got them. She took a banana with her. Greg said Cassie was making breakfast so she would eat when she got there."
I had the chills. "I feel so sick, X this doesn't feel good at all."
"I know baby, but you gotta get up so we can go to the doctors," X said, rubbing my shoulder trying to warm me up.

X helped me up and he helped me get dressed. I had the chills bad so I put on some jeans and a sweatshirt. We were a little behind so X drove my car to the appointment. We made it there exactly at 9am. I signed in and the nurse took me back immediately.

She checked my vitals and said my blood pressure was high. She took some blood and my urine. We waited for the doctor to come in.

"Well, you are definitely pregnant, Deja. Also, you are showing to be anemic. Which explains the fact that you have been feeling extra tired and weak. I suggest a lot of rest, fluids, and eating foods high in iron," Dr. Chang said.
"Thanks Dr. Chang," I said, a little upset that I was officially pregnant.

We left the doctor's office. X got on the phone and called for a chef to come to the house and make us steak with vegetables. He also called Greg and asked if the kids could stay with them for the night as I needed to get rest. Greg said that was fine. X was already figuring out what to do to make sure I was good. He called Alicia to pick up my prenatal vitamins and to get some iron pills too.

Moments like this made it hard for me to hate him when he was trying to do everything to make me feel better. He carried me in the house and took me to the bedroom. He picked out some warm pajamas for me to put on. He laid me in the bed and covered me up. He went downstairs and made me a big jug of ice water. He said the chef was here and he would bring my food up when the chef was done cooking. He went to his office to work, but he said he would come in and check on me. I drank a lot of water and I went to sleep.

I woke up at 12pm. X was in the room and he was bringing me food.

"Thank you, X," I said sitting up to eat.
"You're welcome, baby. If you need anything just let me know. I got a few things to finish up and I will be back to come lay with you."
"Okay, thank you," I said again.

X went back to his office. I ate my food. It was delicious. It was a big steak. I couldn't eat it all but I ate a lot of it. I was feeling better for now. I wasn't as tired anymore, but I still felt weak. I turned the TV on to watch my favorite crime documentaries.

X came into the room a few hours later. He laid down with me to watch TV.

"Deja, how are you feeling?" X said, rubbing my belly.
"I feel better now."
"Good, forgot to mention Alicia replaced the money in your account."
"Okay, she didn't have to X."
"I know but I like to keep the account full just in case you need anything. I told you I will cover everything even if you are buying houses to leave me," X said, being smart.
"X, you won't let me leave you. You find me every time. And how much money do you have anyway?" I said, being smart back.
"Well, stop trying to leave me. Looking for you is hard work. And we have enough money to live this life 3 times or more if you must know."
"Oh," I said, shocked. "And stop giving me a reason to want to leave, X."
"Look at me Deja,"

I turned around to face X.

"I love you. And that will never change. I don't want to lose you ever. But I live a lifestyle that I know I should have introduced you to, and that's why I get upset when you do things your way. Because I am used to females that do what I say and how I want things done. I am used to the submissive type. I know when I met you, I knew you would be a challenge. I don't mean to hurt you, but a part of my lifestyle is to not accept defiance. It angers me when you disobey me or do shit that I don't like. Sometimes it's hard to explain my rules, because sometimes you just anger me with what you say or do. And a part of my lifestyle is getting off on your pain and I hate to say it but it turns me on. I want you Deja, more than you even know. Everything about you turns me on, but when I punish you, it turns me on even more. It's the adrenaline of seeing your reaction and how much you can take. It's all part of my lifestyle in the BDSM world."
"So, why didn't you just tell me this, X?"
"Because it was even more thrilling knowing you didn't know the rules or the lifestyle. Your reactions are authentic and not role play. That's what makes it a thrill."
"But X sometimes you beat me like you hate me. Or the choking is scary, because you're so rough I think you're trying to kill me."
"Sometimes I get really angry and I take it too far, I'm trying to work on that. But some things you do Deja take me to the extreme. And I don't know how to control my anger, because I get so lost," X said, tightening his jaw.

I Am A Survivor: Sex, Lies, and Abuse

I could tell he was getting angry talking about it and I could also feel him getting hard. He was really serious about this lifestyle.

"What made you get into the BDSM lifestyle?"
"I was introduced to this lifestyle when I was 18 years old. I used to be a boxer, because my mom always said I had a lot of pent-up anger from my childhood trauma. She linked me with this guy named Junior that owned a boxing gym. I met this girl named Sharon there, she was 21. She stopped me one day and said she noticed I had a lot of anger in me. She told me she had a way to help me release it. She was a Sub looking for a Dom. She took me to my first BDSM event. We went to several and I started reading up on it. And before I knew it, I became her Dom and I realized releasing that way helped a lot with my anger. My mom noticed a difference. She thought it was from boxing, but it was from the lifestyle. It became more exciting to invite new Subs in as I got turned on by their reactions to the lifestyle and being punished."

I honestly didn't know what else to say. I didn't know a lot about the BDSM lifestyle, but I don't know if I would ever like it. I hated that he was just now explaining it to me. I could only see what he was doing as abuse, not a lifestyle for me anyway.

All I knew is that being pregnant and sick was my safe zone for now. X would be gentle knowing I was sick and pregnant. I was safe from any punishments for the moment.

****

I was 4 months pregnant. X let us stay in Columbus while he was getting busy with his businesses. My parents were glad we were in Columbus and they were happy to be back to spend time with their grandbabies. They stated they enjoyed their 2-month vacation. They were also excited I was pregnant again. They were turning my old room into Amara's room, and making space for the new baby like my kids were their kids. I was just happy they were happy.

So far X was managing with just taking care of me and the kids. He was amazing with the kids. I literally was sick a lot more this pregnancy than my other two. I finally felt normal again when I hit 4 months. I had been getting back to my normal routine of getting the kids up and feeding them and playing with them throughout the day. Before I started feeling better X was doing everything with the kids. I would just sit with them for a few hours and then go lay down, because I couldn't get my energy up. But I was doing a lot better now. My "headache" was finally calming down in my belly. I was calling this baby my headache, because this baby caused so much sickness.

I Am A Survivor: Sex, Lies, and Abuse

But we were good now. Cassie was 7 months and she was calling me every day complaining about the pregnancy woes. I would just laugh as I was a pro now with the 3rd one on the way. We just had her baby shower last week. She let me plan it and it was a success. She got a lot of baby stuff and we had so much fun. Cassie was worried that I was back with X, but I reassured her we were doing good for now. I liked that Cassie didn't treat X any different either. I was worried she wouldn't want to be around him, but she was cool about it.

X just left to take the kids to my parents' house for the weekend. X was excited. I was feeling better and wanted to spend this weekend with just us. I know he was wanting sex, because we slowed down with me being sick. He also said he would take me out tonight. It was 5pm. I jumped in the shower. X didn't say where we were going but he had a dress picked out for me to wear. It was all black, thin straps, open back, and the length of the dress was above my knee. I was going to attempt black heels tonight since I was only 4 months pregnant. My feet weren't swollen yet. And it was the month of August so the weather was okay for heels too.

While I was getting dressed, I heard X come into the house. He came straight upstairs.

"Damn, Deja you look beautiful," X said, coming in the room.
"Thank you, baby."
"I am about to jump in the shower and we will leave once I am dressed," X said, kissing me, before heading to the bathroom.

I finished getting ready. I put some curls in my hair and put on some lipstick. I wasn't big on makeup, but I liked to wear lipstick every now and then. X got dressed. We must have been going somewhere fancy. He was dressed in a suit, but he didn't have a tie on. He actually left his shirt somewhat unbutton to where his chest was showing a little. He looked so sexy to me.

"You ready," X said, coming up behind me grabbing my waist.
"Yeah, are you going to tell me where we are going or is this a surprise?"
"It's definitely a surprise."

We left the house and got in the car. The driver took us somewhere downtown. I didn't know where we were going but we were definitely headed downtown. X was all over me in the car. I think he was excited about having me to himself this weekend. We pulled up to a place called Black Dominance. I didn't know if this was a restaurant or what it was.

"What is this place X?" I said, getting out of the car.

I Am A Survivor: Sex, Lies, and Abuse

"You will see," X said.

We walked in the place and it looked very elegant. Everyone was dressed up and waiting for the doors to the next room to open. I had no clue if we were about to see a play or opera, but it was kind of the vibe I was getting. We were waiting for the show or something to begin. X was not saying anything.

"Welcome to Black Dominance, an experience of a lifetime. You will leave more than satisfied. Once the doors open you will be escorted to a table. We will serve dinner; you will need nourishments for a night of bliss. Once dinner is over you will be escorted to the play room to embellish in your most creative desires," the host spoke before opening the doors.

I was getting an idea of what this could be, but I wasn't sure. The doors opened and we were all escorted to a table. I looked at X, we sat down. He didn't say anything, he just smiled. They brought dinner out and we ate. X encouraged me to eat everything. I would need energy for tonight. I was getting nervous about what else was going to happen. After dinner we all got up and headed into another waiting room. X grabbed my wrist and I could hear my breathing getting heavy.

"Deja, tonight I need you to be on your best behavior. I need you to be a good girl." X whispered in my ear.

I took a deep breath as I could feel the chills and anxiety rising. I was really nervous about what we were about to do with all these people present. A man came around and made us all sign an NDA stating nothing leaves this room. The doors opened and we all walked into another room. The lights were dim. The room glowed a red color. There were private areas and open areas of benches, and couches with adult toys on the tables. I saw whips, vibrators, and other toys I've never seen before. There were also swings and beds throughout the room. What the hell did I just walk into? I looked at X and he just smiled at me. X grabbed my wrist and pulled me over to sit on a bench that had a good view of the whole room. X sat down next to me. We watched as other couples utilized the beds, benches, and swings. I watched, not sure if I should be watching. This man took his girl's clothes off and strapped her in the swing. She laid her head back as he spread her legs wide. She looked at me and smiled. I turned my head, but X moved it back for me to watch. The man took the vibrator and stuck it up her ass and put a strap on her to hold it in place. She moaned loudly. He then slammed his dick in her pussy and within minutes she was begging for him to take the vibrator out so she could cum. I thought this is what X did to me. She continued to beg as he told her no, she needed to be punished, he said. Her whole body was trembling as she kept begging and he just kept fucking her.

I Am A Survivor: Sex, Lies, and Abuse

I looked around. I saw other couples watching the others like we were doing, and a lot of wild sex was going on around the room. Another man had his girl handcuffed and blindfolded to the bed while he had another man eating her out while he was fucking the man's girl. This shit was crazy. My eyes were wide open to everything going on. I could feel myself getting wet and my breathing getting heavy. It was like a live porn show. I watched another man tie his girl up and bend her over while he used the whip on her ass. It looked painful, but she was taking it. I didn't know if I should try to run for the door or try to be a good girl like X said. I wasn't sure if I wanted to partake in any of this. This is what X meant when he said this was his lifestyle. I don't think this is something I wanted to do.

X grabbed my wrist. I gasped. I think he knew I was about to run.

"Deja, be a good girl and spread your legs," X whispered in my ear.

I could feel the chills and I was hot and wet. But I didn't know if I wanted to do this here. I spread my legs anyway. X got up and pulled my panties off. He stood in front of me and put his fingers in my pussy.

"Damn, girl you're super wet," X said, smiling.
"X, I don't know about this. I feel awkward," I said, nervous.
"Be a good girl Deja, and let me do what I want to you."

Fuck, okay I was turned on, but I was also freaking out. X put the handcuffs on me that were attached to the bench. Shit. I wasn't going to be able to run now. X massaged my clitoris as I watched around the room looking at what everyone else was doing. I was super wet and close to cumming. My legs began to shake. I could see people watching us too and I was getting uncomfortable.

"Cum for me, Deja," X whispered.

I closed my eyes and laid my head back as I came for him. My body was on fire. This was all too much, but I have to say my pussy was super sensitive and reacting quickly to X's touch. I was ready to cum again. I moaned as I could feel myself secreting a lot. Shit! I was cumming again and I moaned loud as the sensitivity was crazy.

"She's new to this?" I heard someone say. I looked up to see some man talking to X.
"Yeah, I'm breaking her into it," X said, not missing a beat as I could feel myself about to cum again. I felt so weird as he was talking and still massaging me at the same time.

"I could tell. Her reaction is turning me on. She is not role playing, she is sexy as hell with her raw reactions," the man said.
"Fuck, X," I moaned as I could not hold it, I was cumming again.
"Damn, she's so sweet. Can I get a taste?" the man said.
"Just a taste, fucking is off limits," X said, moving aside.
"X, what?" I said, nervous.
"Be a good girl, Deja," X said, as he pulled out his dick to watch me.

I wanted to cry. What the fuck was happening? The man spread me wide and put his mouth on my pussy. I looked at X and he just gave me this look that screamed obey. I could feel him moving his tongue around on my clitoris and moaning like he was enjoying it. I couldn't stop him. My legs started shaking. I wanted to scream. I looked at X and he was now getting his dick sucked by the man's girl. Shit, I could feel myself about to cum. I can't believe this was happening. What the fuck is going on? I cried out in moans as I came and my body was trembling as the man was not stopping. Fuck, the intensity was getting higher and I was about to explode. "X," I moaned. "Cum for me, Deja," X said. X started to moan when he released too. I fucking came so hard. I couldn't believe this was happening.

"Damn baby you a good Sub," the man said as he got up. "Thanks man. That was a great experience."
"You're welcome and thank you. Your Sub was good too," X said.
"I hope to see you both at more of these events," the man said.
"We will see," X said.

X walked up on me and whispered in my ear.

"You're being a good girl."
"Fuck you, X," I said pissed.

I felt the tears falling. X wiped my face.

"You're going to regret saying that," X said, tightening his jaw.

X uncuffed one of my hands. I stood up, because I was ready to go. I thought X was about to uncuff my other hand but he turned me around and crisscrossed my arms to cuff me back to the bench. My hands were on the bench and X pulled my dress up and bent me over. He slammed his dick into my pussy and started fucking me hard. I didn't know how I felt. I could hear the voices. "Damn he is fucking her." "Shit, she must be on punishment." "Damn, he fucking that pussy good." Everyone seemed to be watching us. I felt humiliated. But my body was reacting to X. I was moaning, crying, and cumming at the same time. I hated this but I couldn't stop my body from reacting. X released and I came one more time.

I felt X pull out. I tried to look behind me. I could see people were staring. I felt so embarrassed. I screamed when I felt the whip. Shit X was hitting my ass with a whip. It hurt and I could feel the sting. He hit me again and I cried out. Fuck, this was all bad. I tried to plead with him "X, please don't do this." X slammed his dick inside me again. I cried out. It hurt from the pain of him hitting me. He just sat inside me not moving. And I felt him hit my ass again with the whip. I screamed and he began fucking me hard and fast. I was in pain, but him fucking me was extremely sensitive. I could feel my legs shaking and my pussy was pulsating. I cried out in moans as I was cumming. X stopped and hit me again. I screamed. I felt my whole-body buckle. I couldn't take, anymore. I could still hear the voices. Someone said "Damn I wish he was my Dom. I would like a piece of that action." I was kneeling on the floor with my hands still cuffed to the bench. X came and put his dick near my face. "Suck on it, Deja." I put his dick in my mouth and he moved back and forth fucking my mouth. I was in tears. All of this felt so horrible. I couldn't believe X was doing this in front of all these people. X fucked my mouth until he came.

When he was done, he leaned down to whisper in my ear. "I'm going to uncuff you now. If you try to run out of here it will be worse when we get home. Be a good girl, Deja," X said.

X stood me up and pulled my dress down. He uncuffed me. He wiped my face as I was crying again. He grabbed my wrist and we walked out of the place. X's driver was outside. X opened the door and I got inside the car. X got in and I immediately started hitting him. I was done. I smacked him in the face and he was trying to grab my arms as the driver pulled off. I was just hitting him. I was so humiliated, disgusted, and I couldn't take it anymore. X finally grabbed my hands and crisscrossed them in front of me as he held me. I was still trying to break free. I wanted to hurt him. But he held me so tight I couldn't move.

"Deja, I'm going to beat your ass when we get home," X said, pissed.
"Fuck you, X. I don't care. I'm done with you," I said, still trying to break free.
"Will see," X said, pulling out his phone. "Yeah, can you meet me at the house?"

I couldn't hear who he was talking to but I wanted to know who was going to meet him at the house.

The driver pulled up to the house. I didn't see anybody waiting. X, still holding me, dragged me out of the car. He carried me inside the house. I was still trying to fuck him up, but I couldn't break free of his grip. I knew if he got me up the stairs, he was going to handcuff me and beat my ass. I kicked off my shoes and tried to grab the railing of the stairs with my legs. It was not working X hit my legs and kept going up the stairs. I wasn't going to give up. He carried me to our bedroom. He loosened his grip trying to get the handcuffs. I pulled away and turned around and slapped him. I ran into the bathroom and locked the door.

I started looking for something I could use as a weapon. I couldn't find anything. X was banging on the door. He was trying to bust the door down. He must have found the key, because I heard him walk away and come back and unlock the door. I threw a can of shaving cream at him. He blocked it and grabbed me.

"Deja, I'm going to fuck you up," X said, dragging me back into the bedroom.

He threw me on the bed and climbed on top of me. He slapped the shit out of me. I grabbed my face. He pulled my dress up and lifted my legs up. He slammed his dick inside me and started fucking me rough. I cried. I was so mad at him. I didn't want my body to react, but I already had chills. My body was trembling, and my legs were shaking. I could feel my pussy pulsating. I was cumming hard. I moaned as I came. "Fuck, Deja, you really pissed me off. But that pussy is so good." X moaned fucking me harder. I felt my pussy jerking as I was cumming again. I heard the doorbell. X kept fucking me. He went deeper and faster. I came again as he released. He handcuffed my hands and hooked me to the head board.

X got dressed and went downstairs to get the door. I tried to see if I could break the headboard and free myself. The post was strong and I wasn't going to break it. I heard footsteps on the stairs. I was getting nervous. Who the hell did he call?

X walked in the room first. "You want to act a fool. I got a punishment for you."

I saw Grace come into the room behind X. What the fuck was she doing here? Why was she even in Columbus? What the fuck is going on?"

"You brought this bitch here?" I said, pissed.
"Deja, be nice," X said, taking his clothes off.
"It's okay Sir, X, I will take good care of her," Grace said, taking her clothes off too.
"Fuck no, X," I said trying to curl up at the head of the bed.

X grabbed my legs to pull me back down. I screamed. Grace came to the side of the bed and X spread my legs. Grace started licking on my clitoris. I tried to close my legs but X held them open. She then started sucking on my clitoris hard. I cried out as my body began to react. I felt the chills, and my pussy was getting wet. My temperature was rising with every lick, twirl, and suck. I was trembling. I didn't want to cum. I hated this. I tried to hold it. I didn't want her touching me. I cried as I felt myself about to cum. "Cum for me Deja," X said. I closed my eyes when I felt my tears falling and let out a loud moan as I came. "That's my good girl," X said. Grace climbed on top of me and started sucking on my breast. I felt X put the vibrator in Grace and turned it on. I could feel the vibration as she sat right on the top of my pussy. She was moaning as she sucked my breast. X got behind Grace and pushed her up some as he stuck his dick inside me.

He started fucking me with Grace in between us. I was shaking as the feeling was unreal. I was getting chills from her sucking and moaning on my breast while I could feel the vibrator and X fucking me at the same time. I was trembling and feeling so many feelings at once. I was about to explode. "Ahh, shit this feels so good. I was about to cum. Deja cum with me." X moaned. I was cumming with X as he said the words. "Oh, shit," I moaned as the feeling was good but different.

X laid back on my legs so I couldn't move. Grace turned around putting her pussy on mine so I could feel the vibrator on my clitoris. I immediately started moaning. The vibrator was making me shake. I watched as Grace began pushing into me as she sucked X's dick. I wanted to beat her ass, but I was already cumming from the vibration on my clitoris. I put my head back to not watch her. My body was reacting to the vibrator as she kept pushing into me. I was trembling, and my pussy was pulsating with the vibration. I was about to cum again. "Fuck," I moaned as my pussy exploded. X also moaned a few minutes later as I saw he was cumming.

I couldn't take anymore X had gone overboard with this dominance shit. I was going to have to leave him. I couldn't do this anymore. Grace got up and X stood up. Grace laid over my stomach and began to massage my clitoris with her fingers. X stood behind Grace.

"This will teach you to not defy me, Deja. What I'm about to do is going to hurt. But you need to obey me and stop being defiant," X said.

X lifted Grace's ass and slammed his dick inside her. I cried. I didn't even know what to say or do. My pussy was reacting to Grace massaging my pussy, but I wanted to fuck them both up at the same time. I came as Grace began to move faster. X was fucking her harder. X released and Grace came with him. What the fuck is this shit.

Chapter Seventeen: Sex, Lies, and Abuse
"What the fuck was wrong with me?"

I woke up the next morning still handcuffed to the post. Grace left after X fucked her and X kept me cuffed because I'm sure he knew I would leave his ass. As soon as he decided to let me go, I was going to leave him. I couldn't stay with him. I just couldn't. X, wasn't in the room when I woke up. I had to pee though. I yelled his name. I heard footsteps coming to the room.

"You're awake," X said, standing at the door.
"X, I have to pee."

X came and uncuffed me. I went to the bathroom and shut the door. My ass stung a little as I sat on the toilet. It had to be from that damn whip. I got up and checked in the mirror. I had whip marks on my ass and my cheek was purple.

"You will probably need some cream," X said as he opened the door to watch me.
"X, what you did last night was uncalled for. Why the fuck is Grace even in Columbus?"
"Watch your damn mouth. And she's here for me. I told her to come to Columbus this weekend."
"For this bullshit?" I said, pissed.

X grabbed my face and it hurt as he grabbed the side he smacked.

"Deja, watch your fucking mouth."
"Okay," I said. He let me go.
"Yeah, she is here for whatever I want her to be here for. She's more submissive than you will ever seem to be," X said, with an attitude.
"So, you been fucking her, because she's submissive?"
"I fucked her last night to punish you, because you're so damn defiant."
"No, you humiliated and disgusted me with everything you did last night at the event and in our bedroom."
"So, you're going to leave me now, huh?"
"Yes, X. I don't want to stay in this fucked up marriage," I said, being bold.
"Deja," X grabbed my neck. "You will never leave me."
"X, you're hurting me. I can't breathe," I said, grabbing his hands trying to pull him away.
"I will not let you leave me ever again," X said, tightening his grip. "YOU HEAR ME," he yelled.
"Yes," I mumbled, barely getting the words out.

X let me go and I grabbed my neck as I started coughing.

I Am A Survivor: Sex, Lies, and Abuse

"Damn, Deja. You're always pissing me off. Shit, baby I didn't mean to hurt you like that, I'm sorry," X said, trying to be apologetic.

I didn't say anything. X went to his office. He said he had to get some work done. I jumped in the shower. The water stung on my bruises. I got out of the shower and got dressed. I grabbed my phone and without even thinking I called 911. I waited in the bedroom for the door. 15 minutes went by and I heard the door. I heard X run down the stairs. I went to the top of the stairs to watch him open the door.

"Hello, I am Officer Creed, and this is Officer Beard. We received a call about a disturbance in the home."
"I'm sorry you must have the wrong house no one called from here," X said, looking confused.
"I called," I yelled, coming down the stairs.
"What?" X said, tightening his jaw.
"I want to press charges. My husband is abusing me," I said, a little nervous.
"Deja, what the fuck are you doing?" X said. "I'm sorry Officers, this is a misunderstanding."
"No, it's not. You can see the bruise on my face and I have marks on my butt too."
"Are you sure you want to press charges, ma'am? There have been many calls about your husband abusing you and no charges have been filed. I just want to make sure you understand what this means," Officer Beard said.
"I'm sure this time. I want to press charges," I said, confident.
"Sir, I'm going to have to place you under arrest," Officer Creed said.
"Deja, tell them this is a mistake," X said, looking at me.
"It's not," I said, backing away as Officer Beard placed handcuffs on X. They read his Miranda Rights to him.

X was cussing and stating his lawyer was going to take care of this. They put him in the car and gave me a police report number to take to the prosecutor. They left with X.

I ran upstairs and grabbed whatever I could think to grab. I locked up the house and left. I didn't know if he would be in jail until Monday or if his lawyer was going to find a way to get him out. I figured I would go to the condo tonight and figure out the rest tomorrow. But this was my only chance to get away. X would probably kill me now if he got his hands on me again. I knew my kids were safe with my parents so I wouldn't worry about them tonight. I also knew X wouldn't hurt our kids so if I had to leave without them, they would be okay. I would come back for them as soon as I could. But for now, I would stay at the condo.

I made it to the condo and parked my car in the garage this time. I put the door stopper at the door so X couldn't get in. I did stop by the store to get some groceries so I put those up. I sat on the couch and it all hit me as I cried. I didn't

I Am A Survivor: Sex, Lies, and Abuse

know if I did the right thing or not but I felt horrible. I laid down on the couch and went to sleep.

I woke up to my phone ringing. I saw it was 3pm. I answered the phone and it was an unknown caller.
"Hello," I said sitting up.
"Hello is this, Deja Thomas," a male voice said.
"Yes, who is this?" I said, curious.
"My name is Detective James Moon. I was calling, because your husband was released 3 hours ago from jail by his attorney. We received a 911 call not too long ago about an intruder. I am at your home now, because your husband has been shot."
"What? What happened?" I said, freaking out.
"It looks like Randy Sawyer, the man who shot you, came back and tried to kill your husband. Your husband was shot during the fight that occurred between them. But your husband was able to grab the gun and killed Randy in the process."
"Oh my God," I was in shock. "Is X, okay?"
"He is being escorted to the hospital; he was shot close to his chest but up towards his left shoulder. I don't know his condition, but he was awake and talking before they left to take him to the hospital."
"What hospital?"
"He is going to Grant Hospital."
"Okay, I am on my way there now. Thank you," I said, hanging up the phone.

I jumped in the car and called everyone I could think of on the way to the hospital. Mike said he was going to get Mama Clara there asap. I called my parents and they said they would keep the kids for however long they needed too, and to keep them updated with X's condition. I called Cassie and Greg. They were going to meet me at the hospital. James said he would be flying out with Mike, Whitney, and Mama Clara. I was panicking trying to stay focused on the road. I couldn't believe this. I didn't know what to think.

Randy was dead, but X was hurt. I made it to the hospital. I ran inside wanting to know what condition X was in.

"Excuse me, excuse me I am here for Xavier Thomas he was brought in for a gunshot wound," I said crying at this point.
"Ma'am take a seat I will give you an update when I know more," the lady at the desk said.
"Please, he is my husband. I just need to know he is okay."
"Deja," Cassie said, coming in the door.
"Oh, God Cassie, they won't tell me nothing," I said, hugging her. I was panicking.
"I will check with them, hold on," Greg said, going back up to the desk.
"Deja, what happened?" Cassie said.

I Am A Survivor: Sex, Lies, and Abuse

"I don't know. I wasn't at the house. The detective called me and said X got shot. And Randy tried to kill him, but X was able to fight back and killed Randy."
"No, Deja, to your face?" Cassie said, noticing my bruise.
"Cassie, it's nothing. I'm worried about X right now."
"Jesus Deja, it never stopped, did it?" Cassie said, upset.
"Cassie, don't do this right now. I just want to know if X is okay first. And we can talk later," I said, worried.
"Fine," Cassie said.

Greg came back and said that X was in surgery right now and they would update us when he was out. I just wanted him to be okay. I needed him to be okay. I didn't want nothing bad to happen to him. We waited for hours and nothing. I was up and down pacing. Cassie tried to keep me calm. Mike, James, Whitney, and Mama Clara showed up. I ran and hugged Mama Clara. She was already crying. Whitney hugged us too.

"What happened to my baby?" Mama Clara said.
"He was shot trying to defend himself from Randy. The detective said he killed Randy in self-defense. The last thing they told us was that he was in surgery, but we have been waiting for 5 hours now," I said, frustrated.
Mama Clara grabbed my chin and looked at my bruise. "Deja, baby, are you okay? You should probably wear makeup before coming outside," She mumbled.
"I'm fine Mama," I said, sitting down.

I couldn't believe she said that, but I was more worried about X right now. Cassie gave me a look like she wanted to say something, but I shook my head no. Cassie was pissed.

We sat in the waiting room for maybe 2 more hours. It was 10:15pm when the doctor came out.

"Mrs. Deja Thomas," the doctor said.
"That's me. Is X okay?" I said, walking up to the doctor.
"He is stable. He is asking for you. We were not able to extract all of the bullet, but we got as much as we could. But he is doing okay. It didn't touch his heart but the shot was right above his heart."
"I want to see him."
"I will take you back there. We are still trying to get him a room. So, I can only take you back for now."
"Okay," I said.

Everyone else waited in the lobby area. I walked back with the doctor. He took me to the after-surgery area. I saw X and ran to his side.

"Hey, X, how are you doing?" I said, rubbing his arm.
"Deja, I am so sorry," X said, grabbing my hand.

"X, don't worry about that right now. I am just glad you're okay."

"Deja, all I kept thinking about was you and the kids. If you were there and he would have hurt you again, I wouldn't have known what to do. I had to make sure he didn't hurt any of us ever again."

"I know X. I know. But I'm so happy you're alive and well."

"Deja, I want to fix this and I want you to come home. I will work on controlling myself. But I love you and I want you to come home. Baby, this has opened my eyes in so many ways and I can't do this life without you," X said, grabbing my wrist.

I pulled away. "X, I love you too. And I will be there for you until you are healed. I want to take care of you. I know that our kids need you and you are a great father to them. But I can't do your lifestyle and I can't handle your anger. I can't come home. And I am being real with you, because I love you. And I need you to respect that and let me go. I just want both of us to coexist for our kids, but this marriage is done," I said as I felt the tears fall.

"Deja, I can't let you go baby. I love you too much for that. Please come home," X pleaded.

"X, your family is out there and they want to see you. Mama Clara and your brothers are worried about you. Let's just focus on that right now. Letting them see you and you getting better. I'm not the girl for you, X, but I will wait to file the divorce so we have plenty of time to explain it to our families. But I can't be with you. Now the doctor said he will be moving you into a room and everyone can come see you. I just want to be supportive for you right now and focus on you going home and getting better."

"Deja, please," X said, crying.

It hurt to see him like this and I wanted to fall right back in, but I knew nothing would be different. X could only be normal for so long. And this time I was not going back.

****

X spent a week in the hospital and we took him home. Mama Clara and his brothers stayed at our house helping out for a month. I stayed at the house just so they didn't think we were not together. But as soon as they went back home, I went back to staying at the condo. I would come over during the day with the kids so X could see them and I helped with changing his bandages and fixing his food. X tried to have sex with me a few times but I refused and with him still being sore he didn't fight me. But X was getting better. He was doing physical therapy to get movement in his arm again. I knew my time helping was coming to an end.

X still begged me often to change my mind, but I wasn't budging no matter how much he wanted to be nice. I knew soon he would go back to being controlling and beating me again. I wasn't going to take that anymore. We had already arranged how we would do visitation with the kids. Until we told everyone we were divorcing we would still be present together for family events and so on. It was now October 17th. I was staying at the condo on a regular basis. X had been respecting my space and we would meet at the house in Dublin to drop off or pick up the kids. I liked that he wasn't forcing me to come home and though he talked about it a lot he wasn't being controlling. I had the kids for two weeks so X could get some rest, but I was meeting him at the house to drop them off for his week. I was now 6 months pregnant.

Cassie on the other hand had her baby last week. She had a healthy baby boy Gregory Jr. and he was a cutie. I did tell Cassie I was not with X, but that we were still pretending for the family until the divorce was filed. Cassie was happy that I wasn't with X anymore. She was really upset seeing my face when we were at the hospital after X got shot. And she couldn't wait to share how she felt about Mama Clara's response. Cassie made sure I knew Mama Clara had some issues too. But she was happy to know I was done with him.

I pulled up to the house to drop the kids off. I knocked on the door. Even though I had a key it didn't feel right just walking in now that we were not together.

"Deja," Grace said, opening the door.
"What are you doing here?" I said, a little upset seeing Grace.
"Not that it's any of your business anymore. But I am with X now and I live here with him," Grace said, with a smart mouth.
"Hmm, where is X?" I said, ignoring her.
"He's upstairs."
"Can you go get him?"
"Hey, Deja," X said, coming down the stairs.
"Hey X, here is the diaper bag for Manny. Amara is working on being potty trained. She has been really good at telling me she has to go to the bathroom, but I still use pullups for her as she had a few accidents," I said to X then I turned to Amara. "Give me kisses baby. You be good for daddy and I will see you next week okay."
"Okay, mommy," Amara said, giving me kisses.

Amara walked in the house and ran to her playroom. I handed X, Manny in his car seat. I gave Manny a kiss. I turned to walk to my car.

"Deja, wait," X said, putting Manny in the house.
I turned around. "What X,"
"Look, I know what this looks like, but I don't want Grace. I want you, Deja."
"X, it's a little weird seeing her here and she's telling me she is living here now. Whatever you two are doing is none of my business. I get it, I'm not coming home and you have needs that need to be fulfilled. I get it, it hurts, but it doesn't change anything. I am not coming home, X," I said, trying to be okay with it.

I Am A Survivor: Sex, Lies, and Abuse

"Deja, I'm sorry. I am back in my anger management classes and I am in counseling now too. I will do whatever it takes to get you back, baby."
"X, I am happy for you. I really am. I'll be back next week to pick up the kids."

I got in my car and pulled off. I cried on the way home. Not because I was mad, but it did hurt to see him with Grace or any woman. I still loved him. I just knew that I couldn't be with him.

I made it home and I called Cassie. I just had to vent and I knew Cassie was the only one who knew what was going on. She helped me feel better by comforting me and telling me I shouldn't go back. And she was right. I couldn't go back. As time would pass it would be easier to deal with. I got off the phone with Cassie and laid down on the couch to watch TV. I fell asleep.

I woke up to my door opening. Oh Shit, I forgot to lock the door. I was so frustrated it slipped my mind. X was standing at the door staring at me. I got up and looked at the clock. It was 7pm.

"X, why are you here? I hope you didn't leave my kids with Grace," I said, frustrated.
"The kids are with Micah. I have a rule when our kids are at the house, Grace goes to her apartment, I got for her."
"Oh, and she is a Sub so she obeys right?" I said, being smart.
"She does, Deja. Look, I saw how you looked at her and I just wanted to come apologize again. I didn't mean to hurt you or upset you. Deja, I miss you."
"X, don't please. Grace is perfect for you. I was just a little taken aback, because I didn't expect that. But it's okay whatever you are doing with her that's between the both of you," I said, trying to sound okay with it.
"Deja, I want you. I want you right now, baby," X said, grabbing my wrist.
"No, X," I said, standing up and walking away from him.
"Deja, baby don't do this. I want you so bad," X said, begging.
"X, I can't," I said as my breathing was getting heavy.

X walked up on me and grabbed my wrist. "I know you want me too, Deja," X said, pinning me to the wall. Hell, he wasn't lying. It had been months since I had sex. "I can hear your breathing baby, and I know you're getting wet for me," X said, touching my pussy through my pants. Fuck, I was definitely getting hot and the chills were all through me. I put my head down so he couldn't see my reaction. X grabbed my face and lifted it up to kiss me. Shit, the sensations running through me had my pussy pulsating. I wanted to fuck him. X, pulled my pants and panties off. He lifted my leg and started eating me out. I moaned so loud as I missed his mouth on me. I was shaking. "Damn baby, you missed me," X moaned as he felt how wet I was. Oh gosh, I was giving in so quickly. But his sex was something else. I moaned as he sucked on my clitoris and massaged his tongue so gently on me. I was trembling with every touch. "Fuck, X," I cried out as I was cumming.

I Am A Survivor: Sex, Lies, and Abuse

Damn, he started moving his mouth faster and I was screaming in moans as my body was shaking and I was cumming again. "Shit, X fuck me," I cried out.

X stood up, turned me to face the wall, and he slammed his dick inside of my pussy. He immediately started moving fast, hard, and rough. I was screaming as my body was so hot and aroused by his movement. I was trembling as his motion was so intense. Damn, my whole body was covered in chills, as the intensity was rising. I was gyrating to his movement and X started to moan loudly too. Fuck, he felt so good. I was about to cum. "Oh shit, X I'm going to explode baby," I moaned. "Cum, Deja, I'm about to cum too," X moaned fucking me harder. I screamed out as I was cumming and X moaned as he released. X pulled out and stood back against the wall.

"Fuck, Deja, that shit was amazing," X said, trying to catch his breath.

I turned around to look at X. He was panting. I could tell he was still a little weak from being shot as he never panted before like that. I smiled at him.

"What, Deja?" X said, coming towards me to kiss me. "What's on your mind?"
"Nothing," I said, wrapping my arms around him. "I did miss you and that was amazing."
"Oh, really,"
"Yeah, really," I said, kissing him.
"I miss you too," X said, sounding upset. "Deja, what will it take for you to come home?"
"Can we please go slow. I want to go to your anger management classes with you. I want to attend counseling with you. Marriage counseling too. I want us to work X, but I need you to understand I can't do your lifestyle. And I won't accept you hitting me or choking me. And if everything seems to go well. I will then come home," I said, trying to give this one last shot.
"Okay, I will do it your way. I want you home and I'm learning I have to respect and support your decisions too."

I put my hand on his head.

"Are you okay? Who am I talking to? Are you sick?" I said, laughing.
"Deja, I'm serious," X said, kissing me.
"Oh, and Grace. She has to go."
"I know. I will let her know in the morning."
"I mean I don't ever want to see her again. All business affairs and everything are done with her."
"Deja, I never did business with her, besides your event. She was just at a lot of the events I attended for my businesses. And I told you how I met her."
"Well, then you're done with her."
"Do I hear Deja, being controlling now?" X said, being sarcastic.
"X, I'm serious."

I Am A Survivor: Sex, Lies, and Abuse

"I know, baby, and I'm done with her."
"Good," I said, kissing him.
"One last thing," X paused. "Can I stay with you tonight?"
"X," I said unsure.
"I know we are going slow. I get it. I'll leave," X started putting his clothes on.
"Okay, you can stay the night," I said, not wanting him to leave.

X wrapped his arms around me and kissed me. We made love the rest of the night and the chemistry between us felt stronger. I felt like for the first time X, may have changed. I was hoping so, because he really seemed different.

The next morning, I heard X talking on the phone in the living room. I looked at the clock and it was 8am. I walked in the living room. X looked at me and kept talking on the phone.

"What are you saying? Greg didn't tell me nothing like that happened," X said. I noticed he was tightening his jaw. "I'll call you back."
"Is everything okay, X," I said, nervous.
"No, Deja. That was Grace. She is telling me that before I came to your art event you were smitten with Abraham and that is why he mentioned he thought you were a free agent."
"X, seriously. I was not even worried about Abraham; he seemed like an asshole."
"Deja, why would she lie about that," X said, walking towards me upset.
"X, you believe her over me? She is probably saying that, because she is mad you are letting her go," I said, backing up.
"Deja, what happened before I came to the event," X said, still walking towards me.
"X, don't do this. We had a really good night and we made plans to attend your classes and go to counseling. You're scaring me right now and this does not make me want to work on anything with you," I said, trying to make my way back to the bedroom walking backwards.
"Deja, answer my fucking question," X said, still following me.

I could see he was tightening his jaw and balling his fist.

"X, nothing happened. He talked to me about my paintings, that's it."

I made it to the bedroom and tried to shut the door, but X was right there and he pushed it open. I backed up and fell on the bed. I tried to scoot myself up, but X grabbed my leg. I screamed. X pulled me towards him and I covered my face when he raised his hand. He punched me in my arm. I cried out for him to stop. He kept on hitting me. He hit me in my stomach, my arm, my face, and my leg. I screamed out trying to get away from him. But he was holding my other leg. So, I couldn't go far. X got on top of me and started choking me. I was losing my breath. I was hitting his hands, but he kept choking me. "X, please, please, I can't

I Am A Survivor: Sex, Lies, and Abuse

breathe," I cried out. I was kicking my legs and trying my hardest to move his hands from my neck. I felt myself going weak. I stopped fighting, I felt my eyes closing. Everything went black.

I woke up to my head hurting and X was not in the room with me. I didn't know if he was still here or not. My whole body was sore. I sat up and I screamed. I saw a lot of blood and didn't know what was going on. I felt a huge sharp pain in my stomach. I started crying. I think I was having a miscarriage. I grabbed my phone to call 911. I fell to the ground as I grabbed my phone from the night stand. I was in so much pain I could barely walk. I called 911 and I passed out again.

I woke up in the hospital. I had a tube in my nose. I felt my stomach and I began to cry as I couldn't feel anything moving. The nurse came in my room.

"You're awake. I will page the doctor, hold on," the nurse said, calling for someone to page the doctor. "Mrs. Thomas the doctor is on the way. I just want to stay with you until she comes in," she said, grabbing my hand to console me.

The doctor walked in.

"Hey Deja," Dr. Chang said. "I just happened to be working a shift at the hospital today when you came in, I knew I wanted to assist. I'm so sorry honey. We tried everything we could, but we could not save the baby. Deja, we had to give you oxygen, because you were very low. Who did this to you?" Dr. Chang said, referring to my bruises.
"I lost the-," I tried to speak. I couldn't get the words out. I was crying at this point. I lost the baby.
"Oh Deja, I'm so sorry," Dr. Chang said, rubbing my arm. "Let's give her a minute."

Dr. Chang and the nurse left me alone. I couldn't stop crying. He made me lose my baby. Why did he do this?

I stayed in the hospital for five days alone. Dr. Chang came in everyday to check on me. She said she picked up extra shifts to make sure I was doing okay. I didn't call anyone to tell them what happened. I didn't even care if X knew or not what he did. I called the police while I was in the hospital to make a report. Detective James Moon came to the hospital. I told him I wanted to press charges. He gave me the report number and said he would put a warrant out for X's arrest. He said he would check his home and try to discuss with him the concerns. He did warn me if X got arrested, he would probably be out in a couple of hours, because his attorney would get him out. He encouraged me to go to the prosecutor's office and file charges asap. I told him this time I would. I wanted X locked up for killing my baby.

I Am A Survivor: Sex, Lies, and Abuse

I knew I couldn't go back to the condo. I had over $500,000 in the account that X had for me and $200,000 in my personal account. I didn't want to involve Cassie; she was married to Greg. So, I figured I would call Stacy for now, when I was ready to get another place. That way it wouldn't be easy for X to find me this time. Dr. Chang was discharging me today, so I would just stay in a hotel for the time being. I knew my kids were safe. So, I would have to wait before I could pick them up. I would figure things out before I had to get them for sure.

Once I was released, the first thing I did was get a new phone. I kept the same number so X wouldn't know I changed my phone. I just wanted to make sure that there were no trackers. I made sure my location was off and I created new passwords for anything I could think X would have access to. I found a hotel in Pickerington far from the northside. I checked in the hotel. I stopped by the condo to grab some clothes and get a few necessities. I also wanted to get my car so I didn't have to use the ride share services all day. I noticed that X had been there. The place was cleaned up. He must have had the maid come by, because the bed sheets were changed and the house was spotless.

I was going to have to get with Stacy today so I could start looking for a place. To my knowledge, X didn't know where Stacy lived. I don't think he knew much about Stacy; besides she used to be my co-worker. I knew he kept up with Cassie, because she is married to Greg and he knew a little about Michaela so I didn't want to involve them.

I didn't call Stacy. I just went to her house. Luckily, she was home. When Stacy opened the door, I could tell on her face she was shocked to see me with so many bruises. She immediately let me in and asked what happened. I told her everything and bawled my eyes out as I couldn't hold back my tears. Stacy consoled me and said she would help anyway she could. She just wanted me to be safe. She offered for me to stay with her. But I told her I was staying in a hotel. I didn't want X to find me at Stacy's house just in case he came looking. And I didn't want her in harm's way either. Stacy did agree to help me find a place and put the place in her name. She said she would call off of work tomorrow and go to the courthouse with me too. I didn't stay long at Stacy's house, because I had many missed calls from X already and he could be looking for me now.

I grabbed some food and went back to the hotel. I sat in the room and ate. I was emotionally going through it as I felt like every 5 minutes I was crying. I tried to watch TV. I kept looking at my phone as X was calling and I had about 10 voicemails. I didn't even care to answer my phone or listen to the voicemails. But I eventually listened to the voicemails, just to make sure he wasn't saying anything about the kids. I knew the kids were safe with him, but I just wanted to make sure. The voicemails were just him complaining about not getting a hold of me. He was cursing and talking about how I needed to call him asap. He mentioned that the detective came over and was trying to arrest him. He said his

I Am A Survivor: Sex, Lies, and Abuse

lawyer stopped that and if I was trying to press charges I was going to pay. I knew I would share that voicemail with the prosecutor. X mentioned on the voicemail that the detective told him I had a miscarriage. X sounded like he was crying and he said he wanted to be there for me. The voicemails just went on and on, one minute he was angry he couldn't get a hold of me, to sounding sad about losing the baby and missing me. He was fucking psycho.

After I listened to the voicemails and none of them were concerning my kids. I went back to watching TV. I laid down and tried to go to sleep around 9pm. I was tired, worn out, and hurting all at the same time. I cried myself to sleep.

The next morning, I picked up Stacy and we went to the court house. I called the lawyer my dad told me about the first time I left X. Tremond Deetz, the attorney, met us there. He helped me with filing for a divorce and was present when I talked with the Prosecutor Maria Sanchez to press charges. The prosecutor stated that X's attorney Eric Caldwell was already in contact with them since he knew I would be pressing charges. The prosecutor stated that I would have to get an assessment completed by a counselor, because X was stating that I was mentally insane and anything I told them was a lie. The prosecutor stated it would be important to make sure that I did everything asked of me; to prove X was wrong and I was telling the truth. She also mentioned that it was good that I had police reports to show the pattern of abuse.

She explained that she knew of Eric Caldwell and he was going to do everything in his power to make sure I looked stupid and unreliable. She explained she wanted to know everything in detail and I should not leave anything out. She said this was going to be a serious fight, because X's attorney was brutal. Tremond tried to reassure me that I had nothing to worry about, because he fights hard too. He was going to support me through it all. The prosecutor agreed with Tremond and tried to reassure me that we had a good case. They both told me to get all my hospital documents together, any other evidence, and to get that mental health assessment completed asap. Maria also mentioned it would be good for me to seek counseling. She also gave me some domestic violence resources and education. I left the courthouse with Stacy, hopeful, nervous, and scared at the same time.

I didn't want to do this or go this route, but I knew X wasn't going to leave me alone. The whole time I was in the courthouse X, was blowing my phone up. I had 20 missed calls and 6 voicemails. I was going to make sure I kept everything for my proof that X was crazy, not me. Stacy drove once we left the courthouse, because I couldn't stop crying. Everything was hitting me all at once. I never thought I would have to deal with this and I didn't know what to do. I was so scared, because Tremond also mentioned that X could get upset and not give me my kids once he found out that charges were filed and I was filing for divorce. He tried to prepare me for every worst scenario and encouraged me to stick it through and not fall for his tactics. Because if I changed my mind, X would win. He also mentioned if I went back, I might not have a next time.

Stacy and I went to look at a few apartments. I didn't want to go through the process of buying a house, because I figured I could just get an apartment quicker. We found one apartment in Pickerington that was move in ready. I told the leasing agent I could pay the whole year up front if she could get me in the apartment asap. The leasing agent was shocked, but she completed the paperwork and Stacy signed the lease. I gave her a year's rent and deposit and she gave me the keys. We put the lease in Stacy's name, and the agent didn't have a problem with that. Once we were done, we went shopping for groceries and things I needed for the place. Stacy helped me get everything in the house. I also scheduled for furniture to come tomorrow.

The place was a good size. It was a 3 bedroom and 2 1/2 bath townhome. I had my own entrance into the place with an attached garage. The entrance opened into the living room and the kitchen was in the back of the place. It was a small kitchen, but it was doable. Between the kitchen and the living room was the half bath. Upstairs was the owner's suite with a walk-in closet and the bathroom was accessed walking through the closet. The other bathroom sat in between the other two bedrooms. I figured this was going to be an okay place for now. I had beds coming for me and the kids and living room furniture. For tonight, I had a blow-up bed for me. I had Stacy ride with me to end my hotel stay, and grab a TV from the condo, and then I took her home afterwards. I thanked her for helping me and gave her $5,000 for her troubles. She said she didn't want it, but I told her to take it anyway. She gave me a hug and told me to call her for anything. She said she was here for me no matter what and just wanted me to be safe.

I went home and set up the TV in the living room and my blow-up bed for tonight. I figured I would sleep in the living room until the furniture arrived in the morning. I put all the stuff I bought for the place up and made sure to put the door stoppers at each door. I cooked my dinner and sat on my bed to watch TV. I decided I would call my parents and tell them everything now that things were in place with filing for divorce.

I called my parents and luckily both of them were at home so I only had to go over it once. My dad was furious. He kept saying why didn't you tell us sooner. I tried to explain I was trying to make it work and didn't want anyone to know until I was done dealing with it. My mom was more understanding and she calmed my dad down. I did tell them that I filed for divorce and pressed charges. I did ask them to please be cordial with X. Since we had to be civil for the kids. I know my dad probably wanted to kill X now, but I explained that we still have to be civil for the sake of our kids. I told them I know X is a good father and until I knew what was going to happen with the case, I knew he would still be in their lives. My parents agreed and stated that they would be cordial for now as long as X was respectful too. I told them once I picked up the kids, I would stop by to see them, but right now I just wanted to rest and get everything in order. They understood. They told me they loved me and they would see me soon. I ended the call telling them I loved them too.

I sat on the bed still emotional. I knew I would have to call X eventually, but not today. I just kept listening to the voicemails he continued to leave and save them for my attorney and the prosecutor. I had the counseling meeting scheduled for Wednesday with Dr. Shannie Mitchell. She was a psychologist that my attorney Tremond recommended. She assured me she would do a thorough assessment and get it over to my attorney and the prosecutor in a timely manner. I also had Dr. Chang write up a thorough report on how I came into the hospital and she provided me with my hospital records. Detective Moon had already sent my police reports to my attorney and the prosecutor. I was trying to get everything together, because X was never going to do this to me or anyone again.

It was now around 8pm when I saw Mama Clara was calling me. I didn't know if I wanted to answer, but I did anyway.

"Deja, baby what's going on?" Mama Clara said, worried.
"Hey mama, it's a lot going on right now, but I really don't want to talk about it," I said, trying to keep my conversation short.
"I understand baby, but X has been calling me crying talking about you left. He's worried that you are mentally not doing well."
I rolled my eyes. "I'm doing fine mama. It's your son that is not mentally doing well."
"What are you talking about Deja?"

I didn't want to say much. I know she was more on X's side; I mean he was her son.

"He's abusive mama and he has been abusive since the day I told you about it. He hasn't changed and I can't deal with it."
"Oh baby, X has been through a lot. I know he didn't mean it and he is hurting without you. That man loves you so much Deja. He told me he was doing counseling now and working on his issues. Please don't leave him."
"Mama, I know you love your son and I can't fault you for that. But you can't be serious asking me to return for him to continue to abuse me," I said, angry.
"Listen Deja, he's trying to change that. He saw a lot of abuse with his bio mother and that trauma has tainted him. He doesn't mean to be that way. He just doesn't know how to process his anger correctly yet. But he told me he is working on it."
"Mama, I have to go. I'm tired and I have a lot to do tomorrow," I said, done with this conversation.
"Deja, just take some time to really think about this, he said you filed for divorce and pressed charges. He is hurting inside, baby, and he doesn't know what to do. This could really hurt his businesses."

I Am A Survivor: Sex, Lies, and Abuse

"Are you serious, mama? He hurt me. I lost my baby, because your son almost killed me. He is a selfish, stubborn ass little boy, who does not give a fuck about no one but himself. Has he shown you proof that he is seeking counseling or attending those classes? Because the boy has not changed his ways. Look, I really have to go. I will talk to you later," I said, hanging up.

I can't believe she would call and say that. I was so done. I wasn't going to stress though, I had enough on my plate, I was not going to try to make Mama Clara see that he was wrong. I was focused on proving that in court instead. I was so frustrated it took me a minute to relax, but eventually I fell asleep.

I woke up the next morning and made myself breakfast. I put my blow-up bed in the closet and got dressed after eating. I knew the furniture delivery people would be here soon. I sat on the floor in the living room waiting for them. About 20 minutes later I heard a knock on the door. I looked out the peep hole and saw the delivery men. I removed the door stopper and opened the door. They brought in all the furniture and set up everything for me. I tipped them and they left. I put the door stopper back at the door. I sat on the couch and put my head back as I knew I had to call X today. He called my phone all night and even this morning.

"Hello," I heard a woman's voice say.
"Who is this?" I said, looking at my phone thinking I called the wrong number.
"You called me. Oh wait, shit this isn't my phone," the voice said.
I recognized it was Grace. "Grace, where is X?" I said, a little annoyed.

X would have been pissed if I ever answered his phone.

"Grace, what the fuck are you doing bitch, answering my phone?" I heard X say and then it sounded like he hit her. I could hear a smack and her scream.

Shit! I didn't know if I should just hang up and call the police, or is this the shit that Grace liked since she was his Sub. I decided to hang up the phone, because it sounded like he was cursing at her and hitting her. I felt bad not calling the police, but I didn't know if I should or not. I picked up the phone to call the police anyway, but X was calling me now.

"Hello," I said, nervous.
"Deja, what the fuck is going on? Where are you?" X said, upset.
"Is Grace, okay?" I said, concerned.
"Oh, so now you're concerned about Grace."
"I mean you were just beating her ass a few minutes ago."
"Grace, tell Deja you're fine," X said, putting the phone on speaker.
"I'm fine Deja, I mistakenly picked up X's phone thinking it was mine, but I'm okay," Grace said.
"You happy now," X said, taking the phone off speaker.
"Why is she there? When you said she isn't there when you have the kids?"

I Am A Survivor: Sex, Lies, and Abuse

"The kids are with my mom, because I thought I was going to be arrested due to you filing fucking charges on me. But my attorney handled that."
"So, my kids are in New Jersey?" I said, nervous.
"No, mama came here to Columbus. She wanted to keep them last night so I let her. She was going to meet up with you today, but she told me you hung up on her."
"Yeah, because she doesn't believe that your abuse is that big of a deal," I said, upset.
"Deja, I am working on it okay. I want you back home and I am working on it."
"You're working on it, but I just heard you beating on Grace. So, how's that going for you?"
"Deja, that bitch answered my phone and she was in the wrong. Look, I'm doing what I need to do to get better at my anger," X said, upset.

I could tell he was tightening his jaw.

"X, you seem like you are really working on it too," I said, being sarcastic. "Look, I was just calling to see if you can drop the kids off at my parents' house on Friday at 10am and I will pick them up from there."
"Deja, why are you doing this?"
"I am just trying to be safe, X. I don't want to see you right now, but I know we have to make an arrangement for pick up and drop off for our kids. So, can you please just respect that."
"Fine Deja, I'll take them to your parents on Friday. But when are you going to stop this bullshit? My attorney told me you filed for divorce and pressed charges. Deja, I'm not signing those papers. If you want more money, I'm not stingy with my money. You can have whatever you want, but I want you to come home."
"It was never about the money and you know that X. I don't care if you don't give me anything else. I just wanted you to stop abusing me."
"Deja, I am working on it. I am doing everything I can for you," X said, getting upset.
"X, you were just beating on Grace a few minutes ago, how is that working on it?"
"Fuck her, she is not you. I fucked up, Deja. I'm sorry," X said, trying to sound sincere.
"X, you killed our baby and left me for dead. You choked me until I passed out. What if I didn't wake up? You showed me how much you cared. You were gone when I woke up. You left me bleeding to death as I was having a damn miscarriage," I said, crying.
"Deja, I didn't know you were having a miscarriage. I fucked up. I am working on my anger, baby. I need you to understand I didn't mean to do that."
"X, we are done. I can't deal with you. I'm not coming back. Please, understand I love you, but I can't come home. We are done. Just sign the papers."
"No, I will never sign them. We will have to go to court and even still I refuse too. You're mine Deja, and you will always be mine. I love you, Deja. Where are you? I want to see you right now."

I Am A Survivor: Sex, Lies, and Abuse

"X, I have to go. I will get the kids from my parents on Friday and then you can pick them up at my parents the following Friday."
"Deja, don't do this. Let me come talk with you. Where are you staying?"
"I have to go, X," I said, hanging up the phone.

I was emotional all over again. It was hard talking to him and knowing he was fucking Grace to sustain his lifestyle. I hated that I was even doing all of this. I just wanted X to be the husband I thought he was going to be without the abuse. It was hard knowing he wasn't going to change ever. I missed the good moments, but it wasn't enough to go back. I was trying to accept this and move forward.

I wanted a girl's night. I called Stacy, Michaela, and Cassie on 3-way. I caught Michaela up to speed, because I knew Stacy and Cassie knew what was going on. I didn't tell them where I was staying. I know Stacy said she wouldn't tell anyone either. I just really didn't want Michaela or Cassie to know, because Cassie was married to Greg and if Michaela knew she might slip and tell Cassie. I know Cassie wouldn't intentionally tell Greg, but if X wanted to know I'm sure Greg could get Cassie to talk. But I just wanted a night of drinking and partying. After I got Michaela up to speed, we all did a crying moment and Michaela tried to console me and comfort me. I had to stop her. I was done feeling sorry for me. I wanted to drink and have some fun. Cassie said she could get her mom to watch her son and we could go to Club Sparrow tonight. I was thrilled. A girl's night out sounded fun and exciting. I just wanted to feel something different than sadness and despair.

I laid around the house after talking with them until around 8pm when I decided to start getting ready. Everyone was going to meet at Michaela's house and then go to the club. I put on a red slim fitting dress that was right above my knee. The back was open and the front of the dress was square at the top with thin straps. I put on some red heels to match. I wore some silver hoop earrings and a diamond necklace. It was cold outside so I put on my black trench coat to cover me until I was in the club. I put my hair in a loose ponytail and curled the ends. I just wanted to feel and be cute, for me. Everything that was going on had me feeling down and ugly about myself. I left the house around 10:30pm. I made it to Michaela's house at 11pm.

I was watching my surroundings. I was worried about inviting Cassie, but I wanted her to be with me tonight too. I just had to be cautious as Greg could have followed her and told X. I didn't see anything suspicious though so I went to Michaela's door.

"Hey, Deja's here," Michaela said as she opened the door. Stacy and Cassie were already inside getting drunk.
"Ugh, where's my drink bitches. You started without me?" I said, grabbing a cup to get a drink.

I Am A Survivor: Sex, Lies, and Abuse

We probably sat around drinking until 12am. We almost forgot we were going out. We were having so much fun. Michaela called us a rideshare since we all were already tipsy. We made it to Club Sparrow at 12:20am. The place was jumping. We hit the bar and then the dance floor as we were all feeling ourselves. I was dancing to the music and for the first time in a long time I felt amazing. The liquor was feeling good and dancing to the music had me hyped. I didn't even notice when a man came behind me and started dancing with me. Michaela, Stacy, and Cassie were laughing as I was so into the music. I jumped when I felt the man grab my waist. I turned around to see this tall dark skin man with dreads. He smiled at me and his teeth were beautiful and white. His smile was gorgeous. He was muscular and he definitely looked like he had a six pack. His arms were all muscle. He was beautiful. It felt weird to even admire another man, besides X. But he had my attention and he continued to dance with me all night.

It seemed like we were moving at the same beat with every groove. He placed his hand on my back and I grinded on him. I wrapped my arms around him. He squeezed my ass and kissed me. I jumped back once I realized what we were doing. He looked surprised. I apologized and said I didn't want to move too fast. He grabbed my hand and we stepped off the dance floor and went outside to the smoking area to talk.

"I'm sorry. I was in the moment and didn't mean to go too far. Your beauty is just mesmerizing. I couldn't keep my hands off of you. My name is Gabriel Johnson, but you can call me Gabe," he said, taking my hand to kiss it.
"Hello, Gabe, my name is Deja Anderson."
"So, are you from here?"
"Born and raised."
"Hmm, I never seen you around here before. Are you from this area?"
"No, I used to live up north. And this is the first time I have been to this club or I should say been out in a while."
"Oh, you're spoken for, right?"
"I'm separated going through a divorce actually."
"Sorry to hear that. He had to do something horrible to lose a beautiful girl like you," Gabe said, smiling.
"Yeah, not sure I want to talk about it. I was coming out with my girls to try to relieve my mind of all of it."
"Understood, I don't want to mess up your night. I just wanted to apologize for overstepping. I was really feeling the moment."
"Yeah, I liked your vibes too," I said, realizing I was flirting.
"Oh yeah, I don't want to interfere or anything with what you got going on. But I was wondering can I get your number? I know you are dealing with a lot. I wouldn't mind if it's okay with you to maybe help you relieve your mind some more by getting to know you," Gabe said. "I mean if that's not too much to ask."
"Yeah, I think that's okay," I took his phone and put my number in it.

I Am A Survivor: Sex, Lies, and Abuse

I don't know if it was the liquor, but I was feeling Gabe. I wanted to at least talk to him again to see if I was really feeling him. We went back inside to the dance floor. He danced with me for a couple more songs and then he said he had to go, because he had to work in the morning, but he would call me. It was getting late and the club was about to close. Michaela got us a rideshare. We made it back to her house at 2:15am. We were all still tipsy. Michaela told us to stay the night she didn't feel comfortable with any of us driving home. The way my head was spinning I knew I was sleeping on her couch even if she didn't offer. Cassie said she would get a rideshare. She said she couldn't stay out. Stacy said she would go home early in the morning. She had some things to do tomorrow.

Cassie left and Michaela got me and Stacy some blankets and pillows to sleep on the couch. Stacy's alarm went off at 7:30am. Stacy got up and put her shoes on. I got up to watch her get into her car since it was still dark outside. She waved and pulled off. I closed the door and locked it. I laid back down. Michaela told me she didn't have anything planned today, so I figured I would sleep a little bit longer before I got up to leave. I heard a knock at the door as soon as I laid down. Stacy must have forgotten something. I opened the door not even looking to see who it was. It was X. Shit! I tried to close the door but he pushed it open.

"X, what are you doing here?" I said, backing away from him.
"What, you think, Cassie was going to go out and Greg didn't know where she was?" X said, tightening his jaw.
"X, Michaela's upstairs if I yell, she will call the police," I said, lying to myself, but hoping he would leave.
"Oh yeah, you sure about that? MICHAELA," X yelled.
I heard Michaela moving upstairs. She ran down the steps. "Yes, Sir X. Oh, Deja you're still here," Michaela said, shocked.
"What the fuck?" I said, remembering Grace called him that.
"Deja, I'm so sorry," Michaela paused and X shook his head yes at her. "I'm so sorry. When that stuff went down with Liz at my house and X came by looking for you. He grabbed my wrist and my insides melted. It didn't take long for me to realize why you stayed and kept going back. He made me his Sub and the sex was amazing. I couldn't say no," Michaela confessed.
"You fucking bitch. You been fucking X this whole time," I said, as I tried to beat her ass, but X grabbed me.
"Not the whole time. We don't fuck as much, because he keeps telling me he wants you. I'm just his Sub. He only fucks me when you leave him. I didn't want this to happen, but he is good at seducing me. I never had anyone like Sir X," Michaela said.
"I can't believe you. You bitch," I said, still trying to get to Michaela but X wouldn't let me go. "Let me go X. This is some real disgusting ass bullshit. I will never come back to you. Grace and Michaela can have your sorry ass."
"Deja, chill," X said, still holding me as I was fighting to get free.
"Let me go," I said again.

I Am A Survivor: Sex, Lies, and Abuse

X let me go. I stood away from him and I couldn't even look at Michaela. I was so disgusted.

"Deja, what the fuck happened at the club?" X said, balling his fist and tightening his jaw.
"Fuck you, X. You worried about me and you fucking Grace, Michaela and who else?" I said, pissed.
"Deja, answer my question."
"I don't owe you no explanation. You do whatever the fuck you want and you get pissed, because what Michaela told your ass I danced with someone. Fuck the both of you," I said, grabbing my coat, purse, and shoes.
X locked the door and stood in front of it. "Deja, what happened at the club?"
"Move X, I am tired of your bull shit. You have shown me enough of who you really are and I am so done. You need to move and let me go."
"Deja, he won't hurt you if you just listen and obey," Michaela chimed in.
"Shut up, Michaela and sit down," X said stern.
"Yes, Sir X," Michaela said, sitting down.

I just stood there in shock as she was serious. She was obeying his commands and telling me what I should do. I wanted to go smack the shit out of her. If X was not going to let me leave, I swear I was going to hurt her.

"X, please move so I can leave. I don't want to be here with her or you. I am getting very angry," I said, trying to stay calm.
"Deja, you are not going anywhere," X said.

I threw my stuff on the floor. I ran around the couch and smacked Michaela so fucking hard. She fell back in the chair she was sitting in. X pulled me off of her, while I was still trying to fuck her up. I started swinging on X. I was pissed. I had enough of this bull shit and I was ready to fight. I scratched his face and punched him. X threw me on the floor. He got on top of me as I was trying to kick him. He punched me in my face. I hit him in his shoulder, the one he got shot in. He fell on the floor and I ran to the bathroom and locked the door. I was trying to get the window open, but it was not budging. I started looking for something to break the window. I hit the window with an aerosol can and it busted. I started to climb out the window, but X at this point busted the door open and grabbed me. I screamed hoping a neighbor would hear. X pulled me out of the bathroom.

He dragged me back into the living room and threw me on the couch. I saw Michaela was sitting in the chair crying like she wasn't allowed to move or something. I just knew she would try to come at me but she just sat there. X walked over to Michaela and rubbed her cheek.

"Michaela, you are a good girl. You do as I say and I will reward you," X said as he stared at me. This man was psycho for real.

I Am A Survivor: Sex, Lies, and Abuse

I sat up on the couch. "What do you want from me, X? As we know you can have anyone you want. Just leave me be. I am not going to be with you."
"Deja, you're my wife. You are the only one I want. These bitches are just my play things to help me conquer my anger," X said, then he punched Michaela in the face. She didn't say anything, she just lifted her face up.

I jumped back worried that he was going to hit me next. But he grabbed her face and ran his hand across her cheek. And then bent down to kiss her cheek. She looked at me and smiled. This shit was freaky and creepy. I kept slowly trying to move closer to the door. I stopped when I saw X walking towards me.

"Deja, you are not leaving me. We will work this out. Michaela is willing to give me the desires I need to manage and that way I won't have to beat you," X said, grabbing my wrist.
"Whatever you say X. I am okay with it. We can discuss this later. I need to go," I said, standing up.
X grabbed me from behind. "You are not going anywhere, Deja."

X lifted up my dress and put his hands on my clitoris. I cringed as I got chills.

"You didn't let that nigga fuck, did you?"
"X, let me go," I cried out.

X pulled my panties to the side and stuck his dick in me. "Hmm, I can feel you didn't give it up. Good girl, that pussy is still mine."

X leaned me over the couch as he started fucking me. I was crying. I didn't want him to ever touch me again. He was going deep and pounding hard. I could feel my pussy pulsating, and my body was beginning to shake. Shit! I was about to cum. "Cum for me, baby," X moaned. I fucking exploded. I tried to hold it in. I just didn't want to do it for him, but my body was in tune with his touch, his stroke, and his words. He kept fucking me as Michaela just watched us for hours. I kept cumming every time he said "Cum for me, baby". I couldn't control my body from cumming on que for him. He just kept going hard and rough. He whispered in my ear, "I'm going to get you pregnant again". I cried out as I was cumming and thinking to myself, please don't. He sped up fucking me faster and harder. He was about to release. My body was shaking, my breathing was heavy, and I could feel myself exploding as he released. "Fuck, Deja that pussy is so good," X moaned as he came.

He pulled out of me. I wiped my tears. When I turned around, I saw Michaela was crying now. X was rubbing her back and whispering in her ear. I didn't understand this shit at all. X was consoling Michaela and not paying me any attention. I ran to grab my shit and opened the door.

"DEJA," X yelled.

I Am A Survivor: Sex, Lies, and Abuse

I ran to my car and sped off quickly. X was left standing in the middle of the street. I called my lawyer immediately to tell him what happened. He told me to meet him at the police station. I got to the police station and Tremond must have called Detective Moon, because he was waiting on me. Tremond showed up minutes later. We went into the detective's office and Tremond encouraged me to tell him everything so I did. Detective Moon wrote everything up and gave me and Tremond a copy of the police report. Tremond said he would get this to the prosecutor and they would make sure to issue an arrest for rape and domestic violence. Of course, they told me the same bull shit his lawyer would get him out of jail, but at least it would be reported. I also had to go to the hospital to complete a rape kit.

Once I was done at the hospital I went back to my place. I took a long hot shower and cried so hard. I was feeling like I was running out of tears. I couldn't believe everything that happened. Tremond told me that the prosecutor was also going to file murder charges for X killing my baby. He was going to pay for everything. I loved him, but I hated him too. I was ready for him to pay for everything he did to me. I was disgusted, worn out, and furious. This man was the devil. I wanted him to suffer more than anything now. Why would he do this to me? I didn't care about what this meant for him anymore. I wanted nothing else to do with him.

I laid in the bed thinking about everything that happened to me until I dozed off.

****

It was Wednesday at 11am. I had to go see the psychologist at 2pm today. Hell, she was probably going to diagnose me as crazy now, the way I was feeling. So much has happened and I couldn't make sense of none of it. The last two days I barely did anything, but slept and ate. I didn't know if I wanted to talk to Cassie or Stacy about what happened. I don't think I felt like telling anyone. I know Michaela would probably tell Cassie if she thinks I told her. But I didn't care. I was not in tune with my phone anymore. I had missed calls and voicemails from everyone. I know my parents were probably worried, but I just didn't feel like talking to anyone. I went back to sleep for a little bit, because thinking about this stuff was making me tired.

I woke up at 1pm and got ready to go. I made it to the appointment at 1:45pm. The psychologist was finishing up with someone. She took me back at exactly 2pm. I talked with her and she completed my assessment. She told me that I did have PTSD, but other than that I had no serious mental health concerns and she would send her report to my attorney and the prosecutor. She also mentioned that she wanted to see me again. She did believe I could also be suffering from depression due to the relationship, the miscarriage, and the abuse. She said it could be a part of the PTSD and she just wanted to see me again to make sure it was only the PTSD. I scheduled another appointment with her receptionists and then I left.

I Am A Survivor: Sex, Lies, and Abuse

I rode around for a little bit just trying to clear my head. I was definitely traumatized and what Dr. Shannie said about not thinking clearly was really hitting me. I felt like so much was running through me all at once I couldn't think clearly. I was overwhelmed with thoughts that I didn't know what to do or how to even stop my thoughts. X, had been fucking Michaela since the incident with Liz. I was really starting to think about everything and how many lies did X really tell me? How many secrets did this man have? And I must have to be the dumbest girl in the world to have stayed with him so long. I knew from the jump it never felt right and yet I continued to feed into his bullshit. I felt humiliated, stupid, and so lost. The sex, lies, and abuse and I still dealt with it. What the fuck was wrong with me?

Chapter Eighteen: Survivor
"Because I am becoming me."

I made it home around 5pm. I was glad to be home. I put the door stopper on the door. I was happy that no one would come here looking for me. I sat in the living room staring at the wall for a minute. I just wanted to listen to the quiet in the house. It didn't last long as my phone was ringing.

"Hello, is this Deja Anderson?" a familiar voice said.
"Yes, it is," I said, still trying to figure out the voice.
"Hi Deja, it's Gabe."
"Hello Gabe,"
"You know who I am right? You weren't too drunk?"
"I know who you are. I remember Saturday night so no I wasn't too drunk."
"Oh, good how are you doing?"
"Honestly, not so good, but I don't want to talk about it."
"Okay, understood. Are you willing to talk about other things?"
"Yes, I am. So, tell me about you Gabe?" I said, happy to indulge.
"I am 30 years old. I am a police officer for Reynoldsburg Police Department. I have been working there for about 5 years now. I have my own house, no kids, and I'm pretty much a boring guy. Besides my one or two nights out a week to free my mind and do something different."

I laughed. It felt good to laugh and to hear someone sound so normal.

"I see I amuse you," Gabe said, confused.
"I'm sorry, I don't mean to laugh. I've just been through so much. It just felt good to hear you explain yourself as a normal person. It made me feel good, but I was laughing at myself," I said, trying to explain.
"So, you're not normal?"

"I haven't felt normal for a long time. But I am trying to get back to being normal. But to explain myself. I am 28 and about to be 29 years old next month. I don't work right now, due to being a stay-at-home mom. I have two beautiful kids. I used to be an accountant. I have my bachelors in accounting. I have been married for a year and 8 months. We are currently separated and I filed for a divorce. I just found out he is fucking one of my used to be good friends. I had been hiding from him but he found me Sunday morning and raped me," I said, beginning to cry. "I'm sorry I didn't mean to say that last part. It just slipped out."

"No, don't apologize. Did you report it?"
"Yeah, when I was able to get free. I called my attorney who met me at the police station and then I had to go to the hospital to complete the rape kit. I know it doesn't sound like a get to know you type of conversation. I didn't mean to bring it up," I said, feeling guilty.

"Deja, it's really okay. I know if it just recently happened. You probably needed to get it out and release it. It's truly okay that you shared that with me. I'm glad you did. You know I like you and if I can help in any way, please I want to help."
"Thank you, Gabe. You really seem so sweet. I don't want to bore you with my problems though. I have to be honest; my husband is crazy and I'd rather be up front with you just in case you want to run away now."
"I'm not leaving unless you want me to."
"Okay," I said, taking a breath. "So, you're 30, no kids, and single?"
"Yeah, my last relationship ended two months ago. She really had an issue with me being an officer and you know putting my life on the line for other people. But yeah, I don't have any kids. I wanted to wait until I was married for kids. How old are your kids?"
"I have a one-year-old daughter named Amara. She will be 2 in two months. And I have my son, we call him Manny. He is 7 months now."
"Your house sounds too quiet for two little ones."
"Oh, they are with their dad right now. I pick them up on Friday."
"So, you have to see him this Friday?"
"No, I already have it set up. He will drop them off at my parents' house so I don't have to see him."
"Oh, that's good to hear you have a plan in place. So, seeing that you will be busy this weekend, would it be okay to ask you out for dinner tomorrow. Only if you feel up to it. I know you've been through a lot and I don't want to rush anything. But I would like to see you again."
"Yes, dinner sounds fine. What time and where?"
"I know a spot called The Social. It's a nice little restaurant in Reynoldsburg. We can meet there around 7pm."
"Okay, I will see you then."
"Alright, you be safe and now you have my number, call me whenever you want to."
"I will, and Gabe thanks for listening to me and my troubles."
"Anytime Deja, I will talk to you later."
"Alright talk to you later," I said, hanging up.

I wasn't going to rush anything, but it felt good talking to Gabe. He just seemed understanding and really easy to talk to. I went upstairs and laid in my room. I turned the TV on and watched some TV. I probably fell asleep around 9pm.

I woke up the next morning around 8am. My body was still sore from X hitting me. I went to the bathroom. I looked in the mirror and saw my bruises were going away, but I still had pain. I still couldn't believe Michaela all this time she was sleeping with X. Like, why did X think I would be okay with any of this? I wasn't going to stress it. I was staying focused on moving forward and just co-parenting from now on. He didn't know where I lived and I was safe for now. I would spend most of today at the library. I wanted to get back to working to keep me busy. I wanted to update my resume and start applying for jobs. And later today I would meet up with Gabe.

I Am A Survivor: Sex, Lies, and Abuse

I left the house to go to the library at 10am. I stayed at the library until 1pm. I left feeling good as I updated my resume and applied for 10 jobs. I was back to using Deja Anderson. I did put that in my divorce paperwork that I wanted to go back to Anderson. I didn't want to keep his name; my kids would have it not me. I stopped to get something to eat and I made a last-minute appointment with my nail salon. I figured I wanted to look decent since it had been a while since I even went on a date. I was open to the date, because I really just wanted to have something else to focus on for this has all been so much to deal with.

I made it back to the house at 4pm after I finished my nails. I figured I would start getting dressed at 5pm since we agreed to meet at 7pm. I got caught up cleaning and watching TV. It was after 5pm when I looked at the clock. I took a long hot shower and it felt so good. I dried off really well, because I knew I was going to have to wear makeup tonight. I put some makeup on my arms and of course my face. It looked good. I couldn't see the bruises anymore. I decided to wear a royal blue pencil skirt. I put it on with a black sleeveless blouse that had royal blue flowers mixed with gold leaves. I had some gold heels that matched well. I looked sophisticated. I wore my hair down and put some curls in it. I left the house around 6:45pm. I made it to the restaurant The Social at 7pm. Gabe texted and said he got us a table. I told him I was walking in. He met me at the door.

"Wow, you look beautiful," Gabe said.
"Thank you, you look good too," I said, complimenting him.
"Our table is this way," Gabe said, grabbing my hand.

We sat down and Gabe picked up the menu to look at what to order.

"I ordered you some water. I didn't know what you would like to drink. But the waiter said he would come back when you got here."
"Water is good for now."
"How was your day?"
"It was good. I went to the library, updated my resume and applied for some jobs."
"You're going back to work?"
"Yeah, I think it's time."
"Are you looking for accounting work or trying something new?"
"I am looking for accounting work."
"Hello, are you guys ready to order?" the waiter said.
"Are you ready to order? I didn't see you look at the menu yet?" Gabe said.
"Oh, I'm so sorry. I need a minute," I said as I forgot I had to order for myself.

X always ordered for us both.

"Okay no worries, would you like something else to drink?" the waiter said.
"No, water is good for me.," I said, picking up the menu.
"Okay, I will be back to get your order," the waiter said, and walked away.

"You know if you're looking for accounting work, my job is hiring for an accountant. You can apply at the Reynoldsburg Police Department website."
"Oh, really. I will look into it. How was your day by the way?"
"My day was good. I had a busy work day but I got a lot accomplished. It's good to end my day seeing you though," Gabe said, being cute.
I smiled. "And what does a work day look like for you?"
"Well, I start my mornings sometimes in group meetings discussing what happened the night before and then checking in on the be on the lookout list. I hit the beat around 9am just cruising my jurisdiction until I got a call on the radio. I only got a few calls today though nothing major. I went back to the police department around 2pm to do my reports and I got everything completed and left at 3pm. I went to the gym and went home to start getting ready to see you."

The waiter came back to take our order. I ordered a steak and potatoes. Gabe ordered a steak and steamed vegetables.

"What made you want to be a police officer?"
"Honestly my father was a police officer and he was the police chief before he retired. So, I was definitely trying to follow in his footsteps, but I loved the stories he shared and how excited he would be when he stopped someone from getting hurt or saved a life. I wanted that excitement."
"Wow, that's interesting. Does your dad like retirement?"
"Not at all. He still works, not in the field but he consults on some of the harder cases to keep himself busy. He was lost when he first retired. My mom tried to do more things with him but he always talked about how he missed the job. So, he finally asked if he could go back to work. My mom didn't care as long as it made him happy. So, he tried to get out of retirement, but the new chief compromised and said he could work as a consultant on the more serious or tough cases. It has been keeping him happy so I'm happy for him."
"Does your mom work?"
"No, she has always been a stay-at-home mom. She had 4 kids so she was busy with us doing everything."

The waiter brought our food out. The food tasted delicious.

"You have sisters and brothers?" I said, taking another bite of my food.
"I have 2 brothers and 1 sister. What about you? Do you have siblings?"
"No, my parents only had me. I was spoiled rotten," I smiled.
"Are your parents working?"
"My mom worked for my dad; he owned his own company. But they are both retired now."
"That's good. They live in Columbus?"
"Yes, they live here. But they have been traveling a lot now that they have all this free time. When they are not spoiling my kids, they are out seeing the world."
"Yeah, my siblings are married and have kids. And my parents' spoil the grandbabies."

I Am A Survivor: Sex, Lies, and Abuse

"Are you the oldest or what?"
"No, my two brothers are older than me. I am the third child then my sister."
"Oh okay. So, what are you looking for when dating?"
"Truthfully, I didn't think I would be dating anytime soon. But when I saw you, I just felt a connection to you. I want to go slow to see where this leads. Since, I know what you are dealing with right now. I am open to just being friends if dating is too much for you. I just really like your vibe and energy and I want to see where this could take us."
"I like that. No rush. I just want to get through my divorce and see what's next."

Gabe smiled and agreed. We talked for hours and finished eating. It felt good talking with him and I liked his vibe too. We left the restaurant around 9pm. He walked me to my car.

"I don't want you to think I am trying to rush anything, but I just wanted to ask if I could kiss you," Gabe said as we stood by my car.

I leaned in and kissed him. It felt so amazing. I felt my whole-body tingle with sensations. He kissed me so good it almost felt like he took my breath away.

"Wow, I didn't know it was going to feel like that," Gabe said, looking at me.
"Same here," I said, taking a deep breath.
"Good night, Deja, I hope to see you soon. I have to walk away before I kiss you again," Gabe said, taking a step back.

I walked up to him and kissed him again. He kissed me back even harder. Damn, his kisses felt so different and so unexpected. I liked the way his kisses felt.

"Yeah, that was good the second time too," I said, stepping back to my car.
"Hell yeah. Text me so I know you made it home safely. And I will call you tomorrow," Gabe said as he opened my car door.

I told him I would text him when I made it home and I drove off. I made it home within 15 minutes. That was a nice breath of fresh air to not talk about my fucked-up life and really get to know him. And his kiss sealed the deal for me. I will definitely see him again. I texted him to let him know I was home. I parked in the garage and went in the house from the garage door. I felt good and I had a really good night. I locked the garage door and put the door stopper on it. I made sure all my doors were secure and locked then headed upstairs. My phone started ringing.

"Hello," I said, not looking at who was calling.
"So, you're dating now?" X said.
"X, where are you?" I said, nervous.
"I'm outside Deja. What, you didn't think I would find you?" X said, laughing.
"Open the door."

I Am A Survivor: Sex, Lies, and Abuse

"No, X you need to go home."
"Deja, I want to hear about your date. How it went? Your first kiss and everything."
"You're sick, X. Go home."

I hung up the phone and called 911. I stood in the living room looking out the window. X was standing by my front door. Shit!

"911 what's your emergency?" the operator said.
"My name is Deja Anderson. My abusive husband has found my location and he is outside my house right now. Please send someone asap," I said, giving the operator my address.
"We will have someone out there soon. Stay on the phone with me."
"I'm scared he might kill me. Shit, he's banging on the door now."
"Stay calm, are there any other exits?"
"I have my garage door but it is also in front. If I go out that way, he might still get me," I said, nervous to leave the house.
"Okay, ma'am I have the police enroute. Please stay calm and try to go to a room where the door can lock. Just in case he gets in."
"Shit, he busted the window. I am going upstairs to my bedroom," I said, running up the stairs.
"Okay ma'am, are you safe in the room."
"I locked the door, but I can hear him coming up the stairs. He is yelling my name. Shit, he's going to kill me," I said, panicking.
"Deja, OPEN THE FUCKING DOOR," X yelled banging on the bedroom door.
"Fuck, he just broke the door down. AAAAAHHHHHHH!" I screamed.

X was already hitting me. I dropped the phone. He punched me in my stomach and I fell to the floor. He picked me up and pushed me against the wall. He was choking me and had me lifted up so my feet were barely touching the ground. I was hitting his hands trying to stop him from choking me.

"Bitch, you think you are going to move on. I told you; you will never leave me. You're mine Deja. And I'm not going anywhere," X said, still choking me.
"X, please I can't breathe," I said, trying to hit his hands so he would stop.

X started unbuckling his pants. He finally let me go. I took a big gasp of air. He still had me pinned to the wall. I couldn't move, because he had all his weight on me. He pulled up my skirt and turned me to face the wall. He pulled my panties to the side and shoved his dick inside me. It hurt. I was not wet and it hurt bad. X didn't stop though he started fucking me hard and fast. I cried and screamed in pain. "You're gonna take this dick bitch and like it," X said, pounding faster.

"Nobody's going to have this pussy but me," X said, pulling my hair. He pulled my hair back forcing me to lean back so he could kiss me. "You're mine, Deja," X moaned. He started moving faster and faster going deep. I was so scared I

I Am A Survivor: Sex, Lies, and Abuse

couldn't get wet and every stroke was causing more pain. I was hoping he was about to cum so he would be done already. I screamed out in pain as I couldn't get myself to enjoy it this time it hurt so bad. He finally released. He pulled out and pulled his pants up. I fell to the ground. X kicked me in the face, my stomach, and stomped on my legs. He stopped when he heard the sirens.

"I'm not close to done with you, bitch. I will be back," X said, then he ran down the stairs.

I was in so much pain. I couldn't move. I tried to crawl to the phone, but it was too far away. I just laid there. A few minutes later I heard the police announcing themselves and entering my house. I couldn't even yell anything. I tried but my voice was gone. I saw an officer come into my room and he ran to me once he saw me. He asked if he was still in the house. I told him I didn't know. I think he may have left on foot. He told me the ambulance was coming and they would assist. I closed my eyes and everything went quiet.

I woke up in the hospital. My whole body felt like it was on fire. My head was pounding. There were police officers everywhere. The doctor came in to check on me and stated he would be releasing me soon. He gave me some prescriptions. I told him I was in pain. He stated he would have the nurse administer some pain meds before releasing me as long as I wasn't driving home. I told him I didn't have my car so I would not be driving home. The nurse came in a few minutes later to give me some drugs.

The officers in the room took my report and stated I would probably have to come down to the station in the morning. I said okay, because I was not up for talking too much more tonight. Only thing was I didn't know where I would be going tonight. I couldn't go to my parents not like this and I couldn't go back to the apartment.

I could only think of one person to call and I wasn't sure I wanted to call them.

"Hello," I said, regretting my decision.
"Hey Deja, it's pretty late, is everything okay?"
"No," I paused. I started to cry and couldn't stop.
"Deja, where are you?"
"I am at the hospital-," I took a deep breath. "My husband tried to kill me."
"What hospital? I am on my way."
"I am at Grant hospital."
"Okay, I'll be there soon."

I hung up the phone and laid back down. My head was still hurting and crying was not making it any better.

I Am A Survivor: Sex, Lies, and Abuse

I looked at the clock. It was now midnight and Gabe was standing at my door. He was talking to the officer. When he looked at me, I began to cry again, because I didn't know what to say or think. I didn't know why I called him. I just wanted some peace. And he just felt like peace to me.

"Deja, the officers said you were ready to go. Are you feeling okay?"

I shook my head no, not able to speak, because I was so emotional.

"They told me your place is pretty messed up. Would you be okay staying with me tonight?" Gabe said, holding my hand.

I shook my head yes and leaned into his chest and started crying again. Gabe wrapped his arms around me. It felt so good to be held by him. We left the hospital. The ride to his house was quiet. I laid my head back and closed my eyes. I felt safe for the first time in a long time. Gabe parked in the garage of his house and closed the garage before we got out of the car. He opened my door and led the way into his home.

Gabe showed me to the living room while he went to make me some tea. I sat on his couch and laid my head back. Gabe came in with a cup of tea a few minutes later. I sat up and thanked him for being there. We sat quietly for a minute.

"Do you want to talk about what happened?" Gabe said, breaking the silence.
"Not really. I just want to-," I paused. "Lay down with you. If that's okay I just want to sleep."
"That's okay," Gabe said.

He put my cup on the coffee table and grabbed my hand. He walked me upstairs to his bedroom. He found one of his oversized t-shirts and said I could sleep in it. I took off my clothes in front of him and put on his t-shirt.

"Damn, Deja, he really hurt you," Gabe said. He noticed all the bruises.

I got in his bed and laid down. Gabe got comfortable and laid down with me.

"Is it okay if I hold you? Do you hurt anywhere?" Gabe said, being gentle.
"I don't hurt right now. I think the medicine is working. Please, I want you to hold me. I feel comfortable in your arms," I said, wrapping his arm around me.

It didn't take long for me to fall asleep.

I woke up the next morning alone in bed. I didn't even feel Gabe get up. I slept so well. I got up to sit at the edge of the bed. I saw he left a note on the nightstand.

I Am A Survivor: Sex, Lies, and Abuse

Hey Deja,

I had to go to work. You were sleeping so peacefully I didn't want to wake you. If you're hungry please feel free to raid my fridge. You can stay as long as you like if you want. I left my spare key on the night stand for you to lock up if you have to leave. I will call you later.

Gabe

I laid back down for a little bit. I wasn't ready to face my reality. I knew I had to go to the police station and I just wasn't up for it. I was still emotional and I was beginning to feel anger. I had been through enough with X.

It was 11am when my phone started ringing.

"Hello,"
"Hello, Deja, this is Detective James Moon. I went by your apartment hoping to speak with you. I was wondering if you could come to the police station."
"Yeah, I have to get dressed, but I will be there," I said, angry.
"Okay, I will see you when you get here. Let's say around 1pm does that work?"
"Yeah, that's fine," I said, hanging up the phone.

Ugh, I was so annoyed. I got up and felt the pain hit me. I didn't fill my prescriptions. I didn't have any clothes either. The clothes I wore were bloody from my injuries. I knew I would just throw them away. I looked in Gabe's closet to see if he had something I could throw on. I picked out a hoodie and some jogging pants. They were big but I was going to make it work. I texted Gabe to make sure he was okay with me borrowing his clothes. He texted back and said yes and told me he had some Nike slides I could slip on if I needed shoes. They were big too, but with some socks I could make it work for now. I jumped in the shower.

I took the key Gabe left for me and got a rideshare to go to the police station. I locked up Gabe's house. I texted Gabe to let him know I had left and was going to the police station to talk with the detective. I told him if it was okay with him, I would be back to stay again. I also told him he really made me feel comfortable and I thanked him for being there for me. He texted back, he would love for me to stay with him again.

I made it to the police station before 1pm. I walked in and Detective Moon was already up front waiting for me. When he saw me, he immediately took me back to one of the rooms. We went into the room and Detective Moon turned on the recorder. And grabbed the folder on the table. I looked at him a little confused and irritated.

I Am A Survivor: Sex, Lies, and Abuse

"You have no idea what I've been through."

"For the record my name is Detective James Moon; Deja do you know why you are here today?" he asked, as he opened up a folder to show me the pictures.

Here I was in the interrogation room at the Columbus Police Department. I have had enough and Detective Moon was not going to be ready for what I had to say.

"Well, Deja Thomas, are you going to answer me?" he asked, irritated.
"My name is Deja Anderson," I said, with an attitude. "And yes, I know why I'm here. I can see the pictures you just laid out."
"Anderson? So, you're divorced already?"
"No, not by law, but when I left him, I went back to using my maiden name."
"Okay, so, tell me what happened? Did you have something to do with this?"
"It doesn't matter what I say. I am a suspect and you are going to find a way to take my words and use them against me, because that's what police do to get what they want even if it isn't the truth. I know how you do things," I said angry.

I was more than angry. This man ruined my whole life and now I am still being blamed and tortured. I had enough.

"Alright, I get it, we are the bad guys. But that's not true. All I want is the truth, Deja. I know from past reports you have been the victim of Xavier Thomas's abuse. And even though he was an evil man we still have to find out what happened to Mr. Thomas and yes, the first person we normally like to talk to is the spouse," Detective Moon said in a calmer voice.

I sat in silence for a minute with my head down. I could tell Detective Moon was getting annoyed, but he tried to stay calm and patient as he waited for me to say something.

"I didn't have anything to do with it," I said as tears rolled down my face.
"So, what do you know? When was the last time you saw Mr. Thomas."
"I don't know nothing. And I have not seen X since yesterday when I called the police, because he found out where I was and you guys took forever to get there. By the time the police showed up he was long gone and I didn't see him again. But he made sure to leave a lasting impression on my damn face," I said angrily, talking about the bruises X put on me when he beat the shit out of me.
Detective Moon paused for a minute. "So, you may have been the last one to see him."
"I couldn't have been the last one to see him, because I had nothing to do with this," I said, pissed off now, because Detective Moon was trying to be slick.

"Deja, let me be real with you. You called the police yesterday at 9:20pm saying Mr. Thomas found your location and he was trying to bust in your house. You disconnected from the dispatcher at 9:30pm. At this point we can assume Mr.

I Am A Survivor: Sex, Lies, and Abuse

Thomas busted in, because the dispatcher heard a loud noise before the phone disconnected. And from your bruises I can see Mr. Thomas was very violent with you. Our officers were on the scene by 9:45pm and Mr. Thomas was already gone. When the police talked with you, you mentioned Mr. Thomas had only left about 2 minutes ago on foot. My officers report that when they showed up, they had another patrol unit circling the block and did not see anyone in a 10-mile radius. Now how is that possible if Mr. Thomas was on foot? So, tell me Deja what am I missing?"

"WHAT DO YOU WANT FROM ME? Huh, Huh?? You have no idea what I've been through."

I was annoyed. I was hurt. I was frustrated. I was in pain. I didn't know X was dead. When he showed me those pictures I felt my heart die inside, but I also felt relief. I had nothing else to say to the detective.

"Deja, Xavier Thomas is dead and the officer on scene said you left the hospital around midnight. Xavier was found dead around 2am. And you're telling me you didn't see him no more that night? Where did you go after you left the hospital?" Detective Moon said, standing up.

Before I could answer, my attorney walked in the room and excused Detective Moon.

"Deja, let's go, they have nothing on you," Tremond said, helping me up.

I walked out to the front of the police station and my parents were waiting on me. I ran into their arms. I started crying immediately. My dad held me so tight. It hurt from the pain, but it felt good to be in my daddy's arms. He cried and my mom cried. We went home. When we got to the house, I saw Cassie. She hugged me and was crying once she saw me. She was in the house with her son and my kids. I grabbed Amara and hugged her so tight. I kissed all over Manny.

"When did you get the kids?" I said, asking my mom.

"Mama Clara said X gave them to her last night. She knew they were supposed to be dropped off to us in the morning so she brought them over when she didn't hear anything from X. We got worried when she said she didn't hear anything from X. So, I called your attorney to check around to see if anything had happened to you. I knew X would have called his mom or something if everything was okay. When Tremond called us back and said there was an incident reported. I called Cassie to come sit with the kids so we could go down to the police station and figure out what was going on," my dad said.

"I'm just glad to see my babies," I said, playing with Manny and Amara.
"So, what happened to X?" Cassie said.

I Am A Survivor: Sex, Lies, and Abuse

"I don't know. The pictures looked like he got shot or something. There was so much blood I could barely see his face."
"Are they sure it was him?" Cassie said.
"The detective said it was him, but I don't know if they did a DNA test."
"Well, hopefully they will get a DNA test and figure out what happened," my dad said.
"I hope so too," I said, a little sad.
"Are you okay baby?" my mom said.
"Honestly, I don't know. I don't know if I should be sad, angry, or relieved. I just don't know how to feel right now," I said, thinking about everything that has happened.
"I'm just glad you're safe now," my dad said, hugging me.

I talked with my parents and Cassie for a little while longer. I was just trying to take everything in and I think they were trying to piece things together. I mean who would have killed X? I thought about it, Detective Moon didn't say where X was found dead. I wanted to know that. I would call Detective Moon later to see if he would tell me where X was found dead. I had no idea who could be the suspect. But no matter the thoughts, the emotions, and the craziness of the day I really did have a small sense of relief.

I stepped away to go call Detective Moon.

"Hello Detective Moon, this is Deja. I wanted to ask you something about X's murder. Where was he murdered and did you verify that the body was X's body?"
"Deja, I'm glad you called. We are testing the DNA. And X was shot 12 miles from your home. He was found outside of an apartment complex called Trail Mills Village. To my correction X was driving a car when he left your home, and that car was stolen after he got shot. We were advised that X's car was found covered in blood 6 miles from where X was shot. I think X was robbed and shot in the process. We will do some more digging of course before we confirm that as our final results, but for now you are not a suspect anymore Deja."
"Well, that's good to know. I still hope you find who did it."
"Oh, I will do my best. And my condolences to you and the family."
"Thanks," I said before hanging up.

I let my parents keep my kids for the night. I just wanted to get away and I know I told Gabe I would come back to his place. I liked it over there. It was really peaceful. I took a rideshare to his place. He was cooking dinner when I walked in.

We ate and talked. I told him X was dead and we talked about the incident. Gabe was very sincere and understanding. He consoled me while I cried. So many emotions were going through me I couldn't keep it together. He really made me feel super relaxed and comfortable around him. We watched some TV in the living room. Gabe had to work in the morning so we didn't stay up too long. He held me again and without a doubt I was asleep in no time.

After a couple of days Detective Moon did call me back to confirm that the DNA matched and X was dead. He still didn't have any more news about who did it. But hearing it confirmed that it was X, I think that's when it really hit. I cried after hearing him say that. I didn't know what to think or say.

A week had passed while we set up arrangements. Mama Clara and X's brother had been staying at the house in Dublin. We were preparing for the funeral together. Mama Clara was heartbroken. Mike, James, and I made all the funeral arrangements. He would be buried here in Columbus. I know Mama Clara wanted him to be buried in New York where he was born, but Mike said he would want to be whereever his family was talking about me and the kids. Mama Clara agreed with that.

We found the biggest venue we could find, because everyone was at the funeral. The place was stacked. I didn't know half of the people that showed up, but X was big in the business world. Some of his friends and his brothers talked about how he was a good guy and was all about giving back. They talked about how he made a way for people and small businesses to grow. They said some awesome things about X and I wanted it that way no matter what he did to me. His funeral was beautiful and the room was filled with people who loved him.

I shook so many people's hands and hugged so many people. Once the funeral was over, we were told to meet back at the Dublin house. My parents took my kids to their house, since we had been staying there anyway. I asked Cassie to go to the Dublin house with me. I didn't know why we had to go there, but James, X's brother, said he was told by X's attorney we needed to meet there.

As we were leaving the funeral, I saw Michaela talking to someone. She looked sick and she was bawling her eyes out.

"I know this is hard for all of us. Are you doing, okay? Where do you live honey, do you need a ride home?" the lady said, to Michaela.
"No, I don't need a ride. I stay close to Trail Mills Village, but I have to go to the meeting place after this and I have a ride." Michaela said.

Shit! I listened to her say the apartment name and I thought to myself she does live right by Trail Mills Village. She is not considered a part of that complex but her apartments share the same entry way as Trail Mills Village. I didn't want to say nothing to her, so I just kept on walking. She looked at me and Cassie but we just left. Cassie now knew what Michaela did, because I told her. Cassie wanted nothing to do with Michaela. Cassie was upset at Greg for telling X we went out that night, but I told her not to be mad, he was just doing his job. Cassie also assured me she didn't tell Greg I was over Michaela's house. I didn't care, because I knew Michaela told X when I found out she was his Sub. But now I was curious if she knew anything about X's death.

We made it to the Dublin house. There were a lot of cars in the driveway. I was confused on how many people got invited back for this meeting. Me and Cassie walked in the house. Eric, X's attorney, led everyone into the back sitting room of the house. Mama Clara, James, Mike, and Whitney were present. Micah, Cash, and Greg was there too. Cassie was taken aback, because she didn't know Greg was invited back to the house too. Alicia, who I hadn't seen in a while, was present. Then I saw Grace, and Michaela were making their way in the house too. I was so confused about what was about to happen. Cassie grabbed my hand as she knew my insides were boiling. We sat down and I didn't speak or say anything to Grace or Michaela. Eric began to talk.

"Well, we all should know why we are here. We just got done celebrating the life of a really good man. And just like any human he had his flaws too, but he tried to stay consistent with being a great man. But he was also a wealthy man and loved to share his wealth with others. That is why we are here right now. Xavier had a Will and everyone in this room was called to attend, because his Will includes you all. I will read through the Will and if you have any questions, please hold until the end of the Will reading." Eric said, taking a pause. "Alright, so Xavier's Will reads as follows. I, Xavier Thomas hold this Will to be true in that my Mother Clara Thomas will receive 10 million dollars."

Eric paused as Mama Clara let out a big gasp. "Oh, my lord, what am I going to do with all that money? I can't believe it. I know he always took care of me, but I didn't know he had money like that."

Eric continued. "And to my brother Mike and his wife Whitney I leave 10 million dollars and my half of the partnership businesses in New Jersey. For my brother James I leave 10 million dollars and the full business of X Factor in New York. To my security team I leave each one of you Greg, Micah, and Cash 10 million dollars."

Cassie grabbed my hand as she heard the amount Greg was going to receive.

"Also, to Grace and Michaela, X, leaves you both 10 million dollars."

Cassie grabbed my hand this time so I didn't jump up and hurt someone.

"Alicia X leaves you 20 million dollars and his half of all the partnership businesses in New York. He also left you with a letter stating how much he appreciated the work you did for him. And how you helped his businesses grow and always kept him in order with things."

I Am A Survivor: Sex, Lies, and Abuse

Alicia was crying. I went to sit beside her and hug her. She was always loyal and good to X.

"Now to Greg and Cassie, X also left you with an extra 10 million dollars to support your growing family as well," Eric paused. "And last on the list, I am to read this verbatim. To my wife and children, if you are hearing this then my time on this earth was shortened. And I truly apologize that I didn't get to grow old with you Deja. I loved you from the first day I saw you and I knew I wanted to give you my whole world. I know I wasn't the best husband and there were some demons I just couldn't let go of. But I hope you know if I had to do this life again, I would always pick you for my wife. Give our babies kisses and tell them I love them. I love you forever, Deja."

I busted out in tears. I was uncontrollably crying. Cassie and Alicia were holding me. Mama Clara had to get me focused and she made me take some deep breaths. I finally calmed down.

"I will finish now," Eric said, finishing the Will. "To my wife Deja Thomas, I leave you 2 houses, a condo, and 3 cars. I also set up a trust for 10 million dollars each for Amara Thomas and Xavier Thomas Jr. I leave you Deja Thomas with my whole world. You will receive 100 million dollars and all the businesses I started and grew in Columbus," Eric paused. "That is the end of the reading of the Will. Now are there any questions."

No one had any questions. I was just emotional. I loved X, and it hurt to hear how much he loved me. I just wanted us to work and be happy. But he said it, the demons had a hold of him and he couldn't let them go. Everyone was getting ready to leave. When I heard a loud scream and turned around to see Michaela hit the floor.

"Oh my God, what happened?" Cassie said.

Michaela was hyperventilating and Mike was trying to calm her down. I didn't know what happened. But Mike got her outside and called her a rideshare to come get her. I walked to the front door myself to leave. Cassie and Greg gave me a hug as they were leaving. I thanked them for being such great friends. Alicia also gave me a hug while she was leaving and told me that they will deposit the money into everyone's bank accounts. She also said if you received any business the paperwork will be in the mail. I thanked Alicia for everything she has always done for X and me. Micah, and Cash hugged me when they left and said they would still be around to look out for me. I thanked them too.

Mama Clara came up to me and hugged me.

"Deja, I misspoke about X's actions. I was just trying to protect him, like I always have. He was special to me. And maybe I was a little softer on him due to his childhood. I did everything I could to show him I loved him. I wanted him to feel loved, but he carried that anger for a long time. I didn't know if he would ever get past his trauma. But I thought he was getting better with you. I thought he was healing having you in his life. So, I didn't want to believe he would hurt you. I'm sorry for not listening to you. I'm sorry for ignoring your concerns. I love you Deja and I hope you can forgive me. I just wanted to believe he was doing good." Mama Clara said, wiping away her tears.

I hugged Mama Clara and thanked her for expressing herself. I was full of emotions. I saw Grace coming to the door and I really had nothing to say to her.

"You know Deja, X was a good man. He loved you with everything in him. He just had a horrible past and he used his lifestyle to deal with that. I'm not saying what he did was always right, but he didn't know how to deal with his demons. And that caused him to have a lot of anger inside of him. But I also want to say that you are a good woman too and I hope that you heal from all of this. I understand that you were not aware of his lifestyle and that was not fair to you. I just want to apologize and I hope that one day you can forgive me. But I just wanted you to know that X made it clear from jump you were his one. He loved you more than anything. And I'm sorry, Deja." Grace said before leaving.

I didn't know what to say and I still didn't know how to really feel. All of what happened was just emotional.

****

"I loved my husband, but I hated him too. At this point I didn't know if I would ever be okay. The trauma of it all just didn't make me feel good. X, was a good man, father, and husband who had a lot of trauma and anger that made him horrible too. I always think about how I wish there was something I could have done to help him change or heal from that. A part of me blames myself for his actions. Maybe if I wasn't so defiant or I tried to learn his lifestyle he would have been different. I just don't know what I could have done to keep him the loving husband that he sometimes showed me. I always think about what else I could have done. I can't help but to blame myself."

"You know Deja, that is what most survivors deal with blaming themselves and not understanding they were the victim at that moment. Nothing you did would have changed him. He had to want to change for himself. Yes, he may have been a victim in his life too, but he also had to find peace and heal from what he went through. And I know it will take some time for you to fully heal and move on from blaming yourself. But you are a survivor and you are seeking help to move forward and be happy. And you will get to a much happier place, because you deserve that. But for now, I will see you back here next week at the same time?" Dr. Shannie said.

I Am A Survivor: Sex, Lies, and Abuse

"Thank you, Dr. Shannie. I will see you next week," I said, before leaving.

It had been 2 months since X's death. I was still meeting with Dr. Shannie. She was a lot of help on my journey to healing. I was now living on my own again with my two kids. I sold all of the houses I had with X. I bought a house in my parents' neighborhood to be close to them. I was running the businesses that X left me with the help of Alicia who was happy to still work with me. I was working on living a happier normal life. I was still talking to Gabe as well. We were taking things slow, but he was good company to be around.

It was a week after X's funeral Detective Moon called me. He said after giving him the information about Michaela living close to where X was found dead. He found out by questioning Michaela that she killed him. She was so distraught about it she told on herself. I guess she wanted X to love her the way he loved me. She hated that he continued to tell her she was just his Sub, and he would always want me. She told Detective Moon she was tired of hearing that and decided if she couldn't have him the way she wanted him then no one would.

Detective Moon said she told him she went crazy. He showed up at her house. I guess after the incident with me, she said they had rough sex. She could tell he was upset about something. She asked him what happened after they were done having sex. He told her that he saw me out with some guy. He explained to her that he put a tracker on my car that morning he found me, at her house. Michaela was so tired of hearing about how X was doing everything to get me back and not seeing her as the one. Michaela said when X left, she pulled out a gun and shot him while he was getting in his car. She said she then called her cousin to help her clean up. Michaela said that her cousin left him on the street and took off with his car to make it look like a robbery. Detective Moon said both Michaela and her cousin Ricky were in custody and charged with murder.

It hurt to know it was Michaela who killed him, but I could see the hurt she felt when he raped me in front of her. She fell for X, just as hard as I did. I just wasn't into the abuse. I guess Alicia told me the money X gave Michaela was transferred into my kids trust, per Michaela's request. Detective Moon said that was something she asked to be done when he arrested her. He said Michaela wanted X's kids to have her money and to tell me she was sorry for taking their dad away.

Everything had been so hard to deal with, that I didn't know how to explain to Amara that daddy was gone. I knew Manny was too young to even know, but I feel like he felt it. I know both of them didn't see daddy around and Amara would cry for him. I finally explained the best way I could to Amara that daddy was gone. I still just try to love on them both even more for daddy and mommy. I know they will always feel that loss of not having daddy, but I wake up every morning trying to provide, care, and love on them just like daddy did.

I Am A Survivor: Sex, Lies, and Abuse

I am a survivor and though the road ahead seems harder than most some days. I have survived the worst. I am a strong, capable, and powerful woman. I will manage and improve my life journey every day for me and my kids. I will continue to push forward, because I have always been worth it. I will not let what happened to me deter me from what is meant for my future. I will be okay, and I will continue to improve who I am. Because I am becoming me.

I Am A Survivor: Sex, Lies, and Abuse

About The Author:
Wanikki "MsNikk" Cabell

Wanikki "MsNikk" Cabell is a mentor, poet, author, and entrepreneur. She is the Co-CEO of Tell Her She's Beautiful LLC., and she is the owner of Poetry Grind Entertainment LLC. MsNikk has her master's in criminal justice and her bachelor's in marketing. MsNikk has published books and has always been passionate about writing. She loves to travel, seeing the world has always been something that has inspired her. She lives by her own mantra "Stay positive, encourage others, and always focus on being a better version of you". MsNikk resides in Columbus, Ohio, where she was born and raised.

I Am A Survivor: Sex, Lies, and Abuse

I Am A Survivor: Sex, Lies, and Abuse

www.ingramcontent.com/pod-product-compliance
Lightning Source LLC
LaVergne TN
LVHW021653060526
838200LV00050B/2334